THE BEDROOM SECRETS OF THE MASTER CHEFS

Irvine Welsh is the author of seven previous works of fiction, most recently *Porno*. He lives in Dublin.

ALSO BY IRVINE WELSH

FICTION

Trainspotting
The Acid House
Marabou Stork Nightmares
Ecstasy
Filth
Glue
Porno

DRAMA

You'll Have Had Your Hole

SCREENPLAY

The Acid House

The Bedroom Secrets of the Master Chefs

IRVINE WELSH

JONATHAN CAPE
LONDON

Published by Jonathan Cape 2006

2 4 6 8 10 9 7 5 3 1

First published in Great Britain in 2006 by
Jonathan Cape
Random House, 20 Vauxhall Bridge Road,
London SW1V 2SA

Random House Australia (Pty) Limited
20 Alfred Street, Milsons Point, Sydney,
New South Wales 2061, Australia

Random House New Zealand Limited
18 Poland Road, Glenfield,
Auckland 10, New Zealand

Random House South Africa (Pty) Limited
Isle of Houghton, Corner of Boundary Road & Carse O'Gowrie,
Houghton 2198, South Africa

The Random House Group Limited Reg. No. 954009
www.randomhouse.co.uk

A CIP catalogue record for this book
is available from the British Library

ISBN 022407587X (Trade Paperback)
ISBN 9780224075879 (from January 2007)
ISBN 0224078003 (Hardback)
ISBN 9780224078009 (from January 2007)

Papers used by Random House are natural, recyclable products made from wood grown in sustainable forests; the manufacturing processes conform to the environmental regulations of the country of origin

Typeset by Palimpsest Book Production Limited
Polmont, Stirlingshire
Printed and bound in Great Britain by
Mackays of Chatham plc, Chatham, Kent

For Elizabeth

Prelude

She Came to Dance, 20 January 1980

— THIS IS THE FUCKIN CLASH! The green-haired girl had screamed into the face of the flinty-eyed bouncer, who'd shoved her back into her seat. — And this is a fuckin cinema, he'd told her.

It *was* the Odeon cinema, and the security personnel seemed determined to stop any dancing. But after the local band, Joseph K, had finished their set, the main act had come out all guns blazing, blasting out 'Clash City Rockers', and the crowd immediately surged down to the front of the house. The girl with the green hair scanned around for the bouncer, who was preoccupied, then sprang back up. For a while the security staff tried to stem the tide, but finally capitulated about halfway through the set, between 'I Fought the Law' and '(White Man) in Hammersmith Palais'.

The crowd was lost in the thrashing noise; at the front of the house they bounced along in rapture, while those at the back climbed on to their seats to dance. The girl with green hair, now right at the front centre of the stage, seemed to be rising higher than the rest, or perhaps it was just her hair, and the way the strobes hit it, making it appear as if a spectacular emerald flame was bursting from her head. A few, only a few, were gobbing at the band and she was screaming at them to cut it out as he – her hero – had only just recovered from hepatitis.

She'd been to the Odeon only a few times before, most recently to see *Apocalypse Now*, but it wasn't like this and she could bet that it had never been. Her friend Trina was a few feet from her, the only other girl so near the front that she could almost smell the band.

Taking a last gulp from the plastic Irn Bru bottle she'd filled with snakebite, she killed it and let it fall to the sticky, carpeted floor. Her brain fizzed with the buzz of it working in tandem with the amphetamine sulphate she'd taken earlier. She roared the words of the songs as she leapt, working herself into a defiant frenzy, going to a place where she could almost forget what he had told her earlier that afternoon. Just after they'd made love when he'd gone so quiet and distant, his thin, wiry frame shivering on the mattress.

— What's up, Donnie? What is it? she'd asked him.

— It's all fucked, he'd said blankly.

She told him not to be daft, everything was brilliant and the Clash gig was happening tonight, they'd been waiting for this for ages. Then he turned round and his eyes were moist and he looked like a child. It was then that her first and only lover had told her that he'd been fucking someone else earlier; right there on the mattress they shared every night, the place where they'd just made love.

It had meant nothing; it was a mistake, he immediately claimed, panic rising in him as the extent of his transgression became apparent in her reaction. He was young and learning about boundaries as he saw his emotional vocabulary extending out in front of him, just a little too slowly. He had just wanted to tell her: to be straight with her.

She saw his lips move but heard little of the detail of his qualification as she'd got out of their mattress bed and pulled on her clothes. Then she'd taken his ticket for the gig from her pocket and ripped it into pieces right there in front of him. And after that she'd gone to the Southern Bar to meet the others, as arranged, then on to the Odeon to see the show because the greatest rock 'n' roll band of all time were playing in her city and she would see it and he would miss it and at least some sort of justice would be done.

A tallish guy with short dark hair dressed in a leather jacket, jeans and a mohair jumper, who had been pogoing next to her, was suddenly screaming something in her ear as the band went into 'Complete Control'. She couldn't make it out and it didn't matter as in an instant she was eating his face off, and his arms felt good around her.

The second encore began with the comparatively rare 'Revolution Rock' and ended with an incandescent version of 'London's Burning' repositioned as 'Edinburgh's Burning'. And she was too, melting with the speed in her brain, which pulsed in the frozen air as they got outside the cinema. The boy was going to a party in the Canongate and he asked her to come along. She agreed; she didn't want to go home. More than that, she wanted him. And wanted to show someone else that two could play at that game.

As they walked in the cold night he talked effusively, seeming fascinated by her green mane, and told her that this part of town used to be known as Little Ireland. He explained that the Irish immigrants settled here, and it was in these streets that Burke and Hare murdered the poor and destitute in order to provide bodies for the medical school. She looked up at his face; there was a hard set to it but his eyes were sensitive, even womanly. He pointed over to St Mary's Church, and told her that many years before Celtic in Glasgow, the Edinburgh Irishmen had formed the Hibernian Football Club in these very halls. He grew animated when he pointed up the street, and told her that Hibernian's most famous supporter, James Connolly, was born up that road and had went on to lead the Easter Risings in Dublin, which culminated in Ireland's freedom from British imperialism.

It seemed important to him that she knew that Connolly was a socialist, not an Irish nationalist. — In this city we know nothing about our real identity, he said passionately, — it's all imposed on us.

But she had other things on her mind than history and he would be her second lover that evening, though by the end of the night she would have had three.

1

Recipes

1

Bedroom Secrets, 16 December 2003

Danny Skinner rose first, restless, having failed to get off to sleep. This concerned him as he usually fell into a heavy slumber after they'd made love. Made love, he thought, smiled, and then considered again. Had sex. He looked at Kay Ballantyne as she dozed blissfully, that long, glossy black hair splayed over the pillow, her lips still carrying the remnants of the satisfaction he'd given her. A swell of tenderness bloomed from deep within him. — Made love, he said softly, kissing her forehead diligently, so as to prevent the bristles of his long, pointed chin from scratching her.

Wrapping a green tartan dressing gown around himself, he fingered its gold-stitched crest on the breast pocket. It was a Harp emblem, with an inscription, '1875'. Kay had bought Skinner it for his Christmas, last year. They hadn't been going out long then, and as a gift it seemed to say so much. But what had he given her? He couldn't recall: perhaps a leotard.

Skinner went through to his kitchen, and from the fridge procured a can of Stella Artois. Cracking it open, he headed to the lounge where he rescued the television's remote from the guts of the large sofa, and found the programme, *The Secrets of the Master Chefs.* This popular show was now in its second series. It was hosted by a famous chef, who toured Britain, asking local cooks to demonstrate their secret recipes for a party of celebrity diners and food critics, who would then pass judgement.

But the ultimate verdict rested with the eminent chef, Alan De Fretais. This celebrated cook had recently courted controversy by publishing a book entitled *The Bedroom Secrets of the Master Chefs.* On the pages of this aphrodisiac cookbook, several internationally renowned culinary experts had each produced a recipe, writing about how they managed to use it to advance a seduction or to complement a lovemaking session. It quickly became a publishing sensation, spending several weeks heading the best-sellers list.

Today De Fretais and his camera crew were at a large hotel in Royal Deeside. The television chef was a giant, with a bombastic, bullying manner, and the local cook, an earnest young man, was obviously feeling intimidated in his own kitchen.

Sipping his can of lager, Danny Skinner watched the nervous, flickering eyes and defensive posture of the rookie chef, thinking with pride how he himself had the measure of this browbeating tyrant; standing his ground on the couple of occasions they'd had dealings. Now he just had to wait and see what they did with his report.

— A kitchen has to be spotless, spotless, spotless, De Fretais scolded, punctuating this with play-rapping cuffs around the back of the young chef's head.

Skinner watched the junior cook hopelessly defer, fearful of the occasion, the cameras and the bulk of the gross chef who harassed him, relegating him to the role of hapless stooge. He wouldn't try that shit on with me, he thought, raising the can of Stella to his lips. It was empty, but there was more in the fridge.

2
Kitchen Secrets

— De Fretais's kitchen is a fucking midden; that's what it is. The white-faced young man stood his ground. His attire, a tastefully blended mix of quality designer clothing, did not so much hint as scream at ideas beyond station and salary. At just over six foot two Danny Skinner often seemed larger: his presence augmented by penetrating dark brown eyes and the black caterpillar brows that sat thickly above them. His wavy raven hair was combed in a side parting which gave him a raffish, almost arrogant bearing; this enhanced by his angular face and a twist to his thin-lipped mouth suggesting levity, even when he was at his most sombre.

The stocky-framed man facing him was in his late forties. He had a ruddy, squarish liver-spotted face topped by a mane of amber-coloured creamed-back hair that was whitening at the temples. Bob Foy was not used to being to being challenged in this manner. One of his eyebrows was raised incredulously; yet in that motion and the expression his slack features had settled into, there was just a smidgen of enquiry, even of mild fascination, which permitted Danny Skinner to continue. — I'm only doing my job. The man's kitchen is a disgrace, he contended.

Danny Skinner had been an Environmental Health Officer at Edinburgh City Council for three years, moving there from a management trainee post within the authority. This was a very short time in Foy's book. — This is Alan De Fretais we're talking about here, son, his boss snorted.

The discussion was taking place in a barn of an open-plan office, partitioned by small screens dividing it into workstations. Light spilled in through the big windows on one side and although it had been double-glazed you could still hear the noise from the traffic outside on Edinburgh's Royal Mile. The solid walls were lined with a few antiquated tin filing cabinets, hand-me-downs from different departments throughout the local authority, and a photocopier that kept the maintenance men in more regular employment than the office staff. A perennially dirty sink was positioned in one corner, beside a fridge and a table with a peeling veneer, on which sat a kettle, teapot and coffee urn. At the back there was a staircase that led to the departmental conference room and the accommodation of another section, but before that a mezzanine floor with two smaller self-contained offices was unobtrusively tucked away.

Danny Skinner glanced at the doleful faces around him as Foy let the report he'd just meticulously prepared fall heavily on to the desk, which separated the two men. He could see the others in the room, Oswald Aitken and Colin McGhee, looking everywhere but at him and Foy. McGhee, a short, squat Glaswegian with brown hair and a grey suit that was just a little too snug, was pretending to search for something in the mountain of paperwork that lay heaped on his desk. Aitken, a tall, consumptive-looking man, with thinning sandy hair and a lined, almost pained face, briefly gazed at Skinner in distaste. He saw a cocky youth whose disturbingly busy eyes hinted that the soul behind them was perpetually wrestling with something or other. Such young men were always trouble and Aitken, counting the days till his retirement, wanted none of it.

Realising that support would not be forthcoming, Skinner considered that it was perhaps time to lighten things up. — I'm no saying that his kitchen was damp, but not only did I find a salmon in the mousetrap, the poor bastard had asthma. I was on my way to phoning the RSPCA!

Aitken pouted as if someone had farted under his nose in the Kirk he served in as an elder. McGhee stifled a chuckle but Foy remained inscrutable. Then he let his eye leave Skinner and settle on the lapel of his own checked jacket, from which he brushed some dandruff, worrying slightly that his shoulders might be covered with the stuff. He'd have to remember to tell Amelia to change that shampoo.

Then Foy looked Skinner squarely in the eye again. It was a searching glance Skinner knew well, and not only from his boss.

That gaze of somebody who is trying to see beyond what you presented to them, trying to read the insides of you. Skinner held his own stare firm as Foy broke the glance to nod to Aitken and McGhee, who gratefully took his cue and departed. Then he resumed his eye contact with a vengeance. — Have you been on the fucking pish or what?

Skinner bristled, instinctively feeling attack to be the best form of defence. A flash of anger came into his eyes. — What the fuck are you on about? he snapped.

Foy, used to deference in his staff, was slightly taken aback. — Sorry, I, eh, didn't mean to imply, he began before assuming a complicit tone, — Have you had a drink at lunchtime? I mean, it's Friday afternoon!

As the Principal Officer, Foy was usually drinking himself on Friday afternoons, in fact he was generally posted missing from about midday, this being one of the odd Fridays when he ostentatiously walked around ensuring superiors and subordinates got a full view of him busy and sober. Skinner therefore felt relaxed enough to divulge, — Two pints of lager with my bar lunch, that's all.

With a ragged clearing of his throat, Foy advanced his proposition. — I hope you didnae inspect De Fretais's place with a bevvy on your breath, no matter how light. He's used to detecting it in his own staff. So are his chefs.

— I did the inspection Tuesday morning, Bob, Skinner said, then stressed, — You know that I would never go on to any site with a drink in me. I just had paperwork to catch up with this affie so I indulged myself with two pints of lager, Skinner yawned, — and I have to admit that the second one was a mistake. Still, a cup of instant coffee will sort that right out.

Picking up the thin file that contained Skinner's report, Foy said, — Well, you know De Fretais, he's our local celeb and Le Petit Jardin is his flagship restaurant. Two Michelin stars, son. How many other restaurants in Britain can boast that?

Skinner tried briefly to think about this, then decided that he didn't know and couldn't care less. *I'm a health inspector, not a groupie for some fucking cook.*

As he bit his tongue, Foy moved around the desk, placing his arm around Skinner's back. Although shorter than his younger subordinate, he was a powerful bull of a man whose frame was only slowly and reluctantly going to seed, and Skinner felt the force on his shoulders. — I'll drop by and have a quiet wee word with him, let him know about cleaning up his act a wee bitty.

Danny Skinner felt his bottom lip curl outwards, the way it always seemed to when he was undermined and forlorn. He'd done his job. He'd told the truth. Skinner was no naive fool, he knew the realpolitik of the situation: some were always more equal than others. But it stuck in his craw that if a Bangladeshi immigrant with a last-orders curry house had a kitchen as minging as De Fretais's then he'd probably never a boil an egg in the city again. — Right, he said miserably.

But maybe he had spiced it up a bit. He didn't like De Fretais, even if he found the man strangely compelling. His copy of *The Bedroom Secrets of the Master Chefs* was a guilty lunchtime purchase, and it lay concealed in his briefcase. He recalled the opening paragraphs of the foreword, which he'd read with such distaste:

> The wisest in our midst have long known that the simplest of questions are often the most loaded. With every student of the culinary arts who comes into my orbit, I endeavour to begin our relationship by asking the question: who is the Master Chef? The responses are never less than instructive and intriguing to me, for in order to assist in my quest for culinary excellence, it's this very question I perennially seem to address.
>
> For sure, our Master Chef must be an artisan: a craftsman who takes a stubborn pride in the painstaking and often mundane details of his *métier*. Certainly the Master Chef is also a scientist. But he is more than just a chemist: he is an alchemist, a sorcerer, an artist, as his concoctions are not designed to remedy maladies of body or mind, but attend to the far more wondrous task of uplifting the soul.
>
> Our vehicle for the achievement of this objective is food, pure and simple, but this journey must take us along the road of our own human senses. So, I contend to my oft-bemused students, and now to you, dear reader, that if the Master Chef

is anything, then he is, and must always be, a complete and utter sensualist.

He's just a fucking cook, and so many of those cunts are too big for their boots.

And this fucking guide to sexy food! That fat cunt! The whole thing's ridiculous, it's been a good few years since that phantom's seen his fucking prick without the help of a mirror! And those fucking anodyne, sexless yuppies would respond to that, they would actually buy it in their thousands and make a fat, rich, spoiled cunt fatter, richer and more spoiled still. And here I am with a fucking copy in my bag!

Watching Skinner's complexion redden, Foy felt a slight unease and removed his arm. — Danny, we can't be rocking boats at this time of the year, so no pub stories from the horse's mouth about how bad our friend De Fretais's kitchen is, okay?

— Goes without saying, Skinner replied, trying to conceal a mounting excitement that in the boozer tonight he'd blab to everyone who would listen.

— That's the spirit, Danny. You're a good inspector and we certainly need them. We're down to five in the inspectorate, Foy shook his head in disgust, and then quickly brightened up. — Mind you, our new laddie starts tomorrow, the one from Fife.

— Oh aye? Skinner raised his brows enquiringly in an unwitting impersonation of his boss.

— Aye . . . Brian Kibby. Seems a nice young chap.

— Fine . . . Skinner said distractedly, his thoughts drifting to the weekend. He'd have a few bevvies tonight; these four pints at dinner time had given him a fair old thirst. Then, barring the football on Saturday, he'd spend the rest of the weekend with Kay.

Everybody had his or her own idea of where Edinburgh ended and the port of Leith commenced. Officially, they said it was the old Boundary Bar at Pilrig, or where the EH6 postcode started. For Skinner though, coming down the Walk, he never truly felt back in Leith until he could feel the hill levelling out under his feet, which was a great sensation, like his body was a spacecraft, landing home after a long voyage to inhospitable lands. He generally marked this from the Balfour Bar onwards.

On his way back home, Skinner decided to stop off at his mother's, who lived across the road from her hairdressing business, in a small cobblestoned alley off Junction Street. That was where he'd grown up, before moving out the previous summer. He'd always wanted his own place, but now that he had it, he missed home more than he could ever have imagined.

The Old Girl's finished her shift and she fair stinks of thon perming lotion. I'd forgotten how much the whole gaff reeks of it, how it *permeates*. She's still got that Indian-ink home-made BEV tattoo on her forearm, making zero attempt tae conceal it, even when she's working directly with her customers in her service industry business. Admittedly, wir no talking fussy client base here: a million miles removed fae the sorts who would patronise, say, fat boy De Fretais's restaurant.

I grew up hanging around that shop, where every old boiler of a regular was a surrogate auntie or gran. I was smeared, like a luxury unguent, intae aw thon meaty bosoms. A wee boy without a daddy: to be pitied, spoiled, loved even. Good old sunny Leith: no place loves its bastards like a port.

The electric-bar fire with its fake coal display throws out some heat, but her big, blue fluffy Persian cat lies sprawled out on the rug in front of it, absorbing all the warmth like the selfish fucker it is. The art deco mantelpiece bordering it is usually the centrepiece of the room, but it now takes second place to an overwhelming, outsized Christmas tree in the corner. On the wall, above the fireplace, hangs a mounted copy of the Clash album *London Calling*. Scrawled on it by Magic Marker ink is:

To Bev, Edinburgh's No.1 punk,
Luv Joe S xxx
20/1/80

The Old Girl's great conceit is that she's a student of human nature, having convinced herself that, in her line of work, she can read a person like a copy of *Hello!*. When they come in and tell her they're thinking of having this or that done to their dry, cracking or lank, greasy locks, she looks them in the eye and goes: 'Ye *sure* that's what ye want?' They'll stare nervously back at her and throw out some hopeful possibilities till she nods approvingly and says, 'That's the one.' Then she'll cheerfully expedite this, cooing 'It's awfay nice', or 'It really suits ye, hen'. And they keep coming back. As the Old Girl often boasts, 'Ah ken thum better thin they ken thirsels.'

Unwelcome, however, is the application of this attitude in her dealings with her solo bastard offspring. She sits in her chair as I slump on the couch, hitting the handset and switching on *Scotland Today*. — That compo money, she begins, narrowing her eyes under those big specs, — suppose that's aw in the hands ay the publicans by now, eh?

The Old Girl's expanding out the way. She's always been a short-arse, but now her face is getting fleshier. As she's always favoured black, she gets no slim-effect pay-off on her middle-age spread. — Grossly unfair, I say as the sports round-up comes on and another Riordan goal bursts the net, — there's a number of bookies who've had their cut.

But she's taking the pish here. She knows how much it cost to put a deposit on that flat. It was *fifteen* grand I got for that accident, no a hundred and fifteen!

— So it's aw been squandered? she says, running her hand through her crimson hair.

I'm not getting into this with her. — To paraphrase a great footballer: 'I spent most of it on drink, women and the horses. The rest I squandered.'

— Aye, right, the Old Girl snorts, rising and putting her hands on her hips, unwittingly mimicking the pose struck by Jean-Jacques Burnel in the Stranglers poster on the wall behind her. — Suppose yir steyin for yir tea?

This is seldom the gastronomic treat she imagines it to be. — What ye got?

— Sausages.

Hud me back. — Beef or pork?

The Old Girl whips her glasses from her face, leaving wine-coloured indentations on each side of her nose. She struggles to refocus, looking like she's just woken up as she brushes the lenses on her blouse. — You wantin yir tea or no?

— Aye . . . awright.

— Dinnae dae ays any favours, Danny, she muses, breathing on her lenses and wiping them again. She puts them back on and heads across to the galley kitchen, where she opens up the fridge.

I get up and move across to the kitchen area, draping myself over the breakfast bar. — Maybe I ought to have invested my money in commodities. Something popular and durable, I stretch across, poking the tattoo on her arm, — like Indian ink.

She pulls away, glowering at me through those specs. — Dinnae start, son. And dinnae think you can be paupin oaffay me aw the time. You've a good job: ye can pey yir ain credit card bills.

Every time I come here I get reminded about fucking bills. My Old Girl still likes to think of herself as a punk, but she's a small businesswoman to her marrow.

3

The Outdoor Life

The bracken was thinning out as the gradient of the hill rose steeply. Brian Kibby, his too large Aran sweater and waterproof anorak flapping in the wind, wiped some sweat from his brow under a baseball cap, which was fastened so tightly that it hurt. He took a deep breath, feeling the cool, mountain air clearing out his lungs. As the life fused through his wiry frame, he stopped at his vantage point, turning to look back across at the great range of Munros, and the sweep of the valley curling beneath him.

As he enjoyed his sense of oneness with the world, a righteous notion seized him: this was the best thing he'd ever done, going along to the hillwalking club with Ian Buchan, his only friend from his schooldays, who remained his special companion. They had met through a shared mutual love – video games – and had attempted to convert each other to their own great passions. Ian was one of the few people who had been allowed to set foot in Brian Kibby's attic, with its much coveted model railway, though Kibby knew he had little real interest. And though he himself only tolerated Ian's *Star Trek* obsession, his devotion to hillwalking was for real.

Brian loved his weekends with that wholesome, hearty bunch, rejoicing under their collective title, the Hyp Hykers. It had greatly pleased his ailing father that he was getting out more and had a pal, even if Keith Kibby was doubtful about the somewhat exclusive nature of his son's friendship with Ian Buchan and even more so about this *Star Trek* obsession. Even up in the desolate hills, his father's condition seldom strayed far from Brian Kibby's thoughts. His dad was very ill now, and had seemed so weak and frail when he'd visited him in the hospital the previous night.

Brian Kibby licked at the salt that was tainting his lips, and after the effort of the trek up the path by the side of the hill, raised the bottle of Evian to his mouth. Looking down the valley in some trepidation towards the biggest mushroom cloud of midges he had ever seen, he felt the mineral water massage the back of his dry throat.

Replete with the sense of himself, he gaped in wonder down across the deep gorge over to the stark, sweeping hills above him, the scene scored by Coldplay's *Parachutes* album, which played on his iPod. Switching off the machine and pulling out his earphones, he let the natural silence, broken only by the faint squawking of some overhead birds, resonate for a bit. Then a sudden sound of thicket crushing underfoot signalled a presence by his side. Assuming it was Ian, he said without turning, — Look at that, it makes ye feel great tae be alive!

— It's beautiful, a female voice agreed, as Kibby experienced panic and elation rising in his breast and vying for dominance. As he turned round he felt his cheeks burn and his eyes moisten. It was Lucy Moore, with her intense blue eyes and those blonde-brown curls, which were whipping recklessly in the wind, and she was talking to *him*. — Eh . . . aye . . . he managed to cough out as his eyes fell on her scarlet slash of a mouth.

Lucy seemed not to notice Kibby's awkwardness. Her composed but piercing eyes scanned the mountains across the valley, the tops of which were dusted white with snow, before settling on the highest point. — I'd love to have a go at climbing it, she said, glancing conspiratorially at him.

— Naw . . . eh . . . hillwalking suits me just fine, Kibby responded lamely, immediately regretting it as he sensed her vague interest in him steadily draining away. Worse, it was replaced by the aura of mild contempt he habitually appeared to induce in many members of the opposite sex. — Mind you, it *is* tempting tae give it a go . . . he added, striving to recover his standing.

— I'd love to, Lucy reiterated, advancing again but more tentatively.

Kibby didn't know what to say and lisped out, — Aye, it would be great, right enough.

There followed a silence of such excruciating embarrassment that Brian Kibby, who had reluctantly managed to get through his teens and the first year of his twenties without so much as kissing a girl, would unquestionably have traded a lifetime of virginity simply to be free from its torment. Blood bubbled in his face, tears welled in his uncontrollably blinking eyes, snot ran in a steady stream from his nose and his throat dried up to the extent that he knew if he attempted to speak his voice would crackle like the dry twigs under his feet.

The impasse was only broken when Lucy asked wearily, — What time is it?

Kibby was so eager to be free of his torture that in his haste to respond he caught the elasticated cagoule cuff on his watch strap, ripping the garment slightly. — Nea-nearly two, he stammered.

— I suppose we'd better get back to the bothy for our meal, Lucy mused, regarding Kibby in a quizzical manner.

— Aye, Kibby trilled, perhaps a little too highly, — or these gannets'll have the lot!

And something collapsed inside of him when he saw the slightly sad smile he elicited from her. For he knew that same look from his sister, her friends, and the girls from the office: he saw it in every young woman of his acquaintance. He took off the red baseball cap and stuck it in his pocket, feeling his temples breathe.

The stone walls of the quarry were steep and grave, as stark as a row of tombstones in a cemetery. From the banks of the man-made lake opposite, Danny Skinner looked at the wizened trees twisting upwards, trying to find light in the foreboding shadow the big stones cast. It had been raining all day. Now it had stopped, leaving a dusky sky with the promise of a damp, shivering night ahead.

A cold was settling into his chest already, aggravated by the cocaine-fuelled stream of mucus that trickled steadily down the back of his throat. He looked around at the three ill-clad men beside him. In a predatory manner, they were regarding two other men who were fishing in the quarry and who were more appropriately dressed for the seasonal inclemencies. Big Rab McKenzie, six foot four and overweight, was his best mate from way back at school, and still his best drinking buddy. Gareth he didn't know that well, they'd only been friends for a few weeks, but Skinner had liked him by his reputation before they had even met.

It was Dempsey who made him uneasy. Despite his relative youth, the diverse circles that he flitted around in meant that Skinner had met quite a few name hard men, even the odd psychopath. He noticed, though, that once they got to a certain stage of development, they generally only swam with other sharks. But there was something ubiquitous and consuming about Dempsey. Very useful in certain street confrontation situations certainly, but definitely miscast here. Or, Skinner reflected, perhaps it was he who was miscast.

They were all football mates and the waterlogged pitches had wiped out the fixture list across the country. But that was what they did; they mobbed up on a Saturday and had a bit of harmless sport; sometimes a punch-up, usually just posturing. But, Skinner asked himself again, what was he doing in a quarry in West Lothian on a pissing December Saturday evening?

The answer had been cocaine. Earlier, in a pub in the city, Dempsey had chopped out line after line as the company had whittled down to the four of them. Then he'd suggested a little adventure in the country. It had seemed fine at the time, a scheme formulated in a warm city pub full of drug bravado. Now, out here, it had gone from exciting to dubious to plain boring. Skinner wanted so badly to be at home with Kay.

He had told her that, in the absence of the football, he was going fishing with some of the boys. It was unlikely but was actually almost true. But he knew that he should be with her now, so he grew anxious. He hopefully recalled that she'd mentioned something about dance rehearsals. They could go on. But he was still fretful, though perhaps not as much as the two anglers seemed to be.

— Well stocked wi pike, the quarry, Skinner, trying to lighten things, explained to the two fishing lads. — Used to be aw perch. So they introduced a couple of pike, like: 'pike–lake, lake–pike', he motored on, scarcely waiting for a reaction but noting Dempsey's twisted smile, — and the cunts tore through the perch stocks. Decimation job. He turned to his friends. — Got so fuckin low oan perch that the locals were flinging in the wooden spars fae their budgerigar cages, jist tae make the numbers up! And Skinner's coffin-plate dazzle of a smile was forming involuntarily as he smelt the fear rising in the angling boys. He sensed they caught the nakedness of his base response and it briefly belittled him.

And the insipid setting sun was covered by another wave of renegade black clouds, sending a filthy shadow racing across the lake causing one fishing lad, one with ginger hair, to visibly shiver. McKenzie, feeling moved to react to this, kicked over the box of fishing tackle and bait. Live maggots squirmed in the mud. — Clumsy ay me, eh?

Skinner gritted his teeth and exchanged a knowing look with Gareth that said: trust McKenzie to let the side down by embarrassing us with such a corny line, delivered so shockingly as well.

— Fae up the coonty, then, boys? Dempsey asked. — No attached tae any mob, ur yis? he enquired of the bemused lads before pointing and raising his voice to one boy: — Ginger cunt! Ah asked ye, what fuckin team dae ye support?

— I dinnae follow football . . . the boy started.

Dempsey seemed to consider this statement for a second or two, nodding his head in appreciation, like a toff savouring a fine wine on his palate.

— Pike are bad bastards, Skinner laughed. — Freshwater sharks. It's in the nature of the beast.

— Ken Dixie fae Bathgate? Dempsey snapped at the ginger lad, seeming not to hear Skinner, who was feeling the stakes slowly rise.

The ginger boy shook his head, the other nodded in the affirmative, both punctiliously avoiding eye contact. — Just by name.

— If you see him aboot tell him Dempsey was looking fir the cunt, Dempsey said, emphasising his own name and seeming somewhat put out that the boys offered no reaction to this disclosure.

In exasperation, Skinner chipped a stone with the outside of his boot and watched it skite a satisfying second bounce across the surface of the loch before vanishing with a thunking sound. They'd had a couple of beers and some charlie and been roped into going out to West Lothian for an obscure vendetta that Dempsey had had with an old acquaintance for years, probably over something neither could remember. They couldn't find a trace of the boy and had gone for a wander. This petty bullying was a result of the frustration that nothing had come off. But it was more than that, it was also about the old guard versus the newer breed, Skinner had decided; a dance of power between McKenzie and Dempsey, and the poor fish-boys were caught in the middle. — Sorry to disturb you chaps, hope the fish bite, Skinner sang cheerfully as he nodded to Gareth and they headed down the road. Ominously, McKenzie and Dempsey stalled.

Gareth grimaced. — Those two should just go on holiday to a little B&B and indulge in the Greek love until the need leaves their systems.

Skinner liked Gareth but elected to smile tightly and keep his counsel. — A man should be able to plunge his rod in peace. Basic human right, he remarked inanely.

They heard some cries and shouting but walked resolutely on, heading quickly back to the car. Some moments later they saw McKenzie and Dempsey hurrying towards them in the rear-view mirror. — Did the cunts, a flustered Dempsey gasped, as they climbed into the back of the car. He had a swollen and bruised eye. McKenzie wore a sharkish grin.

— Did they have a mobby? Gareth asked irritably. — Cause the fucking bizzies will be all over us.

— Might no git a signal here, Dempsey said sheepishly, — the waws ay the quarry.

Gareth started the car, stepping on it as they tore away up the track on to the main road, heading for the Kincardine Bridge. — We take the scenic route. You cunts train it from Stirling, he nodded in the back at Dempsey and McKenzie. Skinner wondered whether he had angered Dempsey by sitting in the front passenger seat. Inevitable, especially given the fact that he was crushed in the back beside Big Rab McKenzie.

— Paranoid cunt! Dempsey moaned.

— You can fuck off, Demps, I didn't come out to this grot-hole to watch you having handbags with civilians, Gareth snapped back.

— Aye, but – Dempsey began.

— But nothing. I thought you were after Andy Dickson. I stupidly agreed to help you in this silly little quest as I was chinged beyond reason, and at any rate have no love for that slack-jawed fool. But were any of the boys there Andy Dickson? No? Thought not.

— They wir gittin fucking wide, Dempsey hissed.

— They were *fishing*, Gareth bit back.

In the mirror Skinner noted that Dempsey's eyes burned into the back of Gareth's skull, but the driver didn't seem to register. Meanwhile, McKenzie recounted the tale of doing the angling lads with enthusiasm. Realising the way it was going, one of them went for it and got in first, cracking Dempsey in the eye with a good right-hander. — The ginger cunt, he expanded with some glee. Then McKenzie went on to explain how he decked the boy's mate with one punch and watched in amusement as a furious Dempsey, almost paralysed with rage and frustration, eventually overpowered and booted the fuck out of his assailant.

Dempsey sat as tense as a coiled spring in the back seat, forced to listen to McKenzie's account. Short of killing the fisherman, he knew that he could do little to erase the memory in McKenzie's head of that first blow, struck in surprise by the ginger guy, even if the boy had eventually paid for his bottle and self-respect. But the story would go forth of how this doss ginger cunt twatted Demps at the quarry. His blow would grow more spectacular and Dempsey's retaliation more puny and inconsequential. It would be a fisherman's tale alright, McKenzie's beaming smile testified to that.

In the car, Gareth, possibly sensitive to Dempsey's humiliation and concerned about an aftermath, relented and drove everybody back to the city. As the bungalows of suburbia turned into the tenements of the inner city, Skinner thought that he should get back to Kay now, but McKenzie had suggested going for a pint. Maybe he would have just the one before heading home.

4

Skegness

Joyce Kibby's goosey eye had drifted from the pan of scrambling eggs, only for what seemed to her muddied consciousness to be a second or two, as she'd glanced in distraction at the picture. It sat innocuously on the ornamental shelf of the Tudor-style fitted kitchen her husband had built with his own hands.

It was a photo of herself, Keith and the kids at Skegness. It would have been 1989 and it had rained most of the fortnight. The picture had been taken by the Crazy Golf attendant. Barry, she recollected his name was. Most visitors to the Kibby home would have seen this as an unremarkable family snap, especially as the house was littered with them. For Joyce, however, it had a magical, transcendental quality.

To her it seemed to be the one picture that captured the essence of them all: Keith with his hard-won cheerfulness; Caroline with that provocative, hawkish glee she exhibited as a child and which had never left her. Then there was Brian's happiness; it always had a precarious aspect to it, as if being exhibited too ostentatiously might precipitate the appearance of dark forces that would serve to destroy it. In short, she reasoned worryingly, he was just like her.

A burning smell twisted into her nostrils. — Drat, Joyce muttered, pulling the pan from the heated ring of the stove and scraping at the eggs with the wooden spoon to make sure that they didn't cement to the bottom. Those pills Dr Craigmyre had given her, to help her cope with Keith's condition; they were making her slow and befuddled.

Where was Caroline?

A thin woman in her late forties, with large, busy eyes and a prominent nose, Joyce Kibby skipped across the slate floor tiles.

Poking her head from kitchen to hall, she shouted up the stairs, — Caroline! Come on!

Upstairs in her room, Caroline Kibby elbowed herself up slowly, pushing her blonde hair from her face. A giant image of Robbie Williams greeted her, smiling from the adjacent wall. She'd always found that particular photograph of him sweet and somehow touching. Today, though, it seemed to do Robbie no favours at all, perhaps even making him look a little simple. Swinging her legs out from the bed she had a second to note the goose bumps on them before Joyce's shrill voice echoed up the stairs again. — Caroliiinne!

— Aye. Aye. Aye, she mouthed in hushed exasperation at the large poster.

Caroline stood up and felt the chill on her for the few steps it took to pull her blue dressing gown from the hook on the door, and wrap it round herself. She instinctively held it tight at her chest as she emerged into the hall and immediately saw that her brother was getting ready – he had the bathroom door open to let the steam from the shower out. There was a dripping Star of David on the mirror. Brian was already dressed in the dark blue suit their dad had insisted that he bought for his new job. It fitted well, its cut making her brother seem more elegantly slim than the painfully thin way he was normally perceived. It added to him, she considered, Brian was definitely meant to wear a suit. — Very smart, Caroline smiled.

Brian grinned at her, showing his big, white teeth. He had good teeth, her brother, she thought.

It was a big day for him. This was an officer's job at a bigger inspectorate than Fife, and was several salary grades higher. Additionally, there weren't the same travel costs to consider. However, it was a big step up in responsibility and in some ways, across his tired eyes perhaps, it looked to Caroline like the pressure was telling on him a little. But they were all suffering from a great deal of stress right now. — Nervous? she enquired.

— Naw, Brian said, then conceded, — Well, maybe just a wee bit.

— Caroline! Joyce's voice, high and nasal, rose again from downstairs. — Your breakfast is getting cold!

Caroline leaned over the rail above the staircase. — Aye! I can hear you! I'm coming, she ticked, Brian Kibby tensely noting the sinew straining in his sister's neck.

Joyce immediately stopped her rustling sounds as a tentative silence rose like hot steam from the kitchen. It was as if a bush sniper had just blown the head off a comrade in her proximity.

Brian Kibby looked at his sister in dismay, but Caroline merely returned his pout and shrugged at him.

— C'mon, Caz . . . he pleaded.

— She gets on my nerves sometimes.

— I think it's because of Dad, Brian said, adding, — It's a big strain.

Now she was finding something patronising and exclusive in her brother's tone and it rankled. — It is for all of us, she briskly retorted.

Brian was slightly taken aback at the edge in Caroline's voice. She had shown few overt signs of their father's illness affecting her. But of course it must, after all she was his favourite, he ruefully considered. In his habitual manner of making allowances, Kibby excused his sister's youth, determining that it was just her way. — And I think she's nervous for me cause of it being my first day of work and stuff . . . he carried on, again imploring, — Try no tae wind her up, Caz . . .

Caroline shrugged non-committally as the Kibby siblings headed downstairs to the kitchen. Brian raised his eyebrows as he saw the large plate of scrambled eggs, bacon, grilled tomato and mushrooms on the table. His mother worried about him being thin, but he could eat anything and never put on weight, considering it a metabolic fate he shared with her. — You'll be glad of it later, Joyce pre-emptively told him as he sat down, — you don't know what the food'll be like in that council canteen. You always said the one in Kirkcaldy wasn't up to much, she mused, turning to Caroline, who loaded some egg on to a slice of toast and pushed aside a rasher of bacon.

Joyce screwed up her face, which Caroline immediately registered.

— I've told you that I don't eat meat, Caroline said. — Why did you put it down for me when you know that I don't eat it?

— It's just one rasher, Joyce replied in a supplicating manner.

— Excuse me, but do you actually *hear* what I say? Caroline asked, looking squarely at her mother. — What do you think the statement 'I don't eat meat' means?

— You need meat. One rasher. Joyce rolled her eyes, looking to Brian who was busying himself with buttering some toast.

— I. Don't. Eat. Meat, Caroline stated for the third time, now adopting a new tone, almost laughing at her mother.

— It's hardly anything, Joyce bristled. — You're a growing lassie still.

— In all the wrong ways if it was up to you.

— You're anorexic, that's your problem, Joyce stated. — I've read all about this daft obsession you ones all have with your weight nowadays and I –

— You can't call me that! Caroline flushed in anger. — That's labelling somebody mentally ill!

Joyce looked ruefully at her daughter. What did she know about illness, the cocky young besom? — There's your dad fighting for his life in that hospital, on drips, and he'd give his eye teeth to be able to get down some solid food . . .

Caroline speared the rasher with her fork and held it up to her mother. — Take it in for him then! She sprang to her feet, storming up the stairs to her room.

Joyce started to bubble, in small, broken sobs, — The little . . . oh . . . and stopped suddenly, as if just remembering that Brian was present, — I'm sorry son, on your first day at your new job as well. I just don't know that lassie any more, she said, looking at the ceiling. — She'd never talk like that if your dad was . . .

— It's okay, I'll go up and speak to her. She's upset as well, Mum. About Dad. It's just her way, Brian reasoned.

Joyce took a deep breath. — No, son, finish your breakfast, you'll be late, it's your first day of work. Your new job. It's no fair, it's just no fair, she said, shaking her head, leaving him wondering precisely what injustice she was referring to.

Brian Kibby was anxious to do just that and get out of the house. Though he had time to spare he bolted his food down and stuck his red baseball cap on his head. The momentum and excitement took him swiftly up Featherhall Road to St John's Road, where he saw a number 12 bus approaching. Sprinting to the stop to catch it, he was fortunate to find a seat and stared out through steamed glass at the cold, sodden city. They crawled in traffic past the zoo, then on to Western Corner, Roseburn, Haymarket and along Princes Street, before he alighted at Waverley Station and walked up Cockburn Street to the Royal Mile. He removed the red baseball cap with the football logo stitched into it, as it didn't look right with a suit, and stuck it in his bag.

His flight from home had warmed him, but disembarking from the bus, the morning's damp chill began to insinuate itself. As he felt the drizzle and haar slowly saturating his clothing, he reflected that sometimes going outdoors in Scotland could be like stepping into a cold sauna. To kill some time he walked down the Royal Mile a little. In the newsagent's he bought this month's copy of *Game Informer*, putting it into his bag. Then he cut down a side street, excitement fluttering in his stomach as he saw one of his favourite shops, with its quaint, painted sign:

A.T. Wilson Hobbies and Pastimes

Brian remembered how his dad enjoyed teasing him about his frequent purchases from this particular shop. 'Still going tae the toyshop then, son? Ye no a wee bit auld for all that?' Keith Kibby would laugh, but there was often a mocking, derisive edge to this humour and it shamed the son, making him more covert about his purchases.

The showpiece model railway in the Kibby attic was impressive, though as Brian had few acquaintances, not many people had enjoyed the privilege of seeing it. As a train driver, Keith Kibby originally thought that his son was sharing in his locomotive fascination, and was disappointed to learn that this passion only ran to *model* trains. But in a misplaced attempt to encourage him in the activity, his father, an enthusiastic DIY man, had floored the attic and put in the aluminium stepladder and the lighting.

Brian Kibby had inherited his father's woodworking skills. Keith's joinery workshop had been on the other side of the attic until he had become too ill to manage up the ladder so frequently and had used the garden shed instead. Therefore the whole floor became devoted to Brian's railway and town complex, apart from a few old cupboards where some childhood toys and books were stored, and a lot of shelving containing his archived games review magazines.

It was very rare for anyone else to go up there, and the attic became Brian's refuge, a place of retreat when he was bullied at school or when he had things, or girls, to think about. Evenings of lonely, guilty masturbation sessions rolled by as his fevered mind conjured up naked or scantily clad images of the girls in his neighbourhood or at his school whom he was almost too shy to look at, let alone talk to.

But his overwhelming passion was his model railway. This, too, he was ashamed of; it was so out of kilter with what the other kids enjoyed, or at least professed to enjoy, the pleasure it afforded was as culpably delicious as his bouts of masturbation. As a result, he became more circumspect and withdrawn among his peers, only really feeling free when he was in his attic, the master of the environment he was creating.

Keith's family jokes about being 'pushed out' the attic concealed much greater anxieties, and not just relating to his own declining health. He worried that he had psychologically bricked his son into the roof space; through encouraging this hobby he'd presented this shy boy with a means of entombing himself.

When Brian got to the age when Keith considered him too old to accompany them on family holidays, the father asked the son where he was planning to go.

— Hamburg, Brian told him eagerly.

Keith thought with concern about the touristy sex-sleaze of the Reeperbahn, but then realised, with some relief, that it was just a rite of passage his son was long overdue, as he cast his mind back to his own teenage adventures in Amsterdam's red-light district. Something then jarred inside him when the boy added, — They've got the biggest model railway in the world there!

But Keith knew that it had been him who had initiated the obsession. He had helped his son build the big papier mâché hills, which the trains ran around and tunnelled under, and had assisted him in making the detailed constructions. Brian's pride was the station building and hotel, modelled on St Pancras in London. It had been part of a woodwork project at school, where it had survived several sabotage attempts by Andy McGrillen, a local bully who had taken a particular interest in persecuting him. Once he'd managed to get it home safely though, there was no stopping Brian Kibby, as everything expanded out from those structures he'd lovingly crafted.

Now Kibbytown, as he often referred to it, also contained a football stadium, which was constructed around a Subbuteo pitch. The rail track ran past it, reminding the onlooker of Brockville or Starks Park. His latest project was the construction of an ambitious modern stand, which would form a bridge over the track, with Lansdowne Road Stadium in Dublin as the model. Brian even shed his antipathy to sport, attending several games at Tynecastle and Murrayfield to look at stadium design.

Keith always seemed anxious when a new phase of construction would begin. He worried that his son might level his papier mâché hills, which he seemed inordinately concerned with, but Brian always built around them. And build the boy did: tenements, tower blocks, bungalows, everything he could think of as his town sprawled across the attic, mirroring the development of the west of Edinburgh where he grew up.

Now, in the morning rain, standing on the street and looking into the window of Wilson's Hobbies, Kibby was instantly mesmerised. He couldn't believe what he was seeing, but there it was! The sleek maroon-and-black engine gleamed as with eager anticipation he read the gold-and-black emblazoned plaque on the side: CITY OF NOTTINGHAM. It was an R2383 BR Princess Class *City of Nottingham*. It had been out of stock due to high demand, becoming an instant rarity.

How long have I been after one of them?!

His heart began to race as he looked at his watch. The shop would be open at nine o'clock, in just five minutes' time, but he was due to report to a Mr Foy at 9.15 a.m. It was 105 pounds and if he left it there, it would be snapped up before he could get back at lunchtime. Brian Kibby charged across the road to the cashpoint and withdrew his money, all the time shaking with excitement and fear, lest some other model-railway enthusiast sneak in and plunder the coveted artefact.

Racing back over to the shop, Kibby saw Arthur, the old proprietor, limp into the doorway and turn the keys to open up. He lurched in after him, unable to contain his excitement, having to stop abruptly as the old man suddenly bent down to pick up the morning mail. Taking what to Kibby seemed an agonising time, he gathered the letters and files together, then said sagely, — Aye, Brian son, I think I ken what you're after.

Quickly glancing again at his timepiece, Kibby was now concerned that he'd be late. He couldn't do that, couldn't make such a bad impression on his first day of work. Getting off on the right foot was important. His dad had always stressed punctuality to the point where it now obsessed Brian Kibby. It was a train driver's thing, he supposed.

Old Arthur seemed a bit put out when the young lad left promptly after purchasing the engine, not staying for a chat as was his custom. Young people were always dashing around, he thought in some disappointment as he had long considered Brian Kibby to be different.

Kibby sprinted across the road, box under his arm. No, he couldn't be late, he kept saying to himself over and over again in an agitated mantra. He was going to the hospital tonight and he had to be able to look his dad in the eye and tell him that everything had gone well on his first day. The clock at the Tron told him there was a bit of time, and he started to relax a little and get his puff back.

Outside the City Chambers some major roadworks were taking place. They were always digging up the cobblestones on the Royal Mile, Kibby considered. Then he recognised one of the workmen. It was McGrillen, his old tormentor from school, wearing a sleeveless quilted jacket as he operated a big pneumatic drill, the vibrations of which showed his powerful muscles rippling in his arms. Kibby contemplated his own puny biceps, and recalled the ridiculousness of his dad saying, — If anybody mucks you about at school, just gie them that, holding up his own scared fist in illustration.

Brian Kibby's grip tightened on the box he was carrying.

As McGrillen looked up and clocked him in slow recognition, Kibby felt rising in him the customary bolt of fear his old adversary's presence engendered. However, as he contemplated McGrillen, it seemed to settle into another, less definable emotion. The contempt in his old tormentor's eyes was still there, but this time, clad in workman's clothes, he was confronted by Kibby in a suit and some repressed bourgeois part of McGrillen's soul was belittled. And Kibby saw it; saw that McGrillen could see his own life elongating out ahead of him, digging roads, while he, Brian Kibby, was in his suit and tie, a man of business and substance, a council inspector!

And Kibby couldn't resist a little smirk, in that, after all the school playground humiliations and the years of crossing the road at the baker's or chip shop, he had now gained some measure of revenge, some kind of vindication. That small self-satisfied smile, how it must be like a nail in poor McGrillen's heart! he thought as he danced over the forecourt, instantly withdrawing his glance and proceeding in a studiedly distracted, businesslike manner, as if McGrillen was somebody he thought he maybe knew but was obviously mistaken!

Inside the impressive hallway, Kibby climbed a mahogany-panelled staircase to a set of lifts. Getting into one elevator, he saw a guy in a suit, his own age, maybe a little older. Kibby thought the boy looked cool, as the suit seemed expensive. And the guy nodded and smiled at him; at *him*, Brian Kibby! And why not? Now he was somebody, an officer of the council, not just an unskilled workie like McGrillen.

The likes of that boy wouldnae even gie the likes of Andrew McGrillen the time ay day!

Then he realised that the boy was with this lassie; well, Kibby felt his hormones race, and she gave him a smile too, before she started talking to the young guy. Wow, Kibby thought, admiring her light brown hair, her busy, big brown eyes and her full lips. What a doll, he gasped to himself, seized with a kind of ecstatic rush so strong, he almost forgot for a few moments about the box under his arm.

At the next floor two men in blue overalls got into the lift and then a hot, fecund stench filled the box they were crammed into. Somebody had let off. It was awful, and the guy in the suit caught Kibby's eye and looked to the boys in the overalls and screwed his face up in disgust. The workmen got off at the next stop. The young guy in the suit said loudly, — That is minging!

A few people grinned and the young lassie laughed. — Danny, she tutted.

— I'm no joking, Shannon, Kibby heard the boy say. — There's nae need for thon. There's a toilet on every floor.

Shannon, Kibby thought, too excited and flustered to turn and see if they were going his way. No, he thought, this was his big chance. They didn't know him; he wasn't going to be the timid boy at school or the quiet apprentice in the office who made the tea for grumpy old guys like in his last job. He was going to come of age here, going to be confident, outgoing and respected. Then he sucked in air and turned to face this Danny guy and this Shannon lassie. — Excuse me . . . can you tell me where the Environmental Health section is? I've an appointment to see Mr Robert Foy.

— You must be Brian, the girl called Shannon smiled, and so, Kibby noted in appreciation, did the boy Danny.

— Follow us, he said.

Just in the door and I've already made pals with some really good people!

5
Compensation

The alarm clock's relentless jackhammering jolted Danny Skinner from one hell into another. His hand shot out, slapping its 'off' switch, but for a while the noise continued to pulse inside his brain. The tormented, feverish dreams had gone, but they were only to be traded for the reality of a cold, stark Monday morning of work. His heavy head started to clear as the dawn shadows began to define the room. A surge of panic exploded in his chest as he reached out by instinct, his bare leg surging into the cold of the other side of the bed.

No.

Kay had not come back, had not stayed the night. She stopped over at his a lot, most weekends, in fact. Perhaps she'd gone for a drink with her friend Kelly; two fit girls, two dancers, on the town. The thought appealed to Skinner. Then a sour smell rose in his nostrils. Across in one corner he saw a pile of vomit. He gave thanks that it was confined to the strip-pine floor, missing the oriental rug with several Kama Sutra positions illustrated on it, which had cost him half his month's wages from an antique shop in the Grassmarket.

Skinner snapped on the radio and listened to the implausibly cheerful DJ slaver on for an excruciatingly long time, before a welcome, familiar tune alleviated his misery slightly. He sat up slowly and looked at his clothes strewn over the floor and hanging on to the bottom of the brass bedstead, with the desperation of shipwrecked men on driftwood. Then he morbidly contemplated the bottle of empty beer and full ashtray by the bed. These dregs were lit up like an abhorrent composition by the thin early-morning sun, which filtered in through the threadbare curtains. A chilly wind whistled through cracked, rattling window frames, stinging his naked torso.

Wrecked again last night. Last weekend. No wonder Kay had elected to go back home. Fuckin dingul Skinner . . . fuckin useless phantom bastard . . . acting like an idiot . . .

He considered that he never used to mind the cold. Now he felt it chipping away at his life force. I'm twenty-three, he thought in nervy desperation, jagged with the hangover. His hand rose to his temples to rub out a twinge of neuralgia he felt might herald the onset of the explosive aneurysm that would blow him into the next life.

It's fucking cold in this place. Cold and dark. It'll never be Australia or California. It's not going to get any better.

Sometimes he thought about the father he'd never met. Liked the idea of him being somewhere warm, perhaps in what they call 'the New World'. In his mind's eye, he could see a healthy and tanned man, perhaps with salt-and-pepper hair and a bronze-limbed family, youthful and blond. And he would be accepted into their midst in an act of reconciliation that would make sense of his life.

Could you miss what you'd never had?

Last winter he was skint and he'd tried to stay in, to stay off the drink. He found himself listening to Leonard Cohen, studying Schopenhauer's philosophical works and reading assorted Scandinavian poets, who seemed to him to be clinically depressed, tortured by those long winter nights. Sigbjorn Obstfelder, the Norwegian modernist who wrote at the end of the nineteenth century, was a particular favourite with those great lines of morbid decadence, Skinner's most memorable being:

> *The day it is passing in laughter and song.*
> *Death he is sowing the whole night long.*
> *Death he is sowing.*

Sometimes he thought that he could see it on the faces of the old boys in the Leith pubs: each pint and nip seeming to bring the Grim Reaper one step closer, while fuelling delusions of immortality.

But what sweet delusions!

And he remembered dragging his girlfriend out to the pub on Sunday afternoon, when all she'd wanted to do was lie around watching television with him.

Skinner, though, had needed to drink off his Friday night and Saturday hangover and he'd all but jostled her out the door and steered her up Leith Walk to Robbie's, where several of his cronies were drinking. Yet Kay sat there, the solitary woman, smiling and uncomplaining, indulged or ignored by those weird and wonderful men who just drank and drank and drank. It was as if some of them had never set their bloodshot eyes on a woman before while others had seen at least one more than they ever wanted to. It didn't concern Kay that much; she was just happy to be with the boy that she loved, wherever they went. She couldn't be like them though. She needed to watch her weight, to stay fit, so that she could dance. She would say, You don't understand, I need to stay fit. He'd say, But you *are* so fit, babe.

But with each drink Skinner had got more boisterous and pedantic. He was arguing with his mate, Gary Traynor, a wiry young man with close-cropped fair hair and a harsh but mischievous face. — They huvnae got a proper mob these days. How many could they pull the gither?

Traynor shrugged, a faint smirk on his face, and sucked at his beer. Alex Shevlane, a torpedo-headed gym rat of a guy who looked like he overdid the weights, surreptitiously clocked his biceps in the wall mirror as he raised his bottle of beer to his mouth. — Last time we wir through thair the cunts never showed up. Fuckin waste ay time, he hissed.

— You're eywis oan aboot that, Traynor grinned, slapping Shevlane's broad back heartily. — Let it go. Ye want tae sue the cunts for damages? Emotional damages for wreckin yir weekend, he laughed, nodding towards a well-dressed, shifty-looking young man who was drinking alone at the bar. — Dessie Kinghorn thair's yir man!

Skinner turned round to clock the solitary Des Kinghorn, who caught his glance with hard, penetrating eyes. Skinner rose and walked over to him as Traynor's face expanded in glee.

— Dessie, how goes it, mate?

Kinghorn looked him over, checked the Aquascutum jacket and new Nike trainers. Gave a slow, evaluating nod. — Awright, he said gruffly. — New threads?

Three years and the cunt's still got the cream puff, Skinner thought. — Aye . . . want a drink, mate? He nodded towards the bar.

— Naw, yir awright, got tae head, Kinghorn said, killing his beer, nodding curtly and moving to the exit.

As he went out through the door into the street, Traynor looked across at Skinner, pursing his lips and rolling his eyes. Shevlane's grin mirrored the shark motif on his black-and-white-striped jumper. Skinner shrugged and opened his palms in appeal. Kay was taking this entire scene in, trying to work out what was happening and why this guy had snubbed her boyfriend. — Who was that, Danny? She asked.

— Just an old buddy, Dessie Kinghorn, he said. Noting that this response satisfied nobody round the table, least of all Kay, he was forced into recounting a tale. — Mind I told you, the summer before we met, I got run over by a motor? Broken leg, broken airm, two ribs, fractured skull?

— Yes . . . she nodded. She never liked to think of such injuries. Not just to him, but in general. She had an important audition coming up. Who could recover after such injuries and dance again? How long would it take? Even now, she sometimes imagined that her boyfriend had an unevenness to his gait, perhaps a legacy of the accident.

— Well, I put a claim in for the injuries. Dessie works in insurance and he put it through for me, like got me the forms and that, put me in touch with a photographer.

Kay nodded. — Like to take pictures of your injuries?

— Aye. I mean, ah wis grateful, telt him there would be a drink in it for him. Well, I got fifteen grand, which I was chuffed about, dinnae get me wrong, but ah wis off work for six months, in traction, the lot, Skinner appealed. — I went tae gie him five hundred quid when it came through. Ah mean, ah appreciated what he did, but every cunt was gaun oan tae me aboot claiming compensation, I just did it through the insurance company Dessie worked for. The way ah saw it was ah put a bit ay business the cunt's way, n offered him a nice wee backhander. The bastard wouldnae take it. 'Forget it,' eh goes. Took the huff and been in it ever since. Skinner gulped on his pint like he was swallowing down his bitterness. — The fuckin fandan was puttin it aroond that he was entitled to half. Skinner turned to Traynor then Shevlane, then Kay, then some others in appeal. — Telt the cunt in McPherson's, 'If ye want half, I'll gie ye half . . . if ah can brek *your* leg, airms, ribs and skull wi a baseball bat. Cause that's the only circumstances under which you'd be entitled tae half.' Bastard went aw para eftir that, thought ah wis trying tae threaten him. He pointed at himself as his eyes widened in outrage. — Me. Threaten *that* cunt. As if. I was only trying to make a fuckin point.

Kay nodded warily. — It's horrible when friends fall out over money.

Traynor winked at Kay, slapped Skinner on the back. — Love and money are the only things worth fawin oot ower, eh, chaps? He laughed loudly.

Two men who were with a young boy who was wearing a green Carlsberg football strip sat at the next table and looked over at them. The men were drinking shorts and pints and the kid was drinking Coca-Cola. Skinner gave them a long, cold once-over and they averted their gaze.

The sugar turns to alcohol.

Kay caught the ugliness in his leer, saw the signs. That guy at the bar had soured his mood. She whispered sexily into his ear, — Let's go back and lie in the bath together.

— Whae the fuck dae ye think ah am? Ah only *drink* like a fish! Lie in the bath the gither, she says! Skinner had retorted loudly, drawing in the company, but instead of coming out witty, jokey and flirty as he'd intended, through the mask of alcohol it was distorted into a gruff reprimand, which Kay took as him showing off to his pals that *he* was the boy. Humiliation twisted like a knife in her chest and she stood up. — Danny . . . she said in one last plea.

Skinner, semi-jolted through his heavy-boned pish-head apathy was moved to add in placatory tones, — You go, ah'll be doon eftir this. He shook his half-full glass of lager.

Kay turned on her heels, left the bar and stole down Leith Walk. She was wasting her time. She could have gone to the studio, worked on the barre, got her mind and body right for the audition.

— Birds, Skinner said to his friends. A couple of them nodded knowingly. Most just pulled thin smiles. They were largely from the local younger team who had taken an interest in the fashionable upsurge in football violence. Most were impressed by Skinner and Big Rab McKenzie's recent tales of hanging out with some of the old school CCS boys. They were as anxious to hear the story of their West Lothian day out with terrace institutions Dempsey and Gareth as Skinner was to tell the tale away from Kay's ears. He was also keen to get the porn film Traynor had got for him, *The Second Coming of Christ,* and secrete it from her view.

He had intended to head home after that pint, but Rab McKenzie came through the door and more tales were told and more drinks flowed. No, drink never questioned.

Until the next morning.

The next morning when there was no Kay.

Skinner rose slowly, showered and dressed. Ironically, he was a tidy, fastidious man who spent hours compulsively cleaning his flat and himself, only to almost completely destroy both with a regularity that to many was simply unfathomable. He surveyed the mess of his flat and cursed in sick self-loathing at the cigarette burn visible on his couch. He'd have to turn the cushion over, but no, there was a worse one on the other side, where somebody had let a kernel of dope burn through.

A fucking cigarette burn on your couch! A good enough reason to stop smoking for ever. A good enough reason to ban any weak, minging chavy cunt whae even smelt ay fags fae coming anywhere near yir fuckin hoose!

The handset was covered in sticky beer stains. It was gummed up and it took some time and effort to press and wiggle it into action. The television presenter came up on the screen, fronting the morning show. Glancing at his alarm clock again, Skinner struggled to get into his clothes and into the day. As he knotted his blue tie and gazed at his appearance in the mirror, his confidence to face the week ahead slowly grew.

I look like a fucking pantomime villain. If I grew a moustache I'd be Dick Dastardly.

Danny Skinner knew that although he was relatively young in his department, his sharp tongue was respected and feared, even by some of his elders and superiors, who had seen it mercilessly deployed on several occasions. More than that, he was good at his job: popular, bright and well liked. And yet he was starting to sense a growing disapproval from some senior colleagues regarding his drinking and his often cavalier, irreverent attitude.

But so many of them are corrupt bastards, like Foy.

He jumped on a 16 bus and got off at the east end of town. In Cockburn Street he met his favourite colleague, Shannon McDowall, coming into the Chambers from the back entrance and they took the lift to the fifth floor. In the workplace she was the one person Skinner really talked to, beyond superficialities, and they often enjoyed a casual flirtatiousness with each other. He couldn't believe how prim Shannon looked in her long brown skirt, yellow blouse and light brown cardigan. Her hair was pinned up. All that hinted at the vivacious, clubby, girl-about-town of the weekends was the shit-eating grin she wore. — Awright, Dan? Good weekend?

— Must have been, Shan, must have been, I remember nothing about it, Skinner said. — Yourself?

— Yeah, me and Kevin were at Joy. It was a brilliant night, Shannon leered.

— Good for you. Any naughtiness?

Shannon's voice dropped to a whisper and she looked around, pulling a loose strand of hair back from across her face. — Just one pill, but I was up all night.

Fuck just one pill, Skinner thought, and then with a sideways glance considered, fuck Shannon as well. But he'd never cheat on Kay, and anyway, Shannon had that boyfriend, Kevin, the up-himself-cunt with the weird hair. No, he'd never deceive Kay, but it would be great to screw Shannon's brains out, just to piss that Kevin cunt off, Skinner thought, then felt a rush of shame.

Shannon's okay, a mate. You cannae think about friends in that way. It's the alcohol: it leaves a taint of sleaze, of dirt in your mind. Mix it with cocaine and in large quantities and over long periods of time and you're probably heading for the beast's register. I've got tae fuckin well –

He remembered the time that he and Kay were at a club in the West End, and they met Shannon and Kevin. It ought to have been a cosy foursome, but he and Kevin never hit it off for some reason, neither, he could tell, did Shannon and Kay. It wasn't so pronounced as to be an instant dislike on either side, as things were superficially friendly enough, but the mutual antipathy was apparent.

Different lassies, Skinner thought. Kay was the youngest in her family with two much older brothers, the spoiled little Princess. When Shannon was a teenager and still at school, her mother had died unexpectedly, her father subsequently going to pieces. This meant that she'd effectively had to bring up her younger brother and sister. Skinner looked at her rounded face in profile, saw that focus and strength in her eyes. She caught him admiring her and shot him a disarming smile, like a sun coming out from behind a cloud.

On the first floor a skinny guy in a blue C&A suit shuffled nervously into the lift. Something about the boy's awkwardness made Skinner feel sorry for him and he smiled at the guy before noting that Shannon did too.

Skinner's guts were in turmoil from the beer and curry at the weekend and a viscous, silent eye-stinging killer of a fart slipped out off him, as poignantly weeping as a lover's last farewell, just as the lift stopped at the next floor to let in two men wearing overalls. Everybody suffered in silence. As the workmen got off at the following level, Skinner seized the opportunity, announcing, — That is minging, looking towards the departing workies. He knew that when it came to farting everybody turned into Old Etonian High Court judges. Men would always be suspected before women and men in working clothes would always be blamed before men in suits. Those were the rules.

Danny Skinner and Shannon McDowall were making their way to the office, when the thin guy in the suit stopped them and asked for directions. He really was an emaciated youth, Skinner thought: all skin and bone. From the front he looked as though he'd been run over by a steamroller, while at the side elevation he displayed a matchstick-thin body with a slightly oversized head. But he was open-faced enough, with freckled skin and fairish brown hair.

— Follow us, Skinner smiled again, making the introductions.

They took the new lad, Brian Kibby his name was, into the

open-plan office. Foy was late, so they made him a coffee and introduced him to everyone. — We won't take you round till Bob comes, Brian, Shannon explained, because he'll have his own induction programme planned. So, how was your weekend?

Brian Kibby started to enthusiastically recount his weekend. After a bit Skinner felt himself switching off, as the hangover kicked in. He noted the copy of *Game Informer* the new guy had taken from his bag, and picked it up. He wasn't a big video-game player, but his friend Gary Traynor had loads, and often press-ganged him into playing. He saw a review of one that Traynor had mentioned, *Midnight Club 3: Dub Edition*. — Ever played this one? he asked Kibby.

— It's brilliant! Kibby said, his voice going high. — I don't think I've ever played a game where you got as much a sense of speed as this one. And it's not just racing; so much of the emphasis is on customising your wheels so you spend a lot of the time in the garage pimping rides.

— Phoar, Skinner exclaimed, — that sounds right up my street, pimping rides!

Kibby blushed red. — It's no . . . it isnae . . .

Shannon cut in: — Danny was only joking, Brian. He's the office comedian, she smiled.

Brian Kibby got back in his flow about the game. Skinner's growing lack of interest turned into mild contempt when Kibby embarrassingly had to open his box containing a model train, after being pressed by Shannon to explain its contents. He also had, in his bag, McGhee had noticed, a Manchester United hat. — So you're a Man U fan, Brian? he'd asked Kibby.

— No, I dinnae like football, but I like Manchester United because they're the biggest team in the world, so you've got to follow them, Kibby squeaked eagerly, remembering a family holiday in Skegness, where he and his father had watched the 1999 European Cup Final in the hotel. It was there that he'd bought the hat, which, since Keith's illness, had taken on a sentimental attachment.

Oh my God, Skinner thought, Shannon will talk to him. He excused himself and slumped into the chair of his desk by the window.

This place is full of annoying, straight pricks who just dae your fuckin heid in with their home, garden and golf bullshit. That churchy old cunt Aitken'll be in soon . . .

. . . and now the new boy, he's as straight as fuck n aw . . .

Skinner acknowledged his disappointment, realising that he'd secretly wanted another drinking partner-in-crime. He glanced across at Kibby.

Fucking incorruptibly straight. The whiny fucking voice . . .

Those big, camel eyes radiated enthusiasm, but Skinner also thought he could witness, on fleeting occasion, a sneaky calculation in them, which maybe afforded a clue to a less wholesome side of this Kibby guy's nature.

As Aitken, then Des Moir, a perpetually cheerful middle-aged guy, trooped in wet and damp and made their coffees and shook hands with Kibby, it seemed to Skinner that only he could see this duplicitous streak in the new boy.

I'll fucking well keep an eye on that cunt.

A volley of hailstones urgently rattled the large windows, which, despite their size, only at certain times of the day seemed to let in enough light. This was due to the proximity of taller buildings on the other side of the Royal Mile, that narrow thoroughfare which ran from Castle to Palace, a place where sovereign powers once sat, but now essentially just a large open-plan museum.

Skinner stood up to look out at the pedestrians below running for cover. A soaked man, his grey suit made black across the back and shoulders, face red with bombardment from hailstones, scurried into an arched close, peering out with impotent belligerence in the face of the weather's assault. It was only when he plucked up the nerve to make the dash across the forecourt and his face came into sharper focus that Skinner recognised him as Bob Foy.

Delighted at his boss's discomfort, Skinner sank into his chair. As befitting his status, it had no armrests. There was a leather-wrapped football tankard on his desk, with a black-and-white Notts County FC crest, in which he kept pens and pencils. As the strip lighting above bounced off the paper on his desk and into his head, how he wished that it was full of refreshing lager.

Just one fucking pint tae get me going. That's all I ask.

He thought about toughing it out till lunchtime, when perhaps

Dougie Winchester upstairs might have similar needs. Winchester, stuck up in his garret, a small office-cum-broom-cupboard at the top of an old staircase, the struggling council piss artist that the non-job had been found for.

Dead wood, just waiting tae be chopped oot by some cunt ruthless enough to wield the axe. And he'll be along soon, no doubt about that, chavy.

In his mind's eye he could see Winchester's ashen face, now almost neckless, and the dead, sunken eyes with the thinning hair swept across the balding pate, a display of vanity so ludicrous that it could only be contemplated by a clinically depressed old fucker. Skinner recalled a particularly dismal conversation he'd had in the pub with him, one Friday after work. — Of course, as ye git aulder, sex becomes less important, Winchester had contended. Skinner looked at him in his shiny suit, reckoning that he was stating the obvious. — Och aye, ye still like the *idea* ay sex, but it becomes too much faffin aboot. Too uncomfortable and sweaty, Danny son. A nice wank, or a blow job fae a tasty wee hoor, och aye, that's bliss. But see aw this tryin tae satisfy a woman; too much ay a burden, too uncomfortable. Ma second wife couldnae get enough. Aw they friction burns on the welt, scrotum and inside ay the thighs. Nae use. Nae use at aw.

In his hard office chair, Danny Skinner squirmed, chilling as he tried to think of how many times he and Kay had made love last weekend. Only once, a violently sweaty hangover-cure fuck on Saturday morning, devoid of any sensuality. No, there was also a drunken one on Saturday night he could scarcely recall.

She should be having sex with an athlete, not a fucking jakey . . .

Sitting up, Skinner saw Foy appear and his torn face mould into an avuncular grin as he noted the presence of Kibby. He winked, rubbed his cold hands together and led the new boy upstairs to the mezzanine and his office.

Another fucking clone, another Foy arse-licking sycophant. Somebody else who'll be right up the hole of cunts like that fat fandan Chef De Fretais!

6

Little France

It snowed last night. Some of the gritter lorries are out but there seems no need as it's all gone into slush. This kind of weather always gets me thinking about how tough it must be to work on a farm. You get an idea of it from *Harvest Moon*. Just a big, long slog, where, before you know it, it's morning once more and you have to get up and do it all over again. It annoys me when they show you farmers on television, always standing around, lazing about or drinking in country pubs. I once said to Dad, 'they don't have time for that,' and he agreed. That kind of life would just kill most people. The likes of us city folk in offices don't know how lucky we are.

Nup, I wouldnae want to be outside in this. We're in Dad's car and I'm driving us out to the new hospital at Little France via the city bypass. We've all been pretty silent on the journey. It's making Mum nervous and she says something about the snow up on the hills at the Pentlands, but Caroline is just sitting in the back reading her book.

— Wonder if it'll snow again later? Mum asks, pushing it. — Looks like snow clouds to me. Then she turns to me and says, — Sorry, son, I shouldnae be distracting you while you're driving. Caroline, a wee bit of conversation from you would be welcome.

Caroline lets out a sharp exhalation of breath and puts her book on to her lap. — I need to read this book for my course, Mum, or should I just jack in the university because I haven't done the required reading?

— No . . . my mum says quickly, and she's sorry, you can tell, because she knows how much Dad wants Caroline to do well at the uni.

It should be good at Christmas; it always was before, always the best time. No now but.

I've got to be really careful about who I marry. It's not something you can just rush into. I've narrowed it down to five candidates:

Ann
Karen
Muffy
Elli
Celia

Ann is sweet and reliable, but I like Karen cause she's really friendly. I sort of like Muffy as well, but I'm no quite so sure about her. I think that she's the kind of girl that Dad would describe as 'dodgy'! Elli's dead nice as well, and though I don't want to rule out Celia, I think she may have to go from the list.

We pull into the car park and Mum and I share the brolly as the rain is now coming down hard. Caroline could share too if she wanted tae, but she just puts the hood up on her red sweatshirt and wraps her arms around herself and strides quickly across the tarmac to get under the canopy above the gateway to the entrance.

When we get on to the ward I'm nervous as I approach my dad's bed. As I see him I feel a terrible force rising in me, it seems like it's coming up from the lino floor through the soles of my leather brogues, and for a second I think that I'm going to pass out. I take a deep breath but it's all I can do to bring myself to look at his gaunt, tired face. Something hangs heavily inside me. I have to admit to something that I couldn't accept before: my dad is fading fast. He's just skin and bone and I see now that we've all just been pretending – me, mum and even Caz in our different ways – that it's all going to be okay.

I'm so shocked at my father's decline it takes me a couple of seconds tae register that there's this guy standing by the side of his bed. I haven't met him before. He's a big man, quite rough-looking, though Dad always says that you can't go by appearances, which is true. He doesn't introduce himself and Dad doesnae introduce him either, he doesnae shake hands, he only nods to us all, then heads off pretty quickly. I think he was embarrassed that he'd intruded on the family's time, but it was good of him to come.

— Who was that guy, Dad? Caroline asks. I can see my mum looking worried, cause she obviously doesn't know who the guy is either.

— Just an old friend, my dad wheezes.

— A chap from the railways it'll be, Mum coos. — From the railways, Keith?

— The railways . . . Dad says, but like he's thinking of something else.

— See, the railways, Mum says, now seeming pacified.

— What was his name? Caroline asks, her brow furrowed.

Dad goes to speak and he seems really uncomfortable, but Mum cuts in, grabbing his hand, and says to Caz, — Don't tire your dad out, Caroline, then she turns to Dad and says, — Tired?

It was unusual cause my dad doesn't have many friends, he's always been more of a family man. But yes, it was good of the man to come.

When I speak I know that I'm trying hard to make it right for Dad, as if to convince him that I'm okay . . . like before we part. But I'm not okay, I know that much. The job is working out fine and they're all very nice, well, most of them, although I wouldn't want to get on Bob Foy's wrong side.

The person I don't get on with that much is that Danny Skinner. It's funny, because he was nice to me the day I started, he smiled at me in the lift and introduced me to everyone. But since then he's been funny, a bit sarky. It's probably cause I get on well with Shannon and I think he might fancy her. I heard that he's got a girlfriend but there are some rats around whae that doesnae make a difference to, they'll just use lassies.

You read in the papers about the likes of David Beckham. There's girls claiming that he's going with them when his wife's having a baby. I used to like David Beckham, so I hope it's not true and that those girls are all just money-grubbers.

I wonder if Shannon fancies me! Probably no cause she's two and a half years older than me, but that's nothing really. I know that she likes me!

I look at Caroline. She has this terrible tension in her eyes. I know things are horrible but she should try and make an effort to smile, for Dad's sake, or even Mum's. I worry that Caroline's getting in with a bad crowd. She did so well in getting into Edinburgh Uni, but I saw her going down the road the other day with that Angela Henderson lassie, her that's working in the baker's now. That Angela's exactly the kind of lassie who would make false allegations about the likes of David Beckham if there wis any money in it for her. I won't let the likes of that drag Caroline down.

Dad's breathing is shallower and quite laboured and he's talking about the railways. He seems dislocated and confused. It's probably all the drugs they're giving him but Mum's finding it really upsetting. He's ranting a little, and I see agitation in his eyes, like he really wants to make a point.

He signals for me to get close to him and he squeezes my hand with a power you wouldn't believe was possible for somebody so ill. — Don't you make the same mistakes I did, son . . .

My mum hears this, starts sobbing and says, — You never made any mistakes, Keith. Never! Then she turns to Caroline and me and forces a strange smile. — What mistakes? Silly!

My dad won't let go of my hand though. — Be honest, son . . . he wheezes at me, — . . . to thine own self be true . . .

— Okay, Dad, I say, and I sit with him as his grip releases and he zones off into unconsciousness. A nurse comes along and tells us to let him rest for a bit. I don't want to, I want to stay here, I feel like if I go I'll never see him again.

But she insists, says he'll be comfortable and needs to rest. I suppose they know best.

We're quieter than ever on the journey back. When I get in I head upstairs and grab the hooked stick, pulling down the attic hatch, freeing the aluminium stepladder. As I got older I could see that it hurt Dad that I still came up here so much. He'd hear the step-ladder being pulled down, the snap of the aluminium, its strain and creaks as I pulled myself up. I know that it angered him, although he seldom said anything. Sometimes a shake of the head from him made me feel so very small. Like I felt outside and at school. But up here I was away from them all, McGrillen and that lot. They picked on me because I wasn't like them. I didn't always know what to say, I wasn't interested in football or the bands that they liked, or raves or drugs, and because I was shy around girls. And the girls could be even more horrible: Susan Halcrow, Dionne McInnes, that Angela Henderson . . . all that sort. I can tell that kind of filthy tart a mile away. I nearly died when I saw Caroline with that dirty tramp of a Henderson lassie. I know it's not really the girls' fault, it's the families they come from that are to blame.

But my sister's better than that.

But up here, in the town I built with Dad, my place, I was safe. Even from Dad's disapproval as it got so as that he couldn't manage the steps. This was always my place, my world, and I feel that I need it more than ever now.

7
This Christmas

The days had worn down to thin bands of light, squeezed relentlessly by the murky darkness. Snow was unlikely, but a dusting of frost would glitter for hours and night would fall before the chill's jab could be removed from the air.

It was the day of the office Christmas meal and Brian Kibby found himself in happier spirits. His father had enjoyed a relatively comfortable night and seemed perkier and more *compos mentis* than on his previous visit. There was an aura of contentment about him as he apologised for his behaviour the night before, saying that he had the best wife and family a man could ever hope for.

This partially restored Brian's optimism. Maybe his father would get well, get strong again. Perhaps he was being too morbid. He was going to have to be strong himself, make more of an effort with the likes of Danny Skinner. Skinner, who looked at him with that expression of thinly veiled hostility, like he knew everything about him.

He doesn't know me. He knows nothing about me. I'll show him who I am; I'm as cool as him or anybody else! I know about music. I hear stuff.

So a buoyant Brian Kibby swaggered playfully into the office, his narrow hips swivelling as he deftly swerved past the corner of Shannon McDowall's desk, nodding at her as he passed. Her response was a lenient smile. All the time Kibby air-drummed, making home-made sound effects by blowing air through his tightened lips. Danny Skinner was by the window, watching his entrance. An air drummer: that shows his mediocrity, he thought in crushing, savage contempt.

Kibby felt Skinner's eyes on him. He turned and dispatched a weak smile, only to have it met with a terse nod. What have I done? Brian Kibby wondered fretfully. And Danny Skinner was wondering much the same thing, as shocked as Kibby by his increasingly hostile reactions to the new lad.

Why do I dislike Kibby so much? Probably because he's a sooky little mummy's boy who'd rim any ass to get on.

Ass . . . what a great word. Much better than arse. An arse sounded more like something you just shat out off, whereas an ass was definitely something sexy. The Yanks had class, no doubt about it. One day I'll go to America.

Kay's ass . . . tight as fuck, but soft as well. Until you've ran your hands over a pair of naked buttocks like that you can't truly have said to have lived . . .

A hangover erection rose instantly, digging into the material of his pants and trousers. Skinner gasped a little at the discomfort, then watched Foy head into his office, thought about Christmas and the hard-on (to his relief) vanished as quickly as it had appeared.

When they arrived in a fleet of taxis at Ciro's restaurant down on the South Side, Bob Foy immediately took it upon himself to choose the wine to accompany the lunch. Though a few soft grumblings were audible the staff seemed generally happy to defer to him in this foible. It was an in-joke that Foy was the ideal man for the job, as he certainly knew his way around a wine list. Various city restaurateurs allegedly benefited from his selectively lax enforcement of health regulations, and were subsequently quick to show their appreciation.

Foy sat back in his chair and scrutinised the list. His mouth was twisting in the petulant pout of the Hollywood Roman Emperor at the Colosseum games who has yet to decide whether or not what he is witnessing amuses him. — I think a couple of bottles of the Cabernet Sauvignon, he finally decided, with a satisfied air. — This particular Californian red is generally reliable.

Aitken gave a slow, tortured nod of approval, McGhee an enthusiastic puppy-like one. Nobody else moved. A deafening silence followed, broken by the only dissenting voice which was Danny Skinner's. — I don't agree with that, he said firmly, shaking his head slowly.

There was deathly hush at the table as Bob Foy's face reddened slowly but steadily in anger and embarrassment, to the point that he almost asphyxiated with fury as he contemplated this young upstart.

In my section for about five bloody minutes. It's the first works dinner this cheeky wee bastard has deigned to appear at! Who the hell does he think he is?

Composing himself, Bob Foy forced his features to mould into an avuncular smile. — It's a wee tradition that we have here . . . Foy hesitated briefly, then elected to use Skinner's Christian name, — . . . Danny, that for the Christmas meal, the section head chooses the wine, he explained, displaying a row of capped teeth, as he casually smoothed down one of the sleeves of his Harris tweed jacket, brushing off a non-existent crumb.

This 'tradition' had been both purely devised and solely enforced by Foy, but nobody was contradicting him as his gaze scrutinised every face around the table.

Except Danny Skinner. Far from being intimidated, Skinner was in his element. — Fair enough, Bob, he said, imitating the same grandiose manner Foy himself had employed, — but this is a social occasion and nothing to do with rank at work. Correct me if I'm wrong, but we all contributed the same amount to the meal, therefore it follows that we should all have the same rights. I'm perfectly willing to bow to your superior expertise in the wine field, but I don't drink red wine. I don't like it. I drink white wine. It's as simple as that. Danny Skinner paused for a bit, saw Foy start to dissolve into apoplexy. Then he turned to the rest of the company at the table and added with a cold grin, — And I'm fucked if I'm paying for other people to drink red if I'm sitting drinking nothing!

As the eyebrows raised in involuntary concert around the table and breaths were sucked in with a quiet diplomacy, Bob Foy panicked. It was the first time he'd been confronted in this way. Skinner, moreover, had a reputation for mimicry, and Foy had been treated to an unflattering glimpse of himself mirrored back in the younger man's disrespectful parody. His voice rose, becoming strident as he thumped the desk. — Right. Let's have a vote then, he squeaked, as his pitch heightened. — Those who disagree with the choice of Cabernet Sauvignon?

Nobody moved.

McGhee was now nodding grimly, Aitken's thin face girning in disgust, and Des Moir, another Foy loyalist in the section, was examining his Christmas cracker. Shannon was peering over towards another group, apparently from the Scottish Parliament, that had just come in and who were being seated at an adjacent table. Skinner pulled his eyes ceilingward in a gesture of derision at his colleagues' craven acquiescence. Foy half shut one eye and, puffing himself up, prepared to speak.

Before he did, a small rasp of a voice said, — Ah agree wi Danny. We've all paid, Brian Kibby almost whispered, his eyes watering. — Eh . . . ah mean, it's only fair.

— White's fine by me, Shannon McDowall sang happily in chorus. — Maybe a couple of white, a couple of red, and see how we go? she suggested, looking to Bob Foy.

Foy completely ignored both her and Skinner. Turning towards Kibby with venom, he slapped the table again and sprang up. — Do what the fuck yis like, he half sang, half snapped, with an incongruously bright, open smile on his face. Then he vanished into the toilet where he wrenched the paper towel dispenser from its mountings on the wall.

THAT FUCKING CUNT SKINNER AND THAT FUCKING CRAWLING LITTLE BASTARD KIBBY!

Bob Foy picked a paper towel from the heap on the floor, wet it, and stuck it on the back of his neck. When he rejoined the nervous group of diners it was as if he didn't even notice the bottles of white wine on the table.

Kibby was shocked by Foy's barely repressed violence.

What have I done? Bob Foy . . . I thought he was okay. I'm going to have to try and get back into his good books . . .

Foy was not impressed with Skinner, a state that this challenge had done little to help. When in conference with his own boss, John Cooper, and also in the company of the council's elected members on the committee, he often had been inclined to undermine the younger man as a ne'er-do-well. These efforts would be intensified from now on.

As an unrepentant member of the sensualists' club, I have long held the belief that the only pleasure to rival making love is the eating of good food. The twin arenas of the true sensualist must, by extension, be the bedroom and the kitchen, and such a person must strive to be the master of both those environments. After all, the arts of cookery and lovemaking must mutually involve patience, timing and a certain instinctive knowledge of one's terrain.

Danny Skinner threw down the book he had been reading, Alan De Fretais's *Bedroom Secrets of the Master Chefs.* He considered that it was the biggest pile of bullshit imaginable, but many of the recipes looked good. He resolved to try some of them out, as he felt the need to attempt to eat healthier.

Now he was in his kitchen, trying to cook a fried breakfast for Kay. He was soon lamenting that his breakfasts seemed designed for hangovers rather than seduction, as he scraped the burned eggs from the base of the pan, bursting a yolk in the process. Slapping them on to cold plates already congealing with grease of candlewax proportions from the sausage, black pudding, bacon and tomato that sat on them, he could feel his pores beginning to clog from the vapourised animal fat that hung heavily in the air. Kay was in bed, in a deep sleep, dealing with her far more modest hangover in a way he never could. He couldn't sleep through it; he just writhed, sweated and fidgeted until he was forced to get up.

It was a raw, but surprisingly sunny Christmas Eve and tomorrow they were going to his mother's for their Christmas dinner. His mother liked Kay, but Skinner always found Christmases hard going.

Today, however, Hibs had Rangers at Easter Road. There was sure to be some trouble, and if there wasn't, he resolved that he'd make some. Noises from the bedroom and then the bathroom had told him that Kay had risen. She was unimpressed by the food he'd prepared, squeezing on to a stool in his galley kitchen and buttering a slice of cold toast, wondering why he couldn't do them while they were warm. It was like chewing broken glass. — I can't eat this shit, Danny, I'm a dancer. She screwed up her face. — You don't live on black pudding and sausage and bacon and expect to get a job on *Cats*.

Skinner shrugged, scraping some butter on to his own toast. — That Lloyd Webber stuff is a load of shite.

— It's what I do, she muttered darkly under her breath, her sharp, clear eyes staring pointedly at him. Having woken up in a testy mood, she was not happy that he was going to the football. — It's Christmas, Danny. Go to the match if you want but don't come back here drunk, or I won't be going with you to your mum's tomorrow.

— It's Christmas Eve for fuck's sakes, Kay! Entitled to a fucking drink at Christmas! Skinner gasped in outraged appeal, the hangover making him edgy.

Glancing up coolly from the breakfast bar, Kay made a token effort on his offerings by breaking the skin of the yolk with the edge of her toast. — That's just it though. You think that you're entitled to a drink every day.

— Well, you just go tae your ma's then, Skinner snapped.

— Right, said Kay, and quickly rose, calling his bluff by heading into the bedroom and throwing her stuff into her backpack. Skinner felt something tighten in his chest but he forced it down like his black pudding, only feeling the need to pursue her when the front door loudly slammed. A cold Stella from the fridge took the edge off this impulse, although he picked up his mobile and called, only to get her answering service. He looked at her wasted breakfast and slopped it into his pedal bin.

Skinner decided that he'd call her again later, once she'd settled down and saw what a nippy cow she was being. Instead, he went to fridge and took out another can of Stella Artois. Then he picked up his mobile once more and pressed Rab McKenzie's number. — Roberto, where's the meet, ma man?

The game was being televised, and this fact, plus the general festive vibe, conspired to decrease the hoolie element on both sides. The mob scoured the grot bars of Tolcross for Rangers boys through for a day out eyeballing strippers, but all they found were some sagging-faced winos singing sectarian songs and renditions of an old Tina Turner number. After half-heartedly thumping a few civilian bigots out of boredom, they headed back down to Leith and the game but Skinner and McKenzie and some others left irked and wearied after twenty minutes and made their way back to the pub which they had made their pre- and post-match base.

In the bar, without realising what he was doing, Skinner found himself smoking a cigarette. He was supposed to have packed it in the other week but had lit up and taken two drags on a B&H before he figured out what was happening. — Cunt, he said, grinding his teeth together as he took a harsh hit of personal loathing in his chest.

The beers slipped down so easily, and Skinner was pleased that he was matching McKenzie drink for drink. Later on, Gary Traynor and his latest sidekick, a heavy-built guy Skinner knew in vague hostility from a youthful negative encounter as Andy McGrillen, suggested going up to a bar in town. Skinner meant to phone Kay but the alcohol and cocaine had kicked in on the way, distorting time, compressing hours into fifteen-minute blocks. — Whae wis the best obscure cartoon character ever? Traynor asked Skinner, running a hand over his shorn skull.

Skinner thought about this for a second. He couldn't think of anyone, so he shrugged.

— Ah liked that cute wee duck oot ay *Tom and Jerry*, McKenzie said.

Skinner shot Traynor a look, both of them quite overwhelmed the big man could be that sentimental. McGrillen, in awe of McKenzie, kept studiously quiet. In order to avoid bursting out in a smirk, Traynor advanced a proposition: — Naw, fuck off, it hus tae be Sawtooth oot ay *Wacky Races*.

— Sawtooth? Whae the fuck's that? Dinnae mind ay that cunt in *Wacky Races*, McKenzie looked doubtful.

— That's cause the cunt's obscure, Traynor explained. — Eh's Rufus Ruffcut's sidekick, mind, in the wooden car wi the circular sawblade wheels. Every cunt minds Dick Dastardly and Muttley, Penelope Pitstop, Peter Perfect, Professor Pat Pending and the Ant Hill Mob, but they aw forget aboot Rufus Ruffcut and Sawtooth.

— Aye! Right! Rufus Ruffcut wis the big lumberjack boy n Sawtooth wis the squirrel thit wis wi um in the motor. Got ye, said McKenzie.

— Naw-naw, Sawtooth wisnae a fuckin squirrel, Traynor shook his head. — Eh wis a fuckin beaver. Tell um, Skinner!

— Best cartoon American beaver since Pamela Anderson, Skinner laughed.

Later, as they were making their way out of the bar, Skinner saw McGrillen push some boy and there followed a flurry of blows between them. McKenzie and Traynor steamed in but something made Skinner step back into the shadows, and watch his three mates take on five guys. They didn't need much help, but Skinner wasn't going to offer any, not for McGrillen.

Afterwards he concocted a set of barely plausible lies, namely that he was having it in the doorway with one guy, but he realised from their silent disappointment that they knew, as much as he did, that he had bottled it. That one moment of fear, of hesitation, could cost you your credibility, he thought in self-contempt. But why? It was more than the fact that the row was instigated by McGrillen, whom he didn't like and didn't regard as one of them.

For a second, all I saw was Kay, my mother, my job, my Christmas and my whole fuckin life: all going down the tubes. I let it get into my head, all that stuff of real life that we row to get away fae. What the fuck am I –

When he got home there was no sign of Kay. Skinner sat up most of the night drinking, before crashing into an uneven sleep on the couch. A trip to the toilet helped orientate him, making him get into his bed. When he awoke, what seemed like only about fifteen minutes later, fully clothed and feeling battered and broken, he tried to phone Kay on her mobile but again he was greeted by her answering service. He fired off a text, wondering if he'd got the wording right:

K, call me. Dx

He showered and dressed, and headed out on to Duke Street and down Junction Street. — Merry Christmas, son, a squat, white-haired woman said as he passed her. He recognised her as Mrs Carruthers, who lived in his mother's stair.

Although he felt like a microwaved corpse, Skinner managed to cough out a gracious, — Aye, you n aw, doll.

When he got to his mother's tenement flat, he found Busby, the old insurance man whom he heartily despised, just leaving.

That vile creature with the bandy walk and that nauseous cheery smile, heading out my mother's stair! There's six houses in my ma's stair, but I ken which one Busby's been visiting. What does that odious little fart want at this time . . . ?

Skinner loathed Busby for reasons he could never bring himself to conceive. Thinking about this as he sat in his mother's cosy, compact living room/kitchen, he started to laugh to himself as she produced two plates full of turkey and trimmings and put them on a table which she had pulled out from a recess and decorated especially for the occasion.

His mother was obviously well nipped, as she had also set a place for Kay. Danny Skinner watched her swollen hands, her fingers pink like uncooked sausages, slam the plates on to the table. Beverly Skinner had never been a big woman until she'd hit forty, then she had swollen up into obesity. She blamed an early hysterectomy, while Skinner attributed it to the wedges of pizza and the TV dinners she consumed. She always said it was pointless cooking for one.

Beverly had gone to a lot of trouble with the food and had put her new dress on, even if it was black like all her others, Skinner noted. Her disapproval at Kay's non-show hung heavily in the air, and she knew who was to blame, whatever he said.

She went back to the oven to switch it off, pointing at the cat, lying in front of the fire. — Dinnae let Cous-Cous up on that couch, he's moulting.

As soon as she was in the recess, the blue Persian stood up and stretched, arching its body. Then it jumped on to the couch beside Skinner. It walked over his legs then turned and repeated this act. He picked the lighter out of his pocket and singed the fur on the beast's belly. It crackled and gave off a smell, and the cat sprang away into a corner of the room. Skinner stood up and knocked over a lit candle, which was on the coffee table, spilling the wax.

Beverly stood back out from the kitchen area, a dish full of sprouts in her hands. Her nose wrinkled at the odour of burning fur. — What was that?

— The cat. He pointed at the coffee table. — Daft fucker knocked over the candle.

— Aw, Cous-Cous, ye didnae . . . She scolded the animal as she put the sprouts on the table.

Mother and son went through the twisted rigmarole of pulling a cracker each and sticking paper hats on their heads. The hollow, shabby frivolity of the gesture seemed to mock them both, as the day was already a tense disappointment to each. Skinner munched his way tentatively through the dinner, trying to get into the Bond movie on the telly, yet keeping himself braced for the inevitable verbal assault to come. When it did, it was initially low-key. — Stinking of drink again. Nae wonder that wee lassie bolted, Beverly remarked observationally, arching her eyebrows as she poured herself another glass of Chardonnay.

— She never bolted, Skinner protested, going over his rehearsed lie. — Ah telt ye, her mother's no well so she went to her family's to help with the dinner. Besides, she cannae stuff her face over the festive period, she's got a big audition in the new year. *Les Miserables*. And the drink you smell was from last night. I had just one pint before I came here, that's all. It's Christmas! I've been working all year!

But Beverly just glowered at him. — It makes nae difference tae you what time ay the year it is, it's just another lost weekend, she snapped.

Skinner said nothing but sensed that his mother was in the mood for a row and wouldn't be satisfied until she had had it.

— You . . . that wee lassie . . . ah cannae blame her, no wantin tae spend Christmas wi a waster!

A kernel of anger blazed in Skinner's chest. — Must be a family trait, he smiled cruelly.

His mother met his gaze with a combative expression of her own, so cold it made Skinner wish he hadn't responded in that manner. The hangover, it made you jumpy. He hated coming here when he was hung-over. You just couldn't deal with people who *weren't* hung-over, they were a hostile race; demonic predators who wanted to rip your soul out. They smelt the weakness from you, sensed the dirtiness, the otherness of you. And his mother was formidable at any time. — What's that meant tae mean? Beverly's words slowly corkscrewed into Skinner.

Even as he thought that he'd better move on to the back foot, Skinner inexplicably found himself saying, — My dad. He didnae stick aroond long, did he?

Beverly's seething face reddened, clashing with the green crêpe-paper hat that topped it. It was like she was trying to keep her breathing even but the action seemed to suck all the oxygen out off the small room. — How many fuckin times have I told you never tae mention –

— I've got a fuckin right tae know! Skinner snapped. — At least you ken who Kay is!

Beverly looked at her son in an expression that Skinner could only feel to be one of abhorrence. When she spoke, it was in a low hiss. — Ye want tae know whae yir father wis? Aye?

Danny Skinner looked at his mother. Her head was cocked to the side. He realised that after all those years, whoever his father was, her sheer hatred of him – complete, abject – it had never waned for a second. Worse, the look told him that he too could come to be as detested by her if he pushed it. He wanted to say it's okay, forget it, let's have our dinner, but no words would come from his lips.

— Me, Beverly pointed vigorously at herself. — Ah'm yir faither, and yir mother. Ah put the food on yir plate and ah cooked it. Ah took ye tae the fitba at the school and kicked a baw wi ye in the gairden. Ah knitted your skerf and ah took ye tae the fitba matches. Ah went doon tae the school when they were on your case. Ah built up a business soas ah could pit clathes oan yir back n food in yir gut. Ah washed and cut the hair oan every scabby auld heid in Leith soas that you could stey oan at school and git the qualifications ye needed tae git a decent job. Ah took ye oan holiday tae Spain every year. Ah bailed ye oot that bloody nick in the High Street when ye were involved in they stupid cairry-oans and ah peyed yir fines! Me! Ah did that! Naebody else!

Skinner fought to keep his mouth shut. But it was true. And he looked at this tough, bitter, loving and wonderful woman, who had devoted her life to his welfare. Thought about growing up with her and her pals Trina and Val, his surrogate punk aunties. Who looked after him and never talked down to him, valued his opinion and treated him like an adult even when he was just a boy. The only bad thing was when they tried to indoctrinate him into their music. The bands they went on about, the Rezillos, the Skids and the Old

Boys. But this was a minor point because the crux of the matter was his mother ensured he got opportunities not only as good as, but better than the two-parent kids around him. He looked down at the food Beverly had made for him and he shut up and he ate.

8

Festivities

Dougie Winchester proffered some good advice during my first festive period in council employ. He told me that the worst time for a drinker to go on holiday is between Christmas and New Year. That's cause it's just one big piss-up anyway, and nobody sensible does a fucking stroke of work. The only ones left are the drinkers; most of the family-orientated people are at home, and they tend to be the bosses or the dinguls who disapprove of a peeve in the workplace, so you have carte blanche approval to get lashed up.

The vibe reminds you of the last day at school: that sense that something amazing is going to happen. Back then, for some reason, we'd all hang around my ma's shop; me, McKenzie, Kinghorn and Traynor, just waiting. It was seldom that anything of note actually occurred, of course, but the anticipation was delicious.

As I stagger in around ten thirty, fucking stewed after a shite Christmas, I could do with something wonderful happening. I'm snowblind and my mouth is like the bottom of a budgie's cage. Shannon's gone to some meeting but is heading for the Housing Department do at lunchtime, but I think I'll need a couple of pints in me before I check that one out. I'm thinking pish, pish and pish again. I'm wondering if Winchester is around or if Rab McKenzie's working in the town. The only problem is that that sooky wee bastard Kibby is in, beavering away at his desk. Don't know what the fuck he's doing here: probably to grass up every fucker to Cooper or Foy!

The big strip lights, thankfully, haven't been switched on, and Kibby fair cuts a Dickensian figure, sitting there alone, working in the lamplight. Suddenly inspired, I lift a manila folder off my desk, heading across to him. As I approach, I'm surprised to see that Kibby looks fucked; it's like he's about to burst into tears at any second. I slide into the vacant seat opposite his. — Alright, Brian?

— Yeah . . . he says warily, his back stiffening as he pats the sides of his hair.

My eyes squint in the harsh light coming from the lamp on his desk. — No on holiday this week?

— No, my dad's no well and I need to keep my holiday time back, he says, and his nose wrinkles, probably under the smell of stale pish on my breath.

— No sae good, chief, I mumble, leaning back, thinking that the little bastard is lucky that he's got a faither, before I go into businesslike mode. — Listen, Bri, I'm off a couple of days next week and I hear that you've got to do some of my follow-ups.

Kibby nods in thoughtful acquiescence, and I push the file in front of him.

— I thought we'd just quickly go through them. My handwritten notes are a Spiderman job. I bend my wrist, shooting an imaginary web to the ceiling. Kibby looks blank, so I elaborate: — Dead ropy.

— Cool, Kibby says in a way that makes me I feel like I've just scraped my nails down a blackboard, as he rocks back in his chair. I wish I knew why that fucking wee fandan just bugs the shit out of me.

— It's all quite straightforward, I explain, as I get my file and stick it down in front of him.

He opens the folder, giving the contents a rodent-like scan. He still has freckles, the fucking little retard. — What about this one? He points at Le Petit Jardin.

— De Fretais. A fucking midden, that kitchen, I explain.

The keen-eyed wee fucker looks carefully at me. If he goes down there that fat poof De Fretais will probably try and ram a load up his skinny white-boy ass. It'll be him getting inspected: bum inspected. I doubt that wee sooky blouse here would have the baws tae stand up tae De Fretais, although he does seem to be a perversely conscientious little fucker. — But he's, well . . . famous. Kibby looks painfully at me.

— I know that, Bri, but you just have to call it as you see it. We're professionals and we're here to serve the public, not some egotistical cook. Anyway, it still all goes up to Foy and it's his decision as to how we proceed.

— But if I write anything too critical in the report, it's down there in black and white . . . Kibby bleats like a spring lamb. Fuck me, De Fretais will probably sauté the little cunt and serve him up with a mint sauce.

— That's why honesty is the best policy. If some poor fucker gets food poisoning, which is highly probable given the state of that gaff, and sues, and remember we live in a litigation era, I lecture, thinking about the possibilities, — then the powers that be will want to look at the officer's report. If your report doesnae chime with mine, either one of us is a liar, and mine was countersigned by Aitken, or De Fretais has, in three months, spent a National Lottery jackpot on his kitchen.

You can see Kibby's wheels turning; painfully slowly, mind you, but turning all the same.

— Telling you, Bri, I almost shat myself when I looked in this big filthy stockpot. I half expected the creature fae the black lagoon tae emerge. Ah pulls up this cook and goes: 'What's that then?' The boy says: 'Aw, it's bean soup.' Ah sais tae him: 'Ah ken it's been soup, ya cunt, but what the fuck is it now?'

Kibby stretches a weak smile across his doubt-ridden coupon. Even the most base humour is way above this dingul's heid. I rise, slapping my arse with the file. — Cover it, Bri, cover it, my son, I say with a pally wink, then throw the file on his desk.

There's something about him . . . I now find myself feeling sorry for him, as the poor wee fucker looks so lost. I see a copy of *Game Informer* on his desk. I pick it up and leaf through it. — What do you reckon to *Psychonauts*? I ask. — Supposed to be quite inventive. You know, not the usual nerd stuff about thwarting terrorist cells and rescuing beautiful princesses.

— Huvnae played it, Kibby says warily, then opens up a little. — My mate Ian, he's got it but. It gets an 8.75 score in the review, he enthuses.

— Aye . . . right, I reply in unease. — Look . . . I'm going over to the Housing Department for a drink, there's a wee party on. Shannon and Des Moir are there. You coming?

— No, I'm going to try and get through some of these inspections, he sniffs.

Fucking pompous little cunt. He'll be welcome round the restaurants at this time of year.

As I head back across to my desk to call McKenzie, he asks, — Do you really think I should . . . with De Fretais . . . ?

— Honesty is the best policy, I grin, collapsing into my chair and picking up the phone. — You know what they say, tae thine own self be true.

As he shuffled down the Royal Mile, the murky sky forming a dark canopy on the stone tenements on either side of him, the throw-away words of Danny Skinner resounded in Brian Kibby's ears, making more of an impression than their perpetrator could ever have envisaged.

Danny's right . . . it doesnae matter if it's one of the best restaurants in Britain and one of its most famous chefs, it's the same rules for everybody!

It was still morning when he got down to Le Petit Jardin, and they were preparing for lunch. A large party of suits had assembled outside, as the dark sky finally started to break up.

Kibby could tell it was an upscale restaurant as it was confident enough to make little concession to the festive season. Only one modest Christmas tree in the corner gave away the time of year. On entering the sedately lit mahogany-and-magnolia-decorated interior, Kibby relaxed somewhat as his feet sank into the lush brown carpet. The dining room was absolutely pristine, therefore he regarded it as completely inconceivable that the kitchen would be as bad as Skinner had contended. His induction period with Foy round some of the city's varied eateries had confirmed what he had learned as a cub inspector over in Fife: if the dining area is looked after exceptionally well, then the kitchen is usually run to the highest standards of hygiene.

But for every rule there was always an exception.

Kibby showed his inspectorate pass to an unconcerned maître d', who pouted as he nodded towards the swing doors. His heart sank as he went through them: he had braced himself for the blast of hot air, but still physically wilted under its assault, and the first thing that he could see was De Fretais himself, idly leaning against a worktop.

The scents of various foods frying, grilling and baking danced in his nostrils, his brain scrambling with sense data as it tried to identify the myriad aromas. The huge chef was watching an overall-clad girl on her knees, who was unloading stuff from a pile of boxes balanced on a barrow on to a bottom wall shelf.

Kibby heard him shooting the breeze in those booming tones he knew from television, and could see the haughty self-conceit in the dark eyes and tight mouth of the Master Chef. For a brief second there was an unlocatable familiarity in that posture he struck, and the jokes, the foul language . . .

Brian Kibby approached the fat chef with an intense air of trepidation. The kitchen did not look in good shape. De Fretais seemed even less enamoured by the intrusion and gave Kibby a distracted once-over. — Oh, so you're the new laddie from the council. How's my old mate Bob Foy doing?

— Fine . . . Kibby squeaked uneasily, thinking again about both Foy's wrath and Skinner's words. But the kitchen was dirty and a dirty kitchen was a dangerous kitchen. Rule one. He couldn't disregard that.

And it was very dirty. Perhaps not as bad as Skinner had made out in his report, but parts of the floor and some surfaces needed not just to be scrubbed but redone. Additionally, boxes and tins of stock were piled up blocking access, fire doors were wedged open and a lot of the staff seemed somewhat cavalier about their appearance. De Fretais himself looked sweaty and unkempt, like he'd just come out of bed or straight from the pub.

I suppose it's the festive period . . . but it's still a restaurant!

De Fretais was as huge and gross as Kibby was thin and frail and he moved uncomfortably close to the young man, making his intimidating mass count. — The council, eh? I seem to recall a rather attractive female kitchen inspector . . . or, sorry, environmental health officer, the fat man said, and Kibby could feel his scented breath as he focused on the black hairs growing from the chef's nostrils. It was so hot and the back of his neck burned like he was on a tropical beach. — What would her name be . . . ? De Fretais considered. — Sharon . . . no, Shannon. That's it, Shannon. Is the lovely Shannon still there?

— Aye . . . Kibby croaked uncomfortably.

— They don't send her any more . . . pity. A great pity. Is she seeing anyone? I wonder.

— Dunno . . . Kibby lied, sleazed up to the point of disorientation by the very proximity of this man. To Kibby, the chef had the teardrop-shaped body of a clown, and while attempting to be superficially jocund, only succeeded in portraying a conceited, malevolent bombast. He knew that Shannon had a boyfriend but he was telling nobody her business, least of all De Fretais.

— Anyway, carry on at your convenience, the Master Chef said briskly, — or should I say our convenience, he added, looking over at two kitchen porters who were standing by a trolley, — BECAUSE THAT'S WHAT THIS FUCKING TOILET IS LIKE! GENTLEMEN! PLEASE!

The two men scrambled into action while Kibby, going diligently through his checklist, observed the full bins, the boxes of stock and produce piled up in the gangways. The kitchen was so hot now: a sapping, baking heat, blasting out from the ovens. No matter how often you experienced it, you were always forceably reminded that nothing prepared a visitor for the temperature and bustle of a busy restaurant kitchen. It was that extreme heat that made working in a kitchen one of the hardest jobs around. And the bodies, anonymous in their overalls: moving around like ants, shouting instructions at each other. The first orders were in, the big party outside, from the nearby Scottish Parliament, had taken their places for lunch.

Suddenly Kibby felt strong fingers grappling him in an almost shocking intimacy. De Fretais had his hands around the young officer's waist. He commenced pulling him into corners and across walkways in a crazed, violent dance, as the cooks brought their stuff together and waiters passed to pick up orders; jostling him with rib-bruising power across the floor in a flimsy guise of benevolence.

And throughout this harassment, Brian Kibby was trying to look out for the signs, attempting to do his job.

To thine own self be true.

9

New Year

I did a stupid thing at the Housing Department party. It was normal office party stuff: a big, open-plan gaff, dealing with rent, housing benefits and the like, tons of booze flying around, amateur drinkers throwing up, people vanishing into storerooms for stolen moments of soon-to-be-regretted carnal lust.

I was talking to Shannon, getting a bit maudlin about life, and she was too, me mentioning Kay, her Kevin. Then some drunken lassie stuck some mistletoe over our heads. A peck became a snog, which lasted all night as we held on to each other like orphaned baby monkeys, whose worlds were crumbling around them. Mine certainly was and it seemed that she was in the same boat.

The next day I went up to Samuel's in St James's Centre and bought a diamond engagement ring. It cost nearly four hundred quid. I took Kay to the Derby match at Tynecastle, and we saw the bells in at her mother's. I took it easy on the drink – not much option in that house. All the pictures of Kay, everywhere; a wee lassie in ballerina costume, a high-kicking *Guys and Dolls* amateur production teenager, her first real job in some experimental dance troupe. I darkly saw in the fussing of the aunties, uncles and gran, and her taking it as her effortless lot in life, just how all the lassies in her school must have secretly hated her. That slender, toned body, shiny hair and perfect white teeth, her boundless, enthusiastic smiles, the can-do attitude; all the things I loved simply because she gave them to me. And I will marry this girl.

I didn't give her the ring though. I resolved that when I went down on the bended knee, it would be her and me, alone, and I would be totally, utterly, perfectly sober.

Now it's business as usual. No gradual phasing in after the festive period; for some cunts in the office it's like Christmas and New Year never even happened. I heard that old wanker Aitken going on about how he hates the festive holiday, and how it's great to get back to the usual.

The usual.

Foy had put my report on to the second inspection roster, in the anticipation that Aitken or one of his other arse-crawlers would do the cover-up job. Invoking this procedure, a stage two, meant that it wouldn't need to be referred to the next tier, namely that humourless cunt Cooper up the stairs.

Now chubby boy Foy is emerging from his office, crazy with rage, and not only is he going to tear that sneaky wee fandan Kibby apart, he's going to do it in front of us all as an example. That's just the good news. The totally excellent news is that I'm ringside!

He throws the report down on Kibby's desk and that motion, before he even opens his mouth, has made the sad wee cunt go all eppy. Then Foy snarls, — What the fuck is this garbage? Do you realise that this is a stage two and it leaves this office? he hisses, jabbing his thumb ceilingward.

— But his kitchen was really dirty, that dippit wee fucker Kibby goes, and it's unbelievable watching Foy almost having a heart attack, seeing that old spunk-bag wonder how he's gaunnae square that yin with fat boy De Fretais. No more discounts at Le Petit Jardin, no more fussy service and best tables!

— That is not the kitchen of a greasy spoon in Kirkcaldy, you stupid wee laddie, Foy roars in flesh-stripping contempt as Kibby physically cowers, sinking into the collar of his shirt. The term 'stupid wee laddie' is, from Foy's lips, more wounding than any curse I've ever heard uttered. — That is Alan De Fretais's kitchen! Foy booms as Kibby stands up, trying to claim back some power, but he's shaking on the spot, red-faced, and with tears welling up in his eyes. Foy steps closer to him, eyes chickenhawk-like, and guess who the chicken is? The fat bastard is really enjoying this. His voice falls almost to a whisper: — Do you have a television in your house?

I'm feeling fucking weird about this. Foy's a bully, an arrogant, overbearing bastard and he's totally out of order. Why am I *enjoying* this so much?

— Do you watch said television? he booms. I can almost see the laurels above his ears.

— Ah . . . ah . . . aye.

Foy takes his voice down even further: — Have you ever watched *The Secrets of the Master Chefs*, on Scottish Television, after the news?

— Aye . . .

— Then you will have seen Mr De Fretais from Le Petit Jardin, who presents the programme, Foy says reasonably.

— Aye . . .

— Then, Foy's voice slows down, — you will know that he is an important man, he contends in a stagy diplomacy, lulling Kibby, who's now starting to replicate Foy's nod, before bellowing in his face, — AND NOT TO BE FUCKED WITH!

Kibby physically recoils and wilts further, and I am sure that boy's white ass is shaking like Elvis's pet jellyfish, then he rallies a wee bit and coughs out in pathetic defiance, — But . . . but . . . but . . . you sais . . . you sais . . . And I have to admit that something's happening to me here. I'm angry, though not at Foy for his bullying, but at Kibby, for fucking well taking it.

I'm willing him: fight back, Kibby, where's your fucking bollocks? Stick up for yourself, you daft wee cunt. C'mon, Brian . . .

— What? mocks Foy. — I sais what? And I feel my own sides convulse in a pain so fucking gleeful because I now realise that I hate this cunt Kibby, and I want him to suffer. I hate him, I really fucking do. Foy's a buffoon, a joke, but Kibby, there's something sneaky about that wee cunt, something sneaky; stupid and pathetic, aye, but it's like there's this covert snideyness there to try and make up for it. And I realise now that I want to see Foy make that fucking insect crawl like it makes my flesh creep . . .

HATE HATE HATE *HATE HATE HATE.*

I don't even know what's being said now, because I can only see their faces. Kibby's fucking silly muppet head, his eyes wide in shock; Foy's crimson coupon, looking like a red-hot kernel of hashish ready to dissolve into his body, to melt right through that tweedy Marks & Sparks torso . . .

Fuckin dingul. How radge is he?

The fun only stops as that cunt Cooper, the big cheese, comes into the office, his presence a signal for Foy to pull himself together. A flustered Kibby goes to the toilet, no doubt to cry his daft wee girly eyes out. I'm tempted to go after him, to witness that little fag squealing like the bitch-slapped wee pussy he is, but no, I'll chill for a bit and make some coffee. I can't explain the rage I have against him, the impulse to precipitate and savour his annihilation, and part of me is horribly ashamed off it: the pathetic nature of it all, the raw, searing illicit pleasure this hatred of him gives me.

10
Sex and Death

Post-New Year in Edinburgh saw a smoky black city sky hanging like a pile of bricks in a flimsy net above the heads of its inhabitants. The citizenry would frequently look up in anxiety, waiting for it to drop its load on them. Yet most Burgh boys and girls still nipped around briskly: they had processed their hangovers and had yet to break their resolutions, enjoying the wave of optimism a new year brings.

One exception was a fur-headed, dry-mouthed Danny Skinner who was writing a report in earshot of a buoyant Brian Kibby, now recovered from his mauling by Foy, and enthusiastically recounting his recent adventures to Shannon McDowall. — The weekend there, Kibby said in his high, almost girlish nasal whine, — we were up in Glenshee, he explained as Shannon nodded indulgently, sipping black coffee from her Pet Shop Boys mug.

A more clued-up soul than Kibby might have suspected that Shannon was bored and humouring him, but having a massive crush on her served to obliterate his antennae somewhat. In his troubled life dealing with his father's illness and the tensions in his family, Shannon, the video games – particularly *Harvest Moon* – the model railway and the Hyp Hykers had become his main sources of respite. Shannon and one Hyp Hyker particularly. — . . . n thir was a bunch of us; me, Kenny, that's the guy who runs the club, he's a great laugh but pretty mad, Brian Kibby chortled, — and Gerald, who really tries tae keep up, he let his face screw up in a slightly indulgent manner, — but we call him slowcoach, n there's Lucy . . . Kibby was about to expand on the main object of his desire when he was cut short by a terse intervention.

— These trips you go on, Brian, they wee treks in the country, Skinner proceeded in prosecution lawyer manner, as he'd learned from Foy, — any rideable females go along?

The elicitation of Kibby's blush had been Skinner's sole intention and he wasn't disappointed. Shannon rolled her eyes and tutted under her breath, busying herself in her paperwork.

— There's some girls that go – Brian Kibby began hesitantly, looking towards Shannon, who was ignoring him, her head bent over her papers.

— Like the fucking clappers, I'll bet, Skinner cut him off.

Kibby stammered, feeling like he'd already betrayed Lucy in some unspecific yet deep way, — Eh . . . I dinnae . . . you cannae . . .

Skinner's mouth tightened, and from Kibby's point of view his face took on a preternatural hue. — Bet there's a few rides there, eh?

Shannon McDowall looked first at Kibby then at Skinner. Her glance was dismissive. Skinner caught it and gestured in appeal.

— There's some nice lassies, aye, Brian Kibby said, quite assertively, and as a result he instantly, for a few precious seconds, felt that he had captured the moral high ground.

Skinner's expression was stony and serious. — Rode any?

Brian Kibby looked disgusted and turned away, but Skinner saw that the attempt to construct a mature façade was a smokescreen in order to cover his virgin's humiliation. Shannon McDowall tutted again, shook her head, rose and marched over to the bank of filing cabinets. Colin McGhee grinned over and let his brows rise, tacitly giving Skinner the audience he needed following Shannon's departure.

— Why so coy, Bri? Skinner said matter-of-factly. — A simple question: rode any birds at this hiking club of yours?

— Nane ay your business! Kibby spat, and stormed off, heading for the toilets, passing Shannon, who moved back to her desk.

Skinner turned to her. — Looks like I touched a nerve!

— Don't be so fucking horrible, Danny, Shannon said. Brian Kibby could go on, but he was a nice wee guy, just a bit innocent.

Skinner winked suggestively at her, causing Shannon to feel a slow pang of desire she wished she didn't. That drunken snog at the Housing Department party. It had just been one of those things, a piece of nonsense neither mentioned again, yet she was reminded of it every time he looked at her in a certain way. Skinner felt it too, and it shamed him. He'd been stupid. He loved Kay, although things were still pretty tense between them after his behaviour at Christmas. Kibby, though, had nobody, Skinner considered with a treacherous, gloating pity. — There's no stigma in being a virgin at twenty-one. For most people, he grandly contended.

Skinner's baiting of Brian Kibby was relentless enough in the office, although it was skilfully presented by its architect as just a series of light-hearted wind-ups, based on a genuine, if obviously patronising, friendship, rather than any real malice. However, at the local further education college on their day-release studies for the Certificate of Public Health Management, his viciousness came into its own. Surrounded by many of his peers, the flamboyant Danny Skinner was remorseless: heckling, abusing and humiliating the tongue-tied and socially awkward Brian Kibby at every turn. It got so that in certain places, notably the college refectory during coffee and lunch breaks, Kibby was literally scared to open his mouth, lest he draw Skinner's attention to him. Other students became either willing accomplices or unwitting stooges, but most were happy to acquiesce rather than face the sharp end of Danny Skinner's tongue.

That tongue, though, also had its softer side, which was envied by Kibby, almost as much as he detested its more brutal aspect. The female workers at the council, or more often, the students in the college, were seldom spared Skinner's verbal charms. Danny Skinner often seemed incapable of letting a girl pass him by without registering a smile, wink or comment.

The abhorrence Skinner had felt towards Brian Kibby, so deep that it often appalled and dismayed him, had grown steadily over the few months of their acquaintance. It had reached the point where he assumed it had evolved to an unsurpassable level. But one incident would elevate this animus to even greater heights.

The engagement ring intended for Kay Ballantyne had been burning a hole in Danny Skinner's pocket. It was a raw, cold Saturday, with searing gales blasting the city from the North Sea, but the town was nonetheless busy with shoppers, taking advantage of the January sales.

— Let's just take a wee walk through the gardens, Skinner had suggested to his girlfriend. As they descended the steps at the floral clock, now barren for the winter, the throb of a bass line rumbled in the air. Something seemed to be going on at the Ross Bandstand. They heard a wavering voice rising, and saw some groups of freshly scrubbed-looking people, clad in clean brushed denim, and ascertained that some kind of gospel rock band was playing.

— Let's check this out, Kay suggested.

— Naw, let's just sit down here for a bit. Skinner pointed at an empty park bench.

— It's too cold to sit out, Danny, Kay protested, stamping her feet, and pulling some windswept strands of hair out of her eyes.

— Just for a minute, I've got something I need to say to you, he pleaded.

Intrigued, Kay followed him, and they sat on the bench. Skinner looked sadly at her. — I've been an idiot, a total arsehole. At Christmas . . .

— Look, we've been through this before, I don't want to talk about it. Kay shook her head. — Let's just put it behind us. It's Saturday and I –

— Please, angel, just listen to me for a second, he urged, fishing a small box out of his pocket. — I love you, Kay. I want to be with you always.

She gasped as he snapped it open and she caught the sparkle of the diamond ring.

Skinner slid off the park bench on to his knees in front of her. — Kay, I want to marry you. Will you marry me?

Kay Ballantyne was in shock. She'd come to believe that he was bored with her, and wanted them to finish, and that this was what all the drinking was about. — Danny . . . I don't know what to say . . .

Skinner looked tensely at her. Fortunately, this was one of the responses he'd considered in his myriad rehearsals. —Yes would work.

— Yes! Of course! Kay screamed in glee, bending down to kiss him on the mouth as he placed the ring on her finger.

Brian Kibby, out with Ian Buchan on Princes Street, was sporting his favourite baseball cap. A roaring blast of wind suddenly ripped it from his head, hurling it over the railings into the gardens. — My hat! Kibby gave chase, heading through some gates down a cobblestoned slope.

At first he couldn't see it, then he registered that it had come to rest underneath one of the park benches at the bottom of the hill, where a girl in a white jacket was sitting alone. Brian Kibby walked up slowly behind her, and bent down to pick up the cap. As he did, he found himself staring, to their mutual disbelief, through the bars on the bench, straight into the eyes of a kneeling Danny Skinner.

Finding themselves practically in each other's faces, both men were stricken by shock. There was a frozen moment of purgatory before Kibby spoke. — Eh, hi, Danny, he said softly. — It's ma hat, it blew away, he inspidly explained, as Kay turned round in her seat. Kibby was trying not to notice that Skinner was on his knees in front of a startlingly beautiful girl. The white leather jacket she wore had a fur trim, and she sported a furry hat with earmuffs. Her pixie-like nose twitched in the cold, and her eyes widened, as if to compensate for the narrowing of Danny Skinner's, who was ludicrously pretending not to see Brian Kibby. The game was up when Kay nudged him and pointed at his colleague, who was now standing up, clutching the offending cap to his chest.

— Oh, hi, Brian . . . Skinner said with the minimum possible grace.

Kay stood up, thus forcing Skinner to do the same, and put her fingertips together. Cocking her head to the side, she looked up at Skinner in an eager, urging smile, then turned back to Kibby, who marvelled at her dazzling white grin and the swish of her shining black hair in the wind, which cascaded on to her shoulders from under her hat and muffs.

Despite feeling the words jamming in his throat, Skinner managed to cough out, — Eh, that's Brian. He works with me at the council. Then he added quickly, — This is Kay.

Kay smiled broadly at him and Kibby almost passed out.

She's lovely, and she's with Skinner, and they're probably in love and there's no justice in this world . . . a lassie like her going out with the likes of that . . . her teeth are so white, her skin's so smooth, her hair's so beautiful . . .

— Hiya, Brian, Kay said, and nodded to his friend Ian, who had appeared by his side. Then she nudged Skinner, who seemed to Kibby to be sick with tension and disgust and said eagerly, — I can't help it, Danny, I want to tell the world!

Skinner gritted his teeth, but Kay didn't notice. She extended her hand to show Kibby the ring; the diamond ring he'd given her in that exquistite moment of intimacy, only seconds ago, which had now been completely ruined for him.

Him! That fucking little arse-licking walking foetus is the first person to know about us, about my cunting engagement! Caught on my knees by that fucking . . . and that cunt he's with . . .

— We just got engaged! Kay sang, as the Christian gospel music soared to new heights.

Skinner stole a scornful glance at Brian Kibby's friend. All he saw was a pair of protruding ears and a prominent Adam's apple.

Another fucking muppet!

Through witnessing Danny Skinner's silent rage, Brian Kibby realised that he'd inadvertently intruded on a precious moment. It was of the type he'd never personally experienced, but had enviously seen in the lovers around him; and he felt, through that glacier, psychotic stare of Skinner's, that he would emphatically pay for this trangression. — Congratulations, Kibby said as warmly as he could, trying to both ingratiate himself to Kay and make a twisted plea for clemency to his enemy. Ian nodded with an awkward smile as Skinner said something like, — Hmmmph, while almost choking in repressed fury.

He's the first fucker to know . . .

The most beautiful and important thing that has happened in my life, and <u>he</u> is the first person to know about it!

Kibby.

And he winced as they departed, dishonoured by Kay's goodwill, her oneness with the world, as she looked at the sparkler on her finger again, and said, — He seems a nice guy.

Skinner watched Kibby, as his workmate climbed the cobbled path up to Princes Street, holding that cap, clutching it fearfully in the wind.

That cunt dies.

Skinner said nothing. When she prompted him by widening her

eyes, he spat out in unbridled repugnance, — Aye, he's awright. And in Kay's look he saw that she had caught something in him, something ugly she'd not been privy to before, not even in his most selfish, drunken moments, and it was what Kibby had brought out in him. Trying to seize control of his emotions and the situation, he suggested that they go for a drink down Rose Street to celebrate their engagement.

One drink turned into several, became more than enough for Kay, but it was apparent that Skinner wasn't for moving. Now it was Kay's turn to attempt to wrestle some mastery back into her life, and she started to talk about their plans for the future, where they would live and such, and was soon decorating their imaginary home.

Though trying to bear this affably, Skinner became vexed, as he generally did, when she started to talk of children. To him, this represented the ultimate slavery, the end of his social life. But there was a deeper anxiety: he desperately wanted to know about his own father before he ever thought about becoming one himself. They started to argue, Kay growing close to tears as she saw her special day being washed away in a sea of lager and Jack Daniel's. — Why do you have to drink like that? she pleaded. — Your mum's not like that. Your dad's not . . . I mean, was he?

Skinner felt something cold bite into him, like a giant insect was crushing his torso in its jaws. He simply didn't know. — No, he said, deeply embarrassed at this ignorance. — He was a straight guy apparently, never touched a drop, he ventured, making it up. Now his rage was shifting in its direction, heading towards his mother. A fatherless child of an only child, all he and Beverly had were each other, yet she would tell him nothing of his origins. She held all the cards and every time he'd pushed the issue she would not back down.

Was it too much tae fuckin ask? Was he a fuckin rapist or a nonce or something? What the fuck did he dae tae her?

— Well then, Kay argued, looking at his glass.

He had heard from Beverly that her own father, whom Skinner had only known as a toddler, before he had died from a stroke, had taken a good drink. — My grandad was an alcoholic, he said defensively, — it just skipped a generation.

Kay looked open-mouthed at him and gasped, — My God, I don't believe it, you're *boasting* about this!

— I wish I could meet my dad, Skinner suddenly said in great sadness. His words shocked him as much as they did Kay. He'd never said this to anyone before, outside of his mother.

She squeezed his hand, and sweeping her hair behind her ear, leaned close into him. — Did your mum ever say who he was?

— She used to joke that he was Joe Strummer from the Clash, Skinner laughed sadly. — She's got this signed album of his, it's her prize possesion. I used to get beaten up at school for telling everybody that my dad was in the Clash, he smiled ruefully at the memory. — Then she said he was Billy Idol, Jean-Jacques Burnel, Dave Vanian; any punk who'd ever played Edinburgh or Glasgow. It got so that I'd look at all the old magazines and try to see a resemblance. But this was when I was young, and she was just taking the pish. I got so obsessed as a kid, I started staring at any old guy in the street who smiled at me, wondering if he was the one. It's a miracle I wasn't kidnapped by some old nonce, he said woefully. — Now she won't talk about him at all. Skinner raised his glass and took a big gulp. Kay watched his thyroid cartilage bobble as more drink went down his throat. — Every few years I ask her again and she does her nut and we have another big bust-up.

Kay nervously pushed her hair back again, looked at her drink, decided that she wasn't going to finish it. — She must really loathe him.

— But it's irrational to hate somebody like that . . . Skinner stopped in his tracks as Kibby's face, with those virgin-fool camel-like eyes, blazed into his head, — . . . I mean, after all that time, he mumbled uncomfortably.

I do hate Kibby. I'm just like her. Why Kibby? What is he doing to me?

If only Kibby would leave, get out my fucking life, go back to Fife or something.

The walls were painted bright yellow. Sky-blue curtains hung from the long windows. But the small room's sedate decor could not deflect the dominance of the aluminium-framed hospital bed. A television screen swung to the side, attached by anglepoise arm to the wall above the bedstead. The only other furniture was a locker on wheels, two chairs and a small sink unit on the wall at the bottom of the bed.

In the bed, Keith Kibby, weak like a punctured tyre, felt his life ebbing away just as slowly and steadily. The saline feed drip-drip-dripped into his withered limb, each drop for him the almost silent ticking of a clock. Outside, the trees were bare, dry sticks, like his arm, he thought, but unlike it springtime would see them reignite with life. Last summer had been good, Keith recalled through a disorientating fog of medication, then, as if in need of affirmation, wheezed to himself, — A good summer . . . But this precipitated a stark, bitter bolt of realisation, and he rolled his bald head ceiling-wards in accusation: — . . . and I've only been allowed to see forty-nine of the bastards . . .

Francesca Ryan, one of the nurses on the ward, entered Keith's room to take his pulse and blood pressure. As she went to work, wrapping the Velcro pad from the equipment around his skinny wrist, Keith scrutinised the facial hair under her lip. A small spark kindled inside him and he considered that she wouldn't be bad-looking if she had it removed.

Electrolysis. That, and losing a few pounds. Aye, then she'd be a comely lass.

Ryan couldn't wait to get away from Keith Kibby. It wasn't his illness that made her squeamish, she was used to imminent death, but there was something about him, a hungry waft coming off him that disturbed her. She preferred old Davie Rodgers next door, although he teased her about being a native of Limerick City. 'Dinnae let that lassie in the operating theatre wi aw they knives or we'll have a bloodbath oan oor hands!'

Old Davie could be a pest, but with him, she felt, you got what you saw. When her back was turned away from Keith Kibby she could feel his eyes on her.

So Francesca was pleased when Mr Kibby's wife, son and daughter arrived. They seemed to her to be a close family, to really love him, and be utterly devastated by his illness. She didn't find him the slightest bit lovable, but then it was a funny world.

She watched as the teenage daughter kissed the father's head. Francesca had heard that she was a freshman student at Edinburgh University, studying English. She sometimes went to dos at the student union and glanced to see if she could place the Kibby girl but her face, conventionally pretty, Francesca thought with a little envy, rang no bells. Caroline saw the nurse staring at her and gave her a tight smile back. Slightly flustered, Nurse Ryan departed from the ward.

Caroline had been considering attending a club event that night at Teviot Row, a dance held by one of the societies, where a local name DJ was spinning. But looking at her dad's worn-out face she wanted to cry. It was only when she noted the tears that were welling up in her mother's eyes that she felt furiously, perversely, empowered to fight her own ones back.

I'm not like her. I'll stay strong.

She noted that her brother had remained silent, but sucked in one of his cheeks, a nervous reaction of his that was familiar to her. Then he started to say something to their father; words that sounded like, — See when you get out of here, we'll . . .

But Brian Kibby never got to finish the sentence as his father went into a gripping seizure. The Kibbys screamed for the medical staff. They were prompt in their response, particularly Francesca Ryan, but they could do nothing as Keith Kibby hurtled into convulsions right there in front of them. In his death throes he battled every inch of the way to hold on to his life, bucking up in bed with an almost supernatural force, his eyes unfocused, as, in their torment, the Kibbys silently prayed for him to let go, to leave this earth in peace. For Caroline, this violent, paranormal passing compounded the unspeakable horror of her father's death. She had assumed that he would go out like the dimmer switches he'd installed in the family home, a slow almost imperceptible ebb into blackness. But as he thrashed around, she could virtually see the life, which now seemed an alien force that had permeated the flesh beneath, rending free from its flimsy cage.

Time seemed to freeze, seconds stretching out into hours, as he died with all their arms around him. Brian, in particular, seemed to hold that bony carriage in a manner that suggested he was trying to shore up any cracks through which the essence of his father might escape. But when it was over, it was as if Keith had ripped some of the life from every Kibby in the room to take with him. A long silence followed, before Brian Kibby, the thin youth with the long-lashed cow-like eyes, hugged his mother and sister to him.

Caroline smelt the sweat on her mother, rank and foul, oddly like her father's corpse, and then the sweet, sharp aftershave on her brother's face. After a bit it was Brian who spoke and Caroline looked up and saw the tears running across the peach fuzz of his cheeks. — He's at peace now, he observed.

Joyce looked up at him, first in a stunned bovine bemusement, then sharply and imploringly. — Peace, Brian said again, tightening his grip on his mother.

— Peace, Joyce repeated, swamped by the mindlessness of grief.

— Peace, Brian confirmed once more, looking at Caroline. She nodded and wondered whether or not she would go to this dance tonight; then she heard her mother recite in a small but eerily defiant voice:

> The Lord's my shepherd, I'll not want
> He makes me down to lie
> In pastures green: he leadeth me
> The quiet waters by.

When she heard her brother join in with 'My soul he doth restore again' she knew that she would not – could not – stay at home with them tonight.

11
Funerals

The old drunkard was a handy cunt in his day. I've seen him knocking around for ages and even on occasion knocking ten types of shite out of other pissheids who got a wee bit too lippy. Aye, he got plenty dangerous for a while, when he was in that last angry menopausal flush of power, just before the physical and mental enfeeblement of old age started to kick in. Then a younger guy he got wide with did him badly and now there's a broken yellow light in the cunt's eyes. I suppose it might be peace but it's more likely to be a fucked liver. Sammy, I'm sure they call him.

Now he's reduced to slavering drivel in old Busby's ear; they're always in here together, in this grotty Duke Street dive. Only Busby's not around today, he's probably up giving my old girl a fucking length . . .

It's just this old cunt; donkey jacket, hands like shovels, Mars bars, mind fuddled by drink, but you still don't want to get too close, cause the last thing that goes with an old boxer is the punch. Worse than that, it's probably the second last, to that bell they hear in their doolally heids at the strangest of times!

I think about the my old boy, how I've always envisioned him: tanned, square-jawed, thick hair, with his well-preserved and impeccably groomed wife in a New South Wales or southern Californian suburb, and realise that I've almost certainly been kidding myself. He's more likely to be some broken jakey, in this very bar. That's doubtlessly why the Old Girl hates him so much; she probably bumps into the cunt on a fuckin daily basis, as he staggers down Junction Street to the foot of Walk, maybe trying to put the bite on her for a few quid. Perhaps she's just trying to save my crushing disappointment, and my father is a man who, when you take away the drink and cigarettes, is just a total void.

They're talking about banning smoking from pubs. You ban smoking from this doss you might as well torch the fuckin place behind ye, because if you don't, sure as fuck the owner will for insurance purposes cause no cunt will ever set foot in here again for trade. Tabs define this place more than whisky or beer: from the nicotine-stained walls to the tubercular hacking, rasping coughs of the locals. Not that there are many in right now, just two toothless auld gimpy cunts on the dominoes in one corner and me and the old boxer at the bar.

— Awright, he growls at me. Aye, Sammy's his name.

Peace, brother. — No bad, boss. Yersel?

The old white hope shrugs in a you-see-it-all gesture and I'm thinking, 'Bad as that, is it?' but I offer to buy him a beer, help the fucking aged, ya cunt. Forget the credit-card problems, a salaried man has to do his bit. He accepts with only a modicum of grace. Then he fixes me in his narrowing eyes, trying to get a focus. — Bev Skinner, the hairdresser; you're her laddie, eh?

— Aye.

— The Skinners . . . aye . . . Tennant Street, back in the day . . . Jimmy Skinner . . . that would be your grandfaither . . . oan yir ma's side. Yir faither wis the chef, wis eh no?

I shudder inside and look the old cunt in the eye. — What?

The old boy looks cautious now, wary that he's said something that he shouldn't have. I've heard this shite before. I remember my old neighbour, Mrs Bryson, before she went totally potty, telling me that my dad was a chef. I half put it down to dementia. I asked both Trina and Val about this but the Old Girl had done a number on them and they denied all knowledge. The auld felly here's got something to say though. — Yir auld man. Wis he no a chef? he warily repeats.

— Did ye ken um, likes?

Some memory seems to play across his mind as his eyes roll into accord like the symbols on a fruit machine. But he's paying out nae jackpot right now, cause the Sammy boy goes aw furtive, and no mistake. — Mibbe ah'm thinking ay somebody else.

— Whae's it you were thinkin ay then? I ask challengingly.

The old cunt raises his brows and I can see the thug that I had presumed long departed, seeping slowly back into the lamps underneath them. — Somebody you dinnae ken.

I can see where this is leading so I drink up. Fucked if I'm bursting chops with an old bastard in a shithouse like this. Win, lose or draw, the only real result is humiliation for even being daft enough to take part. — Right, I'll see ye then, I tell the old cunt, and I can feel that his eyes never leave the back of my head until I'm out the door and into the rain at the foot of Leith Walk.

I stop off in a couple of boozers, throwing back six pints of Guinness and three double JD's quickstyle, the lush charge hitting me like a ton of bricks. When I get back to the flat Kay's there, in tears again, saying some stuff about dancing, her career, her ambitions, how I don't respect them, how they mean nothing to me, then leaving. Everything is muffled and car-crash-like and I want to speak but she's looking through me and I'm looking through alcohol. We're nowhere near each other even as we stumble in tandem through our disintegrating lives.

She came to dance . . .

I couldn't feel her presence, but I sure as fuck notice her absence. I can't stay here alone and I head down the street, passing the Duke Street dive and glancing in where I can now see that big gadgie, swaying in the non-existent breeze, and wee Busby's in now, crouched at the bar, in sour disapproval.

I feel like gaun in thair an . . .

Get up that fucken road . . .

And I cannae remember the walk tae my ma's hoose, can't mind her opening the door and me going in, all I can mind is saying to her, — So eh wis a chef then . . . ma dad wis a fuckin chef . . . a fuckin cook . . .

And we're shouting at each other and I mind of repeating to her, — chef, chef, chef . . .

Then I see something in her eyes, not anger but something harsh and mocking, and I stop and she says, — Aye, son, and how many fuckin meals did eh ever make ye?

I storm out, resolving that I'm never talking to that stubborn, evil auld hoor again, no until she tells ays the fuckin truth . . .

Then when I get round to mine, back up the stairs to my flat,

I see it on the mantelpiece, and I freeze in shock.

It's the ring. The ring I gave Kay.

I'm not ready for this. Can you ever be ready?

My father, my poor old dad. He never harmed anybody, he was such a good man. Why did this happen? Why? But now it's Mum's grief, the sheer power and force of it; it's every bit as harrowing as my father's death. I've not been ready for anything, it's all just happened to me and I haven't coped. I don't know what to do and Caz won't even talk, she won't say a word.

There's a slow drizzle as we wait to go into the chapel. I look around and see that there's hardly anybody here. My dad was a family man and his family was very small. He has no living elderly relatives. So apart from us and some people from the church congregation, there's only a few neighbours and former workmates from the railway present.

It seems so sad and makes me angry that a good man can just go like that and be mourned by so few, when the likes of the big loudmouths on television like that De Fretais would have thousands at their funerals, all weeping and saying how great he was. But it would be crocodile tears, not real grief like this: this horrible, quiet misery and paralysis that can tear people apart.

Dad's old railway friends all say the same thing about him. He was a decent, sober man, who was warm and friendly enough, but who largely kept himself to himself. The men who worked in the signal box at the old railway junction in Thornton, Fife, they are telling me about the side of my dad that is a mystery to me, a man who whiled away his spare hours reading and writing, filling up notepads with doodlings. That seemed to be his great passion, outside of his family. When he became a driver, Dad really appeared to have found his vocation. Sitting alone in the hot seat, taking the train up the West Highland line.

One senior rail official, a Mr Garriock, comes up and says to me and Mum, — They don't make men like Keith any more. You should all be very proud, and he seems overtaken by genuine emotion.

The service is so nice. I said that I wouldn't cry but can't help it when Mr Godfrey, the minister, talks about my dad, how he knew him well through the church activities and what a good person he was and the things he would do for the pensioners in the parish.

I wait outside in the doorway of the church to shake hands with the mourners. Ian shakes my hand but he doesn't stay or come back to the reception. He looks at me quite strangely but I suppose that's what grief brings out in other people, they don't know how to take you. The biting, whipping wind is numbing my head like an ice-cream toothache, and I'm relieved to get into the car and head for the function at the hotel in Ferry Road.

The funeral party isnae busy and Mum's estimates of the amount of whisky, sherry, sausage rolls, egg-and-cress sandwiches, tea and cakes look to be a wee bit too optimistic. Still, Mum did say she could take any spare food down to the pensioners' club at the church. One neighbour, Phil Stewart, raises a glass of whisky: — Absent friends, he toasts.

A few of the railwaymen join in eagerly, while Mum smiles tightly, putting down her cup of tea and raising a glass of whisky that she has no intention of drinking. Dad would have understood, as he wasn't a drinker.

I hold up my glass of orange juice. The railwaymen would probably have disapproved if I'd done this on another occasion but probably just think, like father like son. I shudder with embarrassment as Caroline picks up a whisky glass and knocks it right back, then just grabs another.

What the hell is she –

My stomach's already in turmoil and that makes things worse. I head to the toilets and sit in a cubicle, and I'm cramped over with constipation. It's a terrible struggle to move my bowels. Ken Radden from my Hyp Hykers club always says that it's important for your health to keep your bowels moving.

I'm thinking about the other two chickens I hatched at *Harvest Moon* last night. It's great to get a video game that involves building stuff, not just shooting and destroying things all the time. The Rockstar North people here and up in Dundee who make the likes of *Grand Theft Auto* are so talented but they make such destructive games. And *Game Informer* gave it 10. Why do they have to use their gifts in that way? How can they live with themselves? If I had that ability I'd design games like *Harvest Moon*. Only the Japanese could have made that though; they're different to us over there. It would be great to go to Japan one day. Some of the girls are really beautiful and it's said that they're nice lassies, really clean and they make good wives. And they're meant to like Western men.

That's my problem, finding a wife! I've now ruled out Celia but that still leaves Ann, Muffy, Karen and Elli to consider.

Muffy . . .

From inside the booth I hear two men enter and start relieving themselves at the latrine. Their pee drums on the stainless steel.

— Sair ficht, bonny lad.

— Aye, sad tae see the faimly sae upset.

— That wee blondie, that's Keith's lassie.

— Aye, a wee belter n aw.

— She's beltin back they fuckin nips awright.

— Fuckin belt her back in a minute!

— Hi, you, behave yirself! Mind whaire ye are!

— Jist sayin . . .

— Ah ken what you're like, you jist pick oan somebody yir ain size, Romeo!

The sick cackles of these odious men send shivers down my spine. I just sit here on the cold toilet in a nauseating, impotent wrath. Surely such men couldn't have been friends of my father! But there are so many of them, men like that, they are everywhere. Lowlife scum like McGrillen back at school. Dirty pigs like Danny Skinner, and him with that lovely lassie. And Shannon fancies him as well, you can tell. Somebody even said that they were snogging at a Christmas party but that's just rubbish! How could they . . . how could girls be so daft . . . ? If they kent what I was really like then they'd want to be with me . . . I just ken that they would . . .

12
The Archangel Tavern

A trembling Danny Skinner looked at the pint of lager in front of him. It could take away this pain, this torment. But no, he'd resist, he owed it to Kay. He'd prove that he was stronger than it by just walking straight out of this pub.

Right now.

So Skinner stood up and strode determinedly out of the bar. In Junction Street the cars and buses grinded, honked and roared, while prams and pushchairs steered by robotic, Prozac-stunned mothers threatened to sever his Achilles tendons. He could feel the eyes of hard men from the bookies, bars and bus stops burrowing into him. Old women – witches heading to their bingo – seemed to be hexing him with their disapproval as they passed him in the street.

Fuckin bams . . . no fuckin intae this . . . no at aw . . .

Panic struck in his chest like a bolt of lightning. He stopped in his tracks. Surely the pint would still be there.

The pint of golden nectar. In the pub, that seat still warm, and moulded for my arse-cheeks.

The world was a better place when he emerged from the bar for the second time. The sharp edges had gone. Leith was no longer stuffed with cruel, brutish psychopaths who hated him. They had vanished, replaced by a convivial community of jaunty salt-of-the-earth types.

Now I'm in shape to meet Kay. To explain to her what's gone wrong. To seduce her, even. It's good that she's coming down here and we'll be able to talk. Aye, I'll make it up to her. Some red wine, she loves red wine. Red, red wine . . .

Skinner dived into Thresher's and, thinking of Bob Foy, bought their most expensive Pinot Noir.

There was still some time to kill before Kay arrived. He watched another of the interminably meaningless turkey-shoots of a Scottish Premier League game between the millionaires of the Carling beer-sponsored sides, coffers bloated through years of exploiting religious sectarianism, and their impoverished journeymen opponents.

The label on the bottle of wine looks interesting. Full-bodied. Aromatic. Rich. Fruity. It looks good stuff, right enough, even though I'm not a red man. Surely one glass wouldn't hurt, just to sip, to feel the flavour on my palate. Then when she arrives I'll hit her with that big Danny Skinner smile and an urbane, — Ah, the lovely Miss Ballantyne, my beautiful fiancée. Care to join to me in a glass of wine, my darling?

Kay'll gie me that look, the one which said, 'You incorrigible, lovable rogue, how could I resist?' Aye, and she might even concede that she's been a bit of a spoilsport, a bit of a wet blanket. You're only young once, after all.

But when Kay did enter the flat there was a distance about her and a resolve that he'd never seen before. And at that point a dagger seemed to twist deep inside him and he guessed that it was over before she even opened her mouth.

And as if on cue she delivered the words, — It's over, Danny, with a stark, uncompromising air of finality.

Skinner was crushed by her words. He wished he wasn't but he was. He felt something real, something essential die inside him; felt it actually leave his body. It was a rich, deep and vital energy, a cardinal component of the self. Stricken, he wondered if he would ever get it back, or if that's what life was to be: steady erosion followed by an occasional big subsidence. He was surely too young to feel like this. His anguished gasp was deep, disturbing and primal, shocking both him and Kay. — Whaaat . . . ?

Kay needed every part of her new-found strength and determination not to go to him, to take him in her arms, the way people are conditioned to do when they see a loved one hurting so deeply.

Skinner always thought that he would never beg in a situation like this. And he was wrong, because he was losing everything. His life was draining from him, walking away from him. He wouldn't survive this. — Please, darlin . . . please, Kay. We can work this out.

— What is there to work out? Kay asked, her face still expressionless, nerves cauterised by all the disappointments he'd unremittingly provided. — You're an alcoholic and guess what? You love it. There's only room for one romance in your life, Danny. I don't mean anything to you. I'm just a pretty girl who looks good on your arm. She fretfully chewed on her bottom lip. — You don't care about me or my career, or what I need. I don't like drinking, Danny. It's not what I want. I don't think you even like having sex with me any more, because all you want to do is drink. You're an alcoholic.

The shock of hearing those words from her. Was he an alcoholic? What was that? Someone who drinks all the time? Who can't say no to a drink? Who drinks in secret? Somebody who anticipates the next drink before he's finished the one in front of him? — But . . . I . . . I need you, Kay . . . he said, but he couldn't say what for. He couldn't say 'I need you to help me beat this disease' because he felt that he was a young guy who drank far too much but wouldn't always drink far too much. He didn't feel diseased, he just felt empty and incomplete.

— You don't need me. I don't think you need anything except that. She nodded at the glass and the empty bottle of wine.

And Skinner hadn't even realised that the bottle was empty. He was just going to have one wee glass of that full-bodied, aromatic red . . .

. . . was it full-bodied? Was it aromatic?

Diseased.

How could I have let this happen?

Kay left him alone in the flat. He had no power to try and stop her from leaving any more. He didn't even hear the front door close behind her; it was as if she was already a ghost to him.

Maybe she would change her mind and come back. Maybe not.

Skinner choked back the tears. Self-pity overwhelmed him; he felt small, childlike and bullied. He wanted his mother; not Beverly as she was now, but some younger, abstracted ideal he could submit to and be indulged by. But she too had gone out of his life, until he came back on her terms and played the dutiful son.

The stubborn old cow would never give in . . .

But he wanted her.

He also wanted a drink, but he couldn't leave the flat feeling like this. He'd heard the alcoholic stories before; the accounts of betrayal, of injustices perpetuated on their protagonists by a mother, a father, a lover or a friend. They were all essentially the same tale: a bitter paean to the loss of love, comradeship or money. And then there were the plans, the utopian schemes for the bright future that would be enacted, after the next drink, of course.

The day it is passing in laughter and song . . .

After a while the pisshead was just one big giant whisky glass talking, telling the same, sad stories, over and over again. Alcohol had just the one voice. No matter who it possessed, all it let them do was add their own distinctive tone, before even that was subsumed into a general jakey growl. And that glass didn't need to take responsibility, it only had to sit there and be refilled.

I'm becoming one of them. I am one of them. I have to do something. I have to act . . .

I mind of when first we got together, it was so fucking sensual and I'd take in the scent of her, kissing her eyes, ears, kissing her all over, totally lost in being with her.

Aye, right.

Other times I'd push her aside and roll away grumbling, made dirty, heavy and thick-headed by the drink, needing to sleep it off and never quite getting enough kip to do so.

What am I? A social drinker? Aye, but more than that. A binge drinker? For sure, when I'm not drinking socially or thinking about drinking. A fucking alcoholic. Aye, that's the one.

I'm an alkie. I dinnae do sober so much any more, it's being squeezed out between the two big ones: being drunk and being hung-over. Being hung-over is not being sober. Being hung-over is hell.

In Skinner's anguished mind, he was taking stock of his life and working out some basic propositions that had been close to gnawing him into action for some time. Firstly, he never knew his father. His mother refused to talk about him. All he had was this limited but persistent information, now backed by a strange intuition, that he may have been a chef.

Could you miss what you never had?

Yes. Yes, you could. I'd see them with their dads at the fitba. Their big proud dads. Tense, serious, Ross Kinghorn with his young Dessie, 'How many you gonny score the day, son? How many?' Bobby Traynor with gap-toothed Gary; like his son, always a joker. My Old Girl did her best, standing there by the side of pitch chain-smoking, pretending to take an interest in the game. But there was something missing. Even Big Rab knew where his old boy was, even if it was usually HMP Saughton.

Missing his father, Skinner reasons that he is missing essential information about himself. Who does he come from? What is his genetic and cultural inheritance? Is alcoholism cruelly written into his DNA? Is he just depressed at the lack of filial connection and will all be well if he meets his dad?

If I found my old man, the fucking chef, then I could see if he was a drunk, if this was his legacy.

Fuck my mother, I'll find him myself! I'll show her . . . I'll show them aw!

The Old Girl was a waitress for a while, years ago, she told me. Where the fuck did she work again? . . .

It hit Skinner slowly, in a big wave that seemed to rise up from his bowels. He looked at the glossy, hardback book on his coffee table: *The Bedroom Secrets of the Master Chefs* by Alan De Fretais. He picked it up and read a section as his heart raced.

> Gregory William Tomlin is not only one of my favourite chefs, integrity forces me to add that he is also a close personal friend. I first met Greg back in 1978 in, of all places, the infamous Archangel Tavern in Edinburgh. So how did an American Master Chef and one of the pioneers of the Californian culinary revolution come to be hanging out in a joint like that?
>
> The Archangel Tavern is still a renowned Edinburgh watering hole and eatery. At the time the Head Chef was the legendary *bon vivant* Sandy Cunningham-Blyth. Old Sandy had a thing about passionate young cooks. In addition to employing yours truly, he took on a young backpacking American student who was 'doing Europe' and who, *en route* to France during the height of punk rock, washed up in Edinburgh short of cash.
>
> Greg and I had a similar philosophy of life and grew fond

of sharing tapes, drinks, lovers and, on the odd occasion, even recipes!

Skinner felt the sweat releasing evenly from his ducts with every pulse in his body as he lowered the book on to the coffee table.

Greg Tomlin. Sandy Cunningham-Blyth. Alan Cunting De Fretais. The Archangel Tavern.

Dougie Winchester was positioned at his computer wearing a pained expression that switched to neutrality as Skinner popped his head round the door. Sometimes his office was locked and when quizzed about this a red-faced Winchester would mutter that it was the only way he could get peace to concentrate on the important project work he was undertaking.

Winchester's title was Special Projects Officer (Environmental Health) even though the department currently had no special projects. In established local authority fashion, they simply made one up, as it would have been too costly to sack him. He had managed to wangle a five-year contract in a previous department and now only had eighteen months left till it expired. Winchester had gone round the departments, a man out of time and unconcerned with his work, such as it was.

Dougie Winchester and Danny Skinner were an odd pairing, one man supposedly close to the start of his working life, the other who, though still only in his mid-forties, would probably never be employed again when he left the council. They were, as Winchester had once said, 'related through drink'. Skinner considered that there must have been a time when he used that phrase in irony rather than in a purely descriptive manner.

Now Winchester had uses other than that of a drinking partner and Skinner wanted to draw on his local knowledge. The older man was surprised when Skinner had suggested a lunchtime pint in the Archangel. Although it was not one of their regular spots, as a very well known Edinburgh hostelry, Winchester had used it many years ago.

The Archangel was situated alongside Waverley Station, at a side entrance, and so was more popular with commuters than tourists.

It was really two premises rather than one. The large bar, McTaggart's, was a spartan pub, which could be atmospheric and lively, especially at weekends. Next door, and there was also a connecting passage through shared toilets between the two establishments, was the Archangel itself. It had a smaller bar, which attracted an arty, bohemian crowd, and an upstairs restaurant that had always been renowned for its good food. Skinner had never eaten there but had once inspected the immaculately run kitchen.

It was the smaller bar that Danny Skinner sought to visit, much to Winchester's consternation. — No going in there, he said, shaking his head, — the place is full off arse bandits. Or at least it was back then.

— It'll no be like that now, especially no at lunchtime, Skinner said. — Let's give it a go and if it's shite we can nip next door.

Winchester was less fussy than he made out. His only real consideration was volume, as he liked to get his four pints in at lunchtime. The first one was hammered back in two or three gulps, the second and third drunk steadily and enjoyed, with the fourth usually getting the same treatment as the first. In the afternoon, the door of the office of the Special Projects Officer (Environmental Health) was generally locked.

The little bar's only occupants were one small group of Fife housewives with shopping bags and a couple of young backpackers, but it already looked crowded. The tubby barman wore an old St Johnstone football replica top advertising The Famous Grouse Whisky. He had blond hair, which he wore slicked back; the sort of guy, Skinner thought, who would have had real girl appeal, before the days of the obesity epidemic. He ordered a couple of pints and noted Winchester giving the first one his usual treatment. — Was this an old haunt of yours then? he asked his gulping pal.

— Aye, said Winchester, — everybody used this place back then. Every hoor and comic singer came here. Great atmosphere it had.

— Was that back in the punk era?

Winchester shook his head briskly, his features puckering in distaste. — I hated all that shite. Killed musicianship. Led Zeppelin, the Doors, they were the boys, he waxed. — The Lizard King!

In Winchester's elation Skinner was privy to a hitherto unrevealed side of his associate. He disconcertingly glimpsed a younger, livelier soul, before the reductive powers of ageing and alcohol had done their work. — You remember an Edinburgh band back then called the Old Boys? he asked Winchester. — My ma was into them. I think she hung about with them.

— Naw . . . Winchester shook his his head. — I wisnae interested in aw that shite. Punk was just a noise, he reiterated.

Losing interest in his colleague and turning to the barman, Skinner remarked, — I hear that the grub's got a good rep here.

— Always has had, he agreed.

— Aye, Skinner nodded, sidling closer to the bar as he warmed to his topic, — been reading that De Fretais guy's book, ken the telly chef?

— Aye, he doesnae like ehsel, that boy, the barman sarcastically observed.

Skinner nodded and smiled. — No half, eh. He's written that food sex book, *The Bedroom Secrets of the Master Chefs*. Tells you how to get a bird intae bed by cooking her a meal.

— Spend enough on drinks trying to get them into bed, the barman laughed, — fucked if I'm cooking for them as well.

Skinner chortled in acknowledgement. — I never knew he started out here. He namechecks this auld chef fae this place; the boy taught him everything, apparently. I'd never heard ay the old gadge but he seemed a right character.

The barman rolled his eyes as he saw Winchester had drained his glass and Skinner was making an impression on his. He gave the 'same again' gesture, to which Winchester responded positively, then turned back to Skinner. — Sandy Cunningham-Blyth. That old cunt's the bane of my life, he said ruefully.

Skinner couldn't believe his ears. — He still works here?

— Wish he did, at least he'd be in the kitchen. It's a lot worse than that: he fucking well drinks here. The barman shook his head. — See, if it was up to me, I'd have barred the drunken auld pest years ago, but he can do no wrong in the eyes of the management here. 'An Archangel institution', the boss calls him. He ought to be in a fucking institution if ye ask me, the barman said, rapping out a speech Skinner sensed he'd deployed on several occasions.

— So old Sandy boy is still a local?

— He'll be in here tonight, that's for sure, unless the old cunt's fallen under a bus or something. We can but hope, the barman continued, deadpan, as a Fife housewife came over and ordered a round of gins.

— What does he look like?

— His coupon's like it's been detonated by explosives and stitched back together by a blind seamstress on acid. Don't worry though, you'll hear him before you see him, the barman gravely advised.

Having got their four pints in, Skinner and Winchester sauntered back to the office, observing their customary ritual. Winchester always stopped in at the newsagent and let Skinner go ahead while he purchased an *Evening News*. Then he'd follow on a few minutes later. That way they hoped that they wouldn't be associated as drinking cronies.

Most of the current gossip in the department, however, didn't concern drinking, but focused around the respective losses incurred by Kibby and Skinner. People seemed a lot quicker to empathise with the former's setback than with the latter's and this preferential treatment did not escape Skinner's notice.

After Kay's departure it had not taken Skinner long to commence a half-formed casual affair with Shannon McDowall. Shannon had also had a romantic setback, walking in on her boyfriend Kevin screwing one of her best friends. The colleagues' new relationship consisted of them going out for a drink after work, getting a bit pissed and necking furiously for the rest of the night. Although it always stopped at that point, it was observed by the odd party and became the subject of much salacious chat in the workplace.

That afternoon Skinner had been chomping at the bit after his four lunchtime pints with Winchester and he and Shannon found themselves sitting in the Waterloo Bar on an early finish after work. — It's a shame about Brian's dad. Shannon shook her head. — He's taking it very badly.

Skinner found himself barking at her in hostility. — At least the fucking muppet knew his faither, his venom causing her to recoil slightly. Aware of his heavy-handedness, Skinner shrugged in apology at his *chère amie*. — Sorry . . . it's just that *my* dad, he could be anybody in this pub. He looked around at the chattering groups of drinkers, all animated after finishing work. — My mum never talks about him, willnae tell me a thing about the fucker. That little bastard Kibby walks around like he's the only person on this earth that's ever known pain and everybody goes: 'Awww . . . poor wee Bri-yin . . . '

He could see that Shannon was gauging the extent of his antagonism towards Kibby, and he reasoned that it wasn't a particularly endearing quality to display. But she was also struck by a more powerful emotion, that of empathy. — You know that I lost my mum when I was younger, she told him.

Skinner thought about his own mother, how it would feel if anything happened to her. — I can't imagine how bad that would feel. He shook his head, then thought about Kibby. What must the poor wee fucker be going through? he considered.

— It felt totally fucking shite, basically, Shannon said evenly. — Dad couldn't cope. Had a breakdown. She took a long drag on her cigarette. As he watched it burn, Skinner wanted one but fought the craving. — I had to look after my wee brother and sister. So uni was out, I needed to get a job. This place was reasonably well paid, and they sent you on day release to get the Public Health Management Certificate. I can't say it's what I wanted to do, inspect fucking kitchens, but I suppose it's important work, and I've made the most of it. But that's why my heart goes out to Brian right now. I know what it's like to lose someone like that.

— I'm sorry . . . I do feel for Brian, Skinner said, and he strangely felt the need to have Kibby with them, to comfort Kibby, to *hold* him, and the impulse shocked him. — It's just that I'm not over Kay – he said quickly, then suddenly stalled, realising that accidentally, and by omission, he'd just referenced a relationship they had both steadfastly resisted defining. — That's no reflection on you, you've been great, it's just . . .

Their hands crossed over and entwined. Skinner often had cause to reflect that sometimes a snog could be more intimate than a fuck. Now it seemed that there were circumstances where simply holding hands could imply a deeper pathos still. He looked at the rings on her fingers, then into her large, brown eyes and saw the sadness in them, and felt something inside him stretch towards her.

— Thanks for trying, Danny, but you don't need to. We're both on the rebound and we're helping each other out, having a bit of a laugh, repairing some badly damaged self-esteem. — Let's just leave it at that for now and if anything else happens, it happens. Okay?

— Aye, Skinner agreed, possibly a little too eagerly, he fancied, and the tight grin that pursed her lips told him that this had indeed been the case. Yes, something in his soul was still waiting for that phone call from Kay, although the realist in him knew that it would never come. — Aye, rebound relationships are always dodgy and that. Let's keep it low pressure, he said, then aware of a slightly painful impasse, asked, — You were wi Kevin a while, eh?

— Three years.

— You must miss him, he said, thinking of Kay.

— I do, but it wasn't right for a while. We both knew it. We couldn't fix it, but we couldn't end it. In a way it came as a relief. I suppose I was already feeling the loss of him those last months we were together. If I'm being honest, I miss Ruth more. Her face pinched and her eyes narrowed, — that weak, twisted, treacherous, fucked-up bitch was my best friend.

She lost two of them in one fell swoop. One fell fuck. I lost Kay. I loved her, but couldn't love her properly. I can't love anybody again until I'm a whole person. I'm not complete till I know myself, and I don't know myself till I know my old man. I've got to find that fucking chef, and I don't care what this old fucker's like, I'd rather it was him than De Fr . . .

They smiled at each other and Skinner suggested that they move on to the Archangel Tavern.

— But that place at the top of the Walk has cocktails at half-price during happy hour, Shannon urged. Since she'd split up with Kevin she too was seeking some sort of regular oblivion, this being as much the attraction as anything else in Skinner's consort.

— Wait till you see this place though, Shan, brilliant atmosphere and some real characters, Skinner said with great zest, relishing the prospect of meeting a certain old chef.

— Let's give it a go then, she said with an enthusiasm he found touching, wishing Kay could have shared it. Then again, he gloomily considered, maybe she did at the start.

They walked down into the station, cutting across the overpass. Skinner wondered whether he should take her hand, or put his arm around her. No, it seemed strange them being like that when they worked in the same office together. The intimacy of the pub had evaporated in the cold, night air, like a Hollywood musical where the hero and heroine go through an elaborate song-and-dance act, ending up in each other's arms, only to pull nervously apart when the music stops.

As they crossed the footbridge and decended into Market Street, Danny Skinner thought in mounting anticipation about Sandy Cunningham-Blyth. He pushed open the frosted-glass doors of the bar and ushered Shannon through.

A drunken old bastard. The apple doesnae fall far from the tree . . .

Even though he had never set eyes on him, Skinner knew who Cunningham-Blyth was straight away. This, he reasoned, was nothing to do with any possible paternal recognition, nor even the description furnished by the barman, accurate though it was. In the small, crowded lounge there was an old guy sitting on his own and the only free seats in the house were beside him. He was muttering to himself, as drinkers on either side of the exclusion zone sat with their backs to him in poses of intent avoidance.

Nodding to the barman he'd talked to earlier, who had now changed into a checked shirt, Skinner got up a pint of lager and a vodka and Coke for himself.

— I'll have a large whisky n lemonade. Shannon pointed to the gantry. — Teacher's will do nicely.

— You want to watch that stuff. It completely decimates the prostate gland.

— Danny, I don't *have* a prostate gland.

— I rest my case, Skinner smiled cheerfully as they moved across to the empty seats.

Sandy Cunningham-Blyth gave the arrivals a big smile, like a country host welcoming expected guests. He was a squat, hunched, bearded, broad-shouldered man with silver hair that was thin on top and ran down his back in lank greasy strands gathered into an unlikely ponytail. His few remaining teeth were stained yellow and he stank of old booze and tobacco. Wearing a crumpled shirt, a checked lumberjack coat and soiled fawn corduroy trousers tucked into old boots, he was a man whose own comfort seemed designed to upset any possibility of that state in others. Most of all, and the barman was spot on, thought Skinner, the man had a complexion which suggested a lifelong devotion to debauchery. He eyed Shannon as she sat down. — Come to me, pretty lady, he said in an unabashedly leering greeting. In response she turned snootily away, pretending not to notice, while Skinner laughed in nervous amusement.

— And your name is? Sandy persisted, gently tapping her on the shoulder as she quickly shot Skinner a 'let's sit somewhere else' look before turning to her self-appointed host.

— Shannon, she said in polite terseness, as Skinner pulled his chair round to make a circle, forcing her to turn in.

— That majestic river of old Erin, Cunningham-Blyth waxed dreamily, a trickle of saliva dripping on to his beard, and began to quote, — 'No more he will hear the seagull's cry, ower the bubbling Shannon tide . . . ' Does your family hail from the Emerald Isle?

— Nup, they took the name from Del Shannon. My dad was a big fan, he played in a rockabilly band, she took a delight in explaining.

Sandy Cunningham-Blyth seemed a bit deflated at this news, letting his big shoulders slump forward. Then his face ignited and he said, — So, where do you stay, my little runaway?

— Meadowbank, Shannon said, now slightly warming to the guy. He was just a harmless old drunk, after all.

All the time Skinner was scrutinising Sandy Cunningham-Blyth. *Decrepit, but probably not even sixty, young enough to have had my mother and got her up the duff twenty-four years ago. A definite pisshead and still going strong. If he's my old man I just hope I've inherited the cunt's constitution!*

— I'm Danny, Skinner extended his hand and felt a strong grip, tried to work out whether it belonged to the drink or the man. — This is a rare pub, eh? he said, looking around.

— It *used* to be, Cunningham-Blyth scratched in gravelly tones. — It used to be a place where people with a lust for life would eat and drink and discuss important matters, he continued, looking in reproach at the current clientele. — Now it's just another watering hole.

— Have you drunk here a while? Skinner asked.

— Yes I have, Sandy Cunningham-Blyth said proudly, then let his eyes bulge. — Sometimes I even worked here.

— Behind the bar?

— God, no, the old chef laughed.

— The restaurant?

— Getting warm, Cunningham-Blyth said teasingly.

— You look a creative sort of a guy . . . the type with plenty of flair . . . I'll bet you were a chef.

Cunningham-Blyth was delighted. — I was indeed, my astute young friend, he said, and it was Skinner's turn to be moved by the older man's flattery. Cunningham-Blyth took his smile as all the vindication he needed to tell his story. — I had no formal training, I'd just always loved to cook, loved to entertain. Originally, I had embarked on a career as a barrister and went to the *other* bar, the old chef waved disapprovingly towards the High Street. — And I thoroughly detested it. I reckoned that Edinburgh didn't need another fucking mediocre lawyer, but back then they could certainly have done with a decent bloody cook!

— Funny, my mother did waitressing here, back in the late seventies, Skinner said, testing the water, noting that Shannon was now in conversation with another couple beside them.

— Ah, now you're talking! Those were great times at this place. What was her name?

— Beverly. Beverly Skinner.

Sandy Cunningham-Blyth furrowed his brow, trying to cast his mind back, but it seemed that he genuinely couldn't recall Beverly. He shook his head and sighed. — So many passed through here at one time.

— She had green hair, quite unusual back then. She was a sort of punk. Well, not sort of, she *was* a punk.

— Oh yes! A delightful girl as I recall, the old chef sang, — though hardly a girl any more, I suppose!

— Naw, Skinner agreed, as Sandy Cunningham-Blyth again seized the cue to move back into tales of the restaurant in its heydays. It was general stuff, but Skinner was content to play it cool and develop a relationship with the ex-chef as the drinks flowed.

Then Cunningham-Blyth started to crumble. After a spate of drifting in and out of consciousness, by the time last orders came round he had completely passed out. Shannon turned to Skinner. — I'm going home. Alone, she added, aware that she always had to make that statement in order to fend off his advances at this time of the night.

— Aye, fair enough, Skinner said. — I'm going to get the old boy into a taxi.

Shannon was slightly disappointed not to have to repel Skinner's ardour, though his generosity towards the old drunk increased his standing in her eyes.

Skinner had managed to rouse Cunningham-Blyth, staging an inpromptu farce, which involved getting him across the road, into the station and inside a taxi before he conked out again. It was a pantomime performance with the lead alternately coaxing, cajoling, begging and threatening. Before the alcoholic coma claimed him, the former chef had managed to bark out a Dublin Street address. The worst part was getting him out the cab and up the stairs. There was an excruciating search through the veteran cook's pockets for his keys, but Skinner doggedly persevered. The stairs were a nightmare; Cunningham-Blyth was bulky, moreover his weight would shift, as he would appear in semi-control, before sinking back into total inebriation again. At one stage Skinner feared they would both go crashing down the steep stairs or, worse, cowp over into the well.

After the ordeal of getting him into the flat and on to a bed, Skinner decided to explore Cunningham-Blyth's apartment. It was roomy, with a large, well-furnished drawing room and an impressive island kitchen. This room wasn't used frequently though; opened tins, strewn takeaway boxes and empty beer cans testified that Sandy's parties weren't as lavish as of old.

This flat is fucking minging.

Skinner prepared to leave but then he heard crashing noises and went back to investigate. There was a heaving sound and he saw Cunningham-Blyth puking up into the toilet at the end of the hall, his trousers down at his ankles. — You awright there, mate?

— Yes . . . Cunningham-Blyth turned round slowly and splayed out on the floor, his back resting against the jacks. Skinner couldn't believe what he was witnessing. The old chef jerked like a puppet, and the similarities didn't end there, as he had no genitals: where they ought to have hung there was only some ugly red and yellow scar tissue. On closer examination, Skinner thought that he could make out a sack, which may or may not have had something in it, but there was certainly no penis. Out from this angry formlessness came a tube feeding into a plastic bag, which was attached by a belt to his waist. The bag was slowly filling up with yellow liquid right in front of Skinner's eyes.

Through his drunken fug the veteran chef registered Skinner's horror, immediately noting its source. Prodding at the bag he laughed. — The number of times I had to empty this old bugger tonight . . . still, at least I remembered. Sometimes I forget and it bursts open. On one occasion recently, there was a very unsavoury incident . . .

Skinner was aghast. — What happened to you . . . ?

Cunningham-Blyth, as if sobered by his embarrassment, hiked up his trousers and pulled himself up on to the rim of the toilet pan, where his buttocks perched precariously. Silence hung for a second or two. When he commenced speaking it was in clipped, detached tones. — As a young man back in the sixties, I became interested in politics. Particularly the national question. I wondered how it was that most of Ireland was free, while Scotland was still in servitude under the English Crown. I looked around at the New Town, its streets named after English royalty due to that toady Scott, while a great, Edinburgh native son and socialist leader like James Connolly merited little more than a plaque on a wall under a shadowy bridge . . . ehm, do you really want to know this?

Skinner nodded, urging him to carry on.

— I was always a recipe maker . . . a *concocter*, I suppose one might say. As a gesture, I resolved to fashion a home-made bomb and blow up one of the symbols of British imperialism that litter this city. I had my eye on the Duke of Wellington's statue at the east end. So I made a pipe bomb. Unfortunately, I had the device between my thighs as I was packing it with explosive. It went off prematurely. I lost my penis and one of my testicles, he said, now almost cheerfully, Skinner thought. — It probably wouldn't even have scratched the Iron Duke. Cunningham-Blyth shook his head and gave a resigned smile. — I was eighteen years old and had only known one woman, a strapping wench who taught primary school in Aberfeldy. She had a face like a bag of spanners but there's not a day that goes past that I don't think of her with a song in my heart, and yes, I can feel it, the phantom erection, as strong and thick as an old beat bobby's truncheon. Look after your old fellow, son, the old chef said ruefully, — best fucking friend you'll ever have and don't let anybody tell you different.

Skinner stood paralysed for a few seconds, then nodded curtly to Sandy Cunningham-Blyth and left the flat. His head swam as he snaked down the cobbled streets of the New Town towards the black, oily waters of the Firth of Forth.

I'm finding out the bedroom secrets of the Master Chefs alright, but not the ones I want.

13
Spring

Spring settled cautiously into Edinburgh, as unsure of its tenure as ever. Its citizens, though customarily wary of its fickle bounty, nonetheless enjoyed its arrival with optimism. The staff at the council's Environmental Health Department were no exception. There was expected to be some positive news about the departmental budget, and employees gathered in the conference room to hear John Cooper tell them that this was being increased, in real terms, for the first time in five years. This meant a reorganisation, which would put another Principal Officer post on the establishment. Somebody was on a promotion.

Though it was often joked in council circles that Cooper could make a promotion feel like a redundancy, the news was heartily welcomed by most of the employees present. Skinner looked at Bob Foy and saw a muscle twitch in his face. Wondered if anyone else did. He glanced round at Aitken, impassive, who was retiring, then McGhee, who had stated his intention to go back to his native Glasgow. Then he saw Kibby, looking serious and focused. He'd been working hard to get into Foy's good books lately, and with some success, Skinner recognised. His own promotion prospects were harder to take stock of. His heavy drinking had not stopped but it had certainly plateaued during his developing relationship with Shannon.

So during one of the first genuinely mild nights of the year, the departmental staff found themselves in the Café Royal. Bob Foy, as Principal Officer in the section, had suggested a pint after work to celebrate the good news. One pint, of course, became several, and in the oak-panelled and marble-tiled grandeur of the bar, people soon grew happily intoxicated. Brian Kibby was the notable exception. As was his habit, he chose to limit himself to soda water and lime for most of the night.

Skinner found his cynicism crank up in correspondence with the units of alcohol in his system. Scrutinising his colleagues' faces – bright, smiling, optimistic – his thoughts grew dark. Everybody was keen, especially, Danny Skinner thought, Brian Kibby.

Oh aye, Kibby's keen. If there's one word that's synonymous with him, that's it. They all said it, the old hands: 'Aye, he's keen, that laddie.'

And Skinner felt that Kibby, with this keenness, would shape up to be his closest rival for the new post.

Skinner did what he generally tried to do in these circumstances: shame Brian Kibby into having a drink. — Soda water and lime . . . hmm, ducky! he lisped at Brian in front of Shannon, on whom Kibby still had an obvious unrequited crush. After a long stint on the soft drinks, Kibby eventually relented to Skinner's baiting and sipped two pints of lager tops. It didn't spare his colleague's derision but he felt he didn't stand out so much with a full pint in his hand.

Get lost, Skinner.

To escape the harassment, Brian Kibby went up to the jukebox and made some selections. He was hoping to impress Shannon, because he knew that a lot of girls liked Coldplay, through the postings on the official site.

There's a really beautiful-looking girl who posts on there, from her avatar picture, but maybe she loves herself too much, putting the picture up like that. No as good as Lucy but, or Shannon.

Kibby stole a poignant look at Shannon McDowall, who was laughing at some racy joke Skinner had made, as the track 'Yellow' struck up:

— What fucking muppet put *that* shite on? Skinner screwed his face up, looking around. When he saw Kibby redden, he rolled his eyes in a canny exasperation and turned to Dougie Winchester at the bar, shouting up more drinks.

— Ah think they're no bad, Winchester opined.

— What sort ay music dae you like? Kibby asked Shannon.

— All sorts really, Brian. New Order's probably my favourite band. Do you like them?

— Eh . . . ah dinnae really ken their stuff. What dae ye think ay Coldplay? he asked hopefully.

— They're okay . . . she said, screwing up her face, — but it's like . . . background music. You know, elevator music, supermarket music. It's just a wee bit bland and insipid, she said distractedly, as Skinner passed a glass over to her.

That must mean that she thinks the likes of me's bland and insipid . . . just good enough for the background . . . no like the likes ay Skinner . . .

With the evening suitably soured for him, Brian Kibby finished his drink, made his excuses and headed off. When he got home he drank two pints of water, then had a Horlicks with his mother.

When he went to bed his stomach was knotted, his head buzzed and he couldn't sleep. All he could think of was the Principal Officer's job and the man who would be his main rival for the post.

Danny Skinner.

We got on okay at first, but Danny seems to see himself as the golden boy. Oh aye, he didnae mind me when I was content tae play second fiddle to his wisecracking, but he disnae like it when I get credit in my own right. No, not one bit. And Skinner takes the mucking around at work and college too far, and he tries to bully me, to make me the butt of his daft jokes. Everybody knows that his drinking is out of control. And to think that Shannon went with him, with Skinner. She's crazy. I used to think that she was smart but she's just stupid and easily conned, like so many of them.

Danny Skinner, though acutely aware of the threat Kibby poised, could do little about it. One midweek evening in a High Street pub, his voice took on a weary resignation as he defeatedly agreed to another pint from Rab McKenzie.

I should say no.

He had the presentation tomorrow, the one on the new set of procedures that many in the department were calling the unofficial first interview, as Brian Kibby was undertaking a similar one the following day. Aye, he thought, I should call a halt now and go home; get a good night's sleep so that I'll be on the top of my game. Yet since Kay had walked out of his life a good night's sleep had become something of a rarity. It was hard to sleep in an empty bed. Shannon and he had only slept together twice. On both occasions she'd taken a taxi home after unspectacular, perfunctory drunken trysts.

Not only was there no Kay, but there was still no contact with Beverly either. He'd gone past the shop one afternoon, glimpsed at the chunky body and scarlet head of his mother as she put another woman under the dryer. But no, let her wait. The next time he spoke to her it would be to see her reaction to two simple words: the name of his father.

He thought about the book again, *The Bedroom Secrets of the Master Chefs.*

De Fretais and Tomlin, the American guy, were the only other young chefs at the Archangel who got a mention. Cunningham-Blyth is definitely off the list. Surely it couldnae be that fat cunt De Fre . . .

Naw. No way.

Gloomily looking into his half-full glass, Skinner could project to tomorrow and see his trembling, unassertive figure bowed and sweating under the fluorescent strip lights, feeling himself internally cowering before Cooper and Foy. *No better than Kibby,* he snorted to himself as he watched McKenzie at the bar, obtaining another drink.

Another fucking pint.

Yes, every casual enquiry would be amplified and distorted; decoded by his fevered, racing brain into a harsh interrogation, designed to show him up for the drunken, inadequate malingerer that they believed him to be.

The problem, and paradoxically the solution, to this nagging awareness of the next day's horror, was more drink. The consciousness of the evil to come would leave him with a few more pints. Then they'd stagger on to a club or either back to his, McKenzie's or somebody's they met on the way with a hastily procured carry-out. All this fear would be forgotten, until it returned with savage interest the next morning, as the alarm clock ripped him out of unconsciousness.

And there would be Kibby, in early at the team meeting for networking purposes; fresh, enthusiastic and, above all, keen.

He turned to McKenzie, looking quite sorrowfully towards the full glass his friend was setting down beside him. — Is it worth it, eh, Rab?

— Doesnae matter whether it is or it isnae, it's what ye dae, eh, McKenzie retorted, as stoical and implacable as ever. Vulnerability and Rab McKenzie went together like gerbils and fishcakes.

So McKenzie and Skinner drank with their customary enthusiasm, until Danny Skinner felt the delicious liberation of entry into the 'not-giving-a-fuck-zone'. Yes, work was only a few hours away now, but it could be light years. And what did it matter? He, Danny Skinner, could run rings round all of those second-rate wankers. Aye, he'd show that arse-licking, little bastard Kibby. His presentation was ready, well, as good as, and he'd blow them all away!

They commenced a pub crawl; a besotted voyage of drunken camaraderie with friends and sneering antagonisms with foes. Then after a muddled, timeless passage, a sweating foray through different lands and states of fevered being, he achieved the goal of nothingness, oblivion. It was this condition that often made Skinner retrospectively wonder, as he started to scramble out of its grip into lighter dozing: is that what death is like, our alcoholic sleep?

Auld Perce made the great proclamation:

How wonderful is Death,
Death, and his brother Sleep!

Then the alarm clock thrashed, hammering on the outside and inside of his head as Danny Skinner woke up with both socks still on. As he gasped to fill air into his lungs via a blowtorched throat, Skinner felt a surge of relief to slowly realise, as his confused brain ordered all the objects around him, that at least he was in his own bed.

Then he saw his best deep blue Armani suit crumpled on the floor, the trousers, the jacket. Skinner launched himself up, too quickly, and started to retch and so urgently propelled himself towards the bathroom. The thin rug between his feet and the pinewood floor slid from under him but actually assisted his transit to the big white telephone as he crumpled to his knees. A series of convulsive, strength-sapping retches, that seemed to be trying to tear his soul from him, eventually ebbed into dry spasms.

Flushing away the cruel reminder of last night's excess into the city's drainage system, he attempted to compose himself. Facing the blue wall tiles, finding a newer, more intimate intricacy in their pattern, he tried to control his breathing. Then he stood up, wobbling like a newborn calf, and opened the small frosted window which led into the stairwell. What happened last night? he asked himself, in the shaving mirror, looking into his own red, tear-stained eyes.

NO.

The word resounded in his head, from which he almost expected to find an axe protruding, as he examined it.

NO NO NO.

Sometimes we said no when we *hoped* no.

McKenzie. A quick beer after work. Then the pub crawl. Then we'd run into Gary Traynor. Thanked him for the copy of the religious porn video, The Second Coming of Christ. *Said he had another one for me, that he would drop it round. He was telling me about it and we were laughing . . . what was it called again . . .* Moses and the Burning Bush*! Aye, that was the one. So far, so fair. Then the lassie. She seemed okay. Did ah make a cunt ay masel? Nup . . . well, yes, but so, fuck, I'll never see her again. But no . . .*

OH NO . . .

. . . then . . . NO, NO, NO, I'm not having it. I AMNAE FUCKIN WELL HUVIN IT . . .

NO.

NO.

Cooper.

He'd been in that pub on the Mile yesterday. After the full council meeting.

NO.

With two councillors. Baird and Fulton.

NO.

I went up to them, approached the cunts . . .

NO.

I sang in their ears.

NO.

I'd . . .

NO NO NO . . .

. . . I'd planted a kiss on Cooper's face! On his lips! A contemptuous, mocking gesture which said: 'I'm Danny Skinner and I've nae respect for a wanker like you or your status, or your shitey fucking council.'

Cooper. It couldn't have been worse if I'd punched the cunt.

NO.

Oh fuck, please to God, no.

Now Cooper knew: in that instant of folly, every unflattering rumour that had ever been aired about Skinner was marvellously confirmed. Every piece of gossip whispered into the boss's ear by the corrupt sweetie-wife Foy, it had all been spectacularly vindicated in those few moments of madness. Danny Skinner was now known at senior official and council member level to be a loose cannon, a drunkard; a weak, frivolous young man, unable to be trusted in a position of authority without letting the side down. Yes, he had shown Cooper that all this snide conjecture was, in fact, based on reality. He'd sabotaged his career, his life. The studies, the college, the school. The deferred gratification (and nobody hated deferring gratification more than Danny Skinner), it was all for nothing.

NO.

Skinner clutched at straws. Maybe Cooper was pished as well, maybe he'd remember nothing.

NO.

Sometimes we said 'no' when we hoped 'yes'.

But no.

Cooper seldom drank, and never, ever to excess.

Even more than Foy, he was that sooky wee bastard Kibby's role model.

John Cooper would remember every single part of their meeting in forensic detail. It would be carefully recorded, in some diary, or even on Skinner's personnel file. Because now they were going to snuff him out. Marginalise him, consign him to that limbo where, at best, he'd serve as a piteous example to departmental newcomers as how *not* to develop your career. He thought of Dougie Winchester and many others like him, the guys tagged the office alcoholic; how, when their youth had gone and the dashing bonhomie of their condition went with it, they were reduced to shambling, shameful figures of contempt and ridicule. Stuck in a dead-end low-paid job, working diligently, but without expectation of anything, except the ticking of the clock and the next drink.

I'll be a fucking pariah.

Skinner's raw nerve endings jangled and his overheated brain did somersaults in his head. The only shard of light was repentance.

They loved that. Why not go to Cooper, and play the game?

He ran it over in his mind, like a radio play:

SKINNER: *I'm sorry, John . . . I know I have a problem. It's actually been apparent for some time, but last night really brought it home. When you disrespect, no, when you abuse somebody that you look up to in working life . . . well, the upshot of it is I've decided to get help. I contacted the AA this morning and I'm going along to my first meeting on Tuesday.*

COOPER: *I'm sorry to hear that you think you've got a problem, Danny, but don't make too much of last night. It was a joke, you were just a bit the worse for wear. Nothing wrong with that. Everybody has a blow-out sometime. It was quite funny, you gave us all a laugh. Aye, you're some boy, Danny!*

No.

He could assign his own part with certainty; after all, it was all a game, and trickery and subterfuge were now regarded as legitimate business tools, but the response was unconvincing. Would Cooper have the range or inclination to play the magnanimous, jocular role?

Unlikely.

Cooper maintained a cold detachment from the minions, and the truth was that although he didn't know for sure how he'd react, Skinner couldn't envisage that mask slipping.

More like:

COOPER: *It was an embarrassment for everyone. I'm glad you admit you have a problem. I'll contact personnel and we'll give you all the help we can. Brave of you to come forward et cetera, et cetera.*

No.

Sometimes you said no because you meant no.

Because whatever Cooper did say, Skinner knew that he could never assign himself such a servile part.

It would be a lie; it would be pandering to all the wishy-washy, nanny-state bollocks they paraded in this hypocritical shithouse of a country. It was all that vain, egotistical insincerity of self-reproach. By blaming ourselves we take away the right of others to do the same.

As an old Catholic boy, Skinner remembered that it was the confession, not the priest, that gave absolution. Remembered it more clearly than any of the priests he encountered, to their chagrin, ever could.

Skinner addressed himself in the bathroom mirror, gave an impassioned speech to a receptive audience of one. — The new fascism is coming. And it's not skinheads marching through the inner cities Sieg Heiling, it's being concocted in the café-bars and restaurants of Islington and Notting Hill.

No.

The idea that every tomato juice consumed on a night out would be met with smiles of kind approval while every pissed-up lurch to the bar elicited stares of baleful fake sorrow or I-told-you-so sneers is completely fucking unbearable to me.

In the bedroom, he examined the jacket of his suit. There was vomit on the lapels, insinuating itself into the fine weave of the Armani's delicate fibres, warping it. This could not be sponged out. Nothing short of dry-cleaning (if he was lucky) would come close to restoring it to its former glory. He would need to wear another suit. But the only other one he owned was an ugly, cheap, coarse excuse. No, he'd stick to a jacket and trousers. In the mirror, he studied his face in detail. It was a mess: a series of dried, blooded spots tore down one side of it, like he'd been scraped against a wall.

The presentation, he had to look over the presentation.

NO NO NO.

His case. It was gone. Where had he left it? Which pub? Pivo, the Black Bull, the Abbotsford, the Guildford, the Café Royal, the Waterloo . . . then the premises blurring into the background, replaced by foreground faces: Rab McKenzie, Gary Traynor . . . Coop . . . fuck that, move on . . . the girl with the straw-blonde hair and the huge squint teeth who grew more beautiful as the night wore on. In his pockets loads of change, loads of pound coins. Very few notes, but thirty-seven pounds in pound coins.

But his old leather briefcase . . . the presentation, it was gone. One of the boys in the pubs would have put it behind the bar for safe keeping. Surely. Most of them didn't open until eleven, when he was due to be on. He'd have to phone in sick. Maybe he could be late, Skinner thought, mentally flipping through a wilted box-file of dog-ate-my-homework-style stays of execution.

Then he rang Rab McKenzie on his mobile, affecting a casual demeanour. — Roberto ma man, how goes?

McKenzie saw through the affected nonchalance so completely, he could have been sitting in the same room. — You were in some state last night, ya fuckin lightweight. Tryin tae match me on the absinthe. Leave it alaine, pal.

Of course, those mad, fevered, hallucinogenic dreams of absinthe.

Panic seized Skinner in its iron fist and shook him like a rag doll. — Rab, ma case. The briefy ah hud last night. Ye seen it?

— Ohhh, ah dunno aboot that, McKenzie pursed, his teasing tones simultaneously exposing Skinner to fear and elation.

— You goat it?

— Might have, McKenzie said coolly, evidently enjoying himself.

— So ah wis at yours last night?

— Aye.

— Geez it, ah need it, Rab.

— Well, ye ken whaire ah'll be in half an ooir, McKenzie challenged.

— Right . . . Skinner said, putting the phone down.

And a perverse thought gripped him, the idea that, given certain conditions, he could actually come through here.

Skinner pulled off his socks and staggered into the shower. Yes, it could all still be salvaged, but it needed the exercise of a supernatural will-power that only sheer desperation could engender.

As he scrubbed away last night's shell of scum, he could feel his body kick into gear, working, processing, expelling new toxic trash that would drip from him, its stench wafting up Cooper's nose. Aye, it would be a rare atmosphere for his boss to savour as he recalled last night's humiliation while deliberating, with cold, systematic bitterness, how he'd take his revenge on Daniel Skinner.

McKenzie, a site electrician, was not on a job until the afternoon, so where he would be at eight thirty that morning was the Central Bar at the foot of Leith Walk. The presentation was at eleven and Skinner had to clock in by ten to meet the flexitime deadline. He reasoned that he'd make it in fine time. When he got to the Central, his first sight was of McKenzie, holding up the case by the handle and shaking it. Big Mac was already downing the Guinness.

Skinner looked, with a sickening envy, at the pint of black elixir, perched so temptingly in front of McKenzie on the newly polished, refurbished bar. How he craved its reassuring dimensions in his hand, the sour taste of the liquid in his mouth, its comforting volume in his guts. The Central Bar, with its welcoming booths, its homely atmosphere of tatty splendour evoking the area's wealthy mercantile past and underscoring its present no-frills down-to-earth unpretentiousness. He loved it so much and to be torn from this comforting womb and shunted up the hill to Edinburgh's Royal Mile, to that place of artifice, bullshit and deceit . . . surely he could have *one*. Just *one* pint, to take the edge off his pain. Hair of the dog. Aye, it would improve his performance, therefore it was responsible behaviour.

On the second pint of Guinness, Skinner felt all the drinks from the previous night come flooding back through his system. — Rab, he slurred in foggy concern (but only concern rather than panic, as the drink had restored perspective), — I've got this presentation and I'm fucked again . . .

As so often happened in the drunkard's scene when the protagonist started not to care, it was the comrade, hitherto a marginal player in the drama, who took on the mantle of responsibility. Thus Big Rab McKenzie thrust a wrap of cocaine into Danny Skinner's hand. — A straightener, he smiled.

— Thanks, Rab, Skinner said with genuine emotion, — a wee tickle'll sort ays right oot.

14
Presentation

It was shortly after his death that she'd found them, when she'd been compulsively wandering around the house, like she was looking for Keith. She even went to the attic, climbing the creaking metal steps stiffly and tentatively, almost sick with fear as she had no head for heights.

This factor, and her sense that she was intruding on her son's space, made her more inclined to visit the garden shed. She liked it there, enjoying the paraffin and creosote smells she associated with her husband. She tackled the spiders and their webs and the slugs and their slimy trails, for though those creatures made her squeamish, they couldn't be allowed to desecrate Keith's special place. Growing appreciative of the tranquillity, Joyce quickly came to see what he had liked about sitting in there with a book. She would sometimes take a pot of tea in with her, switching on the oil heater, which gave the place a cosy, intimate warmth the dry central heating indoors couldn't match.

It was in the shed that she came across the diaries, a big pile of notebooks in an old drawer under a workbench that was covered in ringed coffee stains from the edge of his mug. They were a guilty pleasure; she kept them to herself, feeling like a greedy hoarder of a treasure that should be shared.

Joyce had read them many times since finding them, but was still intoxicated with anticipation whenever she picked them up. And she always froze a little on reading his words; pondering and reinterpreting the most innocuous until her head spun and the narrative became meaningless. The journals, which started in 1981 and ended in 1998, were written in a peculiar spidery script that hardly seemed to be his. She found it difficult to make them out and even bought a magnifying glass to help her, despite feeling bad about her intrusiveness. Yet even in the mundane day-to-day observations, a fierce love burned through their pages, vindicating her stance and ultimately never failing to give her anything other than great comfort.

She often whiled away hours poring through them. On this occasion she tutted in self-reproach when she looked at the shed's rusty old alarm clock, putting the diaries back and heading indoors. Upstairs, she loaded the dirty laundry into the washing basket, catching a scent in her nostrils and holding a pair of underpants up to the light. Puckering in sour disgust, she put them back into the basket and didn't look as she squashed them into the washing machine.

It had been a good weekend for Brian Kibby. Working with devoted industry on his offering for Tuesday, he was pleased to see what he considered to be a slick, well-argued presentation come together. Additionally, he'd been able to get up to Nethy Bridge for a Hyp Hykers weekend ramble where he sat beside Lucy Moore on the bus back to the city. Into the bargain, three of his *Harvest Moon* chickens had lain eggs. But when he arrived home from the trip he found his mother crying, with a set of John Menzies notebooks on her lap.

Kibby swallowed hard. Somehow those black-bound desk diaries had a coldly portentous aspect to them. — What's is it, Mum?

His mother gazed up at him, an evangelical stain in her brown eyes. Since her husband's death she'd dug herself deep into the foxhole of her religious belief, rediscovering the literalist Free Church faith of her girlhood, to the concern of Mr Godfrey, her local Church of Scotland minister. Her obsession with spiritual matters, while reducing down to the base ingredients of her beliefs, simultaneously became more eclectic. In town shopping recently, she'd engaged in an intense debate with some Buddhists, and had even started regularly seeing some visiting young Texan missionaries. Those suited, crew-cutted, bespectacled young men from the New Church of the Apostles of Christ came round to the house with pamphlets, which Joyce studied with enthusiasm. They often gave her succour, though not as much as the notebooks she was reading. — Read this, Brian. It's your dad's diaries. I found them in his cupboard in the garden shed. I'd never gone in there . . . I didn't like to . . . it was always his place. I just heard this voice, like he'd be there, and I know it's daft, but I went . . .

Although at that point he saw that his mother's tears were bitter-sweet, Brian Kibby was highly resistant to this idea. — Mum, I don't want to, it's Dad's private stuff . . . he said, feeling as if they were prising the lid off his father's coffin.

Joyce, though, was insistent, infused as she was with an energy and enthusiasm he hadn't seen in her for a long time. — Read it, son, it's okay, you'll see. Just from there, she pointed at an entry, compelling his widening eyes to follow.

> I used to fret about Brian, worrying that his hobbies, all this model-railway stuff, was isolating him from the other lads at school, setting him apart. But I'd rather see him running a model railway than running with some of the tickets I did back when I was a lad. It's great to see him in this hiking club with good kids, getting out and enjoying himself.
>
> Our Brian's a grafter. He'll get what he wants through hard work, that one.
>
> Caroline takes after me but she's got more brains than I ever had. I just hope she uses them and does well at the university. I hope she can curb that wanton, arrogant streak that almost did me in, because she's my pride and joy, that lassie.

Brian Kibby read with tears welling up in his eyes.

— See, son, see how much he loved you! Joyce jaggedly shrieked, desperate that her son interpret her late husband's words as she herself had done.

But they were unambiguous enough. It was true; it was there in black and white. –Aye . . . aye . . . it's great to read it, he gasped in affirmation.

— We should show them to Caroline . . . Joyce ventured.

A ball of unease rattled in Brian Kibby's chest. — Naw, Mum, she's going through a tough time.

— But they might give her comfort . . .

— She needs tae stay focused on her studies though, Mum, not wasting time reading old journals. Let's leave it till she's stronger and got the course out the way. That's what Dad would want!

Joyce Kibby saw the fervour in her son's eyes and was happy to defer. — Yes . . . that was so important for him, she conceded.

Kibby ground his teeth, savouring his assertiveness. He was going to show them all, especially that bully Skinner, what he was made of.

Danny Skinner's heart thudded in crazed rhythm like a child's stick dragged against a long set of railings as he ascended in the lift towards the departmental conference room. The cocaine had been the best idea though; it had given his mind some clarity, and restored his confidence.

What had happened with Cooper was outside of work hours and fuck all to do with anything.

He'd look Cooper straight in the eye when he walked into that conference suite, and if he wanted to say something, then let him.

Either we sort it out through official channels, Cooper ya cunt, or we sort it out outside, man to man. What's it to be, Cooper? Eh? Sorry, what was that? Didnae quite fuckin well catch ye thaire, ya radge, what is it you're fuckin well sayin then, cunt? Eh? Nowt? Aw, so it's 'nowt' wir gittin now, is it? Aye, thought so.

The doors of the lift flew open and Danny Skinner marched stiff-backed down the corridor and into the conference room. On entry he was almost taken aback as the white light from the neon strips bounced off the cream walls and into his wired head, evoking the white room before death, he considered, but without apprehension, as he had the white powder on his side.

Fuck them.

Most of the staff stood around the coffee trolley, waiting to fill their beakers from the urn. He could do with a coffee, but he was late and the fact that many hadn't taken their seats handed him back the initiative. So Danny Skinner flashed a cokehead's grin at Cooper, who gave a slow, expressionless nod in return. Skinner thought that you could hang Tolstoy's complete works into a heartbeat of Cooper's silence.

— Hi, folks, Danny Skinner said breezily, making his way to the overhead projector. A click of his thumb switched it on, as he snapped open his briefcase. His stuff was only half ready, but he'd wing it okay.

Out of the corner of his eye, he saw Foy looking at his watch.

Cooper stood up. — Please be seated, folks, he said gregariously, then gruffly added, — Danny, are you ready?

— Willing and able, Skinner smiled, continuing to stand as the last of his colleagues sat down. He heard a wheeze of laughter and watched Kibby dance into his chair like a puppet on a string, twitching inanely at a remark of Foy's.

They're fuckin talking about me.

Skinner felt his pores open up and bleed like a victim's skin under a psychopath's blade. Despite his nagging suspicion that everyone present saw him as a Victorian freak show, he began authoritatively. — So much of our city's reputation as a major tourist centre rests on the quality of its restaurants and cafés. This, in turn, is dependent on the rigour and vigilance of this department, and, specifically, the quality of its inspection and supervisory teams . . .

He took out his first slide and let the static tear it on to the projector's surface. He looked at the shock on the assorted faces as he turned to see

CCS RULE

in big green letters on the screen behind him. McKenzie, he cursed, then smiled, quickly putting the slide down and picking up the correct one, which showed a flow chart of the current reporting procedure. — We have saboteurs in our midst, he smiled, to largely reciprocated grins. Pleased that his friend's casual subversion couldn't faze him, he continued: — As we know, the quality of our staff is of the highest level. The same, however, cannot be said of some of the anachronistic working procedures we are currently adopting. The reporting procedures, particularly, are in serious need of an overhaul. There's no question about that in my mind. They don't meet my own section's requirements, let alone the broader needs of the department as a whole, he said earnestly, sweeping his hands around the room to magnanimously include colleagues from the other two sections.

Time to kick up a gear.

— Far less do they meet the exigencies of the service, Skinner barked, almost threateningly, watching Foy's face turn the colour of the Forth Bridge. It was common knowledge that Foy had designed these procedures years ago, and had steadfastly resisted their overhaul. — The present system of inspector responsibility for designated units, without rotation, for years, and under the same supervision, leaves far too much room to develop the kind of relationships with restaurateurs that encourages the turning of blind eyes and petty corruption.

As Foy tried to control his shaking and Kibby pouted in hostility, Skinner flicked on another slide and started to outline his alternative procedure, involving cross-checking and the rotation of duties. However, towards the end of his spiel, he started to feel unwell, becoming tired and faltering. His voice had dropped to the extent that they could hardly hear him at the back.

— Can you speak up a wee bit please, Danny? Shannon asked him.

A sharp bolt of betrayal thumped like an arrow into Skinner's chest. He tried to compose himself, but was overwhelmed by the thought that Shannon had also applied for this job.

Surely she's no trying tae set me up, she wouldnae be such a cunt, surely . . .

— Sorry . . . eh . . . a bit of a cold, he said, looking icily at her before addressing the table again. — Eh . . . I think I've run out of steam here. Anyway, that's the suggested procedure. It's in the briefing notes . . . any questions? he slurred, slumping into the seat.

A few quizzical faces flashed looks across the table, but the silence was short-lived. — How much is the new procedure likely to cost? Kibby squeaked loudly, sitting forward in the chair, his big eyes trained on Skinner.

One fucking clean shot at that cunt's face . . . that's all it would take . . .

— I haven't come up with specific figures, Skinner said, so repulsed he couldn't even look at Kibby, — but I'd envisage no significant cost increases.

Skinner felt the limpness of his response in the semi-incredulous faces of those around him.

If only I'd given myself that half an hour with a calculator! That was all it would take to crunch out a set of bullshit cost-benefit analysis numbers to pull the wool over every cunt round the table's eyes. If only I'd just gone the fuck home last night . . .

Foy let one eyelid half close and the other rise like a venetian blind. His mouth formed a crescent. — No significant cost increases? With this extra level of supervision, checking and cross-checking? Foy shook his head in a sadness, which seemed almost earnest. — We're in cloud-cuckoo-land here, he contended, his head still shaking slowly.

Before Skinner could respond, Kibby had started again. — I don't think anybody could ehm seriously ehm argue that there wouldn't be a significant increase in costs. But ehm Danny's making the point that this would be ehm offset by an intangible increase in tourist revenue. The point is that I hardly think that tourists perceive of our restaurants as hotbeds of plague, pestilence and disease. I also think that there's no reason for us to ehm believe that members of staff in this department don't ehm carry out their duties professionally and honestly. If we're to ehm change a system due to the possibility that this system is ehm corrupt, ehm then we ehm have to have evidence that this is indeed the ehm case. If not, apart from ehm costing ourselves time and ehm money, we're also ehm undermining staff morale. So, Danny, Brian Kibby smiled, — do you ehm know something the rest of us don't?

Skinner glared at Kibby in such a stare of concentrated, raw hatred, it froze not only its recipient but also the entire room. And he was going to hold it. He sat there, quietly, coldly; judging Brian Kibby, peering into his soul, watching his eyes water, until Kibby, face flushed, was forced to avert his gaze and look down at the table. Skinner kept staring, and would keep staring silently, for ever if need be, until somebody else spoke. If they wanted to up the stakes and talk about corruption and taking bungs, he was ready to do it. In his mind's eye, the worms were already slithering from the rusty can.

The atmosphere in the room was becoming highly uncomfortable. Then Colin McGhee spoke up. — I think we have to cost the new procedure as a starting point. If there's any concrete evidence of corrupt practices, then the current set of arrangements need looking at in light of that evidence. But we can't shelve a cost-effective set of procedures purely on the basis of daft rumour and speculation.

Brian Kibby wanted to nod in agreement but couldn't move, still feeling Skinner's rapacious eyes on him. Sensing that the meeting had strayed into dangerous waters, Cooper took advantage of the impasse, tetchily calling matters to a close. Skinner hastily gathered up his papers. As he made for the door he heard Foy shout at him, — What aftershave is that you're wearing, Danny?

Skinner spun round to face him. — What?

— No, I like it, Foy smiled reptilian-like. — It's very distinctive. Very strong.

— I'm n . . . Skinner began, stopped and smiled. — Excuse me, I've an important phone call to make, he said, turning sharply and heading downstairs to the open-plan office, the soles of his shoes slapping the insolent pattern of the marble steps.

At his desk, Skinner could feel the coke rushes running down further and the alcohol leaving his bloodstream, and with them leaked away his own sense of omnipotence. Every presence appeared intrusive; every ring of the phone seemed to carry a threat. Foy's laughter boomed and Kibby's snivelling tones stripped the quivering flesh from his back. An adversary so puny, so weak and pathetic now seemed to have taken on inhuman, fiendish powers. Once, when Skinner met his eyes, he was startled to find that they weren't timid and cowed, they were defiant, sly and smug.

So Danny Skinner, unaccustomed to being so unassertive, worked steadily, cleaning up the paperwork he'd let mount up over the weeks, trying to somehow redress the balance, right the wrongs, make himself unimpeachable. Yet he had no head for it; he'd commence one job, only to tire of it and switch to another before sinking in a swamp of choking exasperation as his desk mounted up with half-completed tasks.

As the office started to empty at five, Skinner relaxed a little and became lost in his thoughts, eventually feeling almost too weary to go home. When the phone rang at six, he picked it up. It would be a social call, as everybody else had long gone.

— You're working late, McKenzie accused, then asked the

inevitable, — Fancy a quick pint? As if offering Skinner redemption.

— Aye . . . said Skinner, with hesitant guilt. But he did. He *did* fancy a pint. There were a thousand reasons why he shouldn't, why he just ought to go home, but they paled into insignificance beside the three which dictated that he should have a drink: it was finishing time, he had thirty-seven pounds' worth of coins in his pockets, and he was shaking and he *wanted* one.

In the pub, Rab McKenzie already had a pivotal place at the bar, reminding Skinner in his bearing of a ship's captain on the bridge of his vessel. When he turned to a barman and asked for a pint of Lowenbrau for Skinner, it was like instructing him to proceed at a very high speed of knots.

The drink went down fast and, as he bought the next round, Skinner's rationalisation processes moved into full throttle.

No matter how many of those self-justifying twats write in their lifestyle columns in the mags and papers that you should be this kind of man or that kind of man, that you should have responsibility to your wife, children, employer, country, government, god, delete to taste, not one of them can convince me that Kibby is not a fuckin wanker and I'm not a brilliant cunt. For however they spring-clean this Responsible Man as a New Action Man or Renaissance Man, or a Take-No-Shit Man, in real life he is invariably a fucking insipid bore like Kibby.

Yes, they're all fucking control freaks and sycophants and every one of them is eager to tell you what your responsibility is in one form or another. And Kibby, he is very responsible.

A powerful speculative fantasy gnawed at Skinner: wouldn't it be fantastic if Kibby could take his hangovers and comedowns for him! If he, Danny Skinner, indulged in the pleasures of life in the most wanton, reckless way and fresh-faced, clean-cut, mummy's boy wanker Kibby could pay the price!

How fantastic would that be? Kibby. God, how I loathe him. How I fucking well hate and detest that fucking puerile little fart. I hate him. HATE HATE HATE HATE HATE HATE HATE HATE HATE HATE HATE HATE.

Sitting with his lager, Skinner found those idle, half-drunk ruminations evolve with an *ockenblink* into a violent prayer, the ferocity and intensity of which shook him to the marrow.

I FUCKIN HATE HATE HATE THAT CUNT KIBBY LET HIM GET FUCKED UP.

The low-ceilinged bar seemed to drain of light, which appeared to flush into his head, like water down a drain, as though his hungry psyche or his neurons were ravenously sucking it in. Then he saw Kibby's face flash before him: the open, smiling 'nice laddie' they all liked at the work. For a split second, it became, in contrast, his own roguish countenance. And he watched it alter once more, back to the sly, manipulative sooky little bastard that he believed was the *real* Kibby.

People wanted their arses licked but they didn't understand . . .

His breathing was going and he could see the faces swirling in front of his eyes; Cooper, Foy . . .

Fuck, I've got the DTs now . . .

Then the whole bar suddenly darkened a few shades and seemed plunged into a bizarre slow-mo. He couldn't make anyone out, they were all just pulsating, undulating shadows, until he saw the normally lumbering figure of Rab McKenzie come swaying through the crowd of silhouettes as deftly as a ballet dancer, balancing the drinks and chasers. And Skinner's heart warped in a shuddering spasm so violent that he fancied for a second or so that he was having a convulsive attack.

FUCKIN SHI . . .

— There we go, Skinny boy, get that doon ye, McKenzie boomed, consigning the drinks on to the table with a semi-pirouette.

Skinner was sweating and breathing in a laboured manner as the lights heightened and the room appeared normal once again. A heart attack. A stroke. Something was happening . . . his breath was leaving him . . .

I'M FUCKIN . . . I'M FUCKIN

— You look like you're strugglin, son, McKenzie scoffed. — What is it? Can ye no stand the pace?

Danny Skinner sucked the air into his lungs as McKenzie slapped his back. Skinner put his hand to his face in a gesture to signal his friend to back off. McKenzie looked at his sweating, red-faced buddy in concern, but then as his anxiety appeared to hit its apex, Skinner felt a barrier melt inside him and he quickly resumed his breathing. He looked up at the ceiling before lowering his gaze to face Big Rab. — Was it just me, or did the lights go dim for a bit there?

— Aye, some fuckin power surge or something. Are you awright?

— Aye . . .

Some power surge.

Skinner looked at McKenzie, Big Rab McKenzie, his best mate, who would have been the best man at his marriage, and his best drinking compadre. No matter how much he put away, he could never quite keep up with Big Rab. Never match his intake, his calm, stoical, sinking of pints, his snorting monstrous lines of cocaine, which made Skinner fear for the heart that thrashed in his chest like the pea in an overzealous referee's whistle, every time they went to the toilet.

But *something*, deranged, anomalous, was happening because now it was Skinner who was having a power surge, a charge of the alcoholic's sense of immortality perhaps, that belief transcending decaying mortal flesh, that nothing, truly nothing, could ever touch him. But while he'd known this feeling many times, he'd never experienced it at this intensity. He was going to ride this wave. He flung back the short of Jack Daniel's. — C'moan then, McKenzie, ya big poof, let's see whae can stand the pace!

2

Cooking

15

Mystery Virus

It was the first time he'd left the chickens outside. It had rained and the fence posts had rotted and the wild dogs had got in. Now there were no chickens left.

He wasn't concentrating. He felt dizzy: dizzy and sick. The huge, brightly coloured *Star Trek: The Final Frontier* poster on the wall, the one Ian had given him, which showed a Starship *Enterprise* bursting out of a black hole, it resonated and throbbed, orchestrating the dance of his raw nerve endings.

Rising shakily from his mobile computer desk, he staggered back to his bed, sweating and nauseous under the duvet as he heard his mother's approaching footsteps on the stairs outside.

Joyce Kibby wearily ascended the steps carrying a silver-effect tea tray. It seemed almost too much for her thin arms, burgeoning with a large plate of scrambled eggs, bacon, tomato, a smaller one with a formidable stack of toast, as well as a pot of tea. She steered it into her son's bedroom, startled at how rough he looked today.

— Brought you some breakfast, son. God, Brian, you don't look well at all. Never mind, you know what they say, feed a cold, starve a fever. Or is it the other way around? Anyway, this'll do you no harm, she declared, carefully setting the tray down at the bottom of his bed.

Brian Kibby achieved a pained, reluctant smile. — Thanks, Mum. I'll be fine, he said, trying to reassure himself. He didn't want food. He felt so terrible, his head was pounding and his guts seemed to be blistering and popping inside. He always tried to play a minimum of three *Harvest Moons* before breakfast. This morning he'd barely managed two and now all the chickens had gone.

How could I have been so stupid?

— It must be this virus that's been doing the rounds, Joyce

contended, as Brian sat up, plumped up his pillows and lay back on them. Even with that minor exertion he was perspiring. His mouth was dry and there were knots of cramp and fatigue in his arms and legs. — I feel terrible. I feel like my head's gaunnae explode.

But Brian Kibby also felt guilty. Danny Skinner had obviously been feeling rough yesterday during his presentation, but everybody had put it down to drink, even when Skinner himself had said he felt he'd picked up some kind of cold or virus.

I gave him a hard time when he was feeling rough, I didnae give him the benefit of the doubt. Now I'm being punished for that, Kibby ticked himself.

Skinner has given me his virus.

— I'll phone in sick for you, son, Joyce volunteered, drawing the curtains.

Seized with a panic, Kibby sat bolt upright. — No! You can't! It's my presentation today. I have to be in!

Joyce shook her head stiffly. — You're no in any state to go into work, son. Look at you, you're lying there sweating and shivering. They'll understand; you're never off sick. When was the last time you were off sick? What's the good of it, Brian, what's the good of it?

Brian Kibby *was* never off sick. And he wasn't going to be. He had what he could stomach of his breakfast, then took a moderately warm shower and jadedly got dressed. When he got downstairs Caroline was at the kitchen table, pushing her books in a clandestine manner into her bag as he came into the room. — Mum said you were going to spend the day in bed, she commented.

— I can't, I've got a pres . . . his eyes registered her actions. — Are you still doing that essay from last night?

She pushed her shoulder-length blonde hair from the side of her face. — Just changing a wee bit, she said.

— Caroline . . . Brian Kibby whinged, — ye should've finished that last night. Ye promised you would finish it properly before ye went round tae that Angela's!

Caroline's painted nails scraped the edges of the Streets sticker on her bag. She looked up at him and her thin, plucked eyebrows arched icily. — Promised, Brian? I didn't promise anybody anything as I remember. She shook her head and repeated slowly, — I don't recall promising you a thing.

— But it's your course! Kibby whined at his sister, feeling rough, wondering why he was struggling into work when all she was doing was wasting her time and her talent. — That Angela's no goat any ambition, Caroline. Watch she doesnae drag ye doon wi her. Ah've seen it happen!

Caroline and Brian Kibby were close, and seldom argued. He could go on a bit, but generally his sister put up with it. When she snapped, it was always at her mother, never her brother. But Caroline was feeling the drinks she'd had last night in Buster Brown's nightclub, and was not impressed by her brother's seemingly new-found determination to impose a draconian regime of study on her. — You're no ma dad, Brian. Mind that, she said almost threateningly.

Brian Kibby looked at his sister, saw her eyes glass over, and felt the shared hurt of their loss. They were not prone to invading each other's personal space and the onset of puberty had all but destroyed any tactile contact between them. Now, though, he was moved to put a viral, trembling arm around her. — I'm sorry . . . I didnae mean it . . .

— *I'm* sorry . . . Caroline sniffed awkwardly, — I know you only want what's best for me . . .

— It's only cause it's what he wanted, Brian coughed, fighting back his own tears, as he let his arm fall from her shoulders to land limply by his side, — but you're a woman now, it's up tae you what ye dae, I've got nae right . . . he gulped. — Dad would be really proud of you, ye ken that? Brian said, in some guilt as he considered the evidence of the diaries that he and Joyce had resolved to keep away from Caroline.

Caroline Kibby kissed her brother on his cheek. It still had those thin, duck-down layers of hair on it, like a peach, she always thought. — He'd be proud ay you, cause I am. You're the best brother anybody could have.

— And you're the best sister, Kibby almost shouted back, somewhat spoiling the moment in her eyes by his high, bewailing reciprocity, but she managed to convert a guilty impulse to grimace into a smile.

Both desperate to extricate themselves from the unfamiliar and uncomfortable vortex of emotion that had swirled around them since their father's death, Brian and Caroline composed themselves and said goodbye to Joyce, who had come downstairs having made the beds. They headed off to work and Edinburgh University respectively.

Brian Kibby was hailed as a hero for coming in, Danny Skinner noted bitterly. — Brian looks terrible, like he's got flu, Shannon McDowall observed. Skinner nodded, fighting through a suspicion that when he'd wandered in yesterday it would have been 'Danny looks terrible, it's like he's got flu or something . . .'

That crucial or something. *And in such trivial asides so reputations are made and undermined in corporate life. It'll take a lot to undermine Kibby's though. The benefit of the doubt is all his.*

But Danny Skinner was inexplicably beset with the notion that perhaps time was on his side. He felt surprisingly good, especially after the session they'd had last night. Maybe he was becoming like Big Rab McKenzie, he considered, developing an immunity to drink and drugs.

I'm fucking ready. C'mon, Kibby son, let's see what you've got!

The staff members made their way to the conference room and settled down to hear Brian Kibby's presentation. As he picked up his stuff, Skinner smiled at him and, sidling over, whispered in his ear, — You're fuckin well getting it, cunt.

Only one or two people seemed to notice the quaking, flapping spasm Kibby briefly went into.

No home runs for you the day, cunty baws!

They were all eager to witness Kibby's presentation. Bob Foy gave him an encouraging pat on the back, which Skinner gleefully noticed almost caused its recipient to leap out of his skin. Kibby was never a confident performer, but he compensated by having the life belt of the most meticulous and detailed transparencies, which he could resort to when things got a bit askew. Or he could have, had his trembling hand not knocked a cup of coffee over them, soaking them completely. His subsequent attempts to mop things up merely made even more mess. Oswald Aitken came to Kibby's aid, taking over the clean-up operation and urging him to carry on.

Strike one!

Danny Skinner sat and watched in amusement as Brian Kibby dug himself into a hole.

— Sorry . . . I've . . . eh, I've been feeling a wee bit off colour . . . some kind of virus . . .

— Aye, Skinner said loudly, — a lot of it going around.

— Yes, I've been feeling very peaky myself lately. Oswald Aitken supportively tried to draw Skinner's sting.

As Kibby staggered through a painfully embarrassing presentation, the questions were largely unchallenging, except from one quarter. Danny Skinner toyed with Brian Kibby; his seemingly innocuous questions probing for a detail that his hesitant, tremulous adversary could not bring to mind. Skinner set his mouth in a cruel twist, the pout of a toff who has been unsatisfactorily served, but who will not cause further embarrassment by making a scene. Additionally, he had passed round detailed notes with figures explaining his omission the day before, which served to undermine Kibby even before the presentation started.

Bob Foy sat smouldering quietly, but, Skinner noted, his anger seemed less directed at him than at Kibby, for such an inept defence of his status quo position.

It was Skinner who de facto wound up the proceedings by attacking Kibby's advocacy of the current reporting system. — So, Brian, what you are effectively proposing is nothing. Keep things the same, he said, imitating Foy's weary sadness of the previous day to the point of parody, which everyone bar the boss seemed to notice. At one stage Shannon, who had been treated to those impersonations in the pub, had to stifle a giggle, as Skinner did *that thing* with his eyes. — A lot of people might feel that dragging them in here to say what could have gone round in an email might not be the best use of their time, Skinner continued in growing arrogance, — and by extension the council resources, the efficient use of which you profess to care so much about, he smiled coldly, keeping his grin locked on Kibby's face.

Brian Kibby was dumbstruck. He couldn't retort. His head was pounding and his knees felt weak. Caught like roadkill in a car's headlights, he looked around at the edgy staff.

Strike two!

— If it isnae broke then you don't have tae fix . . . he began weakly, his voice drying to a hiss in his throat.

Colin McGhee turned to Skinner uncomprehendingly, and then to Kibby with the same quizzical expression, which spread round the table like a bush fire.

— Sorry, Brian, Skinner cut in tersely, — I can't hear you. Can you speak up a little please?

— If it isnae broke . . . Kibby lisped recalcitrantly, but he couldn't finish the sentence as he felt something rise up from the pit of his stomach. He tried to cover his face, and by turning away managed to get a lot of the vomit into a waste-paper bin, although some splashed on the desk and bounced on to the sleeve of Cooper's suit.

Strike three and out!

Shannon and Colin McGhee went to Kibby's aid, while Foy wearily shook his head.

— Looks like the mystery virus has struck again, Skinner said in a deadpan way, as Kibby barfed humiliating piles of scrambled egg, bacon and tomato into the bin, while Cooper grimaced and brushed at his jacket sleeve with a handkerchief.

Danny Skinner rose and exited the conference room as if sanctified, leaving behind the distressed Kibby and his squabbling, fussing colleagues. Through his exaltation and excitement he struggled to make sense of things.

What the fuck went on in there?

It was surely just chance. Kibby obviously had the flu, or some genuine virus, while I've put away so much drink recently that my resistance has gone through the roof. It's pretty fucking worrying; it could be the alcoholic's last blast of light, one final big rush of omnipotence before the dark decline sets in.

But . . . Kibby was fucked! Truly, utterly, strung out.

It was the symptoms of somebody who's been caning it!

Nah . . . I'm gieing my mind a treat.

The afternoon flew effortlessly by for him, and he was astonished to find his desk clean at the close of business. Completely spellbound, he stopped off en route home at several of his preferred Leith Walk hostelries; the Old Salt, the Windsor, Robbie's, the Lorne Bar and the Central.

That night in his flat, he sat up denting a bottle of Jack Daniel's with a flat litre mixer of Pepsi, watching *The Good, the Bad and the Ugly* on Channel 4. Something, though, was making him restless through his contentment. Skinner had to be sure. He lit up a cigarette, and after only a moment's hesitation, stubbed it into his cheek. A fierce cry of pain exploded from him. Tears welled up in his eyes. Self-loathing burned him deeper than the cigarette.

How could I have been so fucking stupid? I've probably gone and fucking well scarred myself for life.

He watched the rest of the film in a deep depression, occasionally touching at the nasty burn mark on his cheek.

Skinner eventually went to bed, expecting one of his bruising, fitful sleeps, the type that he tended to have when he was full of drink. But he slept soundly, a deep, rich slumber and woke up the next morning feeling invigorated. In the bathroom he looked at his face in the shaving mirror. Something was wrong. Something was missing. He felt an excitement mount in him so strongly that he had to sit down on the toilet seat fearful that he would pass out, as his head raced with possibilities.

The thing was that it was so damn sore. Brian Kibby winced as Joyce dabbed some germoline at the ugly wound on her son's cheek. — It's a nasty one alright, she said. — You must remember doing something to it. It's like a burn or a bite . . .

It was a vile, dirty pain and it worried him that he didn't even notice when it had been inflicted. It had just seemed to come up in the night. Its sting woke him up and he had put the light on, brandishing a rolled-up copy of *Which Computer*, looking everywhere, under his bed, in his wardrobe, behind the curtains, for some exotic multi-legged intruder. He could locate nothing. — I wish ah did, he whined disconsolately.

— You look terrible, son, Joyce said, with a sombre shake of her head, — I'm sure you're coming down with something. You should go and see a doctor.

Brian Kibby had to concede that he did feel very rough, but he was disinclined to indulge his mother's fussing as, in his experience, it only made him feel worse. The way she mollycoddled him had often been a source of tension between her and his father. Now that Keith was gone Brian was the man of the house and he was determined to at least try and act it. — I'll be fine, it's just a bite from some spring bug with the milder weather coming in. These things happen, he said cheerfully, but he felt so much more weak and sick than he was letting on.

But there were a lot of exciting things happening in his life, and he felt that he couldn't afford to submit to illness right now. There was a Hyp Hykers meeting at the McDonald's at Meadowbank on Friday, which had become a regular haunt for them. Kibby occasionally enjoyed the guilty pleasure of a Big Mac, although he knew it wasn't good for him being full of sugar, salt, fat and additives. Most excitingly, he and Lucy had arranged to go over to the sports centre after the meeting, for a game of badminton.

That'll get them talking at the club!

He felt rough, but his head was already spinning with the advanced, perhaps even ridiculous notion that they were already *bona fide* boyfriend and girlfriend. He might even ask her over to the Golden Gates pub for a drink after the game, although he'd probably stick to fresh orange and lemonade.

Ian had called last night to remind him of the *Star Trek* convention in Newcastle that they were going to attend on Saturday.

Aye, it's shaping up to be an eventful weekend!

The problem of his marriage remained a sticky one. He decided to seek advice on a *Harvest Moon* Internet chat site. Like so many players, his preference was for Ann. He had to admit that there was something about her that was better in the 64 version than in BTN, but as well as being pretty, she was loyal and steady.

A good wife. An asset.

He just couldn't get Muffy out off his head though. He was delighted to see that Jenni Ninja was online. She (he assumed it was a she) was really sensible and knew the game inside out, amassing very high scores.

05-03-2004, 7.58am
Über-Priest
King of the Cool

Hi Jenni babe, still stuck on my marriage decision. It's a big one. It's shaping up to be a battle of the super-cuties, Ann v

Muffy, although Karen and Elli are still in the running. Any advice?

05-03-2004, 8.06am
Jenni Ninja
A Divine Goddess

Yeah. I have to admit that I voted Ann and Muffy, they're both my all-time favourites. I used to like Karen and Celia but not any more. Good luck in your decision Über-Priest and I hope it works for you.

She wrote straight back. And she understood. But who is Jenni Ninja? She sounds really cool and sexy, but maybe she's a lesbian. Wanting to marry other girls and that. But it's only a game! Maybe I should write back and ask her where she's based. But that sounds a bit creepy.

05-03-2004, 8.21am
Über-Priest
King of the Cool

Thanks for your advice Jenni babe. It's a difficult call to make but the King of the Cool here in the Palace of Love notes your words of wisdom.

I'm smiling at my words but I feel a burning sting in my cheeks. I'm tempted to wait and see if Jenni Ninja replies but I have to get moving and I feel awful. I click off-line, then shut the Harvest Moon *game down and switch off the screen. In the reflection I can see the ugly mark on my cheek. My head is spinning and I feel sick and dirty, like dirty inside. Something's no right here.*

So Brian Kibby journeyed groggily into work. At the office he felt very uneasy. Danny Skinner was already in before him and that seldom, if ever, happened. Moreover, Skinner seemed elated to see him, making Kibby self-conscious, as his eyes wouldn't leave his face, where the bite mark was. — That looks a nasty one, Bri, what's that?

— Like you care? he snapped, uncharacteristically irritable. It was this flu, it dried out his mouth, made his head throb, poisoned his guts and frayed his nerve endings.

Skinner threw up his hands in a gesture of mock surrender. — Sorry I spoke, he said, eliciting a sympathetic nod from Colin McGhee, and another from Shannon, although he overcooked things slightly by adding, — Somebody got out the wrong side of bed this morning!

Brian Kibby busied himself by heading out to his inspections. En route to his sites, he read everything he could get his hands on about the council and its workings, as well old committee papers, and reports on initiatives relating to public health. He would be well prepared for this test.

I've got to get this promotion.

Outside an Italian restaurant, a young girl, who wore a plastic vest adorned with the Cancer Research label, smiled at him in appeal. He shouldn't have stopped, but her baleful stare ate into him.

She seems a really lovely lassie, a really nice person.

Sheryl Hamilton was fed up. She felt like a prostitute, soliciting men all day. The ones who stopped were either creepy businessmen, or total victims like this guy. She was even thinking like a whore now, she mused, as she went through her spiel. Kibby learned, encouragingly, that most cancers were preventable and treatable, and that major medical breakthroughs were happening all the time. But, Sheryl added gravely, funds were urgently required in order that progress be maintained.

Kibby dutifully signed on the dotted line, buoyed by the knowledge that he was doing something helpful and useful. He thought about asking the girl if she wanted to go for a coffee sometime, but she was immediately talking to somebody else and the moment had passed.

Later in the day he started to feel a little better. During the afternoon tea break, he sat close to Shannon, marvelling at the red nail polish that she wore, as if she was at a nightclub rather than the office. She was reading a celebrity picture magazine, and Danny Skinner was in attendance, teasing her.

— It's just harmless lowbrow fun, Danny. I mean, it's not the kind of publication that's going to change the world.

— It already has. For the worse, Skinner said, slightly concerned that he was sounding like his mother.

Shannon rolled up the magazine and play-hit Skinner with it, before throwing it on the desk. Skinner felt a bit flustered at their public show of intimacy. He noted the racket sticking out of Kibby's sports bag. — Badders, Bri?

— Yes . . . said Kibby warily, then asked, — . . . Do you play?

— Too energetic for me. I'm off out the night to get hammered, he smirked.

As if I care, Kibby thought, picking up Shannon's magazine.

Kibby noted the American twins, the Olsens, on the front cover of the journal. They were talking about their forthcoming movie. It was considered to be 'the next step', a sentiment the girls, the management team and the magazine's writer all seemed to be in accord with. He thought that the girls looked so sweet and pretty.

Those girls are beautiful. I can't work out which one is the best. They do *look identical.*

Skinner noted Kibby's attention. — Every perv's been waiting for them to hit puberty for yonks, he said conversationally, making Kibby self-consciously turn the page. — It's the twin thing. You want to shag them both just to see if one would be, well, different, right, Bri?

— Get lost, Kibby snapped, though he was a little disquieted.

— C'mon, Skinner said, noting that Shannon was now taking an interest, — you must be curious. Identical twins, raised in the same household, done all the same things, played the same part on telly . . . would they have different sexual predilections?

— I'm not taking part in this conversation, Kibby said snootily.

— Shannon?

— Who knows? Would one of the guys in Bros have a bigger cock than the other one? she said, picking up her phone, dialling one of her girlfriends, oblivious to the fact that her throwaway comment, which Skinner seemed to be pondering, had made Brian Kibby's blood freeze in his veins.

He's got her as bad as him. Turned her. I'll never let him anywhere near the likes of Lucy, never. He's a sick, evil bastard!

16

Star Trekkin

Brian Kibby lay awake all night, cooking to his bones in sweat. A fever raged through his battered body and delirious visions flooded his tortured mind, making him fearful of his grasp on sanity. All he could see was the cruel, mocking face of that psychotic bully, Danny Skinner.

Why does Danny Skinner hate me so much?

At the school he attended, Kibby had been sensitive, shy and insecure enough to attract aggressive kids like Andrew McGrillen, who were tuned instinctively to the scent of playground prey. Yet even at school he had never encountered anyone like Skinner. So relentless, so set in a path of controlled, manipulative hatred against him. But at the same time his nemesis possessed an intelligence and personality that suggested he should be beyond that kind of behaviour. This aspect disturbed him the most.

Why does he bother about me?

Come Saturday morning Brian Kibby was in a shabbier condition than when he'd risen the previous day. He groaned, dragging himself out of bed with reluctance, and headed into town, where he met Ian at Waverley Station. Ian was excited and the friends exchanged their traditional high-five, and he teasingly pulled out his iPod.

— Is iPod on stun? Kibby asked, as was their habit, with Ian replying, — No, man, iPod's on kill! Maroon 5, Coldplay, U2 . . . he said enthusiastically.

— Add Keane and Travis to that list and we got ourselves a party, Kibby wearily retorted, holding up and shaking his own machine. Even this usually zestful ritual was now tiresome, and Kibby apologised for his virus, pulling his somnolent, sweating body on to the train. Normally train journeys occasioned him much delight, but this time he just sat cramped miserably in the seat, perspiring as he tried to read the newspaper.

Ian, in the meantime, talked enthusiastically about the importance of *Star Trek* as an inspiring, idealistic vision of the future, a world without countries fighting each other, without money, without racism, where all life forms were respected. He loved the conventions and the people they met there, their fellow Trekkies.

Kibby listened in silence through a thin, pained smile, punctuated with the odd tired nod. His resentment mounted as his friend seemed oblivious to his suffering. Two Nurofen had helped slightly, but he was still feeling atrocious. The train rattled through a tunnel, producing a repetitive whooshing of sound like special effects for a volley of space missiles. Kibby trembled, and was happy to disembark at Newcastle.

At the hotel, the PlayStation console Ian had brought with him was swiftly connected up to the room's television. His friend loaded up *Brothers In Arms: Road to Hill 30*.

— You'll love this yin, Bri, *Game Informer* gave it an 8.5 . . .

Kibby nodded, coming from the bathroom with a glass of water and washing down two more paracetamols. — 8.5. Not bad, he croaked, sitting down on the bed.

— But I think it should be at least 9, maybe even 9.5. It's based on the real, uncensored story of the Normandy invasion, and I'm up to sniper level. Want to give it a go?

— The graphics look a bit washed out, Kibby said, flopping back on to the bed.

— Okay. Ian rose. — I can tell you want to cut to the chase. Let's hit the gig!

Kibby reluctantly pulled himself up and hauled on his jacket.

At the National Gene Centre, there was much excitement in the air. The lights were dimmed and a formidable sound system rattled with electronic music. Suddenly laser lighting flashed and strobes resonated at a low pulse as the voice of the actor William Shatner filled the air:

> Space, the final frontier. These are the voyages of the Starship *Enterprise*. Its five-year mission, to explore new galaxies and

seek out new life forms and civilisations. To boldly go where no man has gone before.

— That's a wee bit sexist, Ian said as they made their way into the hall. — They ought to have done the Patrick Stewart intro, which says, 'To boldly go where no *one* has gone before.'

The actor DeForest Kelley, who played Dr 'Bones' McCoy in the original series was rumoured to be in the country, and if this was true the chances were that he'd be making an appearance here. As they milled through the crowds, checking out the numerous stalls with their exhibitions, merchandise and sci-fi societies, Ian remarked to Kibby, — It would be great to talk to Bones. I wonder what he really thinks of Leonard Nimoy *as a person*.

They crowded in towards the platform at the front of the hall, to hear the host, dressed as one of the alien species known as the Borg, welcoming them from the podium. — So enjoy yourselves, he urged, — and remember, resistance is futile!

Kibby was jumpy in the busy crowd, but he felt even more so as something brushed against his buttocks.

It's somebody's hand!

He turned round sharply to face a lecherous grin. It belonged to a middle-aged man with fairish hair that was greying at the temples, and who sported a large Zapata moustache. His skin was orangey sunbed-tanned and he wore a T-shirt, which under the lights was as electrically cobalt white as his teeth. It had the words BEAM ME UP stamped on it.

Turning his back again, Brian Kibby caught Ian saying, — It's no DeForest Kelley after all, it's Chuck Fanon who played a Klingon crew member in one of the episodes of *Deep Space Nine*!

Again!

But that touch had now become an undisguised grope. Something in his essence twanged like an elastic band. He should turn round now and punch the guy, or tell him to eff off. But Brian Kibby didn't hit out, didn't swear and didn't make scenes in crowded places. For reasons not known to himself, he was a person who always bore abuse and humiliation in silence. Instead he gave a feeble, — Tsk, and headed out, making for his hotel.

Ian Buchan spun round in time to see Brian Kibby pushing through the crowd, making his defeated egress. He was about to set off in pursuit when he saw that his friend was being followed by that sleazy guy, the one who always hung around the conventions and who was known as a pervert. He hesitated, trying to work out what was going on.

Head down, crossing the bridge with a group of his mates, his collar turned up against the cold, biting wind as he lit a cigarette, Danny Skinner looked ahead, eagerly anticipating the tenements, which would buffet him against the gale's assault. The posturing clouds, heaving and swirling above, closed in like a rival mob intent on inflicting some damage. Then a swirling pocket of air whipped grit into his eyes. He spat out, — Fuck, as he collided with an oncoming lassie: overweight, sour and tutting. A crisp packet danced in front of him, its camp fluttering motion and gaudy colouring mocking his plight.

The word on a billposter above, stark black against a white background, came into focus as his watering eyes expelled the dirt: CONTACT.

— I'll be fuckin glad tae get inside the ground, he moaned to McKenzie, as they approached the turnstiles.

— Aye, me n aw, McKenzie nodded, slapping his huge, cold hands together.

Skinner shared a quick look with Gareth, which seemed to conspiratorially ask how a man of Big Rab's girth could even be expected to get through the turnstiles. He had read somewhere that the British turnstile had gained over a foot in width since the 1950s. The article also said that it still wasn't enough, as more able-bodied people than ever now had to enter through the disabled gates.

He still wanted a pie.

— Thought you'd packed in the tabs, Skinny? Gary Traynor nodded to his cigarette.

— Doesnae seem much point, he smiled. — I've a theory that they're actually good for ye. I reckon it's passive smoking that's the real killer.

From the ramshackle East Stand, or the 'Scabby' or 'Cowshed' as it was more accurately called by its residents, the visiting South Stand was a kaleidoscope of dimly discernible visages. Traynor wished he'd put in his contact lenses. Spotting Aberdeen faces from this range was impossible. As so often happened a fat cunt stood out, beating a nearby baldy and ginger. A chorus of 'you fat bastard, you fat bastard' was greeted with a resplendent curtsy from the obese Aberdeen casual which had the simpletons baying, the psychopaths staring with studied malevolence and the clued-up boys smiling in quiet appreciation.

The wind suddenly changed direction, whipping a spray of rain into the faces of the crowd. A tinny riff of a ringtone intro'd 'The Boys are Back in Town' as McKenzie clicked on his mobile and Skinner, though appearing nonchalant, knew it was his cocaine contact and allowed himself that internal 'yes!' that followed a psychic stoppage-time winner of this type.

Skinner looked around at his friends, who had been subsumed into a larger mob. A good few faces were out today. He felt ready for some serious action, more so than in a long time. A meet had been arranged after the game, down East London Street, and the firms were to make their way there in small groups.

As the Hibs boys started to leave around ten minutes before the final whistle, the Aberdeen lads mounted a surprise attack. Instead of going over the Bothwell Street bridge, they somehow managed to get round the back of the South Stand where they confronted the remaining Hibs supporters.

The majority of the Hibs mob had all but left the Scabby and were heading for the meet but there were a few stragglers, of which Skinner was one, and they were surprised to see the Aberdeen crew charging through packs of terrified scarfers and replica strips on their way towards them.

Here we go . . .

Skinner felt his pulse rising as the adrenalin shot through him. The police were simply *in absentia* as the mob of Aberdeen surged forward. It was going off, Skinner thought excitedly, and in almost seventies- and eighties-style numbers. All around him. A proper old-school row, one which they had spent years preparing themselves for, but due to the ritualisation of the violence with the policing and stewarding, seldom actually happened on any scale outside the pages of newspapers. Not only did Skinner stand his ground, he ran straight into the Aberdeen boys, throwing punches.

C'mon then, ya sheepshagging cunts . . .

Sidestepping a bull-like country boy in a black Stone Island jacket, Skinner found himself exchanging fast and enthusiastic blows with a toothy, skull-faced guy with hard weaselly eyes who was clad in a red Paul & Shark. He'd resolved to keep focused and in the proper scrappers stance, but his opponent connected first with a heavy right-hander on his nose which dazed him and stung his eyes with tears, and Skinner was soon flaying around, windmilling like an amateur.

Bastard . . .

Taking a fair cracker in the eye and another on the chin, Skinner staggered back, briefly noting the insipid sodium street lamp burning wanly against the murky twilight sky. It was only then he was aware that he'd actually hit the ground. Realising that his legs had gone, he sensed that it was unlikely he'd be able to get straight up and so curled into the foetal position. But it wouldn't herald his own demise as someone else was going to get it. Yes, Kibby was going to suffer, because he, Danny Skinner, was now invincible. It was inconceivable madness, but he had the power!

Geez it then, Aberdeen, just fuckin well geez it!

After a few stout boots were sunk in one killjoy shouted, — Fuckin leave it, min, he's had enough!

Fuck off . . . stupid cunt . . .

The rain of blows began to let up and then ceased, as the police sirens filled the air.

Kibby's owe some decent sheepshagger a drink, or more likely the Lothian's finest. Still a fuckin healthy one but . . .

For a while he thought that he'd been stabbed. Some of the blows seemed too sharp and breaching to have been made by fist or boot alone, but he could see no blood as the paramedics lifted him off the pavement. Before they could load his stunned form into the back of the ambulance, two policemen tore him from their protesting grasp, handcuffing him and throwing him into the back of a van, where they removed one cuff, clipping it on to a rail that ran the length of the vehicle. The folly of the Lacoste top, he thought, through a daze of double vision as he sat silently in the meat wagon, the anaesthetic of adrenalin dissipating as he became aware that his head was throbbing and his sides aching. Next to him was his Aberdeen adversary. — Fit, like? the boy asked, looking slightly guiltily at the battered Skinner and offering him a cigarette.

His throbbing, dizzy opponent was happy to accept. — A good show by your chaps, it has to be said, he acknowledged.

— Min, ye took some beating there.

— Ah well, industrial accidents, mate. Anyroads, they breed them tough in Leith, he grinned through his terrible sweet pain.

I hope that for somebody else's sake they do the same in Featherhall.

Eyeing the boy's jacket, Skinner commented, — Smart threads. Is that a new range Paul & Shark? he asked, pointing to the man's chest.

— Aye, got it doon in London, ken? the Aberdonian beamed. Skinner tried to return his smile but his face hurt too much. It wouldn't last though, he thought cheerfully.

Well, no for me at any rate.

Ian Buchan had been concerned when Brian Kibby had gone back to the hotel early. He pondered as to why Brian had left; maybe he should have gone with him. But leaving with that strange guy, what was all that about? Could it be . . . was Brian gay? Surely not, he'd always professed interest in girls, like that Lucy for example. And that girl at his work he always talked about. But maybe . . . it might have been a case of the lady protesting too much.

Returning to the hotel, Ian was disinclined to go up to the room. Brian was an adult, what he did or didn't do was his business. Stopping along the riverside gangway, he watched the moonlight glisten on the Tyne, noting the new waterfront theme-bar zone emerging from under glass and chrome.

Brian might just have that guy back!

He sat up at the bar half the night, with some other Trekkies, talking about conventions past. The party carried on in one of the hotel rooms, Ian waking up fully clothed alongside a Trekkie he vaguely knew.

In a room on the floor above him, the dawn was rising, filtering a tepid light in through the curtains. Brian Kibby tried to lift his banging head from the pillow but his body only snarled back a threatening response. In terror, he recalled the events of yesterday. That weird guy touching him up. He'd felt terrible anyway but with the harassment and humiliation, he'd headed back to the hotel, without even telling Ian. And now Ian's bed was empty, hadn't been slept in.

The creepy guy had even tried to follow him back, had said disgusting things about them having sex together! He shuddered at the recall of the pervert's words: *'I want to burst your arse. I want to make you squeal.'*

— LEAVE ME ALONE! Brian Kibby had howled in his face, exploding into tears and running away, as everyone entering and leaving the hall looked round at the moustached pervert, to his shock and shame.

Then Kibby had gone, nerves jangling, back to the hotel, wondering what was happening to him. He'd curled up into a ball under the blankets. Instead of the settling into a comforting dreamland, he just lay there in a stupor, feeling like he'd been in a car crash. His mouth and throat were completely arid, as if he'd swallowed some hot desert sand. He tried to generate saliva but only managed to weld his tongue to the roof of his mouth. Now he was gagging with the rasping dry heat, which seemed to push right down into his throat and chest . . . he reached for the tumbler of water by his bed but he'd forgotten to fill it up. Exhausted and in pain, he was disinclined to be harassed so blatantly by his needs, but a racking cough grappled him, watering his eyes, and he was compelled to stagger to the minibar and get some mineral water, his legs, back and head burning in excruciating agony.

His lips were strangely numb and swollen: as he sipped the water, it ran on to his chest and pyjamas.

The early-morning hours slowly faded away, just as the night had slipped by in a sleepless agony. Kibby's swollen eyes ached and itched full of sleeplessness's phantom dirt. He squirmed like a beached porpoise on his sweat-soaked bed.

When he heard a knock coming from outside he clambered up, feeling like a parade of drummers were beating out a tattoo on his legs, back, head and arms. Timidly opening the door, he saw Ian's face contort in horror.

Far from being charged for his activity in the row after the Aberdeen game, Danny Skinner had taken such a bad battering that the duty sergeant had sent him straight up to casualty, castigating the officers who'd snatched him from the paramedics. They planned to keep him in overnight for observation. On the ward he talked to a reporter from the *Sunday Mail* who was looking to get information from the wounded. He was a young man, with already thinning hair and terrible pockmarked skin. With his earnest but nervy manner, Skinner felt sorry for him. The reporter sat a tape recorder in front of him and said, — Do you mind? Like he was about to light up a cigarette.

Skinner's line was that as he was leaving the ground he was set upon by Aberdeen thugs. Fortune had smiled upon him as the only conclusive CCTV footage of his involvement in the conflict showed him lying prostrate and being kicked by different individuals. He talked at length as the reporter listened in grave, but detached, concern.

He was given painkillers that night, which seemed to have absolutely no effect on the terrible aches he suffered from. At one stage he needed to go to the toilet but was too tender to move. He lay still until he eventually fell into an even sleep. When he awoke early in the morning, he skipped out of bed and drained his bladder, contemplating himself in the mirror.

Not a mark on me!

Chagrined by his poor show in the row, he took up the stance and practised shadow-boxing for a bit. Then he got dressed and left the ward, discharging himself, embarrassed at the absence of any marks on his face. — The doctor will need to see you before you leave, said the surprised nurse, looking at the notes, trying to reconcile this Skinner with the one her colleagues admitted yesterday.

She went to find the duty doctor, but when she returned, Skinner had gone.

When he got home that Sunday morning, he heard the phone ring three times, but stop just before his messaging service kicked in. He dialled 1471 hoping that it might be Kay, concerned at his injuries, but his mother's number came up. She must have read about him in the *Mail.* He thought about calling her, but his pride stopped him. He reasoned that if she really cared that much, she'd call back.

— C'mon, slowcoach, Ken Radden smiled back at a battered and bruised Brian Kibby who panted and gasped behind the rest of the pack on the West Highland way. — If we don't make that lodge before dark . . . he said ominously, adding, — . . . you should know that more than most.

Ken had never said that to him before. It was their private guilt-tripping phrase, one they often used in the sly condemnation of others whom they perceived were letting the side down. And worse, 'slowcoach', that Hyp Hykers generic term of patronising abuse for someone who wasn't really up to scratch.

Now Brian Kibby felt guilty for his tired snorts of exasperation when Gerald, always Fat Gerald, held them up. How he was always keen to shout words of superficially friendly badgering encouragement to Gerald when Lucy was in earshot: — C'mon, Ged! You can do it, mate. No far now!

And Lucy, all they had done was exchange pieces of chocolate. This time his was a Yorkie, hers a Bournville dark. Now he could see her ahead, trying to wait for him, but unable to help herself as he fell further behind. He watched her orange backpack, moving out of his reach. A swarthy-faced young Hyp Hyker called Angus Heatherhill, whom Kibby had never talked to, was pulling up alongside her. Heatherhill had an unruly mop of black hair, under which a pair of dark and steely eyes were sometimes visible.

Kibby's heart grew leaden, becoming another part of his physical burden, and seemed to drop a couple of inches in his chest cavity. Things were going so terribly wrong. He couldn't understand it. He was waking up every morning feeling so dreadful. And now, the state he was in . . .

And Ian hadn't called. He had been so strange on the return train journey, when Kibby had woken up badly bruised, having suffered what he had since fearfully postulated was everything from some severe allergic reaction to the bizarre improbability that he'd been sleepwalking and fallen down a flight of stairs. His mother, like Ian, couldn't believe it; she thought that he'd been beaten up. She wasn't even going to let him go to the Hyp Hikers!

As he watched Lucy's back grow smaller, and Heatherhill's windmilling arms gesticulating to the side of her, Kibby thought of her sharp, frail features; accentuated under those thin, gold spectacle frames she occasionally wore instead of contact lenses.

He often fantasised about being Lucy's boyfriend. In these sketches, mundane domestic scenarios produced almost as much satisfaction and not so much guilt as full-on masturbatory set pieces. A particular favourite had Lucy sitting next to him, riding shotgun in the car, his dad's old Capri, while Joyce and Caroline sat in the back.

Mum would love Lucy while Caroline and her would be real pals, like sisters, but at night it would just be me with Lucy in our own flat and we'd kiss and . . . but that's enough ay that!

Shaking himself out of his fledgling fantasy, Kibby looked up to the darkening sky.

God, I'm sorry about all my touching myself cause I know it's wrong. If you could get me a girlfriend I'd treat her nicely and there would be nae need to . . .

Kibby gasped again as he looked ahead and saw the backs of the group receding further on the horizon. But somebody had stopped. He staggered forward on his aching legs. It was Lucy! Her almost translucent face appeared to open up as he advanced unsteadily. A cast of disquiet – or was it pity again – seemed to chisel her brittle smile as Kibby felt his legs going. With every step it seemed as if they were shortening or he was submerging into a swamp. But the sodden earth was rushing up and before it met him the last sight he saw was Lucy's mouth forming a perfect 'o'.

He stood at the bus stop, waiting for one of the maroon Lothian vehicles to take him up Leith Walk, full of beans, entertaining the other regulars in the queue with his chat. The Sunday newspapers had mentioned the trouble at Easter Road, now the Monday morning ones were full of it. He'd already made the *Daily Record*, where he was described as Daniel Skinner, Local Government Officer and an innocent victim of Saturday's violence.

A 16 bus rolled in and he saw Mandy, his mother's hairdressing apprentice, disembark as she regarded him in some surprise. — Danny! Are you alright? I mean . . . it said in the paper that you had serious head injuries!

— I've always been a serious head case, he laughed, adding, — Naw, it was a good thing it was only my heid. He banged his skull with his knuckles, quite hard, wondering if Kibby would feel it. — The newspapers always exaggerate, they're full of crap.

At his office Skinner scored brownie points by coming into work in an assured frame of mind, never complaining about his injuries, and strangely, there were no marks on his face. He did have a pronounced limp but it was Dougie Winchester who had noticed that after a few pints at lunchtime it seemed to have miraculously healed.

Brian Kibby, by contrast, had not appeared, calling in sick. This was highly unusual for him.

Beverly Skinner's probing fingers worked the conditioner through Jessie Thomson's steel-wool hair. The label information on the bottle mentioned 'fruit oils', describing them as 'nourishing', and strangely, it did seem that as she massaged the older woman's scalp, some kind of rejuvenation was taking place. Jessie's eyes and mouth were becoming more animated. — Of course, Geraldine's ey been prone tae ovarian cysts. Her sister had them n aw. Martina, mind? Her wi the laddie that died, mind the motorbike? Death traps. Awfay sad though, rare laddie n aw. How dae ye get ower something like that? Ah mean, ma two, thir nae angels but if anything happened tae them . . .

The customer was fishing, trying to get Beverly to open up about Danny's plight. She should go round and see him. The football assault had been preying on her mind all weekend.

I've telt that stupid wee fucker about that fitba nonsense for years . . .

He's all I've got. My wee boy. He wasn't a bad laddie. He was –

Mandy Stevenson breezed in, hair plastered to her scalp and the side of her face, the shoulders on her beige coat dark from a sudden heavy burst of rain. — Sorry I'm a bit late, Bev. Saw your Danny at the fit ay the Walk.

— What . . . how was he?

— He was just getting on the bus for work, Mandy smiled. — He looked fine, you know Danny, always joking aboot.

— Aye, ah ken um awright, Beverly mused. Selfish little bastard, worrying us all for fuck all, she thought, and worked more conditioner into Jessie's grateful locks. — This will *really* suit ye, hen, she threatened as Jessie Thomson fell into an abrupt tense-eyed silence.

Brian Kibby had been prone to hypochondriac tendencies for a long time. As a schoolboy he was seldom far away from the doctors: a sick note procured in order to attain some respite from bullying was a precious commodity. But since then, he had grown shy of visiting his physician and was never off work. Any supposed illness was generally now little more than self-pitying habit, his routine phrase 'I think I'm coming down with something' usually deployed to get some sort of attention from women. Now that he actually had a genuine ailment, and one undiagnosed, he was worried that he might be going crazy.

But that Monday morning, Joyce's promptings and his bruising and terrible pains, to say nothing of his embarrassing collapse while hiking, at last compelled him to visit Dr Phillip Craigmyre, the family physician, at his Corstorphine practice. — Listen, son . . . his mother began uneasily, — mind and put on fresh underpants . . . you're seeing the doctor, mind.

— What . . . ? Kibby beamed bright red. — Of course I've put on clean pants . . . I always –

— It's just that I found . . . boy stuff . . . in your pants when I put them in the wash, Joyce said nervously, — you know the sort of stains boys can sometimes make . . .

Kibby's cheeks burned and he hung his head in shame. She'd mentioned this to him once before, but that was way back in his teens.

— I know it can be difficult, Brian, but it's sinful and it can be very weakening, that's all I'm saying. Remember, she looked to the ceiling, — He sees everything.

Kibby went to speak and decided better of it. He was further mortified as Joyce insisted on accompanying him, and even had to be convinced to wait outside while the GP subjected him to a thorough physical examination. The physician's familiarity gave Kibby the courage to cough out the question, — Doctor, could this be, eh, because I, eh, sometimes, ehm . . . touch myself?

Craigmyre, a hawk-faced man with silver, shorn hair and an air of bustling energy, looked pointedly at Kibby. — Are you referring to masturbation?

— Aye . . . it's just that Mum says it's very weakening and I . . .

Shaking his head, Craigmyre said in clipped tones, — I think there are other things happening here much more significant than common masturbation, before going on to take blood, urine and stool samples, Kibby so chagrined that it took his body a while to part with its waste.

When he was done, Dr Craigmyre invited Brian's concerned mother into his surgery. He described the symptoms diligently, then contended evenly, — Some form of abuse has clearly taken place here, he stated.

— What do you mean? Joyce said.

— Look at your son, Mrs Kibby, he's covered in bruises.

— But he wasn't fighting . . . he doesn't get into trouble, she pleaded.

— Ah dinnae . . . ah dinnae, Kibby broke into a wail.

Craigmyre was unrepentant, removing his stethoscope and setting it down on his desk. — In fact, everything here is consistent with the after-effects of a lost weekend of alcoholic debauchery. He shook his head. — These bruises are of the type you see every weekend in the city's casualty unit. The result of drunken street brawling, he contended, while Brian Kibby and his mother couldn't believe what they were hearing. — And this mark on the cheek, it's like a cigarette burn, of the sort that might be self-inflicted in drunken depression. You were telling me that you lost your father recently . . .

— Aye, but ah dinnae drink . . . Kibby protested.

— Yet your son says that he doesn't drink and has had no alcohol over the weekend, Craigmyre half sneered as Joyce stood agog. — I have to tell you that if Brian does have an alcohol problem, then this is a very serious matter and neither he nor anyone else are helping things by attempting to conceal it.

Now the laddie was being branded an alcoholic in denial, in spite of his tears of insistence that he didn't drink! What kind of doctor was this? Joyce wondered through a seething rage. — But he doesnae even drink! He was at a *Star Trek* convention this weekend, Doctor! she implored, then looked intently at her son for traces of duplicity. — Weren't you?

— Aye! Aye! I wis with Ian! We were together all the time! He'll tell ye I never had a drink at all! Kibby squealed at the injustice of it all, as his face reddened and he started to sweat. — I went back to the hotel on my own for a while when I got a bit sick . . . but I never had a drink!

— I'd like to see some evidence of that, Craigmyre said. He'd seen scores of alcoholics before, some of whom would go to any elaborate lengths to obscure their drinking problem.

— I'll get it for you, Joyce snapped. — Thank you, she said snootily, heading for the door, — C'mon, Brian, and Kibby trailed pathetically behind his mother, puffing and secreting as he went.

It took him till the end of the week until he felt well enough to go into work, and the bruises and swelling were still prominent. But the more he talked about his puzzling malady, the more he seemed to be full of self-pity. At least he was spared Skinner's abuse, his rival had taken two days off to prepare for the interview the following week.

Kibby stayed in most of that weekend, in readiness for his own performance. Apart from that, he just about had the energy to get up the metal stairs to his beloved model railway, and he spent a bit of time watching the *City of Nottingham* going round the loop, imagining the passengers inside the carriage. In his mind's eye it was himself and Lucy in a luxury compartment. Lucy was dressed in Victorian style, with a tight corset racking out her cleavage. Her breasts in real life he had surreptitiously evaluated as smallish, but for the purposes of his fantasy Kibby had substantially enlarged them. Now, as the train headed up the West Highlands – not through Europe *à la* the *Orient Express* – Kibby was pulling down the shutters and picking at the laces on the dress and freeing those mammaries.

Craigmyre seemed to think it was harmless . . .

— Stop, Brian . . . we mustn't . . . Lucy gasped in soft arousal through her fear.

— Can't stop now, babe, and I don't think you want me to either . . .

But this is wrong . . . this is bad . . . I must stop . . .

It was too late. Kibby panted hollowly as his jism pumped into the handkerchief and he lay out on the plywood floor further depleted by his efforts.

I'm sorry, God, I'll try to be good, please stop punishing me . . .

17
Interview

In his office on the mezzanine floor, Bob Foy lurched forward in his leather chair, rose and scanned the Sasco year planner on his wall. It was fastidiously maintained: its keyed system of coloured symbols resolutely adhered to, indicating an organised and ordered inspectorate. Yet like most artefacts of its kind, it tended to depict wishful thinking rather than reality. Foy's countenance took on a doleful aspect. Things were in flux and he didn't like it. The vacant new Principal Officer's post would be interviewed not just by him and Cooper, but by members of the Environmental Health Committee of elected officials, though Foy personally felt that none of the candidates were up to scratch.

And yet . . .

Danny Skinner had been very different over the days following Brian Kibby's extraordinary mishap. He'd smartened up his act, appearing exceptionally bright and early in the mornings. Kibby conversely, his original preferred candidate, had just gone to seed. With Aitken retiring and McGhee finally getting his transfer to Glasgow, it was between Skinner, Kibby and 'the lassie', as Foy habitually referred to Shannon McDowall.

Shannon was the first to be interviewed. She came over as knowledgeable and erudite. Yet she wasn't aware that Foy and Cooper had been busy doctoring the Person Specification to make sure that her skills would not be deemed essential, and had been compiling an advance list of arguments as to why she was unsuitable for the job.

Danny Skinner impressed the committee. He was well turned out, on the ball and bright enough, but above all deferential, taking care to play down his intelligence. Crucially, he came over as diligent, successfully packaging himself as a prototype senior local government official.

Far less impressive was Brian Kibby, who had a nightmare interview. The panel took a collective, synchronised sharp intake of breath when his battered and bruised face appeared before them. He was sweaty and twitchy, and his voice, when audible, was a high, fey hiss. Kibby seemed less a nonentity more a seedy, desperate wreck of a man, in the middle of some personal crisis.

While their colleague was suffering the torture of interrogation, Skinner and Shannon were in the office having a coffee. — Obviously, I want it, but if I don't get it, I hope that you do, Skinner told her. And he was being sincere.

— Thanks, Danny; the same goes for me, Shannon reciprocated, though with less sincerity. Both of them knew that she really should be the one.

She's got more experience than both of us put together. She's able and well liked.

But when he saw Foy and Cooper come into the office shortly after a shattered-looking Kibby appeared and flopped down into his chair, he thought, almost sadly, it's a pity that she's a woman.

It took a few days for the decision on the promoted post to be announced. Le Petit Jardin was deemed by Foy to be the appropriate venue for the celebration lunch. — I'm not sexist but I know that some of the men here are, he said to Danny Skinner, — so I was protecting Shannon from their attitudes. Some of them could never work for a woman boss. It wouldn't be fair to put her in that position and I'm not about to have the section in discord. And as for the restaurant trade . . . do you think somebody like our friend Mr De Fretais here is going to take a woman seriously? He dropped his voice: — He'll have his hand up her skirt and her knickers off before she could say 'Edinburgh Council Health Inspectorate'.

— Hmm, said Skinner, nodding non-committally. While personal success was sweet, it hurt somewhat because of his relationship with Shannon. Their sex sessions had become more regular, often against the better judgement of either. Skinner had pushed it the most; he had just felt so energised, so damn horny all the time. At least till now.

She'd been badly shocked when he'd got the job, but managed

to congratulate him with graciousness which, combined with his own sense of injustice, made him feel rather small.

Foy leaned in close, Skinner learning just how much some men's essence was defined by their aftershave. — And you know lassies, they are *not* natural inspectors. They react to different things. 'Oh, it's a nice tablecloth you've got' or 'What lovely curtains' and all that pish. Never mind the state of the fucking kitchen!

Skinner suddenly felt the blood chill in his veins as the kitchen doors flew open and the bulky, apron-clad figure of Alan De Fretais swept into the dining room and moved towards them. In panic Skinner rose quickly, and made a beeline for the toilet. — Duty calls, he smiled at Foy in hasty departure.

As he left, he glanced back to watch the Master Chef in conference with the council official. In the toilet Skinner did a long pish, thinking about the folly of office relationships. You're fucking her and you've stolen her career, he lamented, as he looked at himself in the mirror. Then he thought of Kibby and asked himself aloud, — What the fuck am I stealing from him?

What do I really feel? Who the fuck am I? What about my old man, would he criticise or praise my behaviour?

De Fretais. He'd approve. I'm sure of that.

What a thought!

Old Sandy was his mentor. No wonder that poor old cunt drinks like a fish! He's well off the list now, but De Fretais is a shagger, that's well known. He might not be the slim, fit suntanned old boy that I imagined, but he's a drinker, and he's successful.

As he returned to the dining room and took his seat, he was relieved to note that De Fretais had gone, replaced by a bottle of Cuvée Brut champagne. — Oh, this is a present from our good friend, to celebrate. Foy raised an appreciative eyebrow.

Skinner was happy to quaff the elixir, as he recalled a passage from *The Bedroom Secrets of the Master Chefs*:

> This set off a line of thought which I was moved to explore over a lunch with my publisher. We were celebrating, over several bottles of Krug 2000 champagne, the fact that my book *A Culinary Quest: Inside the Mind of the Master Chef* had passed

> the 200,000 UK sales mark. My alcohol-assisted hypothesis was that the sensualist, by both disposition and what I suppose we must simply refer to as training, has a certain knowledge and level of skill to pass on in this area. Most Chefs (or Master Chefs as I prefer to call my peers) are by their nature sensualists. If we are interested in love, sex and human relationships (and who in our midst can truly say that they are not?) then my colleagues seemed an obvious resource to draw upon in this quest for erotic enlightenment

The next time the chef returned he was carrying a bottle of vintage burgundy. This, and the effect of the champagne, served to blunt the edge of Skinner's repulsion. — Well done, Mr Skinner, De Fretais said in ceremonious tones, a tight, evaluating smile on his lips.

Skinner stared at him for a few seconds. As their eyes locked, he sank into a strange quagmire of emotions: simultaneously appealed and appalled by the proximity of the large man.

This fat cunt, my faither? Git tae fuck. There's no way!

— Many thanks, he said, — much obliged.

— Think nothing of it, De Fretais said haughtily. — Well, I have to leave you gentlemen; I'm off to sunny Spain.

— Holiday? Foy asked.

— No, sadly, filming another television series. But I'll be back by the twenty-eighth as I'm having a little birthday celebration. Perhaps you'll be able to join me?

Foy and Skinner both nodded affirmatively as the Master Chef departed.

Was De Fretais like me as a younger man, just a slip of a boy who suddenly ballooned in middle age? I can't believe that!

He had wanted to ask De Fretais about the Archangel, about Sandy Cunningham-Blyth, about the American chef, Tomlin his name was, that he'd trained with, but most of all about Beverly. But now the drink was kicking in and, more than anything, he wanted to celebrate. And why not? He was entitled to do so and Kibby was paying the price!

This crazy arrangement won't last for ever; the normal order will be restored soon. I might as well enjoy it while I can. Let that slimy wee rat pay!

Foy turned to Skinner and, holding the bottle in a most proprietorial way, sniggered, — Of course, you don't like red though, do you, Danny?

Skinner slid his glass across the white linen tablecloth. — Maybe it's time I was a bit less conservative, he grinned.

The following Saturday morning Ken Radden rapped on the door of the Kibby household. Joyce answered it, startled and nervous as she looked over his shoulder and eyed a group of faces staring at her from a minibus outside. — Mr Radden . . . eh . . . Brian's just . . .

Brian Kibby was by her side. His face was still swollen, and his eyes blood red.

— Have a good night last night? Radden asked, wrinkling his nose at the cooking and cleaning smells, which wafted out the door.

— Naw . . . naw . . . I was in . . . I stayed in . . . Kibby protested, his heart sagging as he saw the minibus, — it's some kind of virus, I've been tae the doctor's . . .

Of course . . . the trip to Glenshee . . . how could I have forgotten?

— He has, he has, Joyce said too quickly and emphatically.

— It's some kind ay flu, Kibby pleaded. — I cannae make it the day, he said, noting in terrible despondency that the pushy Angus Heatherhill was sitting beside Lucy.

— Fine, said Radden sharply, — we'll see you when you feel better.

But better seemed a long way off. Over the next few weeks, Brian Kibby endured a merry-go-round of visits to different medical specialists, and rounds and rounds of tests. These produced all sorts of speculative diagnoses, where it was mooted with increasing desperation that Kibby had conjectural viruses, Crohn's disease, obscure cancers, adumbrate metabolic and viral dis-orders, schizophrenia, almost anything. In reality, the medical people were stumped.

Although Kibby's health deteriorated, he refused to give in to his mysterious condition. Despite being completely drained, he went regularly to the local fitness centre, working hard on the gym circuit in an attempt to try and build strength and stamina. And his body was changing; as he pumped the iron, people noticed that his skinny frame was putting on weight. In a painfully thin man, this initially looked welcome, but it soon became clear that it wasn't muscle, he was simply gaining paunch and bloating out.

He studied his father's notebooks as compulsively as his mother, though never as openly, sometimes cautioning her that they shouldn't be left around for Caroline's viewing. His sister was drinking; she was as morose with it as he was in sobriety. His illness had made him selfish, he considered. He could see what was happening to Caroline.

The front door rattled, he lumbered up to answer it, only to see two young boys laughing at him and running up the street.

Stupid wee . . .

Brian Kibby went back to the furtive enjoyment of his father's inspiring journals. While they confirmed Keith Kibby's love for his family, they were also full of his writings on various novels he'd read, showing Brian a side of his father he hadn't been aware off. Keith had seemed to be particularly moved by books like Oscar Wilde's *The Picture of Dorian Gray* and Robert Louis Stevenson's *The Strange Case of Dr Jeykll and Mr Hyde.* Yet Brian, who had never been a great reader of fiction himself, could not remember his father reading more than a newspaper in the house. For some reason, literature was a passion that he strove to hide.

Brian Kibby attempted to escape into the novels, but his head pounded and he lacked the concentration. They seemed dry and drab to him, and he ended up going back to computer games. He stopped going to the gym; it took too much effort.

One evening he sat gasping in the armchair, watching *Coronation Street* with his mother. Every wheezy intake of breath from him pulled on Joyce's nerves. She looked at her son with a tired compassion, — You would tell me if you were drinking, Brian, wouldn't you?

— I've telt you, Kibby moaned in exasperation, — I dinnae drink! When could I drink? I'm at work all day, I was in the Royal for tests . . . when do I get the chance tae drink!

— I'm sorry, son, Joyce said, growing concerned, as she'd seen her daughter clearly intoxicated on a few occasions lately, — I just want you to know you can confide in me . . .

— I know that, Mum, Kibby said in gratitude, then added

thoughtfully, — You know those American guys that come round here? The missionaries?

— Elder Clinton and Elder Allen, from the New Church of the Apostles of Christ in Texas . . . Joyce smiled. — I tell them they'll never convert me, but they're such lovely lads.

— They're not allowed to drink or . . . eh . . . go with girls, are they?

— They can't drink alcohol and the other stuff is out until they get married, Joyce said wistfully. She regarded the Book of the Modern Testament as rubbish and its authors as heretics and false prophets, but she was impressed by the moral code of its disciples.

— They're young men . . . they ehm, must get urges.

— I'm sure they do, Joyce said, — but that's what we have faith for, Brian. If you spent more time in church, it might help.

It was not what he wanted to hear.

Shortly after this, Kibby was sitting with a salad in the council canteen, contemplating a new dilemma. He was ravenous, particularly hungry for sugary, fatty foods, but tried to fight these cravings as he felt his gut straining uncomfortably over the top of his trousers. — I can't believe I'm putting on so much weight, he ruminated sadly. Shannon McDowall attempted to console him, telling him that it was just the age he was at. Kibby gaped enviously at a pristine-looking Danny Skinner, tucking into his food. His old rival had been friendlier recently, at least to his face. — It's no fair, you never seem to put on weight, yet you eat like a horse and drink like a fish.

— Fast metabolism, Skinner smiled cheerfully, looking over towards the counter. — I think I fancy another portion of that sticky toffee pudding. Never could resist it!

18
Rick's Bar

Ann would understand . . . but Muffy, there was something about her, Kibby thought, breathing heavily as he dragged his icon into the feed store. The chickens needed grain. Though his eyes burned and stung at his laptop, if he immersed himself enough in *Harvest Moon,* he could almost forget about his pain. It was so acute that he feared interruptions. Dreaded them on a terrible visceral level as well as for practical reasons as he liked to be alone with Muffy . . .

I have to watch though, Mum has those Americans downstairs, it's not like I'm in the attic . . .

Now that he had accumulated a good herd of animals and had some money in the bank, he had to devote himself to the issue of marriage. He spent a lot of time chatting to Muffy, and on the websites devoted to the game she had many enthusiastic admirers.

12-05-2004, 7.15pm
HM #1 Lover
Top Man

Muffy is the best. She's so cute and gorgeous. In the first game I married Ann because she had a purple heart for me but don't get me started on Muffy . . . whoa man, she is hot!

But there were critics too, people who saw another side to this girl:

12-05-2004, 7.52pm
Nijitsu Master
Registered User

I don't like Muffy because she's too flirty. I mean, she calls you sexy. That's kinda gross.

The boy doesnae understand, she would be fantastic . . . so good . . . but it's daft . . . it's just a game. But she's a doll, a beautiful young Japanese girl . . . it would be so great to kiss her and fuck her, show her how a white Anglo-Saxon boy fucks . . . fuck her right in her tight Jap pussy, her sweet furry little minge . . . cause once she's had white cock she'll never want anything else again . . . no . . . no . . . stop . . . sorry, God . . . sorry, God . . .

As Kibby went into extreme palpitations, the piercing sound of the doorbell rang out, almost flaying him alive. But through his fear there was also beautiful expectation.

Who could it be? Surely no Lu . . .

Joyce answered the door. It was Fat Gerald, who had phoned the Kibby home last week, ostensibly as a friend, checking up on Brian's health. Joyce thought that it was nice that the Hyp Hykers rallied round when her son was so sick. She took him into the front room, introducing him to the suited, crew-cutted, toothy Texans, who moved their heads in unison, registering his entry. Then she took him upstairs, announcing enthusiastically, — It's your friend from the hiking club here.

Kibby really hoped, then, given his condition, feared, it would be Lucy. Failing that, Ian would have done, but when Fat Gerald came through the door behind Joyce, Brian Kibby struggled to conceal his disappointment.

In the event, the overweight hillwalker flopped into the wicker-basket chair opposite him before he could react. — Hi, Bri, Gerald said in cold neutrality.

Kibby saw a focused cruelty in those bovine eyes and knew that he'd be in for a rough ride. — Hi, Ged . . . he blew meekly.

Joyce had retired to the kitchen and when she returned she'd brought them two glasses of orange juice, now always in supply in the Kibby household as Elders Allen and Clinton liked it. A plate piled high with McVitie's chocolate digestives and Jaffa Cakes augmented this. She tiptoed across the bedroom as if it was a mine-field, laying the tray at the bottom of Kibby's bed. Gerald's eyes never left it, making a mental inventory of the plate's contents.

— Hope you get better soon, Bri, Gerald said, grabbing a Jaffa Cake. — You're missing a great time, he gloated undisguisedly, proceeding to tell Brian that there had been a disco at Glenshee. Gerald, with some glee, Kibby thought, told him that Angus Heatherhill had snogged Lucy on the bus all the way up and all the way back. — That pair seem to be an item, he said in a conniving viciousness that pummelled Kibby's already battered psyche.

Ged . . . is . . . so . . . fat . . .

Yet he was too sick to fully react, as it seemed like more misery was heaped on to a plate as full as the one his mother had stacked with biscuits, although that was now being steadily reduced by his Hyp Hyking chum. Contemplating the sad inevitability of it all, he just sat in front of Gerald with an ill, wan expression.

Fat . . . fat . . . fat . . .

— Comin to camp at Nethy Bridge? Gerald asked.

— Mibbe, if ah'm awright, Kibby replied angrily.

You are fat and one day I will kill you . . . I will push your gross body off a cliff and watch you fall like a stone and splatter over the jagged rocks below . . . oh God no, what am I thinking, sorry, God, sorry, Ged, I'm no well . . .

And Fat Gerald looked at the sickly creature in front of him, as he stuffed more Jaffa Cakes into his mouth, the sugar hit briefly lifting him out off the depression his diet induced in the long term, enjoying his wallow in malicious contempt. Payback time was being savoured as years of Kibby's low-pressure but still distinctive antagonism burned in him. All Fat Gerald thought was that Bri wasn't cool or smart or good, no, Bri was a loser who was getting it back.

Gerald finally left, at the same time, Kibby could hear, as the Americans, and he thought he might be able to get back to *Harvest Moon*, but Joyce came up to his room and handed him a pamphlet. — It's from Elder Allen and Elder Clinton . . . they said it was a big help to them.

Kibby looked apoplectically at her as he held the tract in a trembling hand. The pamphlet was entitled 'Overcoming Masturbation' by Living Affairs Committee of the New Church of the Apostles of Christ. — You've been discussing me . . . me *masturbating* with strangers . . . with *American* strangers?

— No! Of course not! I didn't tell them it was you! I just said that I had a young nephew who was touching himself a lot. Read it, son, his mother urged, her eyes burning, — it's full of good, practical advice.

Kibby let the pamphlet fall on to the computer desk. He waited until she had exited the room, before picking it up and reading:

> We know that our bodies are temples of God and are to be clean so that the Holy Ghost may dwell within us. Masturbation is a sinful habit. Although it is not physically harmful unless practiced in the extreme it robs one of the spirit and creates guilt and emotional stress. It is self-centered and secretive, and in no way expresses the proper use of procreative power given to man to fulfill eternal purposes. It separates a person from God and defeats the gospel plan.
>
> Be assured that you can be cured of your difficulty. Many have been, both male and female, and you can be also if you determine it must be so. This determination is the first step. That is where we begin. You must decide that you will end this practice and when you make that decision the problem will be greatly reduced at once.
>
> But it must be more than a hope or a wish, more than knowing that it is good for you. It must actually be a DECISION. If you truly make up your mind that you will be cured, then you will have the strength to resist any tendencies that you may have and any temptations, which may come to you. After you have made this decision, then observe the following specific guidelines.
>
> A guide to self-control:
>
> 1. Never touch intimate parts of your body except during normal toileting processes.
> 2. Avoid being alone as much as possible. Find good company and stay in this company.
> 3. If you are associated with other persons having this same problem, YOU MUST BREAK OFF THE FRIENDSHIP. Don't suppose the two of you will quit together, you never

will. This problem must be taken out of your mind, where it exists, and this cannot happen when you associate with others who have the same weakness.

4. When bathing, do not admire yourself in the mirror and do not stay in the bath more than five or six minutes – just long enough to dry and dress AND THEN GET OUT OF THE BATHROOM into a room where you will have some family member present.
5. In bed dress yourself so securely that you cannot easily touch your vital parts.
6. If the temptation seems overpowering in bed, GET OUT OF BED AND GO TO THE KITCHEN AND FIX YOURSELF A SNACK, even if it is in the middle of the night, and you are not hungry. Do not worry about gaining weight, the purpose of this suggestion is that YOU GET YOUR MIND ON SOMETHING ELSE.
7. Never read pornographic or arousing material.
8. Put wholesome thoughts in your mind all the time. Read good books, Church books, Scriptures, Sermons of the Brethren. Make a daily habit of reading at least one chapter of the Scriptures.
9. Pray, but not about the problem as this will keep it more on your mind than ever. Pray for faith and understanding but NEVER MENTION THE PROBLEM IN CONVERSATION WITH OTHERS AS THIS WILL KEEP IT IN YOUR MIND.
10. Exercise vigorously.
11. When the temptation is strong yell STOP and recite a pre-chosen Scripture or sing an inspirational hymn.
12. Make a pocket calendar for a month on a small card. Carry it with you but show it to no one. If you have a lapse of self-control, color the day black. It becomes a strong visual reminder of self-control, which you can reference if you are tempted to add another black day.
13. Try aversion therapy, think of distasteful thoughts that will cancel out what is pleasurable. Think, for example, of having to bathe in a tub full of worms, perhaps eating several of them.

14. It is sometimes helpful to have a physical object, like a Bible, held firmly in hand in bed at night.
15. In very severe cases it may be necessary to tie a hand to the bed frame in order that the habit of masturbating in a semi-sleep can be broken.
16. Keep a positive mental attitude. Satan never gives up, and neither should you. You can win this fight!

The two young girls, sunbed-tanned limbs protruding from tight, short summer dresses, exited from the taxi as the lights of Lothian Road glowed thinly. Disembarking from his own cab outside the Shakespeare pub, squaring the driver, Skinner caught a brief glimpse of one girl's white knickers as she slid out the cab. He met her eye with a rakish grin and was rewarded with a half-smile back.

Fucking fanny city here. Should follow these wee rides . . . naw . . . head down to the Slutland, then maybe over to Rose Street. End up in George Street. It's fuckin hotchin doon thaire these days.

But tonight he had an important engagement to keep.

Rick's Bar was a basement watering hole that had gained national fame from a Condé Nast feature where it was dubbed one of the coolest and most fashionable places in the UK. It never really recovered from that setback, but still enjoyed popularity with some local footballers and the girls who pursued them, as well as a few Scottish media types who believed in hype that wasn't their own.

This evening, Alan De Fretais had booked it for a special drink he had arranged to celebrate his birthday. Danny Skinner, delighted to be invited, was the sole council representative as Bob Foy had flown out to the Algarve for a week's golfing.

For a while Skinner had been thinking about De Fretais, anticipating his return from Spain.

We shared one crucial thing: an instinctive dislike of Kibby. Could this chef be my old boy, right enough?

Skinner felt his blood thicken in his veins and his heartbeat race as De Fretais saw him enter and immediately beckoned him over. It's got to be that fat cunt, he thought in a kind of gleeful disgust as he headed towards the bar where the birthday boy chef and his hangers-on had set up camp.

— Mr Daniel Skinner, Edinburgh Council, the Master Chef announced theatrically, to his appreciative company. Skinner let his head wobble and eyes flicker in some sort of half-acknowledgement to the suits and dresses present.

— Hi, Alan, thanks for the invite. I've been reading your book.

— Enjoying it? De Fretais searchingly asked.

— Very much . . . very much . . . funny, cause I ran into that old boy you wrote about, old Sandy. Still drinks in the Archangel.

— Does he really, De Fretais said frostily, then demurred slightly: — A brilliant chef, and a real character. The man had a remarkable flair for cooking. Could have gone on to do great things, but, well, I expect you saw the condition of him, De Fretais looked worryingly across the room. — He's not here tonight, is he?

— No, I don't think so.

— Good. I do owe him a lot, of which he's always quick to remind me. But sadly, there does come a time with alcoholics when you have to cut them out of your life. It's always the way.

Skinner felt suddenly uncomfortable under the Master Chef's searching gaze. Wondered what De Fretais knew about his drinking habits. *Cut them out of your life*. It seemed too easy to him.

Sensing Skinner's discomfort, he explained, — Unfortunately, it's the scourge of the catering industry and chefs are very prone to it.

Skinner nodded to the glass of wine in his hand. — Hasn't stopped you drinking though.

— It did for a while, De Fretais contended, forcing a parsimonious smile. His skin was tanned. Skinner wondered if it was Spain, or a sunbed. — I had a problem with it, and I abstained for years. Then I realised that I could drink safely. It wasn't the alcohol that was the problem, he said with a smile, sipping the wine, — it was the self-obsession. Alcohol is just the self-obsessive's medicine.

— But surely we're all self-obsessed, Skinner said in a sudden rising panic. — I mean, you're still . . . well, you're no the sort of person who lacks self-esteem!

— Oh, but it's nothing to do with self-regard. That's not what being self-obsessed is about. De Fretais shook his head. — The biggest egotist need not see every single thing only in regard to themselves, while the most self-effacing, timid or even downright nice person can see everything completely in that way, he continued, his eyes scanning the occupants of the room. — We may feel more sorry for the sad, self-loathing alcoholic than the bombastic one who thinks the whole world is out of step bar him, but by and large they're the same creature.

Skinner nodded thoughtfully, then regaining his composure contended, — I've got to say that with the book, it was the shagging bits that interested me most.

He watched De Fretais laugh heartily and then regard him with more interest, raising his eyebrows to encourage Skinner to continue.

— You know, I liked all that stuff about the Archangel Tavern. That must have been some scene back then. Anthony Bourdain wrote about how punk attitudes influenced the development of cuisine in America, but this is the first time I'd heard it about the UK. Do you mind of Bev Skinner? She worked waitressing there at that time. My mother, he added.

De Fretais smiled and nodded, but he wasn't giving anything away. Skinner considered that if there was any emotional connection with his mother, it had long since dissipated. There was evidence of neither animosity nor fondness. — That's one name I do remember. She used to hang around with that local band, the Old Boys. Not a bad band as I recall, but they never got the profile they deserved.

— Aye . . . Wes Pilton, the singer, he's no got a bad voice, Skinner lied. The Old Boys were a band his mother used to inflict on him from time to time.

— So how is your mother?

— Oh, she's fine. Still goes on about punk like music just died after it.

— I soon got sick of punk myself. That sort of thing was an education for six months, but if you didn't tire of it after that, you were a bit of a numpty, he said, then looked hesitant, as if realising that Bev Skinner might still be a hard-core punk. — But give your mum my regards. These were good times.

— She didn't, eh; she and you were never . . . you know? Skinner smiled, trying to appear as non-threatening as possible, although kernels of anxiety were now burning slowly in his chest.

— What *are* you implying, Mr Skinner? De Fretais asked, rolling his eyes playfully.

— Well, you do have a reputation . . . from the book, and I was just wondering . . . Skinner smirked complicitly.

— Hand on heart, no, De Fretais said, and he seemed sincere, adding, — It probably wasn't for want of trying. Even under all the unflattering make-up and dodgy gear, your mum was a looker as I recall. But she only had eyes for this other guy. For some reason it was all very clandestine stuff as I remember, but I think it was another chef, I don't know which one. It was probably that Yankee pal of mine, Greg Tomlin. Overpaid, oversexed and over here, De Fretais laughed, regarding Skinner and venturing, — But your mother was a one-man gal, she was besotted with this guy. Yes, definitely a one-man woman, but you seem to be a wee bit more adventurous by nature.

— I'll try anything once, and if it's good, more than once, Skinner quipped.

— A man after my own heart, De Fretais said, looking around and dropping his voice. — Some of us are going on to a little private club later. A party *in extremis* situ, no holds barred. Interested?

— Too right, gie's a shout when you're ready, Skinner said eagerly.

Fuck knows where the fuck this is gaun, but I've got Kibby tae take the negative shit.

The locusts of the city ligging circuit had soon done their work, devouring everything behind the complimentary bar. It was apparent that very few would be staying on to buy rounds. Although the champagne wasn't of great quality, it was free and Skinner had got a taste for it.

A middle-aged woman in fake fur appeared and threw her hands ceilingwards. — Alan! Darling, that book of yours is amazing. Tried the asparagus recipe on old Conrad and it was better than Viagra! I was planning to thank you from the bottom of my heart, but I'm thinking a little further down might be more appropriate.

— Delighted to be of service, Eilidh, De Fretais smiled, kissing the woman on both cheeks.

Skinner was finding the exchanges wearisome. This was obvious to De Fretais's company, and they responded by keeping him at arm's length. However, they seemed as irked as he did that the free drink was gone. Soon De Fretais caught his eye and they headed for the exit. Climbing the steps to street level, two taxis were waiting. Skinner followed De Fretais, two other men and a woman, into one of them. One of the men was Asian. He was small, but attired in an expensive-looking suede jacket. The woman, who seemed to Skinner to be in her mid-thirties, was well dressed, wearing a tailored suit that he took to be Prada.

The make-up is a wee bit heavy but she looks in no bad nick for her age.

Dinnae fancy the odds but: four guys and only one bird. Dinnae say we're all on a line-up with this old boiler!

The other man had been looking intently at Skinner. He had dark hair and gaunt features with incongruously bulging eyes. With his taut, stingy lips, this gave him a permanently scandalised air. He and De Fretais were discussing food, as the car cruised the cobbled New Town streets.

— I'm prepared to bow to your expertise on this subject, Alan, but one would have thought that the French –

— All derived from the Greeks and Romans, De Fretais intervened. — Keep cutting back to the three main culinary traditions: Chinese, Roman and Greek. The Greeks and the Romans invented our Western way of eating, the ritual and the feast, the games. The idea that every sensual pleasure had to be explored, he said, turning again to Skinner who was now feeling a little unsettled.

They entered a basement building, after De Fretais had rung the bell, barking his name into the intercom. A tall, tanned man greeted them. He had hard brown eyes and short, curling brown hair, greying at the temples. — Alan, Roger . . . you've brought some friends along . . . he purred, looking Skinner up and down.

— Graeme . . . good to see you, De Fretais beamed. — You've met Anwar.

The Asian man extended his hand and the man called Graeme shook it.

— This is Clarissa, and this is Danny.

Graeme then took the woman's hand and kissed her on both cheeks, before shaking hands firmly with Skinner. There was something harsh and predatory in his stare and Skinner felt the power in his grip. Though middle-aged, he looked in good physical condition. Skinner felt uneasy and for some reason kept thinking about Kibby.

De Fretais and Graeme led them into a large room. It was painted white and sparsely decorated, with huge ceilings, impressive cornices, a marble fireplace and an ornate brass and crystal chandelier. There was a long oak table adorned with some plates of food; smoked salmon, diced chicken, rice, various salads and antipasti and the like. Intriguingly for Skinner, he noted oysters, which he had yet to try, lying on beds of crushed ice in several large silver platters. Even more interesting were the copious quantities of champagne, some of it already bubbling in flutes. Beyond the table, the only other contents of the room were a big mattress with a dark purple drape across it, several cushions and a chaise longue. — We have to serve ourselves, unfortunately, Graeme boomed, and nobody was shy in coming forward. Skinner took an oyster for the first time and was instructed in how to eat it by De Fretais, letting it slide slowly down his gullet. — It's . . . I think I like it, he said hesitantly.

— Remind you of something? De Fretais purred.

Skinner smiled wanly, before considering the other chef De Fretais had mentioned in the context of his mother. — That American boy who contributes one of the recipes, I think it's the chocolate dessert one, is he doing alright?

— Greg. Yes, he's Exec Chef and part owner of a highly-rated San Francisco eatery. Alas, he's another one of us who has sold his soul to television and publishing.

Skinner was emboldened now by the drink and ready to ask more about Greg Tomlin, but Graeme came forward holding a plate, which he thrust in front of him. — *Escargots*?

— I'm not so sure about snails. Skinner screwed his face up doubtfully.

— Maybe it's time you tried, Graeme said coldly.

Skinner shrugged and speared one, immersing it further into its garlic sauce before eating it. It looked like a mushroom and didn't taste that different, he thought. The second taxi arrived; in it were two guys and three young women who weren't at the do and whom Skinner reckoned were prostitutes.

— How do you feel about the national question, Mr Skinner? Roger asked him, in an accent Skinner could detect little Scots in.

— I think we Scots have done okay out of the union, he said, thinking that he was in safe territory in a New Town drawing room, a bastion of Unionist sentiment surely. — We give everybody the sob story about how we're the last colony of the British Empire, but we played a big part in it with the development of slavery, racism and the Ku Klux Klan.

— I think it's a little bit more complicated than that, Clarissa sneered, turning away from him.

Graeme, still hovering close, smiled tightly at him, — Yes, not views that will find much favour in this company.

Skinner suddenly felt like addressing one of the girls, to see if they had any positions on the issue, and tried to catch the eye of one who wore a tight blue blouse and whose bare arm was being stroked by one of the men, but Roger shuffled closer to him. — How old are you, Mr Skinner?

— Twenty-five, Skinner said, anticipating that he was about to be patronised and reasoning that an added couple of years might cushion the blow somewhat.

— Hmm, Roger doubtfully mused.

Clarissa turned to them both, addressing Roger, — Have you read Gregor's paper in the latest *Modern Edina Bulletin*? I think it thoroughly debunks some of the crass generalisations, and she glanced at Skinner, briefly flickering her eyes at him, — that have been somewhat blithely made.

— Well, that's me telt, Skinner smiled cheerfully, waltzing over to the table where he refilled his glass with more champagne. Who pays the piper calls the tune, he thought with satisfaction.

At De Fretais's instigation, they relaxed on to the cushions, where Graeme began carefully measuring some clear, slightly bluish-tinted liquid from a bottle into Skinner's champagne. — As you haven't been here before, I'd suggest a little something to relax you, he smiled, but Skinner still felt the glacier in his stare.

Hesitating only for a second, he recommenced sipping the champagne. There was no discoloration, altered odour or taste arising from the addition of the liquid, and the bubbles continued to sparkle.

Thank fuck for Kibby.

And it did relax him. Feeling his muscles growing heavy, Skinner was happy to be helped out of his jacket, by Graeme and Roger. A mild nausea followed by a fleeting sensation of hunger hit him, before he seemed to lose all connection between reality and thought and he felt himself falling, tumbling off the cushions on to the floor, only partially aware that he had been pulled to it by Roger.

This sensation in my chest is oppressive, like my respiratory system is freezing up. I remember somebody once told me that their grandad was on an iron lung. I feel like my lungs are iron. I should be scared, panicky, but there's something tranquil about it all, my head telling me that fear would simply be pointless: what will be will be . . . I'm thinking that it would be a good way to die, to pass over . . .

He didn't resist, although at times he had the illusion that he could, as his belt was unbuckled and his trousers and underpants were slid down to his ankles then yanked from him. He felt his legs being pulled apart like slabs of dead meat. The thick, shag-pile carpet was in his face, making it even harder to breathe.

From a blurred view along the floor he saw shafts of light sweep in from under the door. Then he felt a heavy weight on him, followed by some movement and a stabbing sensation in his anus. Someone was on him, in him even. He fancied it was Graeme, but it might just as easily have been Roger. He could hear the man's teeth grinding together in his ear; it was as if the man was in pain from being entered himself, maybe he was for all Skinner knew. Then he felt the man really breaching him, even through the drug, with an eye-watering force that seemed ready to split him in two. He heard curses that ought to have been sickening, —You dirty fucking North Brit whore, I'm fucking your stinking English-loving hole, you demented little ignoramus rent boy . . . but through the drug they were somehow rendered as tender as a mother's lullaby.

After he was finished, another man took his place. He could vaguely discern that Anwar was giving another of the group the same treatment, was it Roger or Graeme or had somebody else come into the room? De Fretais had raised the woman Clarissa's skirts and the back of his head was going up and down between her legs as she regarded Skinner in an intense, but contemptuous way. Two of the girls he assumed were prostitutes were caressing each other, egged on by male voices that seemed to tune in and out of his consciousness like radio stations on a long car journey.

Then he was asleep, and when he came to he found himself alone in the room. He pulled up his pants and trousers, slipped on his shoes and crept out the door. Every step was agony as a searing, scorching pain burned up his arsehole into his guts. Skinner cried in rage and tears of agony as he hobbled home, and when he got there and put his finger to his anus, it returned bloodied.

He felt foolish, violated and used, until he thought about that strange sleep. What could it do to heal him? He lay in bed, shaking in woeful, twitching paroxysms until it eventually came for him and took him away.

When he woke up he was refreshed. He touched his anus with his finger. There was no sign of any blood, wet or dried. It was like it had never happened.

It was like it had happened to somebody else.

Her own health had never been particularly good. A nervous woman, with a tendency towards viral infections, her almost translucent skin often had a greenish hue to it. She was prone to gagging at certain smells, and public toilets made her particularly squeamish. Indeed, such was her fatalistic demeanour, it was as if Joyce Kibby developed such illnesses as a show of solidarity, first with her husband, then her son. No matter how often she washed her hair it only seemed to alternate between scrawny and oily, or dry and brittle.

She knew that Keith had been a drinker before he met her. Through the AA he'd found the church and, through the church, her. When his illness became rampant Joyce had assumed that it had been his previous heavy drinking that had weakened his internal organs, but with what was now going on with Brian, it made her reassess her husband's decline.

Joyce loved her children fiercely, but was aware that in Keith's absence they would not so patiently indulge her tendency to fuss. She knew that she was often guilty of putting her fears into them and fought hard against her own natural instinct to do this. Joyce saw her late husband Keith's strength in Caroline in particular, and she was reluctant to sap it or to sour the girl through her own weakness. Yet Caroline had come in tired, bleary and smelling of drink on a few occasions lately and while Joyce had noticed this she could not quite understand it. She had made a mental note to address the issue, but like so many of her cerebral self-postings, it got lost in a fog of despair.

Fear had defined her life. Brought up in Lewis in the Free Church of Scotland, she was taught to be God-fearing in the real sense of the term. Her Maker was essentially wrathful by nature, and if bad fate befell you, you spent your time trying to work out what you had done to displease him. As there was nobody else to blame for Brian's condition, Joyce took the burden of guilt upon herself. She worried that she had spoiled him, that her mollycoddling was somehow responsible for lowering his immune system. Apart from this self-reproach, her only other strategies were to listen to the advice of the medical specialists, and pray.

The doctors, though still no wiser as to the causes and possible cure for Brian Kibby's ailment, nonetheless found some unanimity through the observation of his condition. Bluntly, it seemed that Brian was rotting away from the inside. Brain, throat, chest, lungs, heart, kidneys, liver, pancreas, bladder and bowels were all corroding, under a sustained and ferocious attack, but what exactly from remained so phantom and abstruse.

Her relationship with Elder Allen and Elder Clinton (it seemed so strange referring to young men in that way) had cooled slightly, and they didn't visit quite so often, in spite of the formidable meals she prepared for them, which they greatly appreciated. They became disconcerted when she tried to foist Free Church literature on them, which claimed that the Book of the Modern Testament was evil heresy, propagated by false prophets. Her zeal was disconcerting to the young missionaries, who reasoned that they had come to convert, not be reconditioned themselves.

Upstairs in his bedroom, Brian Kibby was trying to follow the advice of the pamphlet on masturbation. But while attempting to engineer distraction from thoughts of Lucy by playing *Harvest Moon*, he met Muffy in the village and his mouth went dry.

She's only an icon . . . she's only a graphic . . . it's just a game . . .

Joyce had been unable to sleep and so had gone down into the kitchen to prepare food. As she ruminated on matters spiritual while making her Scotch broth, upstairs Brian had a searing attack. Sleeplessly sitting at his computer, he had resisted Muffy's charms and was halfway through a game, repairing rain-damaged fences and reaping wheat, when a weird, dopey sensation came over him. Then suddenly, his insides seemed to buckle and twist and he fell off the chair and hit the floor, screaming helplessly in the face of a burning ache in his very core.

19
Dukes of Hazzard

It was a bright, warm morning, although the wind coming off the North Sea was fresh and brisk. Skinner skipped up Leith Walk, nodding jovially if he made eye contact with anyone, whether acquaintances or strangers. His euphoria amplified when he got to the office and saw Kibby standing against the wall, looking in some distress.

His chorus and verse is totally Donald Ducked!

— Brian, Skinner smiled, — we should go through these inspection reports of yours, he said breezily, pulling up two hard plastic chairs which lay by the side of Kibby's desk. — Take a pew.

Kibby shuffled towards him, but didn't sit. Skinner nodded to the seat. — What's up? Duke of Argyll's playing up?

— Naw, I . . . look . . .

— Have you been practising bum banditry or something?

— Get lost, Kibby hissed at Skinner, lurching to the toilet.

Skinner rolled his eyes and picked up a file. Thoughtfully turning to Shannon, he asked, — Do you think Brian Kibby's queer?

— No, he's just a wee bit shy. Stop being so horrible to him, Danny, Shannon said. More than Skinner, she was feeling the ennui of a relationship that was going nowhere. He just seemed to want sex these days, and from what she'd heard, not just with her either.

— I think being a virgin at twenty-one in Edinburgh is about the most pathetic thing I can envisage. People lose their virginity quicker here than any city in the Western world . . . except San Francisco.

Shannon looked doubtfully at him. — Is that borne out with statistics?

— Everything's borne out with statistics, Skinner observed and he scraped his nail down between two of his teeth to dislodge some trapped food. He senses her need, knows that they'll probably fuck tonight. Shannon knows this as well and looks at him, again despairing about the futility of it all. The friends-who-fuck relationship was losing its appeal.

The way he's looking at me . . . Shannon flinched, then stared hard at him. *There's something different about him lately.* Maybe it was the promotion, but he seemed intoxicated by power. And, she had to concede, in spite of its ugliness, it held a fascination for her. But for all the allure, there was something about his proximity that was warping.

— What? Skinner said, and shrugged as Shannon got up and left the office.

Lassies can be so weird.

While immersed in his power over Kibby, Skinner felt that his current life was somehow not sustainable. Perversely, so much of it now seemed to depend on his nemesis. This strange hex, it was holding him back, preventing him from realising what he was coming to see as his destiny.

He wondered about living in San Francisco, where it never gets that cold, where everything is temperate, between fifty-five and seventy-five degrees most of the time. De Fretais's words in the text of *The Bedroom Secrets of the Master Chefs* burned in his ears; Greg Tomlin, overpaid, oversexed, over here. And Tomlin lived in San Francisco. Could the American chef be his father? Skinner thought about the affinity he'd always felt with the USA. The land of the free; where your accent didn't matter. But he supposed everybody related to it; movies, TV, fast-food outlets, you grew up with up it. Cultural imperialism. Yet no wonder everybody increasingly hated it: it was stupid, self-serving and so in-your-face that it was setting itself up to be despised. Greg Tomlin, what was he like? Was he the tall, slim, suntanned man with the new young family, who would take his long-lost son to his bosom?

Would I despise him? Would we get on like a house on fire?

Danny Skinner danced breezily into the toilet and urinated. As he washed his hands, he cheerfully hummed the lyrics to an R. Kelly song:

It's the freakin weekend baby,
I'm gonna have me some fun,
Gimmie some of that toot-toot
Gimmie some of that beep-beep

He knew who was inside the locked toilet trap. Brian Kibby sat in terrorised silence on the jacks, his arse-cheeks spread on the seat, grimacing from the pain that razored deep in the core of him. He had been trying to think of ways he could stop touching his penis, when Skinner came along and inadvertantly helped him, his singing snuffing out all sexual thought. But it only heightened his pain, misery and degradation.

Help me God, please make me strong . . .

Skinner smiled at the closed door. He heard a sudden shower of rain drum against the frosted-glass window outside and wished that he was in San Francisco.

God, I wish I was in Scotland! These pictures just bring it all back. Edinburgh, what a town! Had the sort of weather where you didn't mind being stuck in a kitchen, or a bar. Not like this freaky shit; the Santa Ana winds have brought havoc and the temperature has soared upwards of one hundred degrees. They're having it worse down in southern California. I wonder what the right-wing born-again types are thinking as their homes burn. It might be Judgement Day and they're being punished for voting in Arnie. With so many Christians and so few Lions, I guess that's what fires are for.

But it isn't kitchen weather, no, not at all. I'd rather be on a beach than at work. All day, every day. As soon as I turn my back I've a renegade diva cook who wants to put his own stamp on my seafood risotto. Now I got to be in the freakin place early cause the plumber's coming to unblock one of the sinks.

I have a glance through them again, that set of old photographs I found the other day – or rather Paul found when he was looking through his stuff – from back in Scotland. It must have been around '79, or '80 maybe. Her hair, ridiculous that it seemed so crazy back then, that goofy smile. Him in those silly janitor's overalls. And Alan, I swear you can see the fat gene ready to explode, even back then.

He's doing very nicely for himself now, a clear case of scum rising to the top. I wonder how the others are getting on.

Different times. Old pictures just fill me full of melancholy. I put them back in the envelope and stick it on the small table by the front door. I head outside and go down our front steps, on to the street, looking up Castro. I decide I'll walk into work.

So I stride up Castro, through this curious ghetto, where all the farm boys settled when they were demobbed from the navy after World War II. Once they'd got used to ass, there was no way they were going back home to marry some bovine breeder and live out the rest of their days on a Midwest farm in sexual frustration. No, this point of disembarkation and demobilisation was really our point of embarkation and mobilisation. This was the first real Boystown.

The old bar tempts me, but I pass it by, cutting through to Fillmore, then up on to Haight. I realise that, even after all those years, I'm still entranced by this grand old place, built on gold and sustained on microchips. It makes me wonder why I gave the bar a miss. Years ago, I'd always swing by for a quick drink, or even just to catch up on the gossip.

It's probably because today's Castro, with its gay plumbers, launderettes, butchers and carpentry services, all seems so superfluous to me: just another part of society's obsession with sexualising everything. How we queens have changed the straight world for the worse. If only we'd realised that getting a sink fixed isn't a gay or straight act, it's non-sexual. Very non-sexual.

When I get to the restaurant, the young plumber illustrates this perfectly. His assumption of such a conventionally culturally gay persona is so all-embracing that he comes on like one of the androids from the film *I, Robot*.

— Just *exactly* what goes down this sink, Mr Tomlin, he lisps, covered in rotting food and stinking water.

— It's a kitchen, I tell him. And it is. Not a beach, just a dirty, stinking, white-hot fucking kitchen.

Wobbling, sneezing, burping and farting around the pristine kitchen with his notepad, Brian Kibby pulled himself through the agony of his inspection. So complete was his immersion in his own misery that he was unaware of the impression he himself was making. Maurice Le Grand, Executive Chef at the Rue St Lazare Bistro was enraged as he observed this dishevelled, malodorous creature, who had come to inspect *his* restaurant. This was a joke. How dare they insult him in this manner?

Le Grand was straight on the phone to Bob Foy, who had asked Skinner to sit in on a counselling interview he was immediately conducting with Kibby on the matter.

Danny Skinner found himself savouring the moment Brian Kibby crept shamefully into the office. — Sit down, Foy gruffly commanded, then pushed a paper across the desk in front of him. It was a complaints note. It shook in Kibby's hand as he read it.

— What is this, Brian?

— I . . . I . . . Kibby stammered.

— It's a complaints form. From Le Grand. Calls you a mess. A disgrace, Foy said, lifting an eyebrow. — Should we be concerned, Brian? He scanned Kibby's haggard appearance in contempt, before irrevocably answering his own question. — I think we should.

Kibby went to speak, but his brain seemed to fuse. For the first time he seemed to take cognisance of the stains on his shirt, and the trousers of his blue suit, which was far too tight for him.

What's happening to me?

— Listen, Skinner said, dropping his voice, — is anything wrong?

— It's just this illness . . . I . . .

— Nothing bothering you, like at home?

— No! I . . . I just haven't been well . . . I . . . Kibby hesitated. Skinner and Foy had got rid of Winchester, Skinner's old drinking buddy. They could make life hard for him. — I'm sorry . . .

— You're going to have to shape up, Foy said in a quiet, restrained anger. — You're making this section look pretty stupid, Brian, and we won't have it.

— I . . . I . . .

— Do I make myself clear?

Somewhere, the sense of injustice at his lot seemed to embolden Kibby, and he was able to look Foy in the eye and say, — Perfectly clear.

I'm letting people down. I've not been good at the job lately. I must be tidier. It's just that I feel so sick . . .

— Good, Foy icily grinned.

Kibby looked towards Skinner, whom he'd noted had glanced in slight distaste at Foy. — Look, Brian, consider this an informal little chat, he said, — off the record, if you like.

Tears glistened in Brian Kibby's eyes and, perversely, he experienced a wave of gratitude, which at once repelled him and also made him want to scream at Skinner, at *Danny Skinner*, for help. — Thanks, Kibby coughed out, before excusing himself and heading for his refuge that was the toilet.

What about Kibby today? Fuck sake, that boy is a born victim. You can never be guilty for giving victims what they crave most desperately in life: persecution and, even more generously, martyrdom. If you don't do it the Fates will do it for you. The Fates are seldom wrong. You can count the exceptions on the fingers of a mutilated hand.

De Fretais and my mother, between the both of them I could get the real story. But I'm thinking that it's Tomlin that the Fates have in mind for me. All my life I've known that my destiny was elsewhere, now I think it's California.

What's keeping me here? Things are getting weirder with Shannon. Last night was more like a square-go than a shag. We were kissing on my couch, but in an attacking, nasty manner and she got me, kind of ordered me, to strip off. Then she started sucking my cock, but raking at it with her teeth, biting it, and it was fucking painful and she knew it was. I grabbed a handful of hair: to pull her *away* from, rather than *towards*, my groin area. Her eyes were narrow and cruel and I tore her blouse off, snapping two buttons in the process. I reasoned that she wanted it rough so I started mangling her tits. She gasped and grimaced and bit my lower lip until we both got that metallic taste of blood in our mouths. I got her jeans and pants down and rammed my fingers roughly into her cunt. She grabbed my cock crudely, the sharp fingernails digging into it as she yanked the foreskin up and down with such power I could feel the strand tearing and stinging. Almost as a defensive manoeuvre, I grabbed her wrist and pinned it back on the couch, thrusting myself into her, my knob burning. She pulled on the back of my head, pushing her own forehead into my nose, rubbing it and grinding it severely, till my eyes watered and I was almost certain she was going to break it. I fucked her as hard and relentlessly as I could and clamped her nipple in a callous vice-like pinch between forefinger and thumb. Then she dragged her nails down my back and the side of my body and violently pushed me away as she twisted out from under me. She ordered me to roll over as she gets on top, shouting, — I'M ON TOP, I'M ON FUCKING TOP OF YOU, SKINNER, YOU CUNT, and she fucks me, but she's really just fucking herself into a bitter orgasm. When she's done, she tears away from me like we were two strips of Velcro, leaving me to jerk off so as to come; my spunk shoots all over the couch and some on to her thigh, which she brushes off with scorn, rubbing it on to the cushion. And the worst fucking thing about it is the way she just treats it as normal, coolly putting on her clothes and leaving. And then we see each other in that cunting office the next morning and it's like nothing's happened!

And I keep subtly looking at Kibby, for the marks, bites and scratches that I know I'll find.

It's fucking crazy with Shannon and me, but we're no longer friends! I keep singing that Dandy Warhols song to myself whenever she walks into a room:

A long time ago we used to be friends
But I haven't thought of you lately at all
If ever again a greeting I send to you
Short and sweet is all I intend
A-aah – a-aah – a-aah – a-aah . . .

Now she's got the huff as we sit in the putrescent Leith superpub called the Grapes. Done out like an airport bar but for non-high-flyers; hardwood tables, plenty glass and chrome. The chairs and floor are already looking like they've taken a good beating and the air is thick and blue with smoke. The scabby Junction Street fashion-wear attire of the clientele gives the game away almost as much as the prices, painted chalk-style on various blackboards, advertising cooking lager at £1.49 a pint and Stella at £1.90. I'm at the bar drinking Bulmers cider and Jack Daniel's while Shannon's on Bushmills. To cheer her up I put my name down for the karaoke. I see a familiar figure approaching the bar, and fuck me if it isn't my old mate Dessie Kinghorn. I nod to the cunt and he cursorily returns the compliment with a measured shake of his head. — Dessie! I shout across at him. — How goes? And I'm steering Shannon towards him.

— No bad, he says, as he and Shannon uncomfortably register each other.

I turn to Shannon. — This is Dessie Kinghorn, an old buddy of mine. Shannon is . . . a colleague, I laugh and she looks sourly at me. — I suppose Dessie's an old colleague of sorts too. Represents the clued-up, stylish wing of the movement, I say, looking him up and down, his tatty old jeans, and minging T-shirt which looks like it's spent a good day too long on his back in a festering, sweltering Rio shanty town. A poor show threadwise.

— Fuck off, Skinner, he spits.

— Dinnae be like that, Desmondo, have a beer. I turn to the barmaid. — A pint of your best lager for my old buddy Dessie Kinghorn! Make it Stella or Carlsberg Export. Nothing but premium for Dessie boy! I turn back to my old buddy. — Still in insurance then, Des?

I never really noticed how evil those eyes were before but I do now as Kinghorn's looking at me in downright abhorrence. His mouth hangs open in that glaikit stroke-victim impersonation nutters sometimes go into just before they start flinging punches. — Ah wis made redundant last year. But I don't want a drink fae you. I dinnae want anything fae you!

— Funny, Des, I just got a big promotion at the council, didn't I, Shannon? She looks as pointedly at me as Dessie does. — Big bucks. But you ken me, mate, every penny is needed. Expensive tastes. I finger the lapel of my new CP Company jaiket. — A curse, I suppose.

— Fuck off, I'm warning you. Dessie's eyes narrow. — See, if you werenae wi yir bird . . .

I'm about to pull Dessie up about his rather sexist comment when the wee guy who's running the karaoke holds up a card and shouts, — Danny Skinner!

— Must go, but hold on, I'll be back, I smile, hopping up on to the small stage and taking the microphone from the boy. — I'm Danny Skinner, I shout, catching the attention of some old boys, young gadges and lassies in the nearby seats, — and this is a song I dedicate to my old mucker Dessie Kinghorn, who's a bit down on his luck at the moment. I wink at Des who now seems on the verge of a fit as I launch into 'Something Beautiful'.

— *You can't manufacture a miracle, the silence was pi-ra-ful that day . . . a love is getting too cynical* . . . I turn to Shannon whose expression is now so acerbic that it takes me a split second to register that it's actually her, — . . . *passion's just physical these days . . . but get no sign, love ain't kind, every night you admit defeat . . . and cry yourself blind* . . . I look at Dessie and upturn my free palm as I belt out the chorus as camply soulful as I can, — *If you can't wake up in the morning, cause your bed lies vacant at night . . . if you're lost,* I point at Dessie, — *hurt,* and again, — *tired and lonely can't control it try as you might . . . may you find that love that won't leave you, may you find at the end of the day, you won't be lost, hurt, tired and lonely, somethin beautiful will come your way . . .*

Dessie freaks and charges up on to the stage. I keep hold of the mike but raise my hands, boxer-style, defending my face. He gets a couple of good licks in, one on the side of the jaw, punching through my guard, like back in our boyhood spars at Leith Victoria, but I'm keeping my grip on that mike. — *The DJ said on the ra* . . . The speakers go dead as the boy who runs the karaoke switches off the machine. I drop the mike, and it falls to the floor. Stepping back I raise my hands to the air in innocent appeal as Dessie tries to stick in the boot, misses, feels like a cunt and shouts, — You're fuckin scum, Skinner! And he turns and pushes past the karaoke boy, making a storming exit from the pub! What a diva!

I shrug apologetically at the stunned drinkers, picking up the mike and handing it back to the bemused-looking boy. Shannon comes up to me and says, — You're being such a tedious bastard; I'm off hame, and true to her word departs from the boozer! Another drama queen! Well, fuck her. I go back to the bar and finish the drinks, starting on the pint I got up for Dessie Kinghorn, which he didn't touch.

A long time ago we used to be friends
But I haven't thought of you lately at all
If ever again a greeting I send to you
Short and sweet is all I intend
A-aah – a-aah – a-aah – a-aah . . .

I'm soon flirting with the barmaid, absolutely 100 per cent certain in the knowledge that I'll be shagging her later. She's wearing a black top and black leggings. Perhaps not obese, but certainly overweight with rolls of cold, wobbly beer fat peeking through the spaces between the clothes. It's amazing how some women like to show off a bit of flab, use it sexually, the puppy-fat nonce thing. Yet naebody accuses those fat girls of advancing paedophile chic, that's just for the thin, anorexic waif-like birds. She's drinking a big tumbler of Coke, twenty-two sugars per glass.

Come on now, sugar
Bring it on, bring it on, yeah
Just remember me when
You're good to go . . .

Funny, but I'm hoping that I can really love her, if just for one day. — Whatcha say, I smile, getting her attention. — Ever made love? I ask her.

Love . . .

— Yeah . . . she says looking at me, but in that same empty, predatory soulless way I am probably regarding her. Just wanting her lumb swept, nothing else, probably her boyfriend working away on the rigs or in jail or out on the piss.

But there is no fucking way back. — Want to do it again? I ask.

— Mibbe, she says, and I ask her what time she finishes and have another pint and wait till she knocks off and gets her coat and we head for mine.

She's nothing to do with my shit, but fuck it, none of us are saints and scapegoats are always handy.

And almost as soon as we're at it, I'm wishing that I was somewhere else, with someone else. But her face is flushing up, one of those birds that you can keep the foreplay minimal with and if you just fuck them enough they'll come. It's like humping Leviathan: a fucking war of all against all, a shag of attrition. Eventually she goes off and I shoot my load and, save for a shaving of egotism, am completely unmoved by the experience.

It was bad sex but not as bad as last night with Shannon. Cause then I had really just fancied talking to her or playing Scrabble or watching the telly. Why? We both need friends more than we need shagging partners.

Kay . . .

We did dance, we really did.

Contemplating the girl underneath me, I know that she could never be my friend. Her gasps as she came sounded like mocking laughter, as empty and pointless as I feel inside.

Not only have I forgotten her name, I can't remember if I ever asked it or if she bothered telling me.

Probably not.

20
Black Marks

More chickens had hatched. Despite another attack in the night, he'd risen early this morning and put a shift in on *Harvest Moon*. Kibby was pleased that he'd managed to avoid all the girls, particularly Muffy. It had been a gruelling session, where he'd concentrated on hatching chickens, planting and harvesting crops and mending fences. That was what *Harvest Moon* was really about, it wasn't meant to be a tawdry tool for masturbation. He pulled the small calendar from the drawer under his desk. No black marks yesterday.

It was a clear, raw morning and Brian Kibby ventured outside, slowly and painstakingly walking up Clermiston Hill. With great effort he sniffed deeply through his scrunched sinuses, struggling to get air into his starchy lungs. Yet the effort was worthwhile as the fresh, sharp oxygen intoxicated him. Breathing was sore though, and for some reason his jaw hurt terribly.

The days were stretching out: only seven forty-six on his watch and a slither of blue space separated the sun from the earth. The sky tapered upwards into a bruised yellow-blue skin with a few cavorting white cumulus clouds in the foreground.

Kibby felt a surge of triumph in his soul, briefly transcending the pain of his mortal flesh, as he stood at the summit of the hill. Looking one way he could just about make out the cool metallic sliver of the firth, and the Fife coast behind it. Forcing some more air into his tired lungs, he turned to see the Pentland Hills, still powdered with snow.

I mustn't think about Shannon, or Lucy, or Muffy. Muffy is just part of a game. I'm stronger than those urges. I can beat them. No black marks today either.

Content with his exertions, he walked slowly down into

Corstorphine, letting the momentum take him to the doctor's surgery at the bottom of the hill.

A pint of Lowenbrau and a large Jack Daniel's and Pepsi sat in front of him as Skinner thought with satisfaction: I've beaten Big Rab McKenzie into the pub! Only just though, as the doors of the Pivo Bar swung open and the big man lumbered in. Unusually, Big Rab didn't head straight up to the bar, he came across to Skinner's table.

— It's over, McKenzie said starkly to him.

— What? Skinner quizzed, the cold edge in McKenzie's tone bending something inside him.

Over? What was over? What was he on about?

— The quack. Ah went intae doc. For the pains . . . He rubbed his side and slapped his chest. Skinner had only been vaguely aware of McKenzie recently muttering something about pains. — The boy says, see, if ye drink again, yir deid.

— What dae they cunts ken? Skinner sneered, raising his glass of Jack and looking at his friend for affirmation.

McKenzie shook his head. — Naw, it's over, he repeated with the solemn finality of a minister performing the last rites. They looked at each other for a small passage of time.

Fuck me, what is that shit in McKenzie's eyes! Is it fear? Hatred?

Danny Skinner then said something that, even as it tumbled from his lips, sounded implausibly limp to him: — Sit doon, stey for a Pepsi or something . . .

McKenzie stared harshly at him as if he was taking the piss, and in the current confusion of his life, Skinner wondered if maybe part of him was. — See ye later, Big Rab McKenzie said, and made for the exit, leaving Skinner sitting alone at the table.

— Geez a bell, Skinner shouted after him. McKenzie half turned and grunted something before continuing towards the door.

Of course, he knew that McKenzie would not call him again. Why should he? Skinner was now distancing himself from their Saturday fix of aggro. Outside of that, during the eight-year tenure of their adult friendship the only time they didn't have a drink in front of them was when a line of coke was there in its place, or if they were up on a strong pill.

Big Rab would just have to get intae the blow. A lifestyle change!

Skinner thought about his friend's heavy, doughy flesh and ran a finger over his own taut, unlined skin in reassurance. He had long wondered whether his father was a drinker or not. It was inevitable; chefs always liked a peeve, as De Fretais said. That old fucker Sandy certainly did, although Skinner supposed that having your wedding tackle scorched all over the New Town was a good enough reason to hit the sauce. He wondered whether or not the American, Greg Tomlin, took a drink.

Me out on a session with my chef old man. That would be some pub crawl. A real battle of the heavyweights. No McKenzies need apply! Poor Rab, without the constitution to play hardball with the big boys. Who would have thought it?

Gulping back a large slice of his pint and knocking down the double JD and Pepsi, Skinner sat back in his chair and started laughing. Then he found he couldn't stop. His foot hammered a loud tattoo on the laminated wooden floor of the bar room as the other drinkers regarded him in mounting concern, but he was completely oblivious to the scene he was making.

21
Muffy

Bolting up from under the surface of the pool's turquoise waters, Caroline ripped her wet, streaming hair from her face. As she filled her lungs with air, taking in the white, cavernous surroundings of the indoor pool, she noted that little had changed since her father took her here as a girl; the big electronic scoreboard dominated one wall, standing over the banks of orange plastic-benched spectator seating. The adjacent diving pool was still there.

For a few moments she was even moved by the notion that she could sense her father's presence. There was a phantom smell in her nostrils of the pleasantly musty odour he gave off, the scent she would for ever associate with masculinity. She looked around at the other swimmers, but the perception of his proximity slid from her consciousness like waking from a dream.

This was always their time, as she recollected how she'd learned to swim: his big hands ready to steady her faltering progress. She always recalled feeling so safe in their grip. Yet they were ugly hands, almost like claws: burned a withered yellow and angry red at the fingers, stiff at the joints, due to some accident at work he'd never talk about.

She remembered his jet-black hair which he centre-combed to cover the receding 'V' at his temples before he gave up and had a functional number-one cut, as it started to meet the 'O' at his crown. There was the Desperate Dan growth on his chin, adding to his ever-present aura of strength. It had filled the house, only waning in his sickness, and now that he was gone it had died with him.

At first she gained no empowerment from these memories of him, they only seemed to deepen her sense of loss. It was as if her backbone had been ripped out of her. To find the courage she lacked, she had taken to drinking alcohol in quantities. But this had only increased her sense of jeopardy and disorientation as she had woken up in strange beds with near strangers on a couple of mornings, with little to remember from the encounters.

Gradually realising that what she needed could only come from within herself, rather than the flesh of a partner or the contents of a glass, she slowly began to find strength. *I'm my father's daughter, everybody always said it*, became her mantra. What has he left me? she wondered. And she stopped the heavy drinking, and went back to the Royal Commonwealth Pool.

Now she was swimming again. She loved it here: the water, the freedom and abandonment of it. It seemed to bring her closer to her dad, as this was their thing, neither Brian nor Joyce being swimmers. And the tears flowing from her eyes could be lost in the chlorine waters of the pool, and her sobs of grief could meld into the gasps of extreme exertion as she forced herself through the water until her arms and legs ached.

And like her body, her spirit was becoming stronger.

Brian Kibby shook and twitched with the resonant gratings of the bus; the rancid smell of old leather, diesel and stale bodies queasing him out. It was a simple perennial routine for many, but a hideous, twice-daily dose of hell for his weak but increasingly bulky frame and tortured soul to endure.

Murrayfield and the rugby stadium had given way to Western Corner and the zoo. At the other end of Corstorphine was home. He was lost in his thoughts and realised that, given his disabilities, he had not allowed himself sufficient time to get to the exit door. Moving slowly, to the impatience of those around him, the young man gasped, struggling to get to the point of egress.

By the time he had stumbled his way to the doors, they had closed and the bus was speeding off. He couldn't even shout stop, didn't want to draw attention to his blotchy, bleary, destroyed face with the sunken black eyes, his bent-over stoop, or his profuse sweating and gasping. At the next stop on the Glasgow Road, he creaked as he stepped on to the pavement, forcing breath into his harsh, stiff, shrunken lungs, then sloped across the park, hunched and cold, in the bitter rise of sunlight towards his home.

She'd have soup on, his mother would. *Get some soup, son, that'll put you right.* Joyce Kibby's faith in the recuperative powers of her Scotch broth remained undiminished, in spite of all evidence to the contrary. Like the Christian Scientists with their healing prayers, Joyce had to keep faith in her concoction. Standing over that pot in the kitchen like a sorcerer, subtly altering the ingredients, Joyce hoped to find the winning balance of chemistry that would restore her stricken son to full health. Nor was she above putting the odd prayer into the mix.

Brian Kibby well knew his mother's obsessive foible. And just maybe it would work, he thought hopefully, as he looked up at the pallid sun. Then, as he suddenly stepped out from the buffeting shelter of the sports pavilion, he gasped in the lashing wind, which tore across South Gyle Park. It stung his watering eyes, pushing the very breath he tried to expel right back into his tight and tired lungs, so that he was forced to turn his back on it, simply in order to breathe. It whipped his long coat around him like the big hands of a master butcher wrapping a cut of dead flesh into a sheet of greaseproof paper.

— Maybe it'll work, he sobbed aloud in an exasperated state between forlorn hope and terrified despair as the cruel wind boxed at his ears. It seemed to take an eternity to get home, but when he did, Joyce had sat him down in Keith's old chair, tray on his lap, with a bowl of her steaming hot broth.

He struggled through the soup and dozed in the chair for a little while. When he woke he had the sense that Caroline had come in, and sure enough, her sports bag was on the floor. Trying to order his senses, he turned to Joyce, who was watching the end credits of *EastEnders* and asked, — Was Caroline here?

— Aye, you were talking to her, silly! I think you had just woken up from a deep sleep.

— Was I . . . ?

— Aye. Joyce smiled stoically, as Brian had been talking in his sleep, muttering disturbing things, although it was all just gibberish. — But it'll do you good to get a nap. You said you hadn't been sleeping well.

— Is Caroline upstairs working?

— No, she's just gone round to her friend's.

— To that Angela's, I'll bet.

— I don't know, Joyce shook her head. I'm just about to watch this video I got for us. It's Chinese or Japanese, *Crouching Tiger, Hidden Dragon*. Everybody raves about it.

Kibby had never heard of the film, and he thought of how well he'd been doing lately, with no black marks for several days. Then the two female leads in the movie began to establish themselves and Kibby's brain in his skull soon felt like a joint of meat bubbling in a casserole dish.

Muffy . . .

He looked down, to see his erection poking through the material of his trousers.

No more black marks . . . avoid being alone the pamphlet says . . . I can't go upstairs . . .

— This is so good, Joyce murmured, but although she was enjoying the film, exhaustion was gripping her and she was drifting off, as she always did in front of the television. Soon she'd established a pattern of loud, grating snores.

Kibby looked at his erection, sticking up towards his face, challenging him.

Mum's out for the count, that wee lassie is so gorgeous . . . if I just rubbed the head . . . you want it, don't you, you wee sha . . .

— STOP! Kibby screamed in anguish.

Joyce sprung bolt upright, eyes bulging, chest in palpitations. — Wha . . . what is it, Brian?

Kibby stood up, struggling for air. — I'm going up to bed, he announced.

— Are ye no going to watch the end of the film, son?

— This is rubbish. Crap, Kibby sneered, heading out.

Joyce felt that she could do nothing right. — But it's kung fu, son, I only got it cause it was kung fu . . .

— Walkin on buildings like that, Kibby whined, — nonsense, as he padded up the stairs.

Bed offered him no rest. The computer seemed to be urging him to switch it on, though he knew who would be waiting for him in cyberspace. But anything had to better than lying here, in this torment.

Muffy . . .

Prone in the darkness, Kibby tried to think of mundane reports of site visits, but when he inspected a restaurant, he would be greeted by a waitress in a short skirt who looked like Lucy, and she'd bend over a table . . .

The Lord's my shepherd

. . . or in a Chinese restaurant, the girl from the film who looked like Muffy . . .

. . . I'll not want . . . office . . . office . . . Foy . . . Foy's office on the mezzanine floor . . .

. . . but inside Foy's office was Shannon, sitting on the desk, looking at him, unbuttoning her blouse. — I've been remiss, Brian, I've let Danny inspect me but I haven't given you your turn . . .

— Stop!

He pulled up the duvet and looked at his tentpole erection. Why did it look so robust and taut when the rest of him was so weak, flabby and stricken? He took long deep breaths as he tried to compose himself. He heard Joyce turning in, then Caroline using the bathroom before going to bed.

No black marks . . . no black marks . . .

The minutes dragged and tugged and sleep still wouldn't come. Images of naked Japanese girls kept intruding into his thoughts.

Muff . . .

He remembered the pamphlet's advice: make a snack, even if you're not hungry. The only thing to do was to get up and reheat the Scotch broth. His stomach was full, but he forced more down. However, when he returned to his bedroom, he still found sleep as elusive as ever. He attempted some more prayer but his heart thudded in his chest as he realised his prick was stiffening again.

I mustn't touch it . . . but they want it, Lucy, Shannon . . . the Jap girls. They want to be fucked but why don't they want to go with me *. . . what's wrong with them? But in here, in my head, I can* make them *want me, but it's wrong, it's fucking wrong, it's evil, Shannon's my friend, Lucy's a nice girl . . . Muffy's a computer icon . . . the Japanese lassies are actresses, playing a role . . . I wonder if the director ever . . . no . . .*

He threw aside the duvet and rose again, fetching an old tie from his wardrobe, using it to bind his right hand to the post of his pine bed. And then he put his left hand outside of the bedcover and silently prayed for strength.

The next morning Brian Kibby sat at his desk, miserable, rubbing at a red bracelet of an indentation circling his wrist. He'd tied it far too tight and had cut off the circulation.

That was so stupid and dangerous . . . I could have lost my hand!

Danny Skinner appeared in the open-plan office, emerging from the connecting door to the staircase and the mezzanine floor. As was commensurate with his duties, Skinner was going over the rota for the approaching summer holiday period. He couldn't remember how many pints he'd had last night, but Kibby's sweaty, heavy breathing and hunched silence told him that it must have been quite a few. — You're offski in a couple of weeks then, Brian? he breezily enquired.

— Aye, Kibby said meekly, fighting hard to stop his jaw going into a spasm.

— So where's it you're off tae then? Somewhere exotic?

— No sure yet, Kibby mumbled. In fact, he knew that he was going to another *Star Trek* convention, this time in Birmingham, but he didn't want his workmates, especially Skinner, knowing his business. He was enough of a figure of fun, he thought, as his trembling hand grasped the Volvic bottle, raising it to a set of dry, cracked lips. Ian hadn't called, hadn't even returned the messages he'd left on his mobile. He'd not seen him in ages, since Newcastle, in fact. He was certain that he'd run into him at the Birmingham Convention, and they could pick up where they left off.

But in the here and now Brian Kibby felt absolutely terrible. That was the worse thing about this disease, the cruelty of the periods of remission, where you grasped at hope, then this . . .

They were running more tests at the hospital. They kept plugging the same lines: various unidentified and known diseases, psychosomatic depressive illness, a mystery virus. The insinuation of denial (he was a closet drunk), however veiled, never quite left the agenda, but to his mind it was all nonsense, because they were still as clueless now as they were when it all started.

He had been researching obsessively on the Internet, checking out everything from alternative medicines and obscure religious cults to alien possession, in an attempt to gain some insight into his condition. As he sat furtively at his desk, a pounding in his ears, his hands shaking, he heard Skinner's throaty voice bellow across the office in a loud mockney accent: — I'M ORF TO IBEEFA AGAIN THIS SUMMAH EHND OIM AVIN IT LAWWRRGGG!! And as Kibby turned, he saw Skinner was staring right back at him as he spoke, as if in threat. He clicked off the Internet Explorer quickly, and dragged up an inspection file.

That lunchtime, Kibby made one of his customary visits to the National Library on George IV Bridge. In his personal attempt to explain the inexplicable, he continued his researches during his breaks in a compulsive, aberrant paranoia.

Scanning the newspapers on microfiche, something came to his attention. He noticed a feature on a woman named Mary McClintock, who had lived with seventeen cats in a minging caravan outside of Tranent until the authorities had intervened and stuck her in a sheltered housing complex. Mary referred to herself as a 'white witch' and was considered by some to be an expert on spells. This was all the encouragement Kibby needed and he was moved to obtain a contact number through a girl Shannon knew who worked for the Scotsman Publications in Holyrood.

After work, he set out to Tranent, catching an Eastern Scottish bus from St Andrew's Square. He found the sheltered housing complex easy enough. Mary McClintock was grossly overweight but her eyes were sparkling and busy, seeming ill-fitting for her heavy, slothful body and pudding head. She wore what appeared to Kibby to be several layers of clothing and yet still seemed to shiver, although it was so hot in the complex that he'd had to remove his jacket and was still sweating uncomfortably.

Mary sat him down and listened to him explain his condition.
— It sounds to me like you've been cursed, she said in earnest.

Kibby almost wanted to snort his contempt at her, but he held back. After all, nothing else had come close to explaining it. — But how can I be cursed? he entreated. — How . . . that's silly . . .

— If it's that silly then you'll want tae hear nae mair fae me, she said, her head wavering imperiously.

— I can pay, if that's what you want, Kibby wailed miserably.

Mary looked at him in some outrage. — *Of course* you'll have to pay, and it's no money I'm wanting either, son, that's nae guid tae me at ma age, she explained, her mouth taking on a lecherous twist.

Kibby had seemed to suddenly grow very cold indeed. –What . . . eh . . . I . . .

— You say ye were thin before ye got ill . . .

— Aye . . .

— All prick and ribs, I'll wager. Would I be right in saying that?

— What . . . ? Kibby gasped, his hands gripping the armrests of the chair.

— Dae ye have a nice cock, son? A nice thick cock? Cause that's what I want up me, Mary said, matter-of-factly. — Then I'll give ye a detailed consultation.

Kibby stood up, made for the door. — I think, eh, I've come to the ehm wrong place, obviously. I'm sorry, he said, exiting in panicky haste from the flat.

As he got into the lobby he heard her voice following him, — You're a dirty one, ah kin tell!

He pushed through the exit door, desperate to leave the rain-soaked streets of Tranent as soon as was humanly possible.

She's a nutcase! She's probably senile!

The rain was teeming down outside as he crushed into a busy bus shelter. A bus stopped soon after but he was too wrecked and nerve-shorn to jostle through the packed bodies to get on to it. He dejectedly trudged out into the cascading wet and flagged down a taxi instead, which took a longer time than he thought to pass the bus, enabling him to board it and get back to Edinburgh.

When he got home he had his tea and sat in wretched silence watching television as Joyce told him about her day. It was terrible. He was miserable, jittery, his head pounding in an ache, the source of which seemed to alternate between each temple, and he could hardly breathe. His nerves were like piano wire. Once he felt rested enough he'd go upstairs to *Harvest Moon*. But it was so dangerous . . .

Muffy . . . I want to fuck her so badly . . . no no no, but at least she's not real like Lucy and . . . and that horrible old crone today . . . it's no fair . . . please, no . . .

But a little TV would be nice, a little TV in total silence. But that simple pleasure . . . why can't she be quiet? Why can't she ever stop talking?

And Joyce continued, her words drilling through his skull, becoming another source of torment to his weary soul.

— . . . just some record tokens for Caroline's birthday. I saw a lovely sweater that would have looked great on her, but she likes to buy her own clothes, she can be a proper madam when you try to get her something to wear . . . what do you think, Brian?

— Aye . . .

— . . . or maybe book tokens rather than record tokens. She's enough CDs anyway and books will be far more useful to her in her studies . . . your father always liked books. What do you think then, Brian, book tokens or record tokens, what do you *really* think?

— I don't care! Let me watch the telly in peace! Please! Kibby shouted.

Joyce buckled, looking at him like the last solitary puppy of the litter, left in a pet-store window. Kibby's heart sank as he saw the distress in his mother's eyes.

The silent impasse was broken by a shattering buzz, which almost caused Brian Kibby to jump out off his skin. Joyce also reacted with a start. Then, glad of the break, she quickly got to her feet to answer the door. When she came back, she had a sweatshirted, parka-clad figure with her. It was Ian.

He's here to talk about Birmingham.

— Listen, Joyce said, — I'm just going to pop down the street to see Elspeth and her new baby. I'll leave you lads to catch up.

— Great, Kibby said, flashing his mother a look of apology at his outburst. — And, Mum, I think the book token is a great idea.

— Right, son, Joyce said, flushed with love. The laddie was ill and she did go on. Never mind, Ian was here and he would cheer the boy up.

Ian and Brian stiffly and tensely looked at each other until they heard the living-room door close followed by the front one slamming shut.

— Ian . . . I . . . Kibby began.

Ian waved him down. — Listen to me, Brian, please just listen to what I've got to say.

He was so insistent and grave that Brian Kibby could only nod in response.

— Growing up, around here, in a city like this . . . in a place like Scotland . . . it's not easy for the likes of us.

Kibby thought about his years of lonely isolation at school. Being ignored, shunned or, worse than that, ridiculed and picked on. He nodded in slow agreement.

— It makes it hard to admit things about ourselves. When I saw you down in Newcastle, leaving with that sleazy guy . . . then when I got to the hotel, you were all beat up the next morning . . .

Kibby tried to speak but no words would come from his dry throat.

— . . . I thought, why does Brian have to go with somebody like that? Some dirty animal who doesn't respect him and slaps him around?

Kibby felt an arresting shiver. His teeth began to chatter. — But . . . I . . .

— . . . when there's somebody close to him who loves him, who always has . . . Ian moved forward in his seat and Kibby felt the blood drain from his face. — . . . that's right, Brian, I've been doing so much thinking, so much agonising . . . I love you, Brian . . . there, I've said it, Ian spat, and looked up at the ceiling. — The heavens haven't opened, I've not been struck by a bolt of lightning. I've always loved you. I never knew that you were like me . . . you always went on about girls like Lucy . . . God, every time you mentioned that bitch's name was a nail in my heart . . . if only you could have told me! There was no need for this elaborate smokescreen, this living a lie!

— No! You're wrong! Kibby squawked. — There was –

— No, Brian, no more deceit. Can't you see? For years we were called 'poofs' or 'queers' at school by the likes of McGrillen and we'd done nothing! What can they do to us now? What can they do or say that they haven't already? We can get a flat together –

— No! Kibby screamed.

— You think I worry about your disease? We'll find a way. I'll look after you! Ian implored.

— You're mad! I'm not gay! I'm not!

— This is classic denial! Ian upturned his palms and shook his head. From Kibby's point of view, his Adam's apple bobbled monstrously like an alien was about to burst out of his throat. — I know that your mum's into all that Church stuff and that some elements of Christianity are anti-gay but the Bible provides a lot of contradictory evidence . . .

All Kibby could do was to look his excited friend in the eye and say evenly, — Look, I don't want to be with you . . . in that way . . .

Ian felt the wind being punched out of his sails. He sat for a second, feeling utterly dejected. Then he looked Kibby up and down witheringly as the bitterness of rejection flooded through him. — So you don't fancy me, eh? Who the fucking hell do you think you are? *You* don't fancy *me*? He sprung angrily to his feet and pointed at the mirror above the mantelpiece. — Take a look in that sometime, lardarse. Look in that and see what you are! I was doing you a favour! I'll see myself out, he pouted in acrimony, then turned on his heels as a shocked and shattered Kibby heard first one, then a second door slam shut.

Shannon's tied back her hair. It makes her look severe, but not unattractive. I ask her if she fancies a drink after work. She tells me that she's got an inspection report but that she'll meet me in the Café Royal about five thirty. I've decided that I'm going to tell her that I think my old man might be an American chef, living in California.

It's almost six by the time she gets in, and instead of sliding into the booth beside me, she positions herself in a chair opposite. She's making no effort to remove her jacket. — What are you drinking? I nervously offer.

— Nothing. I'm off home. Alone. It's over between us, Danny, she says, with that detached but intense, stoical look dumpers always put on. I'm getting used to it.

While I nod in understanding, I can still feel the rancorous bile of rejection burning up my chest and guts, like a cheap, harsh spirit.

— It's served its purpose, certainly for me, and I suspect for you as well, she says. — It's time to move on.

A flood of emotion almost overwhelms me. She's right, but I just need . . . somebody. Why is it girls always look at their most beautiful, most desirable, just as they're telling you to fuck off? I feel my eyes moisten. — You're right, I say, sliding my hand on top of hers and gripping it lightly. — You're a brilliant lassie, one of the best people I've ever met, I tell her in utter sincerity, — it just came at the wrong time for both of us, I concede. — I know it's the fashionable kind of thing people say in these circumstances without really meaning, but I really would like it if we could stay friends, and by that I mean proper friends.

— Goes without saying, she says, now a wee bit teary herself through a look of mild disappointment. You can see why; the chucker psyche is that they build themselves up to give you the elbow, going through all the lines in their head. So the very presence of the other party is by its nature disappointing, even before the other person speaks. She brushes her eyes and rises, kissing me on the cheek.

— Not staying for a drink? I ask, it coming out a bit desperate, but I need to talk to someone about this Yank chef.

— I can't, Danny, she says sadly, but with an emphatic shake of the head. — I'll see you at work tomorrow. Goodbye.

She heads across the bar, her shoes clicking on the marble-tiled floor.

Before I have another drink I'm going to go and see my mother. I'm going to ask her about chefs she worked with, mention some names, see how she responds. I doss back my pint and head down the Walk, catching a 16 bus when I get to the point that I don't trust myself to pass another boozer.

I stop off at my place and look again at De Fretais's book.

Compiling this book proved less straightforward than one might have supposed. When I approached my fellow Master Chefs to share with me their gourmet techniques, not merely of cookery, but of seduction, sex and love, there was understandably some disquiet in the ranks. Many thought that this was simply a joke: De Fretais again with his wacky, offbeat sense of humour. Staider spirits were actually affronted, dismissing me as a crank, or a publicity merchant interested only in smut-driven sales.

Yet there are a few bold libertines in my trade, and they

were more than happy to share their secrets with us. And for that, I thank them all from the bottom of my heart. The bedroom of the Master Chef must be like his kitchen: an arena where dreams are manufactured and where exquisite art and sensual enlightenment pours forth out of the order, movement and inspiration we employ.

Fuck me, that cunt is so up himself. No self-obsessed, he says!

When I get round to my mother's the front door's open. I walk inside, down the narrow hall, over the Indian rug I've always admired. She's in the front room at the kitchen area and Busby's here. He's sitting at the breakfast bar, his bulbous nose and cheeks glowing with a whisky hue. The cat glares at me from his lap. His at-home arrogance crumbles with my appearance and he folds up some documents and sticks them into a battered suitcase. — Hello, son, he says anxiously, obsequiously.

I stare at my Old Girl in accusation and she leans back against the kitchen worktops and stares back at me: mocking and sluttish as she blows some smoke from a cigarette. There's a glass of whisky by her side. The song 'Rag Doll' plays on the radio.

What the fuck is going on here? When was the last time that old cunt ever sold insurance?

— Why, hu-low, stranger, my mother says to me, in a totally snidey way. It's like she knows that she's won cause I've come down here to see her, and she's delighting in it.

Something in her behaviour gives the old insurance man confidence. A gleam comes into his eye and his lips twist wickedly as his cigarette rises to meet them. The cat continues to stare at me in solemn, unwavering judgement. The three of them seem like conspirators.

— I can see that you're busy. I'll see ye when yir better dressed, I say, and I can't stop it coming out scornfully.

As I depart I hear my mother say, — Well, goodbye, stranger . . . and their laughter; hers raucous and his wheezily melodious, like an old accordion; it follows me out the house and down the stairs.

I emerge into the street and head across the cobblestones, cutting down to the Water of Leith. I seem to walk for a while without knowing where I'm going till I'm consciously aware that I'm heading down the brae of Restalrig Road towards Canton's Bar in Duke Street. Darkness is beginning to fall and the cold air scours my face.

That fucking cow, that great big fucking horrible sow, I only went round tae talk wi her and she's got that little sleaze-bucket there . . .

Hello, son.

But everybody said that. Busby's always said that to me.

In the pub I order a pint before I realise that for some reason the bar hasnae been fuckin well cleaned since yesterday. The barman tells me that somebody was stabbed in here last night, with the polis treating it as attempted murder. — We just got the all-clear tae open, he says. — Didnae huv time tae clean things up. Forensics n that.

I'm oppressed by the rancid residue of the alehouse's recent drunken, violent past. The nauseous odour of vomit sticks in my nose, along with that stench of stale cigarette smoke and the alcohol, how it permeates into everything. It was obviously shut earlier today: ashtrays remain full and last night's glasses still pile up on the tables. An old girl takes a mop and some Shake n' Vac to the tartan carpet, which is black with blood underneath the jukebox. I think I should go but the barman is serving me drink, so I find a corner and sit, cursing my lot.

Rejection.

Kay, Shannon, my Old Girl, Kinghorn, McKenzie even. Looks like the absentee father set the fucking trend. And wouldn't that be the ultimate fucking slap in the chops, if he wasn't the athletic Californian, but nasty wee Busby.

Hello, son.

If I can do it to Kibby, I can do it to that wee slimeball. I've always hated him. Now I'm focusing my hate on Busby.

BUSBY.

I HATE THAT SNIVELLING, MANIPULATIVE LITTLE CUNT.

I HAVE THE POWER TO DESTROY THAT WEE FUCKER.

HATE BUSBY
HATE BUSBY

HATE HATE HATE . . .
HATE BUSBY
HATE BUSBY
HATE HATE HATE . . .

This spiteful mantra continues until I become drained, and my head throbs. A couple of old boys come into the bar, register my intense stare into space and nod at each other, tossing me an over-the-shoulder glance. — Spot the loony, one laughs.

But in spite of my efforts, there's nothing; no strange alchemy takes place. There is absolutely fucking zero to resemble the immense shattered, dizzying sensation, followed by the surge of energy when I put the hex on Kibby. Now I just feel stupid and self-conscious; aware of the looks I'm getting from the bar.

In spite of it all I just can't muster the same hatred for Busby. Is this because it's him, that thing, that's my dad? Is it that I can't kill my own?

So what is it about Kibby, this obsession? Just who is he to me?

22
Brummie Balearics

The darkness was illuminated by the pearly smiles that Mary-Kate and Ashley Olsen flashed across the screen of the multiplex. The experience was, for Brian Kibby, entrancing and uplifting. *A New York Minute* was one of the best movies he'd seen in a long time. It was the way to go for the twins, he considered. Nonetheless, he worried about the images of them being burned into his brain. Tonight would be a big test. It had been twelve days since he'd last chalked up a black mark. He was doing so well.

On the way home he stopped at a newsagent and had browsed through a magazine, which featured the Olsen girls on the cover. He was horrified to read that one of them was involved in a battle with an eating disorder. On his return home, he was moved to write a letter of support to her mother.

Dear Mrs Olsen,

I was upset to hear about your daughter's illness and I sincerely hope that Mary-Kate recovers from her health problems. My name is Brian Kibby. I am a twenty-one-year-old Edinburgh man who has recently contracted a terrible rare disease, and one that the doctors and medical specialists are at a loss to explain.

I very much enjoyed the movie *A New York Minute*, which I saw earlier today, and please pass on my wishes to the girls for continued success. I hope that we are able to see Ashley and Mary-Kate together again on the big screen soon.

I don't have any motive for writing this note; this is definitely not a begging letter. I just find your daughters very inspiring figures and want you to know that.

Yours sincerely,
Brian Kibby

He sent it care of the magazine, hoping they would forward it.

Due to the progressively debilitating nature of his illness, Kibby had stopped going out with the Hyp Hykers. The summer party, though, was a big event on their annual social calendar. Aware of how he was coming to be perceived, and in spite of his mounting frailty, he resolved to attend.

It had been Ken Radden's idea to book the function rooms in the Zoological Gardens at Corstorphine. — Get two bunches of animals together, he had joked. The proximity of the venue was appealing to Kibby, who walked slowly down the main road, feeling the pain of dragging his aching, worn body with him. And then there were his nerves, those tattered, shredded nerves. They registered everyone who crossed his path as a hostile force, the most innocuous persons coming over to him like a McGrillen or a Skinner.

When he got to the do, he could feel the unease around him. Paranoia tore out of him; he wondered what they thought of him and he tried to make a big show of not drinking alcohol.

Despite his ostentatious efforts with the Pepsi and the orange juices, for the most part he was either resolutely ignored or met with stares of pity. Those who did engage with him only felt comfortable in conversation for a short while, then would quickly head off when somebody more suitable to talk to crossed their line of vision. He was an embarrassment, and felt it acutely.

I thought they were my friends. The Hyp Hykers. The crazy gang . . .

Then he saw Lucy. She was wearing a green dress.

She's better than Mary-Kate or Ashley . . . or as good as . . .

She looked so beautiful, but he couldn't approach her: not as the tubby, suspiring, red-eyed wreck that he now seemed to be. But she caught his eye and looked at him quizzically, the recognition slowly dawning in her expression and she cautiously approached him, tentatively asking, — How are you keeping?

It was a question . . . she's no sure it's me. She doesnae even ken for certain that it's me!

Brian Kibby forced a sad smile of affirmation. — I . . . eh . . . I think I'm getting better but it's slow, he said, finding himself almost moaning at his own lies. He then hopefully added, — Mibbe get a game of badminton again, when I feel up tae it . . .

— Yes, Lucy grinned forcibly, wanting the ground to swallow her up. To think she'd actually liked him, found him a bit fanciable, even. Rescue came in the form of Angus Heatherhill, who skipped across the floor and pushing his fringe out of his eyes said to her, — Hey, Luce, fancy a wee dance?

— Okay, Angus. Excuse us, Brian, she said, and left Kibby with a fresh orange juice which tasted like poison to him.

He watched them for a bit, first on the dance floor, then in the corner of the room.

His hands are all over her. She loves it as well. It's like she's mocking me!

She's just like the rest of them!

Kibby sloped miserably away from the function, wandering into the night. As he headed down a cobbled path, towards the zoo exit and the main road, a screeching noise lacerated his bedraggled nerves. He felt his heart was going to explode in his chest. Then there followed a cacophony of squawks. Huge, murderous grunts heaved from somewhere behind him. The smells were overpowering as he hurried down the path and through the zoo gates. He got home as fast as his weary frame and a slow taxi could take him.

The next morning Kibby struggled through his agony, rose and boarded the train to Birmingham for the convention. He'd booked the ticket in advance and he was determined to confront Ian, who was certain to be there, and explain things to him. But on his arrival he felt too sick to visit the centre; apart from a tired, breathless canal-side walk, he stayed in his hotel room, watching television. It was useless. There was no way he could face Ian or anyone else in this state. He had to go straight home next day. And that evening as he groaned in his bed back in Edinburgh, Brian Kibby noticed something else. He had come out in strange spots, which were like nothing he'd ever seen before.

Dr Craigmyre, called in by Joyce Kibby, could not believe what he was seeing. — Birmingham, did you say? he shakily enquired of the supine Kibby, who groaned in weak affirmation. — It's only that . . . these look like mosquito bites to me!

Mosquito bites?

And Dr Craigmyre saw a strange thing as he looked at Brian Kibby. He saw a small blood vessel in his patient's cheek rise and burst before his very eyes. Kibby felt it as an itch, and his face twitched.

The champagne cork popped as Danny Skinner stuck its frothing neck to his lips, washing down the two ecstasy pills, which were drying out his mouth and throat. The crowd around him on the dance floor let out a cheer as he passed the bottle round.

Skinner had enjoyed a good Ibiza, at least to outside eyes. There he was, just having it every night, and on the beaches during the day also. He never seemed to sleep. But in a club called Space as the morning broke, Danny Skinner himself couldn't understand something. Why was it, in spite of Fatboy Slim hammering, pounding and tweaking the crowd of demented revellers into a frenzied liberation of the senses, he himself was thinking of nerds in anoraks? And how did it come about with the MDMA pulsing through him and with him swamped in a sea of hugs and smiles in a force of goodwill, party hedonism and, yes, pure love that he was mentally scouring the canals and backstreets of Birmingham? And there was just no way that he could envisage why it was that, when he had his hand inside the silk knickers and on the tight buttock of a breathtakingly beautiful girl from Surrey called Melanie, her lithe body bending around him, rubbing in slow rhythmic thrusts against his groin, her burning hungry lips pressing against his, that he was thinking of . . .

No.

Yes.

He was thinking of Brian Kibby, and what was happening to him right now!

Skinner convulsed, almost oblivious to the beauty around him, as he considered the grim truth: he always missed Kibby if they were apart for more than a few days, craved the morbid, knowing fascination of ascertaining how his rival was doing.

For although Kibby would field what he regarded as Skinner's transparently insincere enquiries as to his health, his desperation meant that he would inevitably confide in someone, usually

Shannon McDowall, with whom Skinner was still on good, if now non-sexual, terms. And Skinner would gleefully pump her for information.

No, Skinner was thinking about Brian, about the impact of his work. He was like an artist who couldn't see the effect of his strokes on the canvas. What would that marathon LSD trip have done to Kibby? What about those grimy, badly-cut-with-laxative lines of cocaine? Or that blithe, indiscriminate mixing of the grain and the grape? What about the bottles of voddy at Manumission, or the chasing of some brown on that yacht; that horrible tinfoil would surely play havoc with the weak lungs of his old adversary.

A weekend was enough to wait, enough to savour and anticipate the destroyed presence or the non-appearance of Kibby on those wonderful Monday mornings, truly the best time of the week for Skinner. A week was tolerable. But two weeks! It was doing his nut in. He had to know.

Unlike almost every other holiday visitor to the magic island that summer, Danny Skinner could not wait to get home.

23
High Concept

Her expression seemed preoccupied, even haunted, as she made her way through the crowded bar. But when she saw him beckon her to a seat beside him in the corner, Kay Ballantyne was stunned at just how well her ex-fiancé looked. — And you're just back from Ibiza as well, she said, quite awestruck, then wondered whether there was someone else in his life now. She felt a sense of failure, thinking, Why couldn't he do that for me?

Kay looks worn out, Skinner thought with a cold detachment. There were new lines around her eyes, deeper lines. This made him cast his mind back to the time he first saw her, at the fair on Leith Links. Her long, black shining hair, that red nylon bomber jacket, but most of all, her twinkling smile, her white teeth and her lovely dark eyes.

No. Not true. Most of all it was her arse, clad in those clinging, blue CK jeans as she raised that air rifle and shot at the targets. The way her tight buttocks moulded into those jeans as she shifted her weight. A dancer's arse, the girl from the dance troupe.

Now, sitting with her in the Pivo, almost two years after meeting her in that fairground, he realised that he felt a desperate urge to see her arse again. So overwhelming was it that Skinner engaged in a protracted game centred on getting her to remove her long brown jacket.

— Take yir jaykit off, Kay . . . he smiled, but Kay wasn't listening. She was going on about how it hadn't worked out with Ronnie, how he'd gone to pieces when they'd lost the baby, how she had too, but now she was fighting back and getting control of her life again, and starting a job, even if it was only waitressing.

Control of her life . . . who the fuck is Ronnie? Lost a fucking baby . . . ?

— Take yir jaykit off, it's hot in here, Skinner urged, now in a strange gasp.

— I'm okay, she said and smiled at him, in a way that disgraced and humiliated him. It made him think how beautiful she still looked. And something was rising in his soul as he was moved by her story.

Please take off that jacket . . .

Please go to the toilet . . .

So that I can critically scrutinise your arse, see for signs of overhang, for signs of collapse, so that I can gauge my mortality by your decline, as I do with everything around me . . . bringing to recall the words of the golden poet:

> *The flower in ripen'd bloom unmatch'd*
> *Must fall the earliest prey;*
> *Though by no hand untimely snatch'd,*
> *The leaves must drop away.*

But then Kay started to cry. Just a trace of a tear, then her hand rushed to her eye. For a few excruciating seconds Danny Skinner wanted to wind the clock back, so he'd be able to be the man who could hold her hand, who could raise his own hand to her face and brush away that heavy bomb of a tear. But in his sick loss he realised that he was no longer that man, could never, ever again be that man. Then Kay abruptly rose. — Sorry . . . I have to go . . . I have to go, she repeated, moving away towards the door.

Danny Skinner thought that he should go after her, to try and comfort her, but he nodded back sadly and watched her turn and leave. He looked at her arse, but it was still covered by her jacket. He could still go after her and he did rise, but he had to pass the bar first and, as ever, it got in the way.

It had been a terrible fortnight in the life of Joyce Kibby.

The laddie had come back so sick and ill from his trip down to Birmingham. He stayed only one night. For most of his holiday he's been lying around in bed or groaning on the couch. For almost two weeks! Now it's time for him to go back to work but he's just no able.

The laddie just isnae able.

On the eve of her son's proposed return to work, Joyce had wanted to get Dr Craigmyre out again. Brian could hardly breathe. He lay under the bedclothes, sweating and writhing. — Nae doctor, he gasped in a thin but determined protest.

The tears welled in his mother's eyes. — I'm going to have to phone in again, son, tell them you're not fit for work . . .

— No . . . Kibby muttered faintly, — . . . I'll be fine . . .

The mosquitoes . . .

Joyce shook her head. — Don't be silly, Brian, she said, turning on her heels and heading for the door, oblivious to her son's pleas. No way was he going to struggle into work again, as he had so many times before.

Now her son, swollen and gasping, was delirious and muttering nonsense. — Skinner and the mosquitoes . . . Skinner and the mosquitoes . . . he brought them to Birmingham . . .

Birmingham . . . mosquitoes . . . Skinner . . .

. . . not a mark on him . . .

. . . I need to get married . . . get to Harvest Moon *. . . Ann . . . Muffy . . . finish the game . . .*

Trundling down the stairs, Joyce dialled the city council's number, asking for Environmental Health, only to be snootily informed that the department was now called Environmental and Consumer Services. Brian had always told her to phone Bob Foy, but Joyce had grown to detest his surly lack of compassion with regard to her son's condition. However, there was one man she spoke to once, he had been so kind and comforting.

Danny, his name was, Danny Skinner.

Brian didn't like him and had made Joyce swear that she'd never call him, but she just couldn't face that Mr Foy's cold sarcasm. She gave Skinner's name to the receptionist who put her through to his extension.

Sitting at his desk, Danny Skinner was reading in *The List* about a new high-concept bar which had just opened up in town and apparently did not just push back the frontiers of service and comfort, but threatened to change the whole nature of how we perceived entertainment. And all one had to do to enter this new dimension was simply to turn up. With, of course, plenty of cash or a credit card. He didn't have plenty of cash, only red bills, but credit was readily given these days and he'd pay off his Visa with his MasterCard. Aye, he'd go along there tonight, thinking that it might serve to remove the increasingly pensive thoughts he'd been having.

He couldn't stop thinking about his recent encounter with Kay. It played through his head, over and over again. Maybe he should call her and make sure that she was okay. But she wasn't his responsibility, that chance meeting being the first time they'd seen each other in ages. No, you couldn't go back, you had to let go. There were other people in her life closer to her now. Let them sort it out. But what if . . . what if she was alone? No. That was his vanity talking. Kay was always vivacious, outgoing and popular. She never had any shortage of friends. That Kelly, the other dancer and her, they were tight.

But she doesnae dance any mair.

Naw.

Work. Clear your mind with work. Sometimes it has to be done.

He clicked on the VDU, dragged up an inspection report on another new bar-restaurant, which was due to open on George Street. Then he was distracted by the phone, an external ring and a bit too early for real business. Something made him rise and look out from his office on the mezzanine, and a wicked smile played across his lips as he saw the space at Brian Kibby's desk. He picked up the receiver. — Daniel Skinner, he sang.

Joyce Kibby's voice seemed to run a tortured obstacle course down the phone, from high to low, booming to breathless. — . . . I'm at my wits' end, Mr Skinner . . . he needs to keep his job, he fears being sacked so much . . . my daughter's at the university and Brian made a promise to his dad that Caroline would go through the university . . . he was obsessed with it . . .

That voice, though ragged, edgy and shrill, sounded like a symphony of angels in melodious choir to Skinner's ears. He was paying for his sister to go through college, Skinner thought in a weird sympathy, straddling across completely fake to utterly genuine.

Then he intervened, his tone reassuring, but, he thought, with the correct gravitas: — Hold on, Mrs Kibby, let me tell you not to worry about that. I know that Brian's had a lot of time off, but everybody here's aware of his illness and we're all rooting for him. Brian's got a lot of friends in this department.

— You're so kind . . . Joyce almost cried in gratitude.

— We need to cut Brian some slack, Mrs Kibby. What I want you to do is sit down and put the kettle on. I'll be straight round myself in about an hour. For goodness' sake, tell Brian to take it easy. I know how proud he is. And try to take it easy yourself, he said, in a burst of empathy.

For her part, the song Skinner was singing was also sweet, sweet music to Joyce Kibby. — Thanks so much, Mr Skinner, but there's no need, you must be so busy . . .

— It's not a problem, Mrs Kibby, he reassured. — I'll see you shortly. Bye.

— Goodbye . . .

Skinner stuck the receiver on the cradle. He didn't even realise that he was vigorously rubbing his hands together until Bob Foy came into his office and remarked, — Somebody's had some good news!

— Met a very sexy lady last night, Skinner said, — and she's just got back to me.

Foy's resultant gaze managed to encompass envy, contempt and admiration.

That Mr Skinner is a saint, Joyce reflected, as she put the phone down.

It's so uplifting, in these selfish, amoral times that there are still some good people left in this world.

Joyce Kibby took Danny Skinner's advice and headed for her kitchen, filling up the kettle.

What a genuinely nice, considerate young man. But why is Brian so hostile to him, recoiling every time his name's mentioned? I can't understand it. Yes, Brian was very put out when Mr Skinner was promoted instead of him, but why bear such a silly grudge when the man's been so good to him?

I'm going to visit my old buddy Brian Kibby! It's been over two weeks. The Balearic holiday was excellent, aye, but the consequences of it on Kibby's health have eluded me. Knowing what you gained was delicious, but seeing what you escaped was utterly delectable.

I've got two site visits to undertake but these will now require some delegation. The personnel business to attend to at the Kibbys' is far more pressing. It's going to be strange seeing a stricken and vulnerable Kibby in his home environment. And stricken and vulnerable he surely will be, as I put a good few away last night, with Gary Traynor and Alex Shevlane. There was a fair bit of charlie flying around as well: Kibby's sinuses would have taken one hell of a beating.

As it happens, Shannon's happy to get out of the office and take on the visits. She's cut her hair shorter, exposing her slender neck at the back. Normally I don't like women with short hair but it sort of suits her. — New haircut. Does that mean new felly?

She gives me that I'm-getting-shagged grin as she picks up the folder. Then she puts her finger to her lips. — Shhhh, she says.

More bedroom secrets.

As well one of us is doing okay: I need cheering up somewhat. I'm still reeling from the shock of seeing Kay, those disclosures of hers about new boyfriends and miscarriages that I tried not to hear, but also feeling well disconcerted about the lot of Rab McKenzie, who's simply fucking vanished of the face of the earth. I haven't seen hide nor hair of the fat bastard in the chicken run of the trashy clubs and grotty pubs that are our stomping ground.

Poor Big Rab, suffering from cirrhosis of the liver, now never able to drink again. What a nightmare. That's the problem with intoxication, it's an immediate state, belonging in the present. You can't live your life on the memory of previous consumption.

The idea of Rab being finished is too fuckin weird. It gets me thinking that we are roughly the same age and height, though not weight. Kibby's an inch or two shorter than me and eighteen months or so our junior. Therefore he must be in, or rapidly approaching, the same state of health. That finite resource that was Kibby's body – his nervous system, liver, kidneys, pancreas, heart – it must be well depreciated by now. At first my big consideration had been: what if Kibby died? Now this is becoming: surely Kibby will die. It's inevitable. Everybody does, but thanks to my antics, his time is almost certainly running short. And I can't – won't – stop living my life this way. There's no need, as Kibby is picking up the health tab. I'd be stopping simply to keep Kibby alive, which is a truly perverse notion.

But . . .

But it's murder. Aye, murder of a bizarre, other-worldly and thankfully unprovable nature, but murder nonetheless. And, speculating further: what happens, if, or when, Kibby does pass away? What becomes of this marvellous arrangement I've been blessed with? Will I be able to transfer the burden of pain on to somebody else?

Maybe once Kibby pegs it the spell might work on that little fucker Busby!

Or will I bloat out instantly into a monstrous, sick, wheezing wreck, dying in the street while a pristine Kibby, like Superman, thrashes his way out of a coffin? That, of course, would be the just scenario, but this shit's shown me far too much darkness, too much morbid fascination, to convince me of the possibility of any form of karma.

No.

The mundane and likely scenario is that I'll just have to bear my own burdens. Face up to my mortality. So be it, I can't complain, I've had enough of a head start.

But he can't die, surely not. I can't let him; it was never meant to be that way.

So I take a council van from the car pool and belt along the main Glasgow Road. I've never trusted myself with a motor, even though I passed my test years ago. Now, it's a piece of cake. I turn into the small housing scheme where the Kibbys reside. It's composed of old high-amenity council stock, in a good part of town. There are plenty of bungalows and the tenements are two or occasionally three storeys at the most. I soon locate their home; it has a new door with the number and a very strange wooden, almost gothic-style nameplate with the spindly branch-like letters somewhat hopefully spelling out KIBBY. I look at it for a second and feel my shoulders shake in nervous mirth.

I compose myself and ring the bell.

Mrs Kibby, or Joyce she said her name was, opens up. She's a thin and spindly woman, her face all sharp angles. Her eyes are like his, big and haunted. I scarcely have time to take in the sights, smells and noises of the Kibby household, but my first impression is that I'm in some old public building, like a specialist library reading room, or a dentist's waiting area. It's your standard low-ceilinged inter-war council dwelling with lots of wood-panelled doors, the type where the white paint always seems to be slightly yellowing as if it's magnolia but you know that it's not. The wallpaper is a pastel blue with a yellow floral design, the sort some cunts call 'rustic'. There's a particularly tasteless blue-and-green patterned carpet on the floor, but it feels like reasonable quality under the feet.

Mrs Kibby ushers me through to the kitchen, and puts on the kettle, bidding me to sit down.

— How is he? I whisper in hushed tones.

— Of course . . . Mrs Kibby says. — Let's pop upstairs for a minute. He might be a bit strange, you understand, he doesn't like people seeing him in bed . . .

— No worries, I nod serenely, belying a heartbeat which is kicking up in anticipation. — I'm loath to embarrass him, so I'll just briefly pop my head round the door.

Upstairs, Kibby's room stinks of a rank decay the like of which I have never encountered before. It's both manufactured and animal: a mixed aroma of stale chemicals and rotting flesh. I hear Kibby groan in the semi-darkness as his mother coos, — Mr Skinner's here . . .

I feel so nauseous with discomfort and excitement, I'm compelled to marshal myself with aggressive thoughts, thinking how that lazy fat poof can just lie there in his scratcher while the real men get on with the fucking job at hand.

— Ah cannae talk . . . go away, please, Kibby half growls, half groans in the small, darkened bedroom as I gleefully scan the *Star Trek* posters and lampshade. A laptop computer is on the bed next to him. The dirty cunt was probably online looking at porn sites!

— Please don't speak to Mr Skinner like that, son, he's come to see you! his mother splutters, looking apologetically at me.

If he was a dug we'd fuckin well shoot the cunt.

— Go away . . . Kibby pants.

Joyce Kibby starts to bubble and shake and I'm forced to grab both her trembling hands in mine and lead the poor woman out of the bedroom. But as we go through the door I turn back and whisper in breathless urgency, — I understand, Bri, buddy. But if there's anything I can do, anything at all . . .

A low growl comes from the bed again. I remember now where I'd heard such a sound before. As a child I had a cat called Maxy. Maxy got hit by a car and had crawled, both back legs smashed, under a bush of shrubbery in the garden across the street. When I'd tried to retrieve the poor wee fucker it really let loose; not a cat's hiss or spit, but a low, dog-like growl that shat me right up.

I guide the shaken Joyce Kibby back downstairs into the kitchen and sit her down, though she instantly springs back up and insists on making more tea. — I can't understand it, Mr Skinner. He was such a nice boy as well. It's really changed him, he even snapped at me the other night. And young Ian, who was his best friend, he fair sent him away with a flea in his ear. I was at the shops the other day when I saw the laddie and he wouldnae even stop and say hello!

— Maybe it's the nature of the illness, I venture sympathetically, — a sort of behavioural change, a psychological degeneration to match the physical decline. People at work have noticed that he's much touchier than he used to be.

— Behavioural change, Joyce Kibby considers, putting a cup of tea in front of me. — That's a good way of describing it, Mr Skinner.

— Still nothing from the doctors?

— That Dr Craigmyre knows nothing, Joyce Kibby spits in bitterness. — I mean, he's just a GP but we've tried every specialist known to man . . . she explains, but my attention is drifting in this warm kitchen until she gets it right back by dropping the bombshell, — You've all been so good, but it's over now. He can't carry on. We're going to see the personnel people and take medical retirement on health grounds.

I instantly feel feeble and nauseous. There's way too much milk in this tea. — But . . . he's a young man . . . he can't retire . . . he just can't . . .

Joyce Kibby smiles and shakes her head sadly. She is looking right at me now and I can see that she believes I really care. Like I'm as upset as they all are . . . and the thing is . . . I fucking well am. — It's the only way, I'm afraid, she sombrely replies.

— But how will you manage? I ask, and can hear my voice going high and fey in anticipation. I try to force some coolness into my demeanour. — I mean, you mentioned earlier that your daughter's at the university . . . you were so worried over the phone.

— I'm sorry, I did panic a bit, didn't I? Joyce Kibby concedes, smiling tentatively.

— No! I reply, loudly and abjectly.

But this woman carries on, oblivious to my pain, feeling the gloomily exhilarated liberation of somebody who's just made a terrible decision that had to be taken. — The other night, we all sat down and discussed it rationally. I know Caroline's at uni but she's got herself a job waitressing at nights so she can move into a new flat with some other students next week. We've got a wee bit put by to cover her fees. I'll be looking after Brian. I'm going up to social services this week to get leaflets to check out carers' allowances and benefits.

I open my mouth and almost start to speak, but no words come: I just can't think of anything to say.

— To be honest, I'm glad she's moving out. This is no place for a young woman. Joyce Kibby shakes her head sadly. — It used to be such a happy house as well. When my Keith . . . She chokes and dabs a hanky at her eyes.

I feel a terrible urge, an *ache*, to help . . . or is it that I just want to make myself indispensable to her so I can gloat at Kibby's demise? But I'm over at his mother's side, perched on the arm of her chair, my arm round her thin, buckled shoulders. — There, there, it's okay . . . I'm murmuring, although her posture irritates me, the way she's all sort of bent in. I want to put my knee into her back and pull her shoulders towards me. There's a strange scent from her and I wonder about her personal hygiene and I'm rising and breaking away.

— You're so kind, Mr Skinner, she sobs with real belief.

Now I'm thinking about my own mum, how distant we've grown, how this need I have to know about my father is tearing us apart. And I won't go and see her again, not until I've seen my dad first.

— I'm sorry, but I really should be making my way back to the office.

— Of course . . . Joyce Kibby finally lets my hand go. — I really appreciate you coming. Thank you so much, Mr Skinner.

— Danny, please, I say with a conviction so sincere and massive that it spooks me out.

So I leave the Kibbys' small council house in the Featherhall district of Corstorphine feeling soured and uneasy in what should have been the hour of my victory. After all, Kibby is history; nobody will look at him, the fat diseased cunt, living at home alone with his mother. Never had a ride in his life, and now completely unemployable. All thanks to me! Result!

Yet I feel uneasy and despondent. Everything is changing. Kibby can't do this to me! How will I be able to keep in touch, to see the effect of my powers on him? I . . . can't lose him. I've lost everybody else, never even had my dad. For some reason I can't lose Brian Kibby! But he surely won't really go through with it and jack in the job! It's all he's got! He's all I've got . . .

No, hopefully he'll think again, and maybe I'll help him by having some quiet evenings. The Filmhouse has a Fellini season coming up and I need to try and crack this MacDiarmid collection of verse I picked up last year; how shameful for a Scotsman not to have at least a working knowledge of that shit. I put it off when I found out the boy's real name was different, there's always something dodgy about cunts that change their name. Aye, maybe get some new DVDs, give poor Brian Kibby some respite.

24
Private Festivities

Summer rolled along, the festival coming and going. Like many locals Skinner always hated the start of it. Enthusiastic amateurs irritated him; they got in the serious drinker's way, taking up seats in pubs and blocking access to bars. Taxis one could normally flag down to take one speedily to the next drinking den hurtled by, full of incomers heading for a show. Yet he was always inclined to lament its passing, as the crowds meant plenty of late-night drinking and shagging opportunities.

But he'd missed all this, sitting alone, with his DVDs, the new *Planet of the Apes* making him buy and watch the originals in triple-boxed set. He went through the first three series of *The Sopranos,* almost tripping with sleep deprivation after one weekend marathon, and another Saturday he tried to watch the first complete series of *24* in normal time, passing out in the sixteenth hour. Aside from this, he had his poetry, finding himself particularly moved by the epic romantic verses of Byron and Shelley. Post-festival, he reasoned that if he ventured outside, he would be pushed back to the old bastions, the hardened bevvier's enclaves, with all the petty feuding and squabbles that would entail.

Too many potential scars for Brian Kibby to bear.

The worst thing was that winter would inevitably spin in quickly. But Danny Skinner had resolved that he was staying indoors. He was eating more healthily, and having read that the liver was one organ that could repair itself, was taking regular doses of milk thistle, to assist in this process.

His discipline had been good; he'd even managed to assemble and fit new wardrobes with sliding doors in his bedroom. But as the days following Brian Kibby's absence from work rolled on, Skinner was disconcerted that he heard nothing of his strange nemesis.

What was happening to that wee bastard? He should be fighting fit by now.

There was still no Kibby, although Skinner had abstained, stayed out of the pub and off the drink and drugs save for a few pathetic cans of beer one Sunday, when the Edinburgh football derby had been on Setanta.

Surely Kibby will be back soon!

Then, one terrible late afternoon, Bob Foy beckoned Skinner into his office and told him that it was official. Personnel had worked out a medical retirement package. Brian Kibby was leaving!

No!

This cannae fuckin well happen!

How could Kibby fucking well dae this tae me?

He had come to regard Kibby as his mirror, a road map of his own mortality. No, this surely couldn't happen. But the glee on Foy's face was telling its own story. Skinner could say nothing; he just nodded and went back to his office where he made a desperate call to Joyce, pleading for Brian to think again.

— Oh . . . thanks so much for you support, Mr Skinner . . . Danny . . . but our minds are made up. Just making the decision's taken a lot of the strain away. He's been so much better over the last couple of weeks or so since he's not been thinking about work.

No.

NO.

Everyone in the department was at a loss to understand why Danny Skinner, who constantly teased and harangued him, was so cut up about Brian Kibby's early retirement. — Danny's got a lot of hidden depth, Shannon McDowall explained to another new inspector, Liz Franklin. — He seems a joker, but underneath it all, he really does care.

And in his strange way he undoubtedly did, as Danny Skinner was plunged into a dark and grim despondency. His world was falling apart. It now seemed that there was no way that he could keep seeing Brian Kibby.

I need to see Kibby.

In the meantime, I'll teach him tae fuck aboot with me. I'll give that little shirker something to bleat about!

Thus Skinner headed round to a dealer called Davie Creed's flat and bought two grams of cocaine. Creedo had also washed up a couple of g's and they'd hit the pipe for a bit, Skinner capaciously icing out. As Skinner was an excellent customer, Creedo had flung in a few sweeties buckshee. Danny Skinner was soon rocking and ranting around town, and trawled several pubs before meeting some acquaintances and hitting a nightclub. Afterwards there was a private party up in Bruntsfield, where Skinner had never seen so much booze.

It's probably all been coincidence; I've been gieing ma mind a treat . . .

He picked up a bottle of absinthe and slugged from it like it was water, to the incredulous stares and gasps from those around him.

Ann. The very name seemed to say dependability. Loyalty. Somebody you could rely on who would never, ever let you down. Yes, she was still the front runner. Muffy was dangerous.

Brian Kibby stayed in his room, almost constantly on his laptop; either at his games or online. The attacks had stopped, but they'd left him ill, depleted and depressed. He lay on his bed, propped up on a bank of pillows, his iBook by his side. He was in no shape to go out or to see anyone, and had banned all visits. Fat Gerald was undeterred by this and constantly called him on his mobile phone, gleefully disclosing Lucy's supposed romantic adventures. These got so disturbing that Kibby stopped taking the calls, but then the texts started, and he couldn't resist reading them. Through red eyes, which burned like hot coals in his skull, he read the latest gloating note:

> Aviemore diff class lucy not seeing angus now but ken got off with her. Sly old fox! Shes turned into right slag giving it to anybody snogged her at disco didnt go further – wld catch something! Ken and i finished hyp hykers guide to grampians, will send u copy.

Kibby shuffled in discomfort against the pillows that held him up, and deleted the message.

That guide was my idea! Ken and me were supposed to be doing that together . . . and Lucy . . . he's old enough to be her father! The dirty, filthy wee whore!

Kibby hastily went back online and scoured pornographic websites until he found a girl who resembled Lucy, with the gold-rimmed spectacles. Her name was Helga, or so she said in a Scandinavian accent, which sang tinnily from the laptop speakers. Guiltily lowering the sound, Kibby then masturbated with all the ferocity that his sick body would permit.

Should have had that fucking wee ride . . . she wanted it . . . everybody else was there . . . you dirty wee slut . . . urgh . . .

Following his climax, more of his meagre life force seemed to leave him. He looked up to the ceiling as a dark, hollow sensation rose inside him and lisped, — Sorry . . .

More black marks . . . I was doing so well . . . how could I have been so weak . . .

He picked up the tie again and, hesitating only for a few seconds, bound his right hand tightly to the bedpost.

But that night, somebody really was punishing him for his sins. He awoke sweating, in the most howling, tortuous pain he'd ever known in his life.

Joyce Kibby, on waking to the terrible cries, rose and threw on her dressing gown as her heart thrashed in her chest. Running to her son's bedroom she screamed, — Brian, clicking on his light switch, only for the bulb to pop dead in one brief, insipid flare. — Brian! Joyce cried again.

There was no reply through the darkness, not even a faint sound. When she bounded across and clicked on his bedside lamp she found her son yellow and barely breathing. For some reason one of his hands was tied to the bedpost. –What happened, son, your hand . . . ?

Realising he was in no state to respond, Joyce ran downstairs and called the ambulance, then bolted back up to the bedroom. — Hold on, they're coming, she pleaded, as Brian lay groaning in soft whispers, sweat oozing out of every pore in his body. She untied his hand, then held it, feeling his weak pulse. She had no way of telling how long she sat like that with him before the ambulance came and took his perspiring bulk down on a stretcher, across the small front garden to the van. The air seemed to revive Brian Kibby slightly and he wailed, — Ah jist feel that ah've let everybody doon . . .

Joyce clutched her son's stout body in her thin arms. — There, there . . . don't be silly, son, we love you. We'll always love you . . . you're still my bairn, she cried. His skin was so yellow, and he complained of terrible pains in his back, like he was being hacked open.

25
Meat City

Foy's steak knife slid through the sautéed liver. Raising a forkful to his mouth, he let the succulent meat partly dissolve on his palate. The taste and consistency evoked the sweetness of honey. Foy cupped the goblet of a satisfactorily robust Napa Valley Cabernet Sauvignon in his hand and let its aroma rise in his nostrils. Times like these were what the Council Principal Officer lived for, the engagement of the senses purely for the art of *living in the moment*. They were totally priceless to him. But try as he might, Robert Foy could not ignore the bombshell dropped by his friend opposite him.

— I mean it, Bob, Skinner said, glancing down at his briefcase on the floor.

Lowering the glass back to the table, Foy sighed and let his mask of contentment slip. Gravity moved ruthlessly into the vacuum, forcing his heavy features south. — Danny . . . I feel the same every other day. Sleep on it, at least.

It was as if he had never spoken, as Skinner fished into his briefcase and pulled out an envelope. — It's all here.

Foy arched his brows, curled out his lower lip and picked up the beige envelope Skinner had thrust before him, opened it, read the enclosed letter. — God, you're serious, he finally conceded. — You really *are* resigning. You've already sent Cooper a copy, I take it?

— This morning, Skinner replied impassively.

— But why? Foy was incredulous. — You've no long been made up to Principal Officer.

What can I say to him? Perhaps something like 'There are billions of people on this planet and I'm getting a little fed up running into the same two or three dozen arseholes'. He might take it personally.

— To travel. See a bit of the world, Skinner responded matter-of-factly before elaborating: — I want to go to America. Always have.

Foy sucked in his bottom lip and frowned in concentration. — Well, you're a young man, and you've been here a while now. It's only natural that you want to get away. Spread the wings, he said chewing on another piece of liver, while sipping at his glass of Cabernet Sauvignon. As if to confirm to himself what he was experiencing, he read the label once more, reassuring himself it was really from the Joseph Phelps vineyard, in his book one of the Napa Valley's finest. — This is excellent wine, he contended, picking up the now half-empty bottle. — I can't tempt you?

— No, I'm trying to get in shape, Skinner said, putting one hand over the wine glass and raising the bubbling San Pellegrino mineral water to his lips with the other. — Packed in the fags as well.

— Well, it *is* a special occasion. Come on now, Foy urged, — it'll no do ye any harm! Look at young Mr Kibby, a teetotaller, now he's in need of a new liver. It just goes to show that all this health stuff is garbage. It's all in the genes. If it's got your name on it it's got your name on it, he said, taking another forkful of that sautéed liver.

Skinner looked grimly at Foy, recalling some verse, which he was moved to recite to his friend: — *Wine rots the liver, fever swells the spleen, meat clogs the belly, dust inflames the eye.*

— What's that shite?

— Aleister Crowley. And he's not wrong.

— You only get one life, Foy said, raising his glass again. — But of course youse papes think that you're going somewhere better afterwards!

— It's called California. Skinner toasted him with mineral water, thinking about how he had to get away from here, from all these drinking opportunities. They were all around, everywhere; those expectations that whenever you stepped outside your front door you'd partake of alcoholic beverage. It was as natural as breathing.

And he's over there, across the city at Little France in that hospital bed, where I put him: fighting for his life. Now I have to fight by his side. I have to be with him. That's the cruellest curse of all, what they never tell you about having such a nemesis, how inextricably bound up with them you become. How you eventually have to take on responsibility for them. A real enemy becomes like a wife, a child or an elderly parent. They determine your whole fucking life and you are never free of the cunts.

All these possibilities for intoxication: they were killing Kibby. But this was Edinburgh, Scotland. A cold city on Europe's periphery where it gets dark early, rains a lot and is dull for much of the year, he considered bleakly. Nominally a capital, but the major decisions for the lives of its citizens are still made miles away. All in all, perfect conditions for bouts of self-destructive heavy drinking, Skinner thought. Yes, he had to get away from here.

When he got home he sat down at his kitchen table. Choking with emotion, he wrote his mother a letter.

Dear Mum,

I'm sorry I was drunk when I was asking about my father. When I came round the last time, I wanted to apologise but Busby was there, and I think you'd been drinking yourself and it wasn't the appropriate time. Things have got a bit strange between us, but I want you to know that I love you dearly.

I've decided that I'm not going to ask you about my father again. I respect that you feel the need to keep this information to yourself, for reasons which I'll probably never understand. But I also need you to know, and accept, that I need to find out. I've just reconciled myself to the fact that it's going to be without your help.

I don't know everything yet but I'm closing in. I've talked to De Fretais, Old Sandy, tried to check out some of the old punks. Now I'm going to America to track down Greg Tomlin.

If you do feel the need to say anything to me, please get in touch by next Thursday, because I go away to the States then.

I want you to know that you did more for me than any two-parent family and that my desire to find my dad isn't intended to disrespect you or what you've done for me. I also want you to know that whatever the circumstances of your relationship with my father, nothing could undermine the love I have for you.

Always your boy,
Danny.

He stuck it in an envelope and went to put it through her door, but didn't want to run the risk of meeting her on the stair. Instead he went to Bev's Hairdressing Salon, and stuck it through the letter box, where she'd find it the next morning with the bills and flyers from the local takeaways.

He walked down to Bernard Street, to the squawking and scrabbling of the birds: the restaurants had left piles of garbage from lunchtime outside and the bin men were late. Close to the nervous, belligerent seagulls, an oily blue-black crow had commandeered a large piece of liver, which it pecked at.

Coming across a new café-bar, he went inside, sitting in the corner with a soda water and lime, trying to read the *Evening News*, but lost in his own dramas. His arcane considerations turned to San Francisco, where there was sunlight, outdoor life, body consciousness and health. One could surely do good things over there, things that didn't involve alcohol. How could Edinburgh compare? And in San Francisco there was Greg Tomlin, the Master Chef whom Danny Skinner was growing to believe might just be his father.

I hate the hospital: the nurses, the doctors, and the cheery porters with their banter. I loathe them all. They could do no good, none of them. My dad wasted away here, in this new state-of-the-art facility, this place that was fucked up before it even opened, like our Parliament, or our Hogmanay street party that never was. It seems that nobody does failure as consistently or as spectacularly as we do. It's the one thing we excel at.

Now my brother is in here and they're still doing no good. All their knowledge and their care, it just adds up to nothing. Because let's be honest about all this, our Brian is in a terrible state and they tell us that they're looking for a liver for him. Are they trying hard enough? Looking far enough afield? If we had the money would they try harder? Look harder? They might not find one and the transplant might not be successful even if they do. And might this disease not attack the new liver in the same way that it attacked his last one?

My big brother is going to die. I look at him and see his bloated, yellowing face, hear the wispy strains of his weak voice, with his eyelids shutting as he seems to drift in and out of this life. Most of all I smell that pungent scent; it's the rank stench that I associate with death. I recall its dusky ming oozing from the pores in my father's skin. I know it, I can feel it. And my mother, my poor mother, is going through everything she went through with my dad. Her world is falling apart around her.

All she does is pray. At least those creepy American boys seem to have stopped coming round. But she still stops by that small stone church on the grassy knoll every day. That place that bored the shit out of me every Sunday of my childhood, when I'd wake up with a skull-crushing dread of us going round there. Now she's even started going to that Presbyterian Free Church in town, the crowd she went to as a girl back in Lewis.

Sometimes I try to remind her about the odds that the doctors gave us against Brian surviving. I don't know why; it's like I'm bracing myself for the impact and I need her to know that she's in the speeding car with me. I just can't do blind faith any more. Probably never could. But she doesn't want to know, because that's all she wants, all she needs, and probably all she's got. She seems to believe that Brian's intrinsic goodness and virtue will protect him.

So I leave her in prayer and him in his disturbing slumber and exit the ward, heading for the coffee bar. They don't notice my departure, or maybe they do.

What was she doing here, in this place of worship, talking to this stranger, this man who had never known relations with a woman, at least officially, and telling him everything? And when she'd blurted out the story in its entirety and she asked him what to do, she knew that three Hail Marys would be enough for her, would make her strong enough to keep the secret.

She left St Mary's Star of the Sea, a place where she'd reluctantly been taken as a child, but always humbly sneaked back to in times of stress. Heading down Constitution Street and Bernard Street towards the Shore, sitting and watching the magnificent white swans cruising the black waters, Beverly Skinner asked herself what kind of Catholic she was, and what kind of mother.

But she'd said her piece to the priest. Tonight Trina was coming round and they'd drink Carlsberg Special and vodka and smoke dope and play the Pistols, Clash, Stranglers and the Jam, until poor old Mrs Carruthers thumped on what was her ceiling and Bev's floor with the broom, and all would be well again.

3

Exit

26
Surgeon

Raymond Boyce MD, ChB (Edin) addresses a group of senior medical students at the University of Edinburgh.

When one has made the study of medical science one's vocation and life's work, to encounter a new phenomenon is one of the most exciting things one can hope to experience. But it can also be among the most horrifying. In the case of Brian, a young Edinburgh man I have been treating, this is such a unique circumstance.

Let me recap: Brian is a young man who has an unclassified degenerative disease, which has attacked many of his main organs, but principally his liver. We know the crucial importance of this organ. A healthy liver cleans almost 100 per cent of the bacteria and toxins from our bodies. A liver overburdened and undernourished is thought to be the root cause of many diseases; now we acknowledge the probability that the majority of cancers derive from a liver operating poorly. And with the toxic chemicals in the food we eat, the water we drink and the air we breathe; with the alcohol, smoke, and the preponderance of prescription drugs, the liver's detox system is more overloaded and under greater pressure than ever.

We know that the liver is the one organ in the body that can completely regenerate itself when damaged. In fact, we have known this since ancient Greece. Prometheus, a character in Greek mythology, was condemned to be tied to a rock and have his liver pecked out by the eagles during the day. At night his liver would grow back, only for day to come, when he would undergo partial resection by the birds. This is early evidence of our intuitive knowledge of the liver's ability to regrow. As far we know it was not until the late nineteenth century that Canalis undertook the first scientific liver resection. Over a century later, we are still unclear as to the exact mechanism involved in initiating this regeneration process.

In the case of Brian, this becomes of secondary, academic interest. There is chronic scarring of the liver; advanced cirrhosis. Thus his liver has now deteriorated to such an extent that a transplant is necessary in order to save his life.

Only in the case of extreme and prolonged alcohol abuse have I witnessed such extensive liver damage. And this in a young man who is a non-drinker, and has hardly ever tasted alcohol. I must say that I was as cynical as the next person regarding the voracity of this claim, initially believing the youth to be in the extreme state of denial common to many who suffer from the affliction of alcoholism.

But I have monitored his behaviour under controlled conditions and am in a position to attest to his utter sobriety. At the same time I remain a reluctant witness to his saddening and mysterious physical deterioration during this period. Therefore, I can also vouch for the terrible emotional cost of this disease on Brian and his family. So we have largely discounted alcohol abuse as a source of Brian's degeneration.

Viral disease is an another common cause of liver dysfunction in Western society. Viral hepatitis, as students know, kills the liver cells. However, we have no evidence of any strain of this in Brian. This, too, can be ruled out.

There is a category of disease called autoimmune liver disease, where, broadly speaking, the white blood cells, instead of, or as well as, attacking bacteria and viruses, for some reason suffer a biological confusion and attack the liver. Many more tests have and are being done around this area.

As is always the case in medicine, or in any discipline where our knowledge is incomplete, we have a 'dustbin' category. This is the non-specific designation we refer to as cryptogenic cirrhosis. Sadly, this group is only recognisable by its effect – liver degeneration – and there is little in terms of a cure that can be afforded to sufferers.

What our tests have shown is that particularly during the hours of darkness, Brian's body experiences a great trauma, as if it is rallying to cope with a massive infusion of toxins. These seizures are fascinating, if highly disturbing, and our multitude of tests in this area will continue as long as the patient is able to bear them.

However, the degeneration of Brian's liver has now forced us to intervene surgically. The immediate danger is highly serious; as I have said, a transplant is now necessary in order to save his life. As soon as we have a donor for the liver the procedure will take place.

As I have stated, Brian's other organs are under attack from this condition. How long his kidneys can continue to function normally is open to speculation and we are trying to match new organs of this kind to him and we obviously have dialysis standing by.

One ray of light is that since his admission to the hospital his condition has stabilised somewhat. We can only hope, for Brian's sake, that this is the case.

27
Going Under

For the first time, as he contemplated his predicament, Brian Kibby was feeling real fear: stark and unremitting. The extent of his trembling panic was such that he almost felt as if his essence would shake free from his body. At first he had been too depressed at his condition to be really scared. Danny Skinner, this irrational dislike he had of him, it had been a distraction. Now he was alone, contemplating little other than his immediate fate, as his hair stabbed the back of his neck like needles.

Kibby looked across at the other men on his ward. They weren't like him. They were old, many of them so obviously chronic alcoholics. They generally came in two packages: either painfully thin and wizened, resembling outsize stick insects, or all bloated like jaundiced whales. And he was in here with them. Why had he, a previously fit, wholesome young man, who had led a blameless life, been singled out for this curse? Kibby lamented in sorry bitterness.

Why? And it was a curse, that mad old woman was right! But who would put a curse on me? Why would anybody want to put a curse on me?

His desperate thoughts were interrupted as Mr Boyce came round to explain the procedure for his proposed surgery. Raw despair got the better of Brian Kibby and his discoloured hand fastened on to the surgeon's cuff as he pleaded, — Why, Doctor, why me?

Raymond Boyce touched the back of Kibby's hand lightly, but even that was enough to shame him into withdrawing his grip. — Brian, you must try to be strong, he said firmly. — For the sake of your mother and sister, Boyce added, more irritated than he let on at being referred to as a doctor. As a senior surgeon, he was technically a 'mister'.

— How? How can I be strong? I've done nowt, Brian Kibby moaned in abject misery. — I'm twenty-one years old and my life's over already. I'm a virgin, Doctor, a virgin at twenty-one! Even before all this I was very shy with girls . . .

Shaking off a tingle in his cheeks, the surgeon puffed himself up and said, — One can never say what's around the corner in this life. You can't give up!

As Boyce departed Kibby thought of Lucy and specifically pulling the straps of that green dress from her shoulders.

Fuck Elder Clinton and Elder Allen and their stupid pamphlet . . . I'm dying here, I'm fucking dying! I don't want to die a virgin . . . that old crone, I should have given her it . . . but there's somebody else who should have got it . . .

And in the febrile but vivid eye of his mind, there was just Lucy and him, walking through the hills, her wearing that green dress and heels and carrying a large backpack, which she was struggling with . . .

The racking, bludgeoning cough of an old drunk cut through the stale, recycled air of the ward.

Shut up, you old cunt, shut up and die, it's just me and Lucy on the hills . . .

. . . and she was sweating with the effort in the sun. Beads of perspiration stuck on her forehead. Heatherhill was –

No.

Not Heatherhill.

— Fuck off, Angus, take a hyp hike somewhere else, Kibby sneered arrogantly, dispatching Heatherhill, who skulked off like a beaten dog, vanishing over the horizon. He turned to the sweating Lucy. — Two's company, eh, bitch?

— Brian . . . Lucy started.

— But they tell me you like the conveyor-belt stuff. Maybe after I've finished Heatherhill and Radden and Fat Gerald can come and get their fill. That's what you want, isn't it? A line-up for the boys?

Her eyes and mouth went wide again as Kibby's hand reached out to the straps of the dress, which conveniently sat outside the ones of her backpack. He pulled them down, and as she was wearing no bra, her tits sprang out towards him. Kibby grabbed them roughly for a bit before shifting his weight and pushing into her, at the same time sticking his leg behind her. Gravity and the rucksack did the rest, and she fell backwards on to the damp grass. Her long legs kicked out, but that only helped ride her dress up. She wasn't wearing any knickers.

— And as I go, I love to sing, my rucksack on my back, Kibby smiled as he unbuttoned his trousers and –

Ooooohhhh . . . oooooohhhhhhhh . . .

He felt his sticky waste pump into his pyjamas, seeping through into the hospital sheets and the mattress.

Fuck the hospital sheets.

28

AA

An asthmatic East European clerk, moving ponderously, shows me to my room. As the door opens it confirms my suspicions that this is a big mistake and I won't last a few days without drink or drugs down here. It's ten foot by ten, with a pish-smelling threadbare carpet, a sink, a set of sloping drawers and a bed with a wafer-thin mattress that creaks on urine-rusted bedsprings.

But this minging, rat-infested dive is the cheapest hotel I can find. It's on 6th Street just off Market, so at least it's central, albeit in an area full of flophouses and cheap liquor stores.

I lie down and sleep takes me off. It's trippy but in a nasty way: loads of crap, mundane dreams of missing buses, trying to find toilets and decipher sports results from newspapers written in hieroglyphic scroll.

But the next day I'm brighter and up early out of this grot-hole, walking the streets of San Francisco. Loads of alkies, junkies and crazy people are hanging out around here, desperate to make eye contact, to drag you into their dramas, no doubt with a view of levying an extrication fee. *Caelum non animum mutant qui trans mare currunt.* Fuck that parade; I've enough of my own shit going on to countenance interest in jakey affairs.

I head down to the Mission district for breakfast in a crêperie. Then it's along to Castro, then up to Haight-Ashbury, before going back down Lower Haight, where I stop at a British-style pub for some pasty and chips. Then, mindful of Kibby's needs, I leave it and head over to an American diner where I eat some grilled chicken with salad minus the dressing.

I'm browsing in a second-hand bookstore where I find a rare pamphlet copy of Arnulf Overlands' early poems in English. I'd lap this stuff up in Edinburgh; spend loads of moribund evenings with a bottle of whisky reading the bastards, reciting them over and over until I propelled myself out into the night, the clubs, with big plans for every fucker. Here, though, in the Californian sun, I see them for what they are: quite stirring, *völkisch* verses, pro-German in a post-Versailles, 'we wuz robbed' kind of way. Strange to think of poor Overlands ending up in a Nazi concentration camp. It may not make much sense here, but it will do back home where some other depressive will pay big bucks for it. The dingul sells it to me for three dollars: it could do a wee turn on eBay.

Enlivened by my decent fortune, I find an Internet café-restaurant called the Click Ass. It's a Japanese place and although the Scot in me craves the tempura because of its deep-fried qualities, I settle for the protein hit of the sashimi. The girl serving looks tranquil with collar-length black hair and glasses, her body long and slender. Guys always go on about lassies' curves, and they do rule, but what I like is good lines on a girl; a straight back, like an old-school amateur boxer. Going with a Japanese lassie, how good would that be? I smile at her and her face is as beautiful as a painting but unfortunately as immobile.

When I check my email it's all spam and disconcertingly I realise that it's hardly any time since I left Edinburgh although with the flight and time zones it feels like ages. I look up the San Francisco AA meetings online. There are pages of them, going on all over town, every day! I select one from the Marina, because it seemed a posh neighbourhood, and set off down there. I just couldn't face hearing the stories of the Tenderloin jakeys. I could get that shite back in Junction Street.

At least my wanderings have given me some sense of the city and its people. San Franciscans seem to fall roughly into three categories. There's the rich (practically always white) with their leisure time, nice diets, gym memberships and personal trainers, who are generally slim and fit. Then you've got the poor (usually Latino or black) who tend to be grossly fat as they can only afford to buy the cheap, highly addictive and calorie-rich TV dinners and fast food from the chains. The third bunch are the homeless, mostly black but with some whites and Latinos (though not too many), who, again, are usually very thin, because they can't even afford the shit that the poor eat.

The meeting is taking place in what looks like an old public building, like it should be a library but there are no books. It's some kind of community centre. It's older than most constructions in the area but looks well maintained. I head along what feels like a concrete-floored hall, unusual for San Fran as the buildings are generally wooden for the earthquakes. It's lined on either side with potted plants. Going through two swing doors I come into a wood-panelled hall full of people with their chairs in a semicircle. One guy, who looks Middle Eastern, with dark hair and eyes and a noon shadow, nods at me and to some of the free seats. The others barely register my presence.

The place is full of obviously well-to-do types, younger executives and the like, all Waspish. The chairman guy is the most ethnic-looking person there. I take a seat in between this suited gadge and this lassie, who's about my age. I notice that she's wearing a red-and-white T-shirt without a bra. It has the word GALVANIZE emblazoned on it. She has a prominent nose, which pokes out from this long, black, curly hair. On closer inspection she looks sort of Mediterranean, or maybe even Latin. The guy is a nondescript yuppie; short hair, dark-blue suit, glasses, polished black shoes. I would be phenomenally shocked if he and I ever exchanged a meaningful word in our lifetimes.

People get up and spin out the usual hard-luck stories, which I find hard to follow due to a thickness in my ears, although I hear this girl hiss the occasional 'bullshit' or 'get real' under her breath. Being a Leith boy and raised by a punk rock mother, I'm inordinately impressed by that kind of behaviour. During the coffee break, I note that she's alone so I approach her. — You don't seem too impressed by this, I smile.

She looks at me for a bit, raises her coffee to her lips and shrugs. — It's cheaper than rehab, that's all you can say, but you have to put up with all the fundamentalist bullshit.

— What do you mean?

— This holy stuff, but also this life abstinence shit. I mean, yeah, well, I admit things got out of hand drinkwise with me. But I will drink again at some point, once I get it under control. One drink is not a matter of life and death.

— Aye it is, I tell her.

— Oh that is so gross, she says, and I can see that she has a slightly square but pleasing face, and I like her green eyes and tight slash of a mouth. —You really fucking want Jesus in your life that much?

I have a vision of Kibby on the cross. Then I think about that porn video of Traynor's, *The Second Coming of Christ*, probably because this lassie looks a bit like the bird that played Mary Magdalene's mate in thon threesome scene and I involuntarily giggle a bit. — I want alcohol out my life, I explain, straightening up.

— Well, just watch that you don't get Jesus in the package: that's the way it is with those freaks. Substitute one dependency for another.

Aye, they fair got Jesus right in the poor bastard's package in that flick. That was where one of the crucifixion bolts went through! Sair yin! I pucker my lips and blow out air at the thought. — That would never do, I tell her.

— You gotta watch, she says, looking shiftily around.

I'm thinking that I need friends over here, and sober and female fits the bill nicely. — Listen; speaking of dependencies, I shake the styrofoam cup, — this coffee is garbage. How do you fancy going for a proper one somewhere when the show is over?

She raises her eyebrows and looks challengingly at me. — Are you hitting on me?

— Eh, I'm from Scotland. We don't really do that there . . . I mean, members of the opposite sex can get on socially in my culture without any other agenda, I lie.

She contemplates this bullshit for a moment and says, — Okay, that would be cool. She smiles and I get a wee flutter in my stomach. Ya beauty! —Your accent is pretty neat. I've never been to Skatlin, she tells me.

— Beautiful country, well worth a visit, I contend in a smug flush of patriotic pride, as the meeting resumes. — I'm Danny, by the way.

— Dorothy, she says, as we take our seats for round two.

The stories still seem as disturbing, but Dorothy and I make faces at each other occasionally, usually in response to some of the more banal comments coming from the floor. I'm only vaguely aware of what's going on in the rest of room until there's a pop in my ear, followed by a warm and wet sensation, like I'm bleeding. When my hand goes to the source I feel a hot gunk leaking on to my fingers. My heart rattles in my chest in panic, as I fear that my brains are melting, but it's only earwax. I rub it surreptitiously under the chair. Excusing myself, I go to the toilet where I wash my ear and the side of my face till the waxy smell is gone. I take a piss and it's the same colour and consistency as the wax.

Meltdown!

Disturbed, I go back inside, but at least I can now hear what's going on. Then, after the serenity prayer, we head outside together. It looks like I've a new friend, which is fine by me!

— Do you have a car? she asks.

— No, I just got here yesterday. I'm staying at a divey hotel on 6th Street, I tell her, possibly unwisely.

— God, that is as divey as it gets, she says, lighting a cigarette. — I'm just over here, she points across the street towards a smart, white convertible. — Let's get out of this neighbourhood.

We climb into the motor and set off, Dorothy's hooked nose poking out in profile from that shaggy mass of black hair.

I clock all these bars on 16th Street as we head into the Mission district. Every one of them seems to beckon a warm invite. Thank fuck I have another recovering alcoholic on-side. — Parking in this town is crazy, she says, with an air of intense concentration and she's into this space as soon as somebody pulls out. I've never seen a bird reverse like that before.

As we get out the car we're stopped by Socialist Workers Party people protesting about the war in Iraq. I didn't even know that they had revolutionary socialists in America. — Bush is the axis of evil, a small, thin girl wails at us. A guy by her side earnestly thrusts a leaflet into my hand.

— I like Bush, I tell them, waiting for their faces to pucker in distaste before hitting them with the punchline, — it's just that cunt in the White House I can't stand.

Dorothy shakes her head and pulls me away from the bemused paper sellers. — You can't say that here, she says as we head down the street.

— Aye I can. I know San Francisco is a liberal town but there must still be some people who like Bush. I mean, I don't, I hate all politicians. They're aw cunts.

— No . . . you used *that* word again.

Apparently it seems to be more offensive to use that word over here than it is to buy a handgun. I decide that I've committed enough faux pas for one day and will try and keep my fucking big gob shut.

We go into the coffee shop. It's dark, with big hardwood floors and is finished with a collection of easy chairs and low tables, giving it a ramshackle but slightly decadent aspect. — Nice place, I say.

— Yeah, Gavin and I . . . my ex, used to come here when we stayed in this neighbourhood.

I thought I could smell rebound. No doubt I'm giving off the same whiff myself. Well, not quite with Kay cause at least me and Shannon used each other as buffers. In fact, I've got through quite a few buffers lately. I'm looking at Dorothy thinking that it seems so strange just sitting drinking coffee with somebody. With a lassie. Outside of work! Impossible to contemplate in Edinburgh, at least at this stage of the relationship. The coffee has a pleasing aroma and a strong, bitter taste.

Later, we go for something to eat, in a Mexican restaurant on Valencia called Puerto Allegrie. It's very busy and the food is great. Dorothy tells me that her surname is Cominsky and that she's Polish on her father's side and Guatemalan on her mother's. — What about you?

— Eh, as far as I know it's bog-standard Scottish. If there's anything else in there it's probably nothing more exotic than Irish or English. We don't really bother about ethnic backgrounds in Scotland. Our own, anyway. Incomers, like asylum seekers, we tend to give a hard time for being different.

I think of Kibby, and people like him. We do give them a hard time for being different; especially if we're depressive, alcoholic, self-loathing bullies. But the crucial point is that we're other things as well. We can be better.

God, it is so fucking weird sitting with a girl and no drink or drugs to disinhibit. Dorothy and I are at angles to each other in these seats, no table between us. But it also feels good to have a clear head. And how long has it been since I've not had that streak of rancid alcohol fire inside, searing me from gullet to gut?

— You look thoughtful, she says.

— So do you.

— I'll tell you what I'm thinking if you do the same first.

— Okay, I say, reasoning that I know where this is going, — I was thinking that if we had been in a bar and had had a couple of drinks to unwind then I probably would have tried to kiss you.

— That's nice, she says, and leans slightly into me. I don't need any more of an invitation and close the rest of the gap as we snog for a while. I'm thinking, fuck me, that was easy. All the times that I've had to get half pished and shell out for about six Bacardis to get to this stage! What a fuckin waste. When we come up for air I ask, — What were you thinking about?

She smiles, and there's a cool, evaluating edge in her gaze. — I was thinking that it would be cool to make out.

Dorothy drives us over the Golden Gate Bridge to a place called Sausalito. We pull into a lay-by and watch the sun go down. I soon learn that 'making out' is a generic term that covers snogging but stops short of shagging, though for a minute I thought that I was in as it was easy to get each tit, braless as they were. I'm in no hurry though, quite content to play the long ball game. A gentleman should never try to get his hole on the first date. (Unless he plans that there won't be a second.) That's got to be a universal cultural rule.

It's only when she drops me off at my hotel that I sense my luck has definitely changed for the better. As a couple of jakeys tap persistently on the window of the car and a woman with balloon-like legs pushes a shopping cart past us with her worldly goods in it, Dorothy turns to me and says, — Jesus, you can't stay here.

— I should try and find somewhere else tomorrow, it's just that I was jet-lagged and wasnae thinking straight. I'll be okay tonight, I tell her.

— No fucking way. Dorothy shakes her head and pulls away from the kerb as one of the jakeys shouts something about Vietnam and yuppie bitches and she gives him the finger back. — Fucking asshole.

It's not like I asked him to fight in any goddam war, she scowls, and then she takes me back to her pad up in Haight-Ashbury.

The building reminds me of where my ma's best mate Trina comes from, that part of Pilton they called the Swedish hooses. They're constructed from the same width of timber and it's even painted the same grey as thon Pilton gaffs used to be. Works a fuck-load better in sunny California than it did back home. Fortunately some brainbox in the local authority cottoned on to the fact that painting every dwelling in a Scottish housing scheme grey may not be the best way of boosting local morale and I think they're all done in bright colours now. Inside, Dorothy's gaff is amazing: the rooms have high ceilings and are painted in bold, strong tones, although I only really get to see the bedroom with the impressive wooden-vented built-in cupboards as she takes me straight there and fucks my brains out.

Normally after a good shag I'm right off into nodland, I've never been one for post-coital inquests, but with the jet lag, excitement and a heavy chicken burrito in my guts, sleep just isn't happening. I can't help thinking, as I watch her in a deep slumber, that this is one hell of a result for Mr Daniel Skinner, native of the port of Leith and former Principal Officer of Edinburgh Council.

I look out from the window of her pad on Upper Haight, over to Castro and Twin Peaks. Then I get up for a bit, watch some television, marvelling at how there can be so many channels, all with pure shite on them. I soon feel the tug of sleep and get back into bed with Dorothy. She stirs and I kiss her, then I feel her wrapping herself around me. I get a feeling that she doesn't want me to go anywhere fast, and I must say, I'm in no hurry.

In the morning we have breakfast, then Dorothy goes off into her work downtown. She runs a software consultancy service, Dot Com Solutions. I've already decided that I like her very much. She has a very American kind of confidence and way of addressing the world that appeals: not as narky and sarky or just plain depressed as many British women, but she won't stand for any crap either. I like that style: confrontational, but diagnostic, rather than aggressive. In Britain we tend to disrespect the other person in the transaction when we get into the ascendancy. Can't fucking well help but sing when we're winning when a wee bit of decency and humility might –

Fucker.

Now I'm hoping that Brian Kibby is singing like a lark. Mindful of the time difference, I head out and buy an international phonecard, thinking it would be a bit of a liberty to use Dorothy's blower. It takes yonks; you have to dial about nine hundred digits. Eventually, I get through to the office in Edinburgh and ask for Shannon's extension. — Shan, Danny.

— Danny! How's California?

— Great. I'm having an excellent time. How's Brian? Any news?

— As far as I know he's just going under the knife now.

As I hear her words I feel a tearing pain across my back. My head swoons, my stomach is nauseous and the receiver I'm holding is sliding out of my sweating hands. — Shan . . . running out of credits . . . I'll email you . . . bye . . . bye . . .

I hear her concerned goodbyes as I slump down on to the pavement, my body heavy and head spinning. I lie groaning for a while, unable to speak, nobody stopping to help. I'm totally immobilized; all I can do is squint up at the warm California sun in my face and try to breathe slowly.

I close my eyes and seem to be falling into nothingness.

It's so cold and I'm quivering in these robes on the gurney as they wheel me into the ante-room of the operating theatre. The anaesthetist tells me to count backwards from ten. But it feels like this stuff has no effect on me: I'm shaking with nerves, even through the pre-med, which is meant to relax me! And it doesn't look like him! It doesn't look like Dr Boyce under that mask! — Doctor . . .

— It's okay, he goes. — Just count. Ten.

Nine.

Eight.

Seven.

Six.

Fi –

I'm outside my house in Featherhall, passing the park, then about to go into my stair when I see Angela Henderson looking at me. She looks like she's been crying. — I thought we were pals, she says to me.

You're not a nice girl you're a bad girl and I was told to keep away from the likes of you.

But she seems nice sometimes.

Angela is sobbing and she turns and walks away from me. I can see her head bent and her blue cardigan and her checked skirt and tights with the patterns up the outside leg.

I try to go after her but I hear a voice and I stumble and fall.

YOU'RE NOTHING, KIBBY.

I'm not nothing . . .

I'm no . . .

I'm no . . .

But I'm falling fast into a void of nothingness . . . I don't know where I am now. It's not home, it's just nothing and I'm still falling . . .

. . . then the air around me seems to thicken into a gas, then moisture, then a liquid which becomes a syrupy substance, slowing my descent and I then think I've hit a glass floor but it starts to give and my velocity picks up again and whenever I try to shut my eyes I can't, I just keep seeing objects and people, then faces, hurtling past me and I'm going to hit something and smash to pieces like a broken glass . . .

. . . and I'm bracing every fibre of myself for impact before I realise that I'm slowing down once more . . .

I feel a sickening sensation, all around me, inside me . . .

I've gone away. I know I have . . .

Somewhere so far away I'll never get back.

Too far out. Too far gone.

I want to go home.

Then the voice comes. It seems to be from inside my head but it's not my voice, it's not my thoughts. I'm thinking that I don't want this, I don't want to be here, I want my mum, my sister . . . my dad, I want things to be like they were before . . .

It sounds like my dad.

It doesn't look like him because there's nothing to look like, but it is him. He's telling me to hold on and that I'll be alright and that Caz and Ma need me.

I'll hold on. I'll keep on.

It was one of the three large municipal crematoriums in the city. Like the other two, it had a chapel, a garden of remembrance and a small graveyard. A strong sun had been blazing but now it had gone behind a dark cloud and Beverly Skinner was suddenly cold. She looked up, trying to trace the cloud's trajectory, hoping that the sun would soon re-emerge.

She laid the bouquet of flowers down on his grave, on the simple headstone she'd visited on so many occasions, always in secret solitude. And even after all this time, the tears still flowed readily. It wasn't natural, it wasn't right; she'd only been a girl at the time. But he was such a great guy, and it was horrible it ended like it did. Could she have saved them all this pain if she had just forgiven him, there and then? If only she hadn't gone with –

No.

It was too late now, she thought, looking down at the tombstone.

DONALD GEOFFREY ALEXANDER
12 JULY 1962 – 25 DECEMBER 1981

She looked back up at the clouds and thought about her son. Wherever he was, she prayed that he was safe, and that he would forgive her. The cloud around the sun now seemed to be breaking up and dispersing, but looking north she noted that darker, stormier ones were coming in from the horizon.

I look out towards Potrero Hill and see some dark clouds gathering. Chances are that it would rain heavily over there while we'll be basking in the sunshine down here. Microclimate. I love the light here; it's busy and it swarms, shimmers and pours, earning its keep as the main player in the city's constantly unfolding dramas. Not that I get to participate in them; I never see enough light with the goddam shifts I work.

Paul always says that I put in far too many hours, and all I can do is remind him that I'm a chef. A chef works while others play. And now he's going and I've got a book coming out.

A lover or a book; a life or a career.

You never think of life in terms of those choices. They seem possible to defer for a while but they always catch up with you. Then you realise that you've already made your choices without intending to.

Now I have to leave my kitchen in Luis's care, not to go to Key West with Paul, but to go on the road to promote this book. Go forth and promote Greg Tomlin! But I wasn't that interested in Greg Tomlin on television or Greg Tomlin in publishing, all I ever wanted to do was cook. But that's what I do now: I present and I publish. Why is it not enough simply to cook food people want to come along to eat and enjoy, and run my own kitchen?

Because something happens to you when you're in demand. You can't stand the thought of not being in demand any more. So you do what they want you to do.

And my kitchen and my bedroom: how they disintegrate around me, as my smile gets bigger and my heart emptier.

I'm lying on a soft bed. A bed of my own bones, which seem to have melted and merged into the mattress. I feel naked except for something covering my groin. Kay is standing above me, wearing that grey-corded short skirt I always liked, and nothing else. She hikes the skirt up and her pubic hair is shaved . . . no, waxed, smooth, porn-star-style. — You never shaved . . . even when I asked, I croak, but she puts her finger to her mouth and says, — Shh . . . secrets . . . Then she bends over me with her long, black hair and her small firm breasts moving into my face like a sensual flood . . . she smells fresh and warm in the sun . . .

I hear noises and squint my eyes open and the golden light blinds me.

I'm on the pavement, where I've been slumbering like a booze-filled, kip-exhausted jakey. I manage to haul myself up. Maybe it was the jet lag, maybe the heat. More likely the pish withdrawal finally hitting home, or the lot at once. Perhaps over here I don't have Kibby to take all the bad shit; maybe he's out of range.

Despite the heat, I'm cold and shaking. I stagger on to the main drag where I pick up a cab and get back to Dorothy's. I'm weak the rest of the day, lying on the couch, going through the *San Francisco Chronicle*, hopping around six hundred channels of shite where the best I can come up with is *Changing Rooms* on BBC America 163. Thankfully Dot comes back early but she heads straight to her little office at the rear of the apartment. — I gotta do some shit, honey, she says semi-apologetically, like I'm already the fixture in this gaff I most certainly aspire to becoming.

— Cool, babes, I wink cheesily, belying my nausea. Eventually I get up and out on to the porch to take in some air. Reasoning that my blood sugar might be low, I go back inside and pour myself an orange juice, make some coffee and toast a bagel, which I have with banana and peanut butter. I then scrape off some of the peanut butter as it has a very high fat content and that might not be good for our Mr Kibby right now. Suddenly thinking about the caffeine, I take the coffee through to Dorothy.

— That's so sweet of you, honey, she says, — I run on this stuff, she informs me before turning back to her screen.

I take the hint and depart, returning to my food, thinking about Brian Kibby, how even here across the pond, I still have his fate in my hands. Or maybe not. Maybe the damaging power of the hex really is weaker from across here, or maybe he's completely out of my range. Out of sight, out of mind, away from damage. Maybe my future's here in San Francisco with Dot Cominsky.

I'm sitting at the marble-topped table, browsing through the paper, hoping some life comes back into my listless body. When I get to the book review section, I see this arresting caricature and I can't believe it! It's a man in a chef's hat, with a dark curl snaking out from under it across his forehead. He has two black eyebrows, a pointed chin and the Dick Dastardly pantomime villain moustache.

I could be . . .

Fuck sakes.

I'm instantly energised. It's Greg Tomlin, which I knew before I looked at the heading and sub-headings, which herald a full-page review of his new book. This cunt has to be my old boy! I know it! At the bottom of the article it says that he's doing a book signing at this place in town tomorrow night. I'll be there!

29
Van Ness

The bookshop is a brightly lit L-shaped place in this small modern mall on Van Ness Avenue, a wide road full of snarling traffic that rips right through the city centre, the cold pin in the butterfly. I felt I had to level with Dorothy about my quest to find my father. She was excited and intrigued about my disclosures, and she told me that she'd once dined in Tomlin's old restaurant. She was very keen to come with me, but I reasoned that my first meeting with Greg Tomlin should be between just the pair of us.

Before I left we made love. I went down on her, working her hole with my tongue, then her flaps, then her clit, holding back, teasing slightly until I felt her hips thrusting into my face and the pressure of her hand on the back of my neck increase exponentially. — You goddam fucking tease, she said and I think I said something like, — Mmmmmhhh, in reply, but I kept her on the boil for a bit before bringing her off repeatedly, taking a delight in her orgasms like they were exploding pearls on a string. Then I went up and started to fuck her until we hit a viscous, demented climax together, prolonging it till we were spent and lay prone on the sweat-drenched bed. She was blown away by it: I left her doolally, mumbling like a drunk in the semi-dark behind the closed Spanish colonial shutters. Being off the peeve makes you much better at shagging, no doubt about it. It's not just to do with the energy levels being higher; as it's the only form of enjoyment left you want to make it last, which means the lassie needs to have loads of orgasms before you blow your muck.

I'm still slightly dazed myself as I take my seat among a crowd of largely older dinner-party types, only about fifty or so of them. There are one or two bored yuppie housewives in the mix as well. I'm still flicking through the copy of Tomlin's book that I got earlier: worried like fuck about the homosexual shit it's peppered with.

My troubling speculations are broken as Tomlin comes out to polite applause and sits in a big leather chair, joined by another guy in an identical one opposite him. The guy introduces himself as the bookshop manager. As my eyes hungrily scrutinise Tomlin, I can't help feeling more than a wee bit disappointed. Bad enough him being an obvious fag, but he also looks too short-arsed to be my old man. The author photo on the cover is obviously an ancient one, and it's evident that the caricature in the newspaper is based on it. The black, curly hair of the Tomlin of this vintage is going grey, as well as thinning and receding. He has a florid coupon lit by burst blood vessels. He's either the demented, stressed-out chef with high blood pressure, or no stranger to the good life. Whatever, he certainly isn't my cool, tanned healthy Californian dad.

After a brown-nose intro from the store manager, Tomlin steps up to the lectern to read. He starts off jerky and not too confident, but he soon finds his stride, performing engagingly as the crowd warms to him. He goes on way too long for my likes but by the time the question-and-answer session comes along, Tomlin's your archetypal, self-consciously witty queen who's OD'd on Oscar Wilde.

There isn't that much cooking in the book. It's largely a memoir with a prominent highly personal sexual content; a buftie version of some UK tabloid Page Three slapper's *Cocks I Have Known*, recounted in words of more than two syllables. I was obviously most interested in the Archangel stuff, particularly the lines:

> That wonderful den of chaos, gossip, and scandal became, and I suppose still is, my spiritual home. I learned to cook and a lot more besides: I had carnal relationships with kitchen and waiting staff of both sexes, all ages and all races.

I would expect that a certain green-haired punkette would have been one of them. The thing is, do the dates fit? Where was he and, more importantly, who was he fucking on Sunday 20 January 1980, nine months before Daniel Joseph Skinner popped into the world?

Despite the nature of the book, the audience questions are mundane, focusing on the token recipes and the best ways to cook this or that, with no one particularly interested in the biographical details. Tomlin seems a bit disappointed, but what the fuck does the cunt expect? He's just a cook; these cunts get all up themselves but at the end of the day all we want from them is a decent fuckin scran. We're after their kitchen secrets, not their bedroom ones, although I'm the one exception in this audience. Blissfully it doesn't go on, as Tomlin has product to shift and at nearly forty bucks a throw it doesn't come cheap.

I stall to the back of the line (as the Septics call a queue) and hold my copy up to him for signing. Tomlin looks even rougher, older and shorter from close up. Yet his eyes are lively enough as he regards me, taking the proffered book. He has a gold ring on his finger with G.W.T. inscribed on it. — Who shall I make this out to? he asks, and his accent is a gayer, posher version of the character Mayor Quimby in *The Simpsons.*

— Just sign it for Danny, I tell him.

— Wow, he says, — that's a Skarrish accent. Edinboro, right?

My accent snares the old fruitbat, and after putting up with his obligatory crap see-you-Jimmy impersonations, we decide to go for a drink. He asks me to excuse him for a second while he has a brief communication with the guy who was chairing the event. I browse at some books for a bit, flicking through Jackie Chan's autobiography. Then the buftie chef comes over and says, — Ready for that drink?

I nod and follow him towards the exit. The chair gadge waves at us, so does another of the bookshop staff who looks a mincing ferret of the highest order, pouting in a disgruntled manner at me like I've just nicked his bird. Tomlin smiles and gestures back in departure but says under his breath, — What an obsequious asshole that man is!

As we walk down Van Ness Avenue my head is spinning. I can't see how this man can possibly be my father and I can't see how he can not be, both at the same time.

For months now I've felt death around me, closing in on me. I fear that I'm becoming like Moira Ormond and all the other girls at our school whom I used to detest. The goth lassies who read too much Sylvia Plath and listened to too much Nick Cave and wore too much black clothing. They were my enemies and I wonder what their lives are like now. Was it just teen angst or had they known all this kind of stuff I'm learning about now, all this death and decay? Surely some kids must experience loss in their adolescence and it must affect them. I wish I'd taken the trouble to find out before being so dismissive.

Thinking about Moira, the strange beauty in her luminous eyes, her imperturbable determination to disregard the maltreatment we would dole out, a horrible anxiety comes over me, rising from the pit of my stomach, going through my spine and spreading up my back like a shivering rash. I have an urge to contact her and apologise and tell her that I understand now, but she'd probably just look blankly at me or laugh in my face. I'd deserve no less.

Two porters stand at the entrance of the hospital, smoking cigarettes. An older, chunky guy and a younger, thin one. As I approach they're all big smiles but my sadness seems to transmit to them and their faces slacken and drop. I'm like a plague of despair. Misery loves company and I'm dreading seeing my brother.

When I was in yesterday, with all those tubes going in and coming out of him, his face gnarled with tape and the monstrous breathing hose spewing from him like an emerging parasite caught heading off to richer pickings, I thought that he would never wake up.

My shoes click almost indecently across the floor against the morgue-like silence of the ward. The first thing I'm relieved to see is that my brother is still alive. And it's better; death's grip seems to have loosened just a little. Now, as I move by his bed, I can see that his eyes are open. At first I thought my own were playing tricks on me, but no, he's looking right at me, regarding me in an almost guileful, collusive way. The tubes are still coming out of him and he can't speak because of the mask taped to his face but he winks at me, and his eyes are full of strength, hope and a life in him that I've not seen for a long time.

I find his hand under the covers and squeeze it. He squeezes back. Yes! It's strong, and maybe I'm seizing at hope but this isn't the grip of someone who's dying! I'm smiling now, not noticing the tears in my eyes until they start to roll down my cheek. I grin at him and, clearing my throat, say, — Hiya, Bri. Welcome back.

30

Fags

Don't take this the wrong way, I've nothing against fags, you know what I'm sayin? In fact, watching two guys getting it on is really cool. Not a turn-on, more really fucking beautiful, cause those gay guys are always so goddam buff.

Danny's thin, but he's built, like he works out himself. And he does all this moisturising and flosses his teeth. And I gotta admit that boy is hot in the sack. Knows how to use his fingers and his tongue.

— Where did you learn those tricks, baby?

— Leith, he says. — It's just one big school of sex. Our motto is: persevere.

— You certainly do, honey, I tell him. God, he's a dreamboat. But this shit about his dad kinda gets me. An overrated quest for sure: I never knew my old man, although we grew up in the same house. He was at work when I got up for school, still there when I went to bed and worked most of the weekends. The asshole divorced my mom when I was eight. Now he sometimes calls when he's in town on business and takes me to lunch. Or tries to: I always insist on splitting the check, which really makes the jerk uncomfortable. We talk about our jobs, his new family, the menu, and food in general. So Danny never knew his father. It's maybe best like that. Sometimes it's like, well, what's to know?

So now we're at this Tomlin guy's restaurant, this fag chef who's supposed to be Danny's old man. Or maybe not. Tomlin is a fag okay, although that counts for nothing nowadays. My ex, Gavin, well, he was a faggot who went straight, then went back to being a queen again. So yeah, I'm not that well disposed towards ambivalents these days.

They're talking about this bar that he and Danny's mother worked in, back in the late seventies. Danny was born in '80, a couple of years after me. The dates fit. But instead of answering the sixty-four-thousand-dollar question, 'Did you engage in unfaggot-like activities on Sunday 20th of January 1980 in Edinboro, Skatlin?' this Tomlin guy just seems to get off on shit-talking every asshole he ever worked with.

I'm getting a little frustrated listening to this bullshit. Tomlin is one of those guys who is dripping with need from every pore and Danny can't see it. And he can't see it because he's blinded by his own goddam need. He seems to *want* to believe this asshole is his old man. I'm impatient and irritated and I know it's not my place, but the champagne he's provided, which Danny's refused, is going to my head. Whatever, I cut to the chase. — So, Greg, did you and Danny's mom – what's her name, Danny?

— Beverly, Danny says curtly, and he's looking disapprovingly at my drink, which I do not need right now. I remember Gavin used to say, 'Why can't you keep your mouth shut when you've had a drink?'

I got a lot of satisfaction in telling him that the problem wasn't drink and my open mouth, but drink and his open asshole.

— Did you and Beverly Skinner get it on?

Tomlin rolls his eyes and looks wearily at me. He's the kind of secretly woman-hating queen who likes fag hags that make a fuss of him but can't deal with the sort of bitch who'll be upfront about his bullshit. — It's very hard for me to be definite, he lisps. — It was an exciting time, punk was big, we were all young, it was pre-Aids and all very free and easy. We drank loads of booze and had some very wild parties.

I feel my eyebrows arching and I'm thinking: yeah, you and just about every other sucker in this universe, pal. It's called, like, *youth*. Tomlin gets my vibe and looks pretty damn uncomfortable, his wide fag eyes seeming like refugees from someone else's face.

— What I'm saying, he clears his throat, — is that I slept with a lot of people round then, men and women, and it's more than possible that Beverly was one of them, he says, and it sounds like a fucking recital to me.

— So you could be my dad, Danny nods.

— It's more than possible. Tomlin smiles the TV grin of the

professional sleazebag. I'm sure I saw this creep once on that food channel. Making some faggoty dish, Hawaiian Roast Macadamia Nut Tempura or shit.

This smells like bullshit to me. I want to say, well, let's get it on with the DNA testing then, asshole, but it's not my place as Danny has to see through this bum himself. But he seems to want to believe it so much, and I don't want to see my tartan toy boy getting hurt, so I'm gonna watch this Tomlin motherfucker. 'I slept with a lot of people.' Bullcrap! I'm not as old as he is, but unless you've got dementia, you always remember who you've fucked. And this creep looks nothing like Danny, nothing at all.

31
Gymnasium Days

Dot and I have been having a great time, hanging around, shagging and smoking dope. But her work seems to be frustrating her right now and she's a bit moody when we go out to eat. In the restaurant, she doesn't like the table or the decor, and you suspect that she won't find the food up to scratch either. — Post-dot com, she winces huffily in this now admittedly slightly tawdry yuppie pad in the Mission.

Yes, it is like it's just past its best and they've sort of given up. A stain on the ceiling from water leakage has only half-heartedly been painted over. One cracked pane of glass in the partition dividing the dining area from the kitchen has not yet been replaced. I point these blemishes out to Dorothy. — That's pretty gross, she frowns. — If a place like this stops trying . . . then her face ignites in an almost theatrical smile as a waiter approaches and she almost sings, — . . . but the food is always so-oh goood!

Dorothy has been conditioned, perhaps by recent experiences, to disapprove, but has a sort of in-built self-regulatory mechanism. Almost in spite of herself, there is music in her soul and it plays loudly. — The seafood is a good bet. Try the warm lobster Martini with cilantro, orange and champagne sauce.

— Anything less boozy? I ask, considering my friend across the pond.

— God, it's only flavouring, and in any case the alcohol boils away when they reduce the sauce. Don't be so goddam obsessive, she scolds, as her eyes involuntarily stray to the bottle of red wine at an adjacent table. The waiter is making a meal of pouring it and the recipient couple are really hamming it up; all long, languid post-coital grins and husky purrs of appreciation. I look at Dorothy's face, her greeny-hazelnut eyes, eager and hungry, and

I'm thinking, maybe I should up the ante a bit here.

Then she catches me and gives me a gently urging look but the waiter is by our side and my moment has passed. He hands her the wine list and she waves it away with an upturned palm saying, — We won't be needing that, and the poor cunt's eyes bulge like a sad dog who's been beaten for something he doesn't understand.

The finality of it all makes me feel both elated and totally despondent. I look at the menu again, and the beef looks nice, a soy-glazed fillet with an eggplant and pepper marmalade, but that means red wine. Curse you, Foy, curse you and your education. Red meat always means red wine to me. Chicken or fish, I can resist the temptation of white and stick to the sparkling mineral water, but red meat . . .

— You don't look too comfortable Danny, Dorothy says, almost challengingly.

— Eh, I'm fine.

— You didn't really want to come out, did you?

— I . . . I start but find myself drying up. What can I say? I can't tell her or anybody else about my relationship with Kibby and alcohol. They'd think I was a nutter; twisted, delusional. Maybe I am. It doesn't make any sense, and from here even less than before.

— You have to face up to temptation. We still need to go out. We can't spend our lives cooped up in my apartment.

I smile, thinking about it. Is that to be the nature of my disease, locked up in exile in her pad in order to protect Kibby, on the other side of the world, with his new liver? And why not stay, marry Dorothy, get the green card, take citizenship classes, swear allegiance to the flag, maybe head out to a small town in Utah, get hooked up with some religious order, live a pish-free existence. Wife, kids, car, church, home, garden. Isolate yourself from the evil out there, the devil in the bottle, the demon drink.

— I know, I know, it has to be done, I agree. — You're a very cool girl, Dorothy, I tell her. Then I add, with feeling, — You make me strong, make me better than I am.

She leans back in her chair, slightly uneasy. — You're weird, she says, and yes, I am. I look across to the couple beside us and if I whipped that glass of wine off their table and knocked it back I'd probably be firing a bullet into the back of a poor wanker in Edinburgh, Scotland.

— Sorry. I'm a bit socially awkward at times, but I just wanted you to know . . .

— But nice weird, she smiles.

After the meal we go straight home, and to bed. The sex is very good and the endorphin rush certainly won't do Brian any harm. It's also the closest to a ride the poor wee cunt's had or is likely to get for some time, at least on *that* side of his body. Lying with Dorothy, Kay's ghost has receded, perhaps supplanted by a strange guilt that I didn't do better by Shannon or, for that matter, some of the lassies I went through quite callously back home.

There's always fucking something. Scotland: the recipe for disaster. Take a cut of Calvinist repression, sprinkle on some Catholic guilt, add lots of alcohol and cook in a cold, dark, grey oven for three-hundred-odd years. Garnish with gaudy, ludicrous plaid. Serve with chivs on the side.

The next morning I rise early and check my email for news of Kibby. There's nothing, but Gareth has got in touch.

To: skinnyboy@hotmail.com
From: gar.f-o@virgin.net
Re: Goodbye Mister McKenzie

Hello Danny

I hope you are having a great time in sunny California. I'm very sorry to be the bearer of bad news but I have to tell you that Robert McKenzie died suddenly in an accident in Tenerife. He was on holiday there with some of the boys. Dempsey, Shevy, Gary T, Johnny Hagen, Bloxo and I think Eric the Red and Peter No Tool were there.

Details of Big Rab's demise are sketchy right now.

Sorry about that. Things have been dull here otherwise. It's very cold. Took the kids to see Hibs v Alloa Athletic in the CIS Cup. 4–0 Hibs. Easy street.

Best wishes

Gareth

Big Rab . . . he must have gone back on the peeve with the boys, the silly cunt . . . or maybe he got done over by a rival firm out there . . . naw . . . you have to be very fucking unlucky to get seriously injured in a football row . . . Brian Kibby unlucky . . .

His heart might have packed in, but he was supposed to be in good nick now . . .

I decide to head outside and call Gary Traynor. It's a scratchy call as it's on his mobile, but I need to get the details.

— Gary, Danny. Heard about Big Rab.

— Skinny! he crackles exuberantly.

— Aye, Big Rab, I remind him.

— Sair one.

— Fuck sakes . . . how?

— He was in the fitness room at the hotel, pumping iron on the multigym. The big man had been daein that twenty-four/seven since he went off the peeve. Bloxo and Shevy wir wi him, ye ken what they bouncer types are like for the weights. Anyway, this fuckin mosquito comes along and bites the big felly. He suffers an allergic reaction and goes intae shock.

— Fuck sakes . . .

— The boys see the mozzie. It's that full ay his blood that it can hardly fly. In true bouncer fashion they escort the fucker tae the door . . .

— Traynor, what are you talking about? I laugh. This cunt takes nothing seriously.

— Just a wee fuckin joke tae illustrate how big yon mozzie cunt wis! Anyhow, they took the big man to the hospital but he died shortly eftir, eh. Extreme allergic reaction, one in eight million chance. Poor Rab. Done by a puny insect.

— Could've been worse, I say, getting into it and we join together in unison, — might have been a Jambo!

I feel a shudder of guilt, but the big felly would have liked that one, of that I'm sure.

— Ye gaunny get back ower for the funeral next week? Gary asks.

No, that would be too much of a potential piss-up for me to endure and I have to find out more about Greg Tomlin, to see if he really is the one. — I'll see, I say, — but it might be hard to get a flight at short notice. Will you send flooirs for me?

— Nae bother. It's a long wey. The big yin would have wanted ye tae enjoy your holiday.

— Aye . . . cheers, Gaz, I say, letting the phonecard run down.

32
Pulled Up

The shafts of brilliant, golden light pour in through the gaps between the blinds in Dorothy's front room. That great Oasis line springs to mind: *Nobody ever mentions the weather can make or break your day.*

I'm checking out her extensive CD collection. Homesick, I look for something with a Skarrish bent, but there's no Primal Scream, Orange Juice, Aztec Camera, Nectarine No. 9, Beta Band, Mull Historical Society, Franz Ferdinand, Proclaimers, Bay City Rollers . . . the only thing I can find is one tartan cover. The artist is 'Skarrish' American country and western star 'Country' George McDonald and the album is called *Savin' For Another Rainy Day*. I play the title track. It has a catchy chorus:

Ain't expectin nuthin no good's ever gonna come my way,
So I'm just savin for another rainy day.

It's followed by a number called '(You Could Get) A Bottle of Whisky (For the Price of That)' and then a cover version of George Harrison's 'Taxman', which seems heartfelt and inspired.

Dorothy comes through wearing a green bathrobe with her hair wrapped in a towel, and catches me reading the sleeve notes. — Oh, you found Country George's album. I got that in Texas. He's Skarrish.

— What's his story then?

— Oh, he just got out of jail. Something to do with the IRS, I think, she explains as she files her nails. — I keep breaking these bastards, she informs me, — it's the keyboard.

Dorothy's working today, and I've got to go and meet Greg for lunch. I get ready at my leisure and hook up with him at a café in North Beach. It's a busy place, brightly lit, full of strip pine and chrome, one of those sorts of gaffs crammed with yuppies and students with laptops and folders, all beavering away, more like a fucking office than a coffee shop. These cunts that say all self-righteously: I work from home. *Do they fuck* work from home, they're in everybody's faces; in cafés with their laptops, in the streets and on the trains barking into their mobile phones about orders, sales profiles and consolidated accounts, forcing us all to reference their boring shit. Soon there will be no division at all between work and leisure. Each shithouse will have a built-in computer terminal with webcam so that you need never be off-line or uncontactable.

Greg looks that orangey sunbed-tanned way and orders a San Pellegrino, and I follow suit. — My head's in a mess, I tell him. — It's so much to take in.

— Tell me about it, he says in a way that makes him seem really gay, as in an ultra-howling buftie boy. It strikes me that I've never really known a homosexual before (though Kibby's rectum might sing a different tune) and it's now quite possible that my old boy is one. Or is that really true? Growing up there were probably a load of repressed bufties who realised that a place like Leith wasn't the most fertile ground for their sexuality and who shot the craw to some other metropolis when the hee-haws got to critical mass. All those slightly funny-spoken guys who kept themselves to themselves then mysteriously vanished . . . — It's strange, your being gay . . .

— Not to me it isn't. It's stranger you being hetero.

Cheeky auld shit-stabbin cunt. But I think about this for a second. — Naw, but in the books you play up your heterosexual side. You come across as a top shagger, but now you say that you were with that Paul guy for ten years.

Greg looks uncomfortable, then stares quite forlornly at me, running a hand through his thinning hair as if to sweep it out of his eyes. I suppose there once was enough of it for those purposes and that old habits die hard. — In the beginning I wanted to please my family. My own father was, is, I suppose, a south Boston Irish hard ass who hated to see men cook. He thought just that in itself was enough to qualify you as a pansy. So back then I cultivated a very macho, hetero image, but it was a lie. I realised I was messing my life up by trying to please a bigot I didn't even like or have anything in common with. I didn't really know myself until I came to San Francisco.

I'm starting to feel a bit uneasy here. — What about Scotland? You were really a friend of De Fretais?

Tomlin grins evenly. — Only in so far as Alan has friends rather than favoured rivals.

I nod in acknowledgement. De Fretais is the sort of person whom it's really hard to imagine anybody genuinely liking. At least I know that cunt couldn't be my old man, not with a gut like that. It's Hobson's Choice, but I've rather have a screaming queen than a fat fucker any day of the week. At least I know I won't go *gay* in later life. But did he ride my ma?

—You know, I came to Edinburgh meaning to stay for a weekend but I liked it and got a job at the Archangel. Strange, because it's probably the most inhospitable place in the Western world for homosexuals, or it was at the time, but that was where I sort of came out. I drank in the Kenilworth and the Laughing Duck.

— So you were at the Archangel in January 1980, but?

— Oh yes, most certainly. I left to get a job in Lyon in France, then went on to California . . . he says evasively, then stops in his tracks. — Danny . . . there's something I have to tell you. He looks steadily at me. I know this fucking look, from Foy when he was my boss, from teachers at my school, from polis but most of all from barmen after last orders. It's not a good look. Not at all. — I never went with your mother. I never went with a woman while I was in Edinburgh.

I feel that the laminated floor has been taken away from under my feet, as well as the joists it rests on, and the dirt below it. There's a sensation of falling, subsiding. I look away and see the rubber face of a pansy waiter, laughing and lisping. I turn back to Tomlin's stupid, gaudy puss. There's a ringing in my ears that means I can't make out what Tomlin says next, I just see those rubbery fag lips pursing. How could that cunt be my father? —You never, ever went with a woman in Scotland? I say, and my voice seems dead in my own ears.

— No, but I knew a few, and there was one woman I was quite friendly with. Your mother, Bev.

My ma. A punk fag hag. Surprise, surprise.

— But she had a boyfriend at the time. She would meet him when they finished their shifts. I think he was in the catering industry, I –

— Who was he? I ask in searing urgency, feeling my guts ulcerating.

— He was a nice guy as I remember, but I can't recall his name . . .

Anger is now stiffening my posture as I take a deep breath. — What was he like?

— It was a long time ago, Danny, Tomlin says, now looking concerned, — I just remember that he was a nice enough young guy . . . I don't recall much else –

— Try!

— I can't . . . I genuinely don't remember, it was over twenty-five years ago. I've led you up the garden path enough, I'm not making any more up. Danny . . . I'm sorry that I can't be the person you want me to be . . . he almost begs, then puts his head in his hands. — You know what the weirdest thing is?

I say nothing. He's the weirdest thing, that fucking monster.

— I had a picture, of your mum and her boyfriend, back at my house but Paul . . . he took my photos to Key West . . . picked them up by mistake when we split and he left . . . He looks up at me with tears welling in his eyes. — God, this all sounds so impossibly lame.

— Fuckin right it does, I say standing up. Fuckin sad old poof, I think, stringing me along just cause he wants his fuckin arse, and for a few seconds I hate Tomlin as much as I've ever loathed anybody. But I know where hate gets you and all I do is nod thoughtfully and exit, leaving the simpering chef at a table waiting on two orders of food coming.

I'm out and walking fast down the road, feeling it important for me not to let him come after me, because if he does I'll have the cunt. I'm tearing down the hill, down Grant, through Chinatown, watching the vans unload their produce into the shops, seeing all those Chinese people going about their business. I'll bet half of them have never even been to China but *they* all know where they come from. The sun is strong and I'm walking for ages and at some point I cross Market and make the mistake of going off the main streets and it's broad daylight but deserted, with old abandoned warehouses all round, well, almost deserted as the boy jumps out of a doorway and stands in front of me. — You! Gimme your fuckin wallet! Now!

Fuck me, the boy has a sort of a gun in his hand, well, no sort ofs about it, it *is* a fucking gun, and he's my age, maybe younger, perhaps older. It's hard to tell. He's not badly dressed but his mouth is blistered and scabbed. He seems to have the bug-eyed crackpot stare, but it could just be the excitement. — Don't have a wallet, mate, I tell him quite smugly, like it's some kind of private joke. That cannae be a real gun surely, it seems too fuckin wee.

The boy is thrown a bit by the accent but he spits out: — Just gimme your fuckin money, you asshole, or you'll be sorry the day your mother ever had you!

I'm thinking of my mother, Tomlin and all the shit I've had to put up with. — You've never seen my mother. I'm sorry already, I laugh, and then challenge, — Shoot. Gaun then, fire away. I extend my arms. — I'll take a fuckin bullet. Gie's it then, cunt!

The ultimate test.

— You fuckin . . . you . . . he gasps, his primal eyes way short of human. His life is as much on the line as mine. If he doesn't use it he knows I'm going to take it off him and just blow the cunt away. I know he can see it in my eyes.

He cocks the gun and I think of Kibby.

The ultimate test.

No way . . . too much despair, too much loss.

No, no . . .

— No, don't . . . take my money, please, don't shoot him. Don't kill him . . . I fall to my knees. I'm dry-sobbing heavily, hyperventilating, and my breath is catching in my chest as I urgently tear the notes from my pocket and stretch my arm out towards the guy, my bowed head staring at the cracks in the pavement.

I wait for the bullet, thinking of my Old Girl, Kay, Dorothy, just waiting to hear it smash into my brain, surely too much damage with the exploding bone fragments and splattering grey matter ever to be reassembled by the crazy nocturnal alchemy of the spell and transferred to poor Kibby . . . Joyce coming into the hospital and seeing his brains blasted out across the pillow . . .

I'm waiting . . . I'm waiting . . . then I feel the notes being torn from my hand.

—You are one sorry fucked-up asshole . . . the young guy shouts, as he pockets the money then nashes away down the road, only once looking back at me still on my knees. He doesn't know that I'm praying, praying for that boy's soul. Praying for Kibby's, and even for my own. Yes, for my own. Beware the man who cries, he cries for himself alone. No, not just himself . . . it's the love prayer.

LOVE

LOVE

LOVE

LOVE

Insanity laughs under pressure we're breaking why don't we give love one more chance –

Why don't we –

Nothing seems to be happening but the sun suddenly comes out from behind the top of the building, spreading a blinding light where before there was only cold shadow. Agitated and elated, I lurch to my feet, walking unsteadily on to the main drag of Market Street then on some more, until I find the Click Ass Internet café.

To: skinnyboy@hotmail.com
From: shannon4@btclick.com

Danny,

First, I'm really sorry to hear about your friend Rab. I never really knew him. I only met him that once in the Café Royal but he seemed a nice, big friendly guy.

I've been in touch with Brian's mum and he seems to have come through the operation very well. He's still in intensive care but it seems to have been a success, and touch wood, it's like the new liver is taking.

I need to tell you that I'm seeing somebody, I have been for a while. I kept it from you because it's someone you know and I worried that it might piss you off. It's Des, Dessie Kinghorn. You were inadvertantly Cupid, it was the night of the karaoke at the Grapes where you behaved badly and chased us both away! We were distressed and on our own in the street. We got talking and went for a drink and it just happened slowly from there.

I don't really want to get involved in any dispute between you and Des, as it's your business. But it's now got right out of hand and you should both put it behind you. Funnily enough, Des agrees. He showed me some old pictures of you both as wee boys and he's still got a lot of time for you.

He was also, obviously, very upset at what happened with Rab McKenzie.

I know from your emails how concerned about Brian you've been. You really are a lovely person, Danny, underneath the hard, jokey act. I know that it all comes from your background regarding your dad and I hope you'll be able to resolve that to your satisfaction.

You know that you always have a friend in me.

Love
Shannon XXX

Jesus fuck almighty . . .

All you can do is type. Type and gape, spending our whole lives addressing the screen: inspection reports, telly, video conferencing, downloading tunes, email . . .

To: shannon4@btclick.com
From: skinnyboy@hotmail.com

Shannon,

Glad to hear that Brian's rallying. We never hit it off and I was probably a bit too hard on him due to my own fucked-up-ness. I really do pray for him.

Thanks so much for your kind comments about Big Rab. The Big Man will be sorely missed by us all.

Your comments about me were very insightful and generous. I value your friendship greatly. I must admit that I was a bit worried when we became more intimate and was concerned that it would affect us as friends. I feel that I was a bit cavalier at that time when we were both emotionally quite raw. I just want you to know that I meant no disrespect to you. It was just that we were reacting to the same thing but in opposite ways, yours being the appropriate one.

I was surprised, but not unpleasantly, to hear about you and Des. I now have to hold up my hand and admit that I was selfish about the division of the compensation money. I still maintain that Des, for his part, was highly unrealistic, but that doesn't negate my own selfishness: you can only take responsibility for your own behaviour. Anyway, I don't want to go into all that again here. Please convey my sincere apologies to Des for my behaviour that night. He's an excellent guy who once was a very good friend, and I hope he can be again in the future.

I wish the two of you all the best.

Love
Dan X

Dessie stole my fuckin bird! Cunt! Wonder how much that rates in his insurance man's mind? A grand? Two grand? Does it even make us square? He'd probably say something like, 'Naw, youse were really just only fuck buddies so it's only assessed at five hundred quid, plus incidental celibacy damage, but I understand that you rifled the fat tart behind the bar shortly after this, which negates that particular clause.'

Ah well, at least he'll be better for her than I was. I was a bit of cunt to Shannon, but she wasn't exactly Ms Sweetness and Light either. But I'll be better to Dorothy, cause here I'm free from Kibby's curse, his curse on me, which pre-dates mine on him. Here there's none of that irrational, all-embracing hatred, distorting my life, fucking everyone I come into contact with. Here I can do good things and we can both be at peace.

But first I have things to sort out. I have to know about Kibby and this shit that's going on with us. And I have to find my old man, and he sure as fuck isn't out here. Tomlin is off the list, gone the way of old Sandy. I have to bite the real bullet and confront De Fretais, and beat it out of that slimy fat fucker if necessary.

I have to go home before I can do anything else.

4

The Dinner

33
Autumn

Edinburgh in autumn seemed to him a city stripped of its pretensions, cut back and pared down to its essence. The festival tourists had long gone, and it had little appeal for anybody passing through. As it grew cold, wet and dark, its citizens shuffled around its streets like frightened novices in a boxing ring, anticipating punches from every quarter but unable to do much about it.

Yet he felt that the city was more at ease with itself at this time than at any other. Freed from external definitions dubbing it the 'arts capital of the world' (festival) or the 'party capital of Europe' (Hogmanay), its populace were simply allowed to get on with the prosaic but remarkable business of everyday life in a North European city.

And Danny Skinner had flown back into town feeling more disorientated than ever. For the entire flight he was thinking about Dorothy, the traumatic tearfulness of their departure at San Francisco airport shocking them both in its intensity. His mind danced with the wonderful possibilities and cruel improbabilities of a long-term, long-distance romance. But his quest was incomplete. Greg Tomlin had been removed from the list, but he knew that his mother had been in some kind of serious relationship. While it warmed his heart to think that he might have been the product of a real, if fleeting, love, rather than a cider-and-speed fuck, he couldn't bring himself to confront her again, at least for the time being. De Fretais was the one he wanted.

When he got back to his cold flat in Leith, he switched on the central heating, then took some sleeping pills and knocked himself out. The next day he called Bob Foy, finding out that De Fretais was currently filming in Germany. The next person he phoned was Joyce Kibby and he was still jet-lagged when he met her for a coffee in the St John's café in Corstorphine.

Skinner learned that Brian Kibby was healing nicely, with the new liver doing its job. And while he listened to Joyce prattling on, he wanted to tell her, *It's all because of me that he's fucked, but I've sorted him, I've not been drinking*, but of course he couldn't do that. All he could do was think: Why can't I like Joyce Kibby more? But as she sang, — We're getting him home, Mr Skinner, Brian's coming home next week! he felt himself sharing her joy.

Giving her hand a spirited squeeze, Skinner trumpeted, — This is great news! And please, for last time, it's Danny.

And Joyce Kibby blushed like a schoolgirl because in ways she couldn't quite understand she really liked young Mr Sk-, Danny.

I head on the number 12 bus from Corstophine back to Leith finding myself glowing in elation at the improvement in Brian Kibby's health. It gets so intense that I opt to alight at the West End, to pick up a copy of the Gillian McKeith book, *You Are What You Eat*. I intend to use it as the basis to make up a sensible proxy diet plan for him. I also pick up more milk thistle from Boots. Later, at the Internet café at the foot of the Walk, I send Dorothy an email detailing some fairly advanced sexual propositions. Hopefully they'll float her boat and at least I'll have it in writing if she backs off later.

I idly trawl the Net for news of some of the local punk bands I know my mother was into, reasoning that ageing punks might even have better recall than ancient chefs. I find a piece on the Old Boys, which interests me:

THE OLD BOYS' REUNION GIG

The Old Boys were an Edinburgh punk quartet who gigged on the local circuit from 1977 to 1982. Most punk bands belted out rabble-rousing anthems of teen rebellion, urging hedonistic escape from a corrupt state and nihilistic acts of depravity and self-abuse in order to combat the boredom of modern life. The Old Boys, though, led by charismatic singer Wes Pilton (Kenneth Grant), took a very different tack.

They sang highly reactionary songs about social decline; lamenting permissiveness, drug-taking, single parenthood and the irresponsibility of youth. They extolled the virtues of wartime Britain: heroic boldness in face of the enemy, *esprit de corps* and an empire on which the sun never set. All this was cause for concern, particularly as the band played every number with deadpan conviction, making them outcasts on the punk scene, an anathema to its self-professed radicalism. However, some mavericks saw them as the true spirit of punk: bold enough to take the piss out of themselves and antagonistic enough to wind up their own audience. They played at being every old bore you had ever met in the pub, criticising your fashion sense. They would dress as their grandads, the sort of proud old man who would wear his best suit to go down the local on a Saturday. Wes Pilton sported a dodgy tash and wore a flat cap and a mackintosh, with a Remembrance Day poppy in its lapel all year round. In between songs he would talk incessantly about his pigeons.

Their first album, *The Old Boys*, brought them some recognition beyond their home town, although opinion was divided on the band and their motives. Were they simply mocking and undermining the generations before them in the cruellest possible manner, or were they a reactionary Trojan Horse within the castle of punk?

The Old Boys themselves never gave the game away, though several critics were pushed too far by the inflammatory and racist single 'Compulsory Repatriation'. In response to a near riot at Nicky Tam's Tavern which, it was claimed, was instigated by Anti-Nazi League members, Wes Pilton came out with the classic quote: 'Has nae cunt in this fuckin doss ever heard ay irony?'

This summed up the Old Boys. They were a band ahead of their time: postmodern piss-takers in a more deadpan, serious, political era. Perhaps due to the frustration that nobody really got them, they started to parody themselves, with attendant declining returns.

It seemed as if this sordid chapter signalled the beginning of the end for the band. They staggered on until the inevitable split came in 1982 when Pilton was briefly sectioned under the Mental Health Act and committed to the Royal Edinburgh Hospital in Morningside. Mike Gibson, the band's guitarist, left to study accountancy at the city's Napier College. Steve Fotheringham, on bass, was the one Old Boy who stayed in the music business. He now works as a DJ and producer. Pilton returned with a solo album entitled *Craighouse*, a concept offering based on his experiences in the mental institution.

The band had the sort of luck with drummers that sounds like the inspiration for *Spinal Tap*, both of their skins men tragically having taken their own lives. Donnie Alexander, the original drummer, left the band in April 1980, following a horrific workplace accident which left him badly disfigured. He was found dead in a gas-stinking bedsit in Newcastle upon Tyne some eighteen months later. His replacement in the band, the unfortunately named Martin Smelt, committed suicide by throwing himself from the Dean Bridge in the summer of 1986. A keen Hearts supporter, he was said to have suffered from a deep depression following the footballing events of that year.

Over twenty years later, the Old Boys are playing a comeback gig, Smelt being replaced on skins by Chrissie Fotheringham, the American spouse of Steve, so at least there'll be no excuse for the rhythm section not being in time.

It says that gig is next week at the Music Box in Victoria Street. I'll definitely check that out and also pick up the *Best of . . .* CD that's recently been issued.

I head outside and I'm finding it bitingly cold here after California, and it's getting dark so quickly. Nonetheless, I'm still feeling quite chuffed until I get round to Duke Street and see that slimy little ratbag, shuffling jauntily down the road.

Busby. What's his profile? What does that ruddy-faced nonce drink?

Export. Whisky. You decide.

I duck into a shop doorway and watch him going into one of the old gadges' howfs that are struggling to stay open in the face of being undercut by the big Wetherspoon's toilet on the corner, with its happy-hour pitchers of cocktails for thirty-eight pence or something like that. Yet as soon as the old gaffs shut down the prices will rise okay, make no mistake.

Busby.

I'm looking in on him through the long windows of the pub; greasy where fish-supper-eating squinty-eyed drunks have pawed at it with their grubby mitts, trying to balance themselves as they attempt to see if there's any cunt inside that they can tap off ay.

Wee Busby, sitting there under the lights of some old Leith fleapit of a pub with his half of heavy and wee gold yin. The thin layer of sweat – or is it grease? – on his face. His strawberry nose. His busy, mocking, sneering little eyes, so at odds with that clamshell smile.

The insurance man.

What is the insurance man offering? He's offering insurance against being ourselves. Which is no insurance at all.

I'm looking in, watching Busby sit there with Sammy. The big fella: chunky and bemused as his life has slid slowly into alcoholic debauchery. He's scarcely noticed the departing years, wife, kids, girlfriends but now he's feeling their absence and all he has left is that most loyal yet treacherous of bitches: who else but Dame Peeve?

Even worse for him, Busby, the skinny-framed sweetie wife, now has the measure of this hulk, a man he probably avoided for a large part of his young life. Things change though, sometimes so gradually that you don't even notice, especially for auld cunts like them. Somebody as sly as Busby will always become the master of someone as slow as Sammy if he's patient and takes care to insinuate himself enough.

And why not? Busby's no threat, he's got nothing Sammy wants, save the stolen nights with bored or lonely single women like my mother. Then as Sammy's alcoholism and confusion grew, he'd find in Busby a strange companion. Deferential at first: *Aye, you'll soon be back on your feet, Sammy, they cannae keep a good man doon and you've ey been one ay the best, Sammy . . .*

Now, though, the contempt is showing. It shows in the sneering glances that Sammy is too languorous and alcohol-fuddled to notice. Or the odd barbed aside that cuts through his muffled layers of consciousness because suddenly Busby's approval has become so important for Sammy as it's now the only quasi-affirmative show in town.

And I see in Busby and Sammy how fucked up things are when you take responsibility for somebody else, how much you can come to rely on them. For Busby and Sammy, read Skinner and Kibby. Or every cunt and any cunt in every grotty bar in every town and city in this country. Everybody who has missed the boat and has nothing left but each other and their own sad dramas full of loathing and dread to fall back on. You can enjoy a mocking dance with somebody, but it's such an albatross around your neck. Especially when the music stops and you find yourselves so deep in each other's desperate embrace that you can't untangle.

Not yet twenty-four years old and I can see that it's all fucked already. My twin curses, Kibby and alcoholism, have taught me that. Is alcoholism the product of bastardism, or is it just another fucking excuse? Discuss, discuss, discuss.

But I so want to go in there and buy a drink for auld Busby and Sammy. Take the old boys on a trip down memory lane. Listen keenly, yes keenly, as Sammy slobbers and even gets coy as sneaky auld Busby's rubber mooth becomes even slacker with drink as the secrets get coughed out.

'Aye, you could be ma laddie right enough. Aboot then that ah cowped yir ma. Wee punk rocker she wis at the time n aw. Mind ay her, Sammy! Nice pair ay tits oan it! Wir you no thair n aw? You wir eywis a Slade man but, eh no, Sammy? Noddy Holder. "Cum On Feel The Noize"? Mind ay that yin, Sammy? "Skwueeze Me Pleeze Me"!'

Just to give me permission to stand up and smash my fist into that face, that twisted rubber mouth which has talked its way out of a thousand such punches, to watch as the dentures or the last remaining teeth hurtle across the bar like bullets. But no. Because I'd need to take a drink myself for that yin and one is never enough and a thousand is too much.

I'm saving Brian. Denying myself to save Brian, and not just through fear of reciprocity, which is real enough. It's more than self-interest or self-preservation. I simply don't want him to die, I never did. Because he doesn't deserve to die. All he was wis an annoying sooky wee cunt. All I ever wanted to do was boot him up the arse.

But the pull, oh my God the fucking pull, aye, much stronger in dingy auld Edina than in sunny Cal-i-for-nigh-ay. One can of lager. Just one fucking cool pint of Michael Philip. I'm heading up the Walk, passing the Lorne Bar now. The Alhambra, with its door wedged open. Duncan Stewart's perched on the bar stool; I see the back of his shaved head. Every bar I pass containing a face: a memory, a story, and the fabric of a life. More than the alcohol I'm addicted to that way of life, that culture, those social relationships. I can't go in there, though, and just drink water or lemonade. I can't go in there. I can't stay here, the invisible hand of expectation guiding, cajoling, pushing and thrusting me in the same direction, or directions. I've backtracked and I'm heading the way I came, back doon the street. I'm at the crossroads but all the roads lead to the same place. Cause it's everywhere. Where do you go from the foot of the Walk? Up the Walk to the Central, Spey, et cetera, et cetera, or along Junction Street to Mac's, the Tam O'Shanter, Wilkies, et cetera, et cetera? Or perhaps Duke Street to the big Wetherspoon's or the Marksman, et cetera, et cetera? Or maybe Constitution Street to Yogi's although it's no his any mair, or Homes or Nobles et cetera, et cetera?

It's everywhere.

A good pint. Aye, they dae a good pint in here, son. A fucking great pint! It contains syrups, corn sulphites, pyrocarbonate, benzoate, foam enhancers, amyloglucosidase, beta-glucanase, alpha-acetolactate, decarboxylase, stabilisers, ascarbonates. Might even also contain: malt, hops, yeast, water and wheat. Maybe. Don't bet on it though.

And it's fucking well everywhere.

It had been an amazing transformation. Now he was sitting up in bed and eating solids. The new liver was functioning efficiently and, more importantly, there had been no further night seizures. All the medical and nursing staff to a man and woman were shy of employing the term 'remission' but Brian Kibby's rapid progress and the stretched resources of the NHS were such that the surgeon, Mr Boyce, estimated that he'd be home within the week.

Joyce was delighted at the news, and couldn't remember when

she'd last been so happy. Her prayers had been answered. Her faith, shaken as it had been by Keith's death, and tested to breaking point by Brian's illness, had emerged intact, even renewed. But worry and concern were by nature and circumstance so well embedded into her psyche that she felt somewhat exposed without their accompanying presence. Brian Kibby knew his mother well and saw that even through her glee there was a spectre at the feast. — What's up, Mum, is there something wrong?

His mother was aware that her son's question had just made her physically recoil, so any attempt at concealment would be folly. — Son . . . I know you said not to bring this up, she began cagily, — but it's Danny . . . Mr Skinner from the office. He really wants to visit you.

Brian Kibby's face contorted into such a twisted parody of itself that Joyce immediately regretted her disclosure. Sitting rigidly upright in the bed, struggling to contain himself, he looked evenly at his mother, wearing a hitherto unseen expression that chilled her to the marrow. — I hate him, he said to her, — I don't want him anywhere near me.

— But Brian! Joyce shrieked. — Da- . . . Mr Skinner was phoning from America all the time he was out there. He emailed that nice girl at your work nearly every day to ask about you!

It was now Brian Kibby's turn to be concerned at his mother's reaction; upset as he was by the way his response had aggravated her. — Let's not talk about Skinner. I just want to get home; just you, me and Caroline, he said, all the time thinking: *What does Skinner want with me?*

34
Shock and Awe

It's a raw, freezing day, but at least it's a brutally honest one, devoid of spirit-crushing icy rains or torturous winds. The last of the weak sun is fading and the sulphurous sky is turning mauve. My feet scrunch on iced-up patches of pavement as soon as I turn off the main St John's Road, down the winding backstreet towards the Kibbys' gaff.

I've come here to see Joyce, who'd called me up, very concerned about Brian's behaviour. She said I didn't need to, but I insisted, as I wanted a nose around Kibby's pad before he gets home from the hospital the morn.

I chap the door and as it opens . . .

Jesus fuck almighty . . .

. . . I get a big shock as a stunningly beautiful girl of about nineteen, twenty, appears before me.

What a honey! She has straight, blonde hair pinned back on one side with a gold clasp. Her large grey-blue eyes ooze a soulful depth. Her pearly teeth are dazzling and she has the smoothest skin I've ever seen.

Fuck sakes.

She wears a green top with green-and-black camouflaged combat trousers.

What the fuck's gaun on here? I am . . .

She raises her eyebrows quizzically at me in lieu of a response that's some time forthcoming as her very presence has knocked me right out of sorts.

Ya cunt that ye are.

Aroused, not so much sexually as emotionally, I struggle to maintain my cool, forcing a clamped smile. — I'm Danny. I, ehm, work with Brian at the council, I explain, almost moved to describe myself as a friend of his, but managing to stop short in time.

— Come in. I'm Caroline, she says, and she turns in an easy twist and heads into the house. I'm so shocked that this, *this*, is Kibby's sister. I'm following eagerly, desperate to remain close to her essence and, of course, to ascertain her curves in detail.

Joyce Kibby, who is already in the hallway beside us, interrupts my eyeful. She's as nervy and jumpy as her daughter is poised and graceful. — Mr Skinner . . . she says.

— Danny, please, I reiterate, more for Caroline's benefit than hers. The dopey cow should really have managed to dispense with the formalities by now. I get no response from Caroline though, who saunters into the living room without further acknowledgement.

— How's Brian? I ask Joyce, ready to follow Caroline, but I'm ushered into the kitchen. As I reluctantly sit down I catch a glimpse of her daughter through a crack in the door. She's more than just a looker; I can't recall having a reaction like that to a woman before, ever.

Well, maybe Justine Taylor in second year. Or Kay. Or Dorothy. But even they were different somehow. This is fucked. I can't just –

Joyce is bringing the kettle to the boil. It's probably cause of her daughter, but I'm scrutinising the old girl now, trying and failing to see a younger, tidier self. I see only the tight, prissy curls and that stiff, jerky manner. — He's getting better but he seems really confused mentally, she tells me in that shrill voice of hers, which dovetails with the sound of the kettle whistling.

— Oh, not so good. How so?

Joyce puts two spoonfuls of tea into the pot, then adding one for luck, in the style of the Old Girl. Come to think of it, she too must be ages with Siouxie Sioux, although you'd never believe it in a million years. This woman was probably born old, or maybe it's just this cloak of uptight solicitude she's shrouded in. — He has a strange obsession about his old job, she says. Then she looks at me quite shamefully, disclosing in a low, cagey voice, — This is so embarrassing . . . it's just that he's been really horrible about everything you've tried to do for him. He just doesn't seem to realise that you're here to help! I cannae understand why he's so set against you when you've been so good to us and so concerned about him. There's no good in it, no good at all, she says, her face flushing and her head shaking as she puts the cup down in front of me.

— Joyce, this has been a terrible ordeal for Brian. He's bound to be confused, I advance in a conciliatory manner. The tea is in a silly little china cup that holds fuck all with a handle so small that it's almost impossible to pick up.

— Yes, Joyce Kibby agrees vigorously, and continues rabbiting one thousand apologies on her son's behalf. But all I'm thinking of right now is her daughter. She is gorgeous and übercool, a fucking megababe; everything that Brian Kibby and his dopey mother aren't.

Caroline Kibby.

Brian Kibby.

And it just comes to me in a blinding flash of inspiration! There was a way that I could keep monitoring Brian's progress, a legitimate reason to continue visiting them! It would be killing two birds with one stone, and a labour of love. It would also, in all probability, get right up poor Brian's nose.

— It makes him seem such a bad person, Mr Skinner, and he's not, he's a fine young man . . .

Caroline.

That divine and splendid prefix which, to my hungry, restless mind, now totally neutralises the toxicity of that previously sickening word 'Kibby'. There is no sugar in this tea but I've yet to taste a sweeter elixir. If I was seeing, *dating*, Caroline Kibby, I could come here if I wanted to, and Brian could do jack shit about it. I could take care of him, at least until he was strong. Eat healthily, get plenty of rest and good lovin' and watch him thrive. And while doing this I could get to understand him, find out why I have this strange and terrible power over him!

— . . . he never gave me or my husband, God rest his soul, a bit of trouble . . .

Caroline Kibby.

No, it wasn't a bad word at all. Quite beautiful really: Kibby, Caroline Kibby. Yes, I could make Brian strong before I go home to San Francisco . . .

Dorothy.

In some ways it seems so far away already, but it was so real, so good.

— . . . and his attitude towards you . . . I can't explain it . . . if he knew you were here even . . .

— Okay, I say to Joyce, — least said, soonest mended. Brian's still very ill and the last thing I want to do is to upset him. I'll take off now and I'll keep away from the hospital. Provided, of course, that you keep me up to date with his progress.

— I certainly will, Mr – Danny, and thanks again for being so understanding. Joyce looks at me in that imploring way.

And for the first time I'm thinking about how there might just be some wonderful divine purpose behind this strange curse. I finish my tea and as I take my leave, stop off and poke my head around the door of the front room to say a cheery, — Bye, to Caroline, dropping her a smile.

— Bye then, she says, turning up from the table she's sat at, at first quite puzzled, but then she returns the smile and I'm thinking, whoa, that is a fucking exceptional lassie!

I'm floating out of the Kibbys' on cloud nine, almost oblivious to Joyce's cooing and clucking. Then I seem to fall a thousand feet through my own body as I think again of Dorothy over in San Francisco. I don't know what the fuck I'm going to do.

35
The Leaning Tower

Friends expressed great surprise, not just that Danny Skinner had come back so early, but that he was hanging around Edinburgh and was still sober. He emailed Dorothy frequently, but was on the phone to Joyce every other day, checking Brian Kibby's progress. The odd coffee with Shannon McDowall was his other main social activity. Shannon had been promoted to his old job, but only on a temporary basis, which irked her, as it was subject to yet another review. Aside from her vitriol at what she regarded as the discriminatory employment practices of her bosses, she only seemed to want to talk about Dessie, and this had limited appeal for him. He found it unsettling having his old friend and rival cast in the role of new man.

Skinner had still not attempted to see his mother, nor had he heard from her. People he bumped into in Leith Walk or Junction Street would tell him that she was doing okay, but he studiously avoided passing the shop. He was keeping doggedly to the resolution that when he did see her next, he'd speak that one name to her, then see how she reacted.

One thing he did resume were his Friday soirées with Bob Foy; an Old Town Italian restaurant, the Leaning Tower, being the current favourite rendezvous point, even if he stuck resolutely to mineral water.

Foy's absolute delight that Kibby certainly wouldn't be returning to the council's employ was still very much in evidence. — That office stink of BO and God knows what else has gone. It's quite literally a breath of fresh air, he rejoiced, waving the laminated menu around theatrically.

Skinner was having none of it. — It's a fucking tragedy what that poor bastard's been through. I'm just delighted that he came through his op okay, and if he gets better, you could do worse than have him back.

Foy puckered his lips and topped up his glass of Chianti. — Over my dead body, he scoffed.

Skinner and Foy finished their meal in some tension, and went on for a few drinks, soft ones in the former's case. Foy eventually headed off in a taxi disappointed and still a little bemused at this teetotal incantation of his old dining partner.

Skinner also had another mission. He may not have been drinking but there were still bars to trawl, especially in the student quarter.

The Grassmarket was busy. Skinner squeezed into one café-bar and had a soft drink when he was accosted by a couple of old faces, Gary Traynor and the chunky young man he knew as Andy McGrillen. They were clearly intent on making a night of it and were surprised and disgusted to note his choice of fuel.

McGrillen . . .

He recalled that fight he had instigated on Christmas Eve, when Skinner hadn't got involved. He didn't like McGrillen. Now his memory danced in recall of the boyhood confrontation they'd had on a train coming back from the football at Dundee. They were just kids, as it had been almost ten years ago, but he had never forgotten the incident. McGrillen, with some mates, had got wide with him. Skinner, who'd lost McKenzie and the rest of his friends on that occasion, was alone and had been forced to back down. It was a minor humiliation but one that still burned him, particularly now that McGrillen was hanging around with Traynor. Once McGrillen had realised that Skinner was connected he'd been civil enough, even attempting to develop a friendship of sorts. Both of them knew, however, how history could weigh heavily and they had largely tacitly agreed to keep out off each other's way, discounting that one time at Christmas. Now, catching McGrillen looking disapprovingly at his glass, Skinner felt the burn again.

A fuckin Burberry baseball cap. What a total chavy cunt. How auld is he? Twenty-one? Twenty-two? Probably cause McKenzie's no longer around, he thinks he can get quoted with our crew!

— C'mon, Danny, have a fuckin pint, Traynor urged.

— Naw, just an orange juice is fine, Skinner insisted.

Traynor seemed to catch the vibe coming from Skinner towards McGrillen and tried to lighten the mood by talking about the most recent religious porn film he'd come across. — *God, He Likes to Watch*; it's the fuckin best yet, ya cunt.

Andy McGrillen shrugged and smiled at Traynor and went to the bar. He let his somewhat intimidating bearing clear a space among the drinkers, some of whom recognised him as one of the boys and possible bad news. He soon came back with the drinks, plonking them on the table.

— Cheers, boys, Skinner toasted. — Good to see youse again, he said, managing to include McGrillen, with just about enough conviction.

Skinner found sipping at his orange juice strangely comforting. He was getting into Traynor's patter again. His old buddy turned to McGrillen. — Tell ye a great Rab McKenzie tale, mind this yin, Skinny, he nodded to Skinner. — Us two and Big Rab went back wi they posh birds, that Paki lassie you wir wi, what wis her name?

— Vanessa. And she's Scots-Asian. Her dad's from Kerala and her mum's from Edinburgh, Skinner corrected.

— Awright, Mr PC. Traynor playfully punches Skinner's arm. — So wir back up this big posh gaff up in Merchy; big indoor pool, auld man n auld girl away oan hoaliday, n wir aw cavortin aroond in the skud. It's the first time we've seen the Big Man without clathes, n, well . . . ye kin imagine. Bit they lassies are aw horned up, this big posh bird Andrea, and that Sarah lassie, n every cunt starts gittin frisky. You went away wi that Vanessa, eh, Skinner.

— Aye, but nowt happened. We just snogged for a bit and talked; that's aw.

— Talked, eh sais! Aye, that'll be right.

— We did, Skinner protested. — She wisnae up for shagging, no big deal. I had a nice night; she was an interesting girl.

— Fuck off, Skinner, Traynor laughed, pushing him in the chest. — Well, while you were *talking*, ah'm fired intae that Sarah, giein it the message oan the lilo. And the posh bird Andrea – tidy, but no that sharp – Traynor tapped his skull, — she's gittin it oan wi the Big Man. Thing is, ah mind ah'd been sayin tae um earlier that posh birds are eywis game, and dirty as fuck n aw, dae anything, ya cunt. Traynor's toothy grin expanded. — So Big Rab's obviously taken aw this tae heart. Ah jist hears the Big Man gaun: 'Ah'd like tae fuck you up the arse.' Then the posh bird says – Traynor puckered his lips and put on a tea-room accent: — 'What *exactly* does that involve?'

McGrillen laughed loudly and Skinner did too, although he'd heard that story many times. He took another sip of his orange juice. Something was wrong here. He sniffed it and tasted it again. There was alcohol in it.

Vodka!

Looking up, he saw McGrillen's stupid, leering expression, then briefly savoured the change in it as he looked down his arm while ramming a solid right-hander into his face. It was a good punch, Skinner pivoting into it and following through with his body weight, and McGrillen went crashing off his stool on to the deck.

Gary Traynor looked at the shocked, recumbent McGrillen, then back to Skinner. — Fuck sakes, Danny . . .

Skinner was still shaking with anger. He threw his glass to the floor and it missed McGrillen's face by an inch. — What d'ye think yir fuckin well playin at, tryin tae fuckin well poison – and he looked around and saw the scene he was making and said, — Sorry, chaps, then swiftly departed, rubbing at his stinging knuckles.

He stepped out into the street feeling the elation of the adrenalin buzz leaking from him as the guilt started to kick in.

It was taking liberties. McGrillen didnae know the score, how could he? But why can't some cunts understand that no means no?

Quickly heading across the road and into another bar, Skinner ran into a group of chatty girls he knew vaguely from the council. One of their pals was on a hen night. Two of them were very talkative but soon he was only half listening to them, distracted as he was by one of the waitresses.

Caroline Kibby had about quarter of an hour to go until her shift ended. From one of the tables, she saw a recognisable man watching her. Yes, she knew him. He smiled, and she smiled back. Then he approached her and invited her to have a drink when she finished up.

It's the guy who was round at Mum's the other day, him from the council. The one Brian's being so weird about.

She was happy to accept.

He'd just eaten a big Italian meal with Bob Foy. However, after a few more soft drinks Danny Skinner was happy to suggest that he and Caroline grabbed a bite to eat at what he was inclined to describe as an 'excellent old-school Chinese' called the Bamboo Shoots up in Tolcross.

Sitting opposite her in the restaurant, he still found it hard to believe that Caroline was Brian Kibby's sister. As she ate in deliberate, poised, economical movements, there were times he just wanted to scream that at her: *You are so fucking beautiful, how can you be related to that sneaky wee fandan, Brian?*

Caroline, for her part, was equally taken by Danny Skinner.

He's quite handsome, in a funny sort of way. He's got that startled expression but it makes him look like he's fascinated rather than perplexed by the world. He must spend a fortune on clothes. It seems ridic that he's a couple of years older than our Brian. He looks years younger: fresh-faced and in pristine condition. There's something about him that's quite imposing; something that makes me think that I might have some of that!

Later on they walked across the Meadows, through a cool darkness lit up by the moonlight and the sodium lamps. They were in no hurry at all, talking unselfconsciously and listening intently to each other about almost anything that came into their heads. Caroline felt the tiredness of her shift peel from her and her eyes, sore from burning an essay out of the computer, began to regain their sheen. Fearing the end of the evening, she said, — I've got some hash here if you fancy a blow.

I'm no really a hash-monkey but a smoke would do her brother good, relax him, and perhaps bolster his appetite.

— Back to yours? Skinner quizzed, the South Side being within walking distance and Leith a taxi ride away.

— Eh, maybe yours would be better, I've only just moved into my flat and I'm not really sure about my flatmates yet, if you know what I mean . . . Caroline said uneasily.

A peg of trepidation was suddenly hammered into Skinner's chest.

He should have been completely made up about this news, getting this girl back to his Leith love nest, but somehow he was experiencing an unsparing discharge of unease.

Why am I so keen to look around her place and her mother's, but feel awkward about letting her see my base? It's better than that mausoleum she comes from!

He nodded in the affirmative and they flagged down a taxi in Forrest Road and headed for the port.

— Have you lived in Leith long? Caroline asked.

— All my life, Skinner replied, thinking about San Francisco, and Dorothy, and how he'd love to live there. It wasn't that he didn't like Leith; in some ways he adored it, but he enjoyed the idea of living somewhere different and always having it to come back to. Maybe you can love something without wanting to be close to it all the time, he considered.

Caroline walked into Skinner's hallway. She saw that the flat was neat and fastidiously clean.

Fucking hell. This is domesticated. Does he have a cleaner?

Mindful of dope kernels on the settee, Skinner went through to the kitchen and got two large pub ashtrays. Caroline followed him, noting the expensive units. — You lived here long, Danny?

— Four years.

— You've got some nice stuff, Caroline said, obviously impressed, looking at his slim, taut arse in his black trousers. A dizzying spasm briefly pulsed through her.

Mmmm-hmmm.

— Aye, Skinner said as they headed into the living room. — I was in a bad road traffic accident a few years back. A car hit me, knocked me unconscious, broke my arm and leg and fractured my skull. I got some decent compensation so I used most of it to do this place up, he explained, thinking with more guilt about Dessie Kinghorn's meagre five hundred quid attempted pay-off.

Maybe a grand would have been a fair result. Or even fifteen hundred. Ten per cent.

Caroline asked him the details of the accident and he recounted them, omitting the fact that it was caused by his own recklessness, as she skinned up while scanning the front room. It had old gold-painted walls and was dominated by an L-shaped black leather settee. A glass coffee table sat in front of it. A flat-screened television was next to a period fireplace with a big wall-mirror above. To the sides were built-in cupboards; one containing a music centre, and above it shelves full of books and CDs, the other housing yet more books and videos. A small replica model of the Statue of Liberty stood on the mantelpiece.

Taking a long draw on the joint before passing it over to Skinner, Caroline got up from the couch to check out the CDs and books. Skinner had already explained his rap and hip-hop tastes so there was no shock in the music department: Eminem, Dr Dre, NWA, Public Enemy. The open CD on the coffee table caught her eye. The band was called the Old Boys. Some of track listings sounded strange to her: 'Compulsory Repatriation', 'Remembrance Day', 'A Penny From the Poor Box' . . . — What's this like? she asked, waving up the index case.

— Utter crap, Skinner said. — I bought it the other day because my ma was a big fan. They were a local punk band and I think she used to hang out with them. But it's not my thing at all.

Moving back to the shelves, apart from copious volumes of poetry by Byron, Shelley, Verlaine, Rimbaud, Baudelaire and Burns, and a big, obviously unleafed one of MacDiarmid, Caroline noticed that the books were mostly American novels, ranging from Salinger and Faulkner through to Chuck Palahniuk and Bret Easton Ellis. — No Scottish fiction? she asked.

— Not for me. If I want swearing and drug-taking, I'll step outside the door and get it. But as for reading about it . . . Skinner smiled, for a second seeming to her oddly spooky and clownish with his long jaw.

That strange smile of his . . . something feels not quite right here, but fuck it, what's the worst that can happen? I get shagged by this fit lad in a nice flat in Leith . . .

— Are we going to go to bed, or what? she asked him.

Skinner was taken aback. Perhaps he had seen Caroline as Joyce's daughter or Brian's sister and therefore found it hard to believe that she could be so at ease with her sexuality. — Aye . . .

He took her hand and they walked through to the bedroom, too lost in their growing mutual discomfiture to realise that they looked less like lovers and more like concentration camp victims walking into the gas chamber.

In Skinner's bedroom an outsize Old Glory hung on the wall over the brass-framed bed. The bed was topped with what Caroline felt was an outlandishly bad-taste orange duvet. The room on the whole represented an odd lapse, as it seemed so different to the rest of the house.

Skinner was methodically taking his clothes off, wondering, in mounting distress, exactly what was happening to him. His erection had become like his father: he was painfully aware of it by its absence. Caroline looked out the back on to the green. — This is nice, she said, now also feeling very self-conscious. She cursed inwardly at this type of weak, bland remark her mother might make.

What the fuck is going on with me?

— Apart from the pigeon shit, Skinner smiled ruefully as he pulled his trousers and shirt off and slipped under the sheets. For some reason he kept his briefs on, possibly because she was making no effort to remove her clothes.

— You get them everywhere . . . Caroline said, — . . . except the tropics. That would spoil a tropical paradise, if you had them cooing away at your feet while you were sipping your cocktail by the pool.

Skinner laughed at this, perhaps a little too emphatically, she thought. She looked at him sitting up in the bed. His body was lean and muscular and she fancied him. Yet she found it strangely hard to undress in front of him. And she sensed that he was as freaked out as she was. Eventually, she kicked off her pumps and peeled off her jeans, keeping on her T-shirt as she got under the sheets.

— Cold? he asked.

— Yeah . . . I think that blow's a bit strange. I've come over a wee bit weird, to be honest, she explained in rueful, confused shame.

Feeling his own inexplicable otherness, he concurred. — Yeah, I know what you mean . . . maybe we're rushing things a bit here . . . I really like you . . . there's plenty of time for, you know . . . let's just have a hug and a blether again . . .

— Okay. Caroline smiled tightly as she moved closer to him. He looked at her again; she didn't remind him of Kibby at all. She *was* beautiful but fuck him if he wasn't as flaccid as he was when confronted with a stage one inspection report.

Striving to create some intimacy into the mood, Skinner swept her hair from her face, but felt her tense up under his touch, as if the gesture was unwelcome and intrusive. Deciding to revert back to their old safe theme of pigeons, while shocked at the inanity of it, he found himself pointing to the window and saying, — In America they don't let vermin nest on public buildings and shit all over us from that vantage point. They have those thin spikes they put on ledges to deter them.

— They've started doing that here as well, Caroline said more dreamily, — but down here it must be the seagulls that are the big problem . . . She liked being beside this guy; she was just being weird.

Skinner, experiencing port loyalties kick in, felt oddly compelled to mount a defence of the seafaring bird. As they seemed to be relaxing a little, he resisted the temptation.

Caroline was thinking about her favourite band, the Streets. How the guy in the Streets was called Skinner as well, Mikey Skinner. There was a line he had about calling women birds not bitches where he came from. It made the male, working-class culture which had often appeared to her to be misogynistic seem beautiful. It depended on what kind of bird though. She suddenly heard herself ask, — Did you like the American girls when you were over there?

— Gorgeous, Skinner admitted, thinking of Dorothy. Was she really the one? Was this why he couldn't make love to Caroline? — But most American girls don't know how to dress, like European women. Even the best-looking of them just can't seem to wear clothes for some reason.

Caroline's mouth seemed to turn up a little at the corner; it probably wasn't what she wanted to hear, he considered.

But Danny Skinner was feeling like he hadn't felt with a girl since he was about fifteen. He was awkward and nervous. They kissed, and it was okay, and then they went into a strange, long sleep in each other's arms, so beautiful and peaceful it was like they'd been drugged by something more prolific than the hash they'd enjoyed.

It was Skinner who woke first in the morning light. Immediately he marvelled at Caroline's slumbering pulchritude but was soon once again beset by a terrible unease, feeling compelled to get up and leave the bed. He went to the kitchen and started to fix breakfast, laying out some cereal, yogurt, orange juice and green tea. Skinner felt strangely relieved through his disappointment when she emerged wearing all her own clothes, rather than one of his T-shirts.

Yet through their breakfast they chatted in a relaxed manner, and it was only when Caroline was ready to depart that the awkwardness set in once again. For some reason Skinner could only give her a chaste peck on the cheek. — Can I see you again? he asked.

— I'd like that, she smiled, wondering why this was all so clumsy. *Was it because of Brian and his strange dislike of this guy?*

Skinner was tempted to say tomorrow, but he needed some time to think things through. His head was in a mess. — What about Thursday?

Caroline Kibby was as anxious to have a moratorium as Danny Skinner was. — Thursday's fine.

She set off on her way back to her new home on the South Side. A while after she'd gone, Skinner remembered that he was going to see the Old Boys on Thursday. He didn't want to start messing Caroline around at this stage, so he thought that they could go together. He noticed that she'd left some hash behind on the coffee table. He skinned up another joint and felt his head bubble. It *was* strong gear.

Fucking sabotaging Edinburgh soapbar! It's as good as any California grass I had with Dorothy. Probably some home-grown hydroponic shite or whatever dopeheads call it.

He rolled up another joint and sucked on it.

36
The Old Boys

It's getting cold, but it looks more like a summer's day. The sky is almost blonde. A starling, twig in its beak, flutters from the corner of the roof extension next door, across to the willow tree at the bottom of the back garden. It'll have to watch for the likes of Tarquin, the cat who lives next door. He's caught a few of them.

I'm getting stronger. I've started going for wee walks now. I climbed to the top of Drum Brae yesterday. Today I put on a T-shirt, a fleece, trainers and tracksuit bottoms and head outside, going down the Glasgow Road. I call into the PC World computer superstore wondering whether or not to upgrade my *Harvest Moon* to the newer edition. I decide against it, I don't feel comfortable spending money on luxuries now that I'm no working.

One of these lassies with the clipboards is outside. She wears a waterproof with OXFAM on it. She gives me a big smile. — Can you spare a minute for Oxfam?

— No.

— No problem, she smiles.

— Correct. It is no problem. It's part of the solution, I tell her.

She raises her eyebrows and gies a closed-up grin. I can feel my neck burn as I depart, but I feel satisfied to have resisted. They always want something. Always. I've stopped the other direct debits as well!

I cut through by the church on to the Gyle playing fields. Aye, I'm getting stronger but I'll never be the same again. The disease has stolen so much from me. I miss my job, and the people in the office. Except Skinner, only I hear that he isn't there any more. Supposed to be taking time off to travel. Why doesn't he just do that then?

I fucking well told Mum not to bring him into our house! If he comes again, I won't be in. What is he playing at, hanging around me and my mother? He's nothing to do with me. He never was!

What does he want?

There's a football match on at the Gyle Park, two teams running around kicking a ball about. How I'd love to join them, even though I never liked the game. It was always too rough and fast and aggressive for me. They shouted at me because I was slow and couldnae trap the ball. I was just a bit nervous and awkward. Now, though, I'd just get right into it. Get stuck right in like my dad used to tell me to. I wouldn't care about hurting myself or anybody else. Because I know now that doing things doesn't hurt you; you get hurt by avoiding them.

Whatever comes my way in life now, I know that I'm done with hiding.

By the time I get home it's getting dark. Mum's got a basket of dirty washing as she heads into the kitchen, looking at me as if she's going to say something, then thinking better of it.

— What?

— Nothing . . . Did you enjoy your walk?

— Aye . . . I head up to my room and fire up *Harvest Moon*. It's New Year's Eve and I'm straight round Muffy's, no messing about to check fucking chickens or cattle or crops, I'm courting her, bringing her cake and flowers . . . but what do I get back, baby? What do I get from you?

Take off your dress.

Slip off your little white panties . . . I know you're wearing them . . . that's it . . .

Bend over that fence . . .

. . . that's it . . .

I've got a big cock; a big, dirty cock that I think is made for tight Jap pussy . . .

. . . that's it, you fucking Jap bitch . . . take this, baby, take it . . . fucking bitches with your big doll lips and your tight pussies . . . your big eyes, every one of you bitches has such big fucking doe eyes . . . ohhh . . . ohhh . . . ohhhh . . . YA FUCKER . . .

Oh.

My spunk is all over my thighs . . . wasted spunk, spunk that should have gone to make beautiful white Christian babies? Like fuck, spunk that should have been swallowed by fucking sluts like that fucking Lucy Moore whore and that filthy Shannon bitch who went with Skinner . . .

THAT'S THE FUCKIN WASTE.

I'm gasping and my head is spinning but I'm going to fuck every bitch on this fuckin farm. Then tomorrow I'm going back to PC World to buy *Grand Theft Auto: San Andreas.* There's a reason why *Game Informer* gave it ten out of ten.

From behind the pane, cracked and mottled with dirt, a judging sky hung threateningly in bruised layers over the city. Skinner considered that he needed to get those windows clean. He could just about make out a row of broken chimney pots on the tenement roofs opposite, holding each other up like a group of partying drunks heading to the next bar. Better take the raincoat, he thought, as he prepared to go outside.

The top of Waverley steps, Skinner pursed sourly, then laughed at his own stupidity.

What fuckin tube arranges to meet a bird at the top ay Waverley steps? She'll probably have blown across to Fife by the time I get up to that fucking wind trap. You dipstick, Skinner!

As he bustled up the Walk, negotiating the grand thoroughfare in even strides, he tried to recall Caroline, to see if, when he conjured up this image of perfection of her, it would chime with the one that greeted him in the flesh at the top of the steps. Or had his mind been playing tricks on him?

When he saw her standing there, approaching her profile, he realised right away, almost with a sense of disappointment, that it hadn't. He was confronted with someone who was approaching the zenith of their beauty without spoiling it by coming anywhere near that awareness.

Her hair is white blonde and looks like silk. Her neck is a slender white stem where the hair tapers out into soft down. Two small silver earrings with tiny ruby-coloured inserts sparkle in her plump lobes.

Skinner wanted to graze on them idly, remembering he thought about doing just that when they were alone in bed the other night, but somehow couldn't. He looked at her fingernails, which were so long that he fancied she could pick locks with them. He was aware that his gaze was all over her and he checked himself, making eye contact as she turned and registered his approach.

Caroline smiled at him and Skinner saw himself like De Fretais's pan-seared tuna steak, burned on the outside, mildly tenderised internally.

He took her to a cocktail bar, a proper American-style one, not a trashy British office workers' haunt, as he derisively described one she mentioned. Sensing a growing harshness in his soul, Skinner tried to check himself. Why was he behaving like this? Was it a way of trying to marshal his inner self in front of a girl who excited strange, indefinable passions in him? To hell with Brian Kibby and Gillian McKeith for a short time: he ordered a vodka martini made with vermouth and crushed ice. Skinner couldn't work out why he was unable to just make love to this beautiful girl he cared about. How hard could it be? He had one drink, then another. Then one more, Caroline matching him all the way for consumption and mood. He went to the machine, inserted his coins and wrestled out a packet of cigarettes.

They tried to negotiate the maelstrom of emotion swirling about them. Role-playing around it, they alternately acted harsh, blasé and aggressively flirty. The drink was their prop in this terrible theatre.

The fourth martini arrived; two green olives, skewered by a cocktail stick, straddled the glass. He picked up the cocktail stick and popped one olive into his mouth. Her eyes met his and a charge surged through him, hopelessly emboldening him and he pulled Caroline to him and transfered the olive into her mouth, almost spitting it in. She pulled away for a bit, because it felt not like it should, like she would expect, but intrusive, even creepy. Something was far from right here.

I've got such strong feelings for Danny, but . . .

Skinner cursed himself internally at the inappropriateness of the gesture, felt a terrible void growing between them.

Screw the nut, Skinner, you fucking tube . . . you fuckin . . . stay cool. C'mon, it was a bad move, but not a disaster.

He contented himself with looking at her again as they sat by each other on bar stools. They seemed to settle into a relaxed intimacy, but one that they sensed would send them scampering away like rodents with hair-trigger nerves, whenever it crossed a sexual line. It had to be real slow, he reasoned, and he got her to touch palms with him. — Almost as big as mine, he said, marvelling at the fluidity and luminosity of her eyes.

I wonder what they would be like when we make love, whether or not they would roll up behind their lids at her key moment, that deathly ethereal, yet arousing effect some women, and for all I know, men, display when they climax.

Danny Skinner was still a young enough man not to realise that his vanity could, on occasion, easily outstrip his sophistication. He'd also been sober long enough to forget that with alcohol it could happen so readily. And although Caroline Kibby was a younger woman, she was still a woman and moreover an inherently mature one whom circumstance had forced to grow up quickly. And as they headed down towards Victoria Street, she sensed that something was deeply wrong between the two of them.

It was Skinner's idea to go along and see the Old Boys. They staggered into the venue, very drunk, but anxious to lose their embarrassment in yet more alcohol and the music. He couldn't believe the crowd, loads of old punks, most of them contemporaries of his mother. Some still dressed like they did twenty-five years ago, while others were quite smart and straight-looking.

The space was spartan, and Skinner and Caroline tucked themselves by a pillar at the back of the house, close to the bar, as the band came on to rapturous applause.

It's the audience who look so old. Even the stick-thin guys who'd kept their stupid hair didn't realise that they looked ancient and ridiculous in their punk threads, the way old cunts never manage to dig. The Old Girl said they used to laugh at old Teds as well, but it was age they were laughing at as much as style, the fucking hypocritical non-sexist, non-racist, non-ageist old fuckers!

The good thing about the band, though, is that they *haven't visibly aged. They looked like old fuckers then; they* are *old fuckers now. Chrissie Fotheringham cuts a cool demeanour on the drums, with her headsquare, overcoat, woollen mittens and NHS glasses, but she's a good decade younger than the others. The singer, Wes Pilton, he's the star of the show and he gets the crowd going with 'The War Years':*

Days of glory, days of hope
Days without porn and dope
Of discipline by birch and rope
Those were the war years.

Days when we lived without fear
No rampaging yobs on beer
The beat bobby would clip your ear
Back in the war years.

Pilton marched, stiffed-backed, to the front of the stage and bent down as he crooned the chorus:

Britain stood alone
Fought against the foe
People shed their tears
For those killed in those years.

He leapt up, quite energetically, Skinner thought, before going back into scathing, snarling punk mode with the verse:

Now our country's breaking down
Lawless thugs in every town
National service would straighten those clowns
Just like the war years.

Taking the bows, Pilton gave a straight military salute to the crowd. — My pigeons have died, he announced to the audience cheers and laughter, — but we're still here, well, most of us. This is for those departed, our old drummers Donnie and Martin. He winked as they launched into 'A Penny From the Poor Box'.

Skinner drifted over to the bar to get some more drinks, where he witnessed Sandy Cunningham-Blyth, swaying around, stupefied with alcohol. Even the hardest-line veteran punks were giving him a wide berth, he noticed. The seasoned chef was the oldest person present and Skinner met his gaze, but Cunningham-Blyth didn't recognise him.

When he returned with some rum and Cokes in plastic beakers, he found Caroline sweating, her eyeliner smudging. She was distressed by the tunelessness of the band. — This doesnae seem your thing, Danny, she shouted in his ear.

— Naw, I'm just looking for my old man.

— Your dad? Where is he?

— Fuck knows. Probably up on that stage, Skinner said, and that was what Caroline thought he said, although it couldn't have been that, she considered. Perhaps she'd misheard him over the racket and through those muffled layers of alcohol.

37
First Drink

It was back. The disease.

It had its own stamp, a particular way of making him feel: like he was shabby and dirty inside. It also seemed to pollute the rest of the world, which became a vile place, full of the cold, callous and uncaring. Bolts of fear rose in him, battering his body in high-impact waves. But this time he decided that he couldn't stay here in his room and lie down to it.

And so Brian Kibby pulled his lumbering, shivering bulk into the Centurion Bar in Corstorphine's St John's Road. On his entry he was hit by a smoky fug even more pervasive and impenetrable than the frozen fog he'd emerged from. This, and the loud, raucous banter, almost made Kibby turn on his heels, but the nervous young man stood his ground as the tired, appraising eyes of the seasoned drinkers took him in, cursorily classifying him as one of their own.

Thinking about his reduced circumstances, Kibby moved uneasily to the bar. All his young life he had work or school or college to go to; now he had nothing, just this.

It has all been taken away, even Mum and now . . . Caroline. They're all under his spell!

On reaching the bar he hesitated for only a second or two before requesting, — A pint of lager and a double whisky please.

The barman didn't know him, but recognised a drinker's build and bearing, dispatching the order with economy.

Sipping the whisky, he wanted to retch as he felt its queasy, nauseating burn all the way from mouth to stomach, but he swallowed hard, washing it down with some gassy beer, which was scarcely more palatable to him. But the second whisky was much better and the third was like nectar, and then Brian Kibby was flying. His head buzzed and his hand tightened around the glass, the knuckles growing white. The pains were still there, he could feel them, but they didn't hurt him, their sting cushioned by the alcohol. Almost to his shock, he found himself in the grip of a vicious anger. In the past this even-tempered young man had occasionally felt these uglier emotions teasing at him, but he had never allowed himself to succumb to them. But now, in his warped spite, Kibby felt a delicious liberation.

Caroline. Seeing him.

His sister was seeing Skinner. This horrible picture wouldn't shift. For so long his lonely illness had dominated his thoughts, but now they were consumed by this new terror. It made Brian Kibby reflect malignantly, yet again, on his rivalry with Danny Skinner.

Skinner. They're under his spell. His curse . . .

And by the sheer, consecrating intensity of his violent thoughts, something, some deep, bizarre truth seemed to settle into the core of his psyche.

Skinner's done it!

He's done this to me!

It was irrational, but strangely all the more powerful, profound and important for that. Yes, he eagerly ratified to his own hungry consciousness, it *was* Skinner.

SKINNER . . .

And perhaps, at some level, Brian Kibby had always believed this. In some unspecific way, purely on an emotional, intuitive level, he had always suspected that Danny Skinner had something to do with his terrible penance. He'd seen Skinner looking at him, studying him in that disconcerting way with his smug face appearing like it understood everything. At one stage he believed that Skinner might be poisoning him. There was a time when he would eat or drink nothing that Skinner could have been around or might have tampered with. But it had proven impossible: this hadn't stopped his decline. Yet, somehow, part of him had remained convinced that Skinner was responsible.

It was *Skinner!*

And now Caroline's going out with him, and my mother is so pleased. She's so delighted that she can't stop talking about it, like a silly wee lassie! Now Skinner's coming for a meal at my house next Wednesday! He's taking over, trying to become part of the family!

Only the gesture for another round could break off Kibby's rancorous meditations. — Same again, he told the barman in an offhand slur of anger.

He was oblivious to the raising of the man's eyebrows, could only see his hand going to the optics. Inside his skull burned with whisky and thoughts of violence against Skinner.

I'd like to see that . . . that bastard . . . I'd like to see him get punched and kicked and stomped . . .

Then his train of thought smashed so suddenly into a set of psychic buffers that Kibby shook spasmodically with the force of the revelation. He realised that Skinner had been beaten up before, beaten badly, and it had been in the newspaper.

The football, and there wisnae a mark on him afterwards!

There were still some windows lit mawkit yellow in the adjoining tenements; lonely ragged teeth in a big, dark, cavernous mouth. As his heavy eyes blundered into slow focus through a repetitive throb in his skull, Skinner could just about make out the differing shades of the darkness he'd learned to navigate his life around. As his trembling hands ripped into the sooty douts in the McEwan's Export ashtray by his bedside, crumbling and breaking shreds of unburned tobacco to roll into a single skin, he contemplated those long hours of blackness, seeming to stretch out into infinity.

Alcohol, he considered, as he raised his smoke to his lips, was the only mechanism by which he could avoid running into the all-engulfing darkness. On those early mornings, it was the drunkenness of the previous night that caused him to sleep in and miss getting up for work and emerging into that cold, biting and dreary blackness. And the only occasions when he could escape from the workplace before the late afternoon's night settled around him was when his need for a drink moved him to duck out early.

What else was there in this dreich, drookit place? he caustically considered, feeling the puny, stale tobacco push into his lungs. The weather levelled us all down into depressed jakeys, bent and scowling under a suffocating cloak of darkness. Where was the respite? Where else was the comradely, raucous laughter, and if you were lucky, the welcoming smile of a pretty girl? All under one sick, nicotine-stained and alcohol-sodden roof. The place where even the mocking sneer of the adversary at least let you know that you were alive: everything took place in the public house.

He'd not been to such a place for a long time. But now Danny Skinner had woken up feeling like he hadn't felt for ages: sick, exhausted, shaky, tired and seedy. He could feel it in his body: its degenerative, corrupting influence. It must be a virus. But no, surely he had Brian Kibby for all that.

He pulled back the duvet and allowed the stench of his alcohol-corrupted body to waft upwards. A shudder started to vibrate in the small of his back as the image of a stricken Brian Kibby briefly flared in his mind. It was like the flashbulb of the police photographer at the scene of a homicide in an old Hollywood movie.

Naw . . . surely tae fuck naw . . .

Could it mean that Brian Kibby was finally gone . . . dead as the morning outside; his heavy body and troubled psyche ultimately crumbling under the strain as his life ebbed from him . . . ?

No . . . steady on . . . surely Caroline or Joyce would have phoned to tell me.

Through his sour gunge-filled mouth, Skinner, dabbing out the cigarette, sucked in a thin, icy breath, which burned his raw throat and made his bubbling stomach heave. Then, as his pulse kicked up, turning on some tap, opening those glands that swamped him with perspiration, a searing realisation hit him.

Kibby. The dirty wee cunt is . . . fighting back.

Yes, Danny Skinner was hung-over. So did the powers not then have a reciprocal nature? He felt the muscles in his tired but still tight arm. They'd fairly sprouted up back in the day when Kibby was tanning it in the gym. He'd just laughed it off, put it down as a time-of-life development. But no, far from it being a futile exercise, Brian Kibby had been actively pumping Danny Skinner up! Now Kibby was on the piss, and he was suffering! It made the perverse sense that only this bizarre condition could, and Skinner found himself conceding that it said a lot for Kibby's priggish sobriety; a lesser man would have hit the bevvy ages ago.

Shuddering up the Walk into town, Skinner sat at the Internet café on Rose Street, writing emails, battling to ignore those seedy demons that gnawed at his brain and body, occasionally trying, by his condition, to gauge the amount that Kibby had put away.

It was useless. He couldn't write to Dorothy. Skinner found himself in the old position he was often in at work: skiving, avoiding tasks simply because his edgy, hung-over self didn't possess the mental fortitude to concentrate and cope with even the most minor of social interactions. Asking for change for the coin machine when the Internet time expired was way too much hassle. And prior to this he was doing what he would have done at the council: having a day of vicious paper cuts and picking up burning coffee mugs and dancing to desks with them. Through his seediness, one emotion came to dominate: *if Kibby wants it, he'll fucking well get it.*

Fortified by the spirit of battle, Skinner left the café and strode up the North Bridge to hit the Royal Mile's pubs. By the time he'd left the first of them it was already difficult to distinguish the early-night sky from the medieval-looking stone tenements on the street.

Later that night, exiting from his last hostelry sodden with drink, he looked up, watching the weathervane on a church spire cut the moon into several pieces. Contemplating the luminous hollow sky, the tendrils of cloud providing so rich a Gothic background to the ridged steeple, Skinner fancied that all type and magnitude of diabolical forces could be concealed within its folds. Cold blue cobblestones clicked under the reinforced heels of his leather brogues as he meandered down the Royal Mile from the castle to the palace, his dragon breath freezing in jets in front of him. He'd pause occasionally at a close mouth to check the pulse of city life at closing time, strangely reassured if he spied a couple engaged in a knee-trembler, a vomiting drunkard or some youths meting out a senseless kicking to a stranger.

As he savoured his intoxication and thought of the bottle of Johnnie Walker that sat in his flat, Skinner's grin expanded to the width of the street. He was back on home territory.

If Kibby wants tae row, then let's just see what the fuckin wee fandan's got!

He was looking forward to his forthcoming visit to the Kibbys'.

How he'd enjoy that little showdown, he cackled as he danced in the shadow cast by the cold, luminous, silvery moon.

Brian Kibby needed a drink. He'd been at the computer upstairs in his bedroom. Through his sweating pain he'd managed to plug in his laptop. This time, though, he didn't load up *Harvest Moon* or any of the other video games. He went online to www.thescotsman.co.uk and signed in and found the *Evening News* section and searched for Skinner. And eventually he found what he was looking for: the occasion some months ago when Daniel Skinner was taken to hospital after the Hibs–Aberdeen game. He was involved in a brawl, they said, and had 'serious injuries'. But Skinner had not a scratch on him that Monday morning, the morning Brian Kibby had woken up in Newcastle, after the convention, looking and feeling like he'd been hit by a truck.

Kibby shivered as he looked through the article.

It cannae be . . . it's impossible . . . but somehow it is Skinner. Skinner somehow kens aw aboot this! He's fucking well cursed me!

He left his house, making his way up to the Centurion Bar. All those years and he had never set foot in this place. Now it already felt as much of a refuge as his attic ever did.

— Hair of the dog, eh, Raymond Galt, the barman, grinned as he dispensed Brian Kibby another double Scotch.

— Aye, Kibby replied in a gruff mumble that sounded like someone else, his mind absorbed for the first time with the drinker's dilemma. It helped, took away the pain, albeit only for a while. But when life was all pain, any pocket of respite, however brief, needed his embrace. And this time he *really* needed a drink; Skinner was coming to his house, coming for tea.

He was with Caroline. Had she slept . . . ?

NO!

Kibby threw down the nip and then a few more, before lurching out of the bar where he almost collided with a woman and a toddler in a pushchair. His subsequent apology came out as a weird slur, as the woman's angry, contemptuous gaze scorched him briefly. But soon he was back in the exclusive domain of his own self-loathing as made his way home in the weak light, stopping off at the off-licence, to get more whisky.

Surely Caroline wasn't sleeping with Skinner . . .

Kibby felt the effects of the whisky in his head, heard Skinner's sneers in mocking flashback, telling all in that college refectory about the 'birds' he'd shagged . . .

. . . that Kay, she was lovely and he treated her like shit . . . Shannon . . . what are they to him, just spunkbags, disposable . . . I'll bet he gives them marks out of ten . . .

Embittered, Brian Kibby alternately staggered and lurched purposefully down the hill, into his housing scheme. A short distance from his home he got out of breath and had to stop for a rest. He was adjacent to a swing park where several kids were playing, supervised by some adults. Kibby was standing there, panting heavily, staring off into space. One of the adults, the sole man, a wiry guy in his early thirties took a couple of steps towards him. — You! he shouted at Kibby, before thumbing down the road. — Keep movin!

— What? Kibby said, at first bemused, then almost fretful as the injustice of the situation hit home.

And Kibby felt fear, and fought through his lack of breath and headed down the road. It wasn't the man he was scared of – his own wrath was now too great – but he feared being branded a pervert, disgracing his mother and sister in their neighbourhood.

Maybe I am a pervert . . . wanking like that, like an animal, a creep . . . how long will it be before I start touching up kids . . . ? no . . .

When Kibby got home the place was empty. It was likely that his mother would be out shopping. He hauled himself upstairs and stashed his whisky under his bed. Going back downstairs, he half slumped, half laid his expansive body out on the couch. After a while he heard a scrabbling, followed by the groaning twist of a key in the door. The sound never used to bother him, but now it was a major source of misery. He would have to oil that lock.

Dad would have . . .

Kibby sat sweating on the couch, breathing hard and low, wishing he'd had just *one* more whisky, and was tempted to go upstairs and get one, but in his guilt he worried that Joyce would instantly smell it on his breath. Yet he could not stop a defiant, belligerent twist moulding his mouth as the door opened.

However, it wasn't Joyce, it was Caroline. He remembered she had said that she'd give their mum a hand with the meal before Skinner came by. Brian Kibby's spirits rose. This was the first time he'd been alone with her in ages. Now he'd be able to tell his sister what Skinner was really like, before he destroyed her, just as he had surely done to him!

— Caroline, he wheezed in acknowledgement.

Caroline Kibby caught the whiff of drink from her brother. Scrutinised his cheeks: rougher, drier and ruddier than usual. —You okay?

— Aye . . . it's good to see you, Kibby sniffled, at first contritely, before a tickle of the alcohol in his brain produced a speculative half-smirk. — How's the course going? he said in sombre exaggeration, attempting to root himself.

The room is sort of spinning but it's no really bad, it's like . . . who cares?

— It's a bit of a drag, Caroline shrugged, instantly reassured that her brother's old concerns were intact. Now vague and distracted, she sat down in the big armchair, curling into it, picking up the remote and clicking on the TV. The mute control was on and a newscaster mouthed in silent sincerity followed by footage of Middle Eastern women and children crying in a pile of rubble. The next picture showed an American soldier, armed to the teeth. Then it cut to a disengaged, constipated-looking George Bush and finally to a simpering Tony Blair, surrounded by suits, at some sort of function.

Kibby felt something rising inside him, through his watery, bloated flesh, across the yards of dulled space that seemed to exist between each cell, each neuron.

They get other people to do it for them. They have the money, the power and they exist to indulge themselves and their vanities. But it's no them, it's no their sons or daughters who have to go and fight and murder or be hurt or killed to indulge those conceits. It's the people who have nothing, those who cannae fight back, who are made meek . . . and you can watch a thousand Harry Potters *or Steven Spielbergs or Mary-Kate and Ashleys and Britneys and* Big Brothers *and* Bridget Joneses *and you can ignore it by wanting to be the next Principal Officer at the council . . . ignore that you're not empowered, you're not enfranchised, you're a slave, a slave to those egotistical, pious, sanctimonious murdering bastards and the world they've created, a world as selfish and cowardly and vain as they are . . . like Skinner . . . they get other people to deal with the shit they make through their own twisted vanity . . .*

Then the distance suddenly closed and a force fused and crackled between the gaps as Kibby's head rattled.

There's Caroline, my sister, part of this lazy, complacent decadence, wasting opportunity while my dad sweated his working life away and deprived himself to ensure that she had those chances . . .

— You always liked your course . . . he whined.

Caroline shook her head rapidly, her mop of blonde hair tumbling and swishing and falling back into place like nylon static, only a couple of strands displaced from its original position. — I do like it, it just gets on my nerves at times. It's just work, work, work, she shrugged, letting her face take on first a speculative, then a wicked aspect. — I just feel as if I need a bit of pampering sometimes, she smiled.

— And that's where *he* comes in, is it?

Caroline gazed at her brother, in a way she never had before, curling her lip, and Brian Kibby instantly saw himself through her eyes. What he saw was a freak; a corpulent, mournful, possessive failure whose wreckage of a life trailed behind him like the slime of a snail.

They thought I was a dirty child molester, outside by the park.

On cue, Kibby felt his treacherous pores chuck more icy, toxic sweat over him.

Not Caroline, though. No Caz. Wee sis.

How close they had been in a quietly undemonstrative and understated way. Then, on occasion, sickening sentiment would crush them into making the odd gesture that mortified them both: how Scottishly close they had once been.

Caroline. Wee sis.

From Brian Kibby's point of view, all he could do was stare at his sister as she turned away and assiduously focused on the television. The American troops were preparing for a surge on Falluja in the run-up to the US elections as they had disclosed that over one hundred thousand Iraqi civilians had died as a result of coalition activities. He wanted to talk to her about this; he never usually talked politics with her because he always felt it was a distraction and that people should be happy with their lot instead of complaining or trying to change things all the time. He was wrong, though; he wanted to tell her that he was wrong and she was right.

But he was realising that he couldn't build a bridge, couldn't make a connection, because his hatred of Skinner had a life of its own, beyond intellect, beyond reason. It forged every grimace, framed each sentence, in fact, it determined all possible responses. It was an entity he was powerless to fight. And before he gained cognisance of it, this force was speaking for him, talking through him. — He's evil . . . he's . . . he whimpered breathlessly.

Caroline turned back to her scrutiny of Brian, then shook her head slowly.

He's finally lost it.

We've been through so much together as a family and now it's taken its toll. I'm so glad to be out of this madhouse, this crucible of fear and loss; to have finally cut loose and let go. God, what does Danny think of them, what does he think of me? It's as well that he's so understanding, so able to empathise with our losses.

— You're sick, Brian, Caroline concluded in deliberate detachment. — All Danny's ever done is tried to help you, tried to be a friend to you. It was Danny that kept you in a job all that time, just because he knew you needed it. *We* needed it, she said, warming to her theme. — Because that's the kind of person he is!

— You dinnae ken! You dinnae ken the kind ay person he is, Brian Kibby squealed in rage and terror.

Caroline's face twisted into a demonic parody of itself. Kibby had seen her bad moods, from toddler pouts to teenage tantrums, but he could never have imagined that his pretty and serene sister could possibly have ever looked so grotesque. — I can't stand it, Brian, I can't stand your puerile jealousy of Danny!

— But he's no what you think! Kibby wailed, looking ceilingwards towards heaven as if for confirmation.

But none was forthcoming as Caroline picked at some of the dry skin around her fingernail. Corrected herself. She'd have to stop that. — I know Danny, Brian. Aye, he likes to go out and have a good time. And he's popular. So people get jealous, start making up nonsense.

Brian Kibby's heartbeat rose and his sweat ducts gushed again. He winced as he got a whiff of that horrible stale scent rising from him. Skinner was doing it again, attacking him, weakening him somehow. — He's using you, Caz, he's just using you . . .

Caroline glared fiercely at her brother. — I've had a couple of proper relationships, Brian. I know a bit about that side of life. Don't presume to tell me about it, she snapped at him in undisguised distaste. She didn't need to say anything about Kibby's own distinct lack of familiarity with emotional or carnal issues; this was as implicit as could be. — And don't make a scene today, she warned, lowering her voice and glowering at him. — If you can't show any decency to Danny or to me, then at least think of Mum.

— It's him that's no goat any de–

— Shut up! Caroline hissed, nodding to the door as their mother's key turned in the lock.

Joyce Kibby deposited two large shopping bags in the hallway and opened the front-room door to find her children sitting in there together, watching television. It was like old times.

Danny Skinner arrived shortly after this, clutching a bottle of full-bodied, quality Bordeaux purchased from Valvona & Crolla, and some flowers, which he presented to an almost orgasmically welcoming Joyce.

It was Skinner's third appearance at the house, though the first two had been brief visits and this was the only time he'd properly set foot in the front room. He drank in the surroundings. The furnishings were old, but spotless. It told him what he could have already guessed: the Kibbys weren't into spending cash on luxuries, nor were they prone to throwing wild parties. A large, patterned three-piece suite dominated the room, though it was a bit big for it, and it gave the place a somewhat cluttered feel.

His biggest impression, though, was that this was a house of ghosts. The most prominent one, however, was not Kibby's father; most of the pictures of him were sun-faded due to having been taken in an era of poor-quality prints. No, it was the ghost of Kibby past. To Skinner, portraits of the young, gangling, *keen*, much-hated Kibby seemed ubiquitous.

Did he ever really look like that?

Sneaking a sideways glance at his grim, bloated, adversary who had just panted into the room and stared at the guest as if Skinner's sole purpose of visiting was the liberation of the family silver, he looked back at the picture. Infused by a sense of unease, Skinner just about managed to convert it into a thin smile.

Joyce had set the table up nicely in the front room, and a bottle of wine sat on it. She then placed the one Danny had brought alongside it, making Kibby, whose bearing alternated between aggressive and sullen, first give a disapproving start at such a lack of frugality, then quickly light up in anticipation of a pain-easing drink.

— I know we shouldn't, she said, glancing furtively at her late husband's picture, — but what's it you sometimes say, Brian: a little of what you fancy does you no harm at all? I mean, with the meal . . .

— Yes. Kibby spat the validation of his endorsement out through clenched teeth.

— I'll drink to that, Skinner seconded.

— Me too, Kibby said slowly, deliberately.

— Brian . . . Joyce pleaded.

— One willnae hurt. I've a new liver, he said, suddenly rolling up his jumper to expose a large scar which snaked in and out of his rolls of fat, fascinating Skinner, — a clean sheet, he added threateningly.

— Brian! Joyce's eyes briefly bulged in horror but she was relieved as her son quickly pulled down his jersey. In spite of her nervous, spastic jerks she managed to fill the glasses up as Caroline looked on, obviously in extreme discomfort which was only eased slightly by Skinner's indulgent squeeze of her hand.

They sat down to dinner. Though the meal – Joyce's carbonara sauce and pasta – was bland to his indulged palate, Skinner forced himself to make appropriately positive remarks. — Nice food, Joyce. Bri, Caroline, your mum's some cook.

— I expect your mother is too, Danny, Joyce obligingly cooed.

Skinner had to think about his response here. He knew that he himself was a better cook than his mother had ever been. It was simply a matter of availability of different ingredients and a more comprehensive knowledge of food, a generational thing. — She has her moments, he said, thinking with some guilt about Beverly.

The sense of trepidation that hung around the table was broken with the drink, into a nervous then hostile irritation on Kibby's part. — So, it didnae work out for you in America then, Danny?

Skinner refused to rise to the bait. — Oh, I loved it, Bri. Planning to go back. But . . . he turned towards Caroline and smiled, — . . . you know how it is.

Kibby sat seething in silent fury at this response. It took a good couple of minutes before he decided to have another pop. Changing tack, he asked pointedly, — So, Danny, how's Shannon getting on, encouraged to see that Caroline was now looking quizzically at Skinner.

— Fine . . . but I haven't seen much of her; he thought about Dessie Kinghorn. — Obviously, I've been in America.

— Shannon works, or should I say, worked, with us, Kibby snidely hissed.

— Yes, Joyce said tensely. — I spoke to her on the phone a few times when you were in the hospital. She seems such a nice girl.

— Her and Danny were very close, eh, Danny?

Skinner looked evenly at Kibby. — Correct me if I'm wrong, Brian, but didn't *you* and Shannon spend a lot of time together? Didn't you go to lunch together regularly?

— Jist in the canteen . . . she was a colleague . . .

— You always were a dark horse, Bri, Danny Skinner winked, almost with affection, even feeling confident enough to spread his grin around the table.

Kibby was so frustrated and drunk, he had to fight to avoid dissolving into a hyperventilating spasm.

This behaviour hardly registered with Joyce, so happy was she to have that vacant seat at the table, long empty, once again occupied. She thought that Danny Skinner was charming, he had such a friendly and dignified bearing and that he and Caroline looked so good together.

Caroline Kibby contemplated the wheezing, sweating mass her brother had become. She thought about the constant embarrassment he'd been to her over the years, whenever she'd brought school or college friends round. At least then he'd tried to be friendly in his inept way, but the vexation then was nothing compared to the discomfiture his behaviour now induced. In those acid comments and bitter asides she saw how much her brother had changed.

Skinner found it hard to stop scanning the room, feeling like an anthropologist attempting to ascertain the social fabric of some strange tribe. Yet the proximity to Brian Kibby made him uncomfortable. It was disconcerting being so close to that reeking, wobbling flesh and it was he who was loath to make eye contact with his old enemy.

This was not at all easy due to Kibby's omnipresence, particularly on that fifties tiled art deco mantelpiece, which was lined with so many of his portraits. While the heavy drapes on the windows shut out much of the light, as if in acknowledgement that Kibby was best appreciated in shadow, one picture dominated and it seemed to keep catching Skinner's glance. Once again it was a large portrait of the Kibby of old; the thin, cadaverousness of his complexion contrasting with the large, liquid eyes of almost incomparable luminosity – in fact, just like Caroline's were now – and the thin, fine features of the mouth and the nose. The current vintage caught him engaged with the image of bygone days and issued a derisive look so knowing that Skinner at first felt worried and then disgraced by it. Real guilt pricked at him as he considered what he had once put Kibby through with his bullying, recognising that he had inflicted considerable pain even before you contemplated the peculiar and devastating hex.

Yes, this thing opposite me is surely a different fuckin species to the youth in the photo. It's a Frankenstein monster, and one created purely by my own indulgence! Sometimes, though, I can feel the presence of this other Kibby, the young cunt I'd been workmates with, gone to college with, eaten in the refectory with. The guy who'd blushed and coughed as I chatted up the hairdressing and secretarial studies lassies. The sap that looked mortified as I casually mentioned the explicit details of some sexual encounter, which I'd never been prone to doing in most company, but couldn't resist due to the effect it had on poor Kibby. Yet afterwards this made me feel so crass, which, in turn, only made me detest Kibby even more. I remember what I once told Big Rab McKenzie about the young Kibby: that I hate him because he brings out the bully in me, brings out a side of me that disgusts and repulses me.

Rab, God rest his inherently minimalist soul, had an immediate suggestion: 'Well, burst the cunt's mooth then.'

If only I had taken the big man's advice. I did much worse: I burst his soul.

Skinner made a pointed decision to ignore that haunting picture and go back to the real thing. For all the short-term jolts of discomfort Kibby's barbed comments and looks induced in him, they were passing irritations, failing to draw real blood. Instead, Joyce's gratitude at his simple appreciation of the food and Caroline's indulgent smile, to say nothing of the wine, were having an intoxicating effect.

Indeed, he clicked back into that sickeningly wonderful false mode, which, he knew with a bitter-sweet sadness, he was just too weak to resist. — Tell you what, Bri, I hear you're sorely missed in the office.

Brian Kibby moved his big, bulging-eyed head up slowly. His mouth hung open, framed by his slack, rubber lips. Yet there was something incongruent in the eyes: a resigned, brutalised pain, way beyond anger. Skinner saw it as a last leak of outraged defiance coming from Kibby's beaten psyche, drip-feeding into the fetid atmosphere of the room around him.

Aye, Caroline was well out of here, Skinner thought, glancing at her and feeling like a knight in shining armour.

Kibby panted softly. The faintest of light tortured his eyes. The most routine burst of sound from outside caused him to start like a dog that had been disturbed by a high-pitched whistle. The sweet odour of the fresh-cut flowers Skinner had brought for Joyce sickened him, while his own bodily smells induced nausea. In the morbid acuteness of his senses only the most bland and insipid food was tolerable to him. And here was Danny Skinner, at his table, torturing him like a matador does a lumbering, wounded bull. And his own mother and sister were screaming '*Olé*' with every flourish, cheering this arrogant poseur on. It was too much for Brian Kibby.
— Aw aye, ah thought ye might have found somebody else tae be the butt of your jokes by now, he spat.

— Brian! Joyce pursed, looking apologetically at Skinner.

Danny Skinner, though, threw his head back and laughed off the intervention. — Pay no heed, Joyce, it's just that old Brian Kibby sense of humour we all know and love so well. We're all used to it by now. He can be such a grump!

There was a wave of cloying laughter from Joyce as Brian quivered again, in that uncomfortable hard chair, feeling it digging in treacherously as his monstrous buttocks spilled across its hard edges.

Skinner is in my *home, fucking* my *sister, eating at* my *mother's table and the bastard has the audacity to invent a fictitious camaraderie which is at best spurious nonsense, and at worst the most blatant attempt to deny a systematic campaign of bullying and abuse . . . and . . .*

— Well, I think it's inappropriate, cantankerous and obnoxious, Caroline sniffed fractiously.

Kibby looked her with a heavy heart. She was a woman; mature, bright, alive, cool and he . . . well, he had never been able, had never been allowed to become a man.

But maybe I can.

After dinner Brian Kibby made his excuse of fatigue and headed up to his room. From under the bed he fished out a whisky bottle. He took a slug at it. The golden elixir burned: thick, strong and nasty in his blood. Hardening him. Making him harsh, squalid, arrogant and, for all he knew, as immortal and timeless as those qualities.

38
Muso

The successful, the semi-successful and the shameless blaggers of the city had gathered in their habitual uneasy federation on the opening night at Muso, Alan De Fretais's newest bar-restaurant venture. De Fretais himself had arrived in a foul mood, which was only now being assuaged by some excellent Chablis. The builders had promised him that the enterprise would have been ready for a grand opening during the Edinburgh Festival, and a host of visiting celebrities and the national press had been lined up. Now it was considerably later, in the autumnal dead zone, and he was stuck with the local Z-listers and burning with spiteful reproach in the knowledge that it would take that elusive third Michelin star to give him anything like the coverage he craved. — My own little Holyrood, he remarked acidly to a *Daily Record* entertainment correspondent, who looked as disappointed as he did.

But the fruity grape, given its distinctive character by the localised Kimmeridge clay soil, was working its considerable charms on De Fretais. Soon he was soothingly reflecting that it was a good turnout for the time of year, when many of the city's cognoscenti were still recovering from festival burn-out or anticipating the Christmas headache.

Skinner entered with Bob Foy, who had told him the welcome news: the Master Chef had returned from his German excursion. They had enjoyed a cocktail at Rick's Bar, and so arrived a respectable twenty minutes late, though not late enough to miss out on the supplies of free booze. His fragile nervous system told him that Brian Kibby had obviously put a few sneaky nips away last night, and he had needed a decent drink to take the edge of his hangover. Skinner had almost forgotten how polluting and weakening alcohol could be. At least it was quite dark in here, he considered, regarding the suitably subdued lighting with gratitude.

That wee fucker must have a peeve stash in that fucking midden of a bedroom of his. I'll get Caroline to search for it . . . or Joyce even. I'll stop that fucking dingul in his tracks! Daft wee shite doesnae ken what he's doing, how dangerous this is!

The bar area was imposing enough in a minimalist sort of way. Although the walls were an uninspired light blue, the old bar had a nice slab of marble on it and the gantry was oak-panelled. An impressive stripped and gloss-effect wooden floor and a series of sunken lights completed the look.

Skinner glanced around at the company thinking: so far, so dull. He was habitually checking out women, trying not to think of Dorothy in San Francisco or Caroline closer to home. Without success.

It's fucking peculiar with Caroline and me. We just can't seem to get it on. Probably cause she reminds me of Kibby. Once I get him back in his sickbed where he can't hurt me, it'll be full steam ahead; his sister will get legged for Scotland. If it turns out to be just a sex thing, then I'm right back over to California. First I need to get steamboats, and this shithouse is as good a place as any to load up in.

Could go a ride though. No sign of Graeme or any of that crowd. Maybe a full-on ungreased erse-tanning might slow Kibby down a bit!

In the rhythmic sips of the confirmed dipso, he quickly disposed of his first proffered glass of champagne. Disturbed by a digging elbow in his side, he turned to see Foy draw his attention to the high ceiling, where a series of musical instruments hung suspended from the roof. There was an electric guitar (which Skinner fancied as a Gibson Les Paul of some vintage), a large harp, a saxophone, a double bass and a set of drums, all at measured heights, as if a troop of gravity-defying musicians could just float up there and strike up a tune. But most impressively and implausibly, there was a white grand piano, hanging about fifteen feet above the bar, joined to the roof by four cables going into a single large hook which he thought must be bolted through one of the ceiling joists.

In spite of himself, Skinner felt some sense of awe.

Suddenly a voice came into his ear, so close he could feel the heat of its originator's breath. — You're thinking: how did we get that up there?

— I certainly am, he admitted to his host, the Master Chef Alan De Fretais.

De Fretais moulded his face into a languid, obsequious grin. — The answer is: with great difficulty, he mused, shaking his head at his own wit before heading off into the crowd.

Wanker, thought Skinner, but without any real hostility, tracking the chef's meanderings. Only a tube, and a coked-up one to boot, could find that shite funny. Which, in essence, was exactly what he thought De Fretais was. There was surely no way that such a twat could be his old man. He reflected that it was how they talked to semi-strangers in such scenes, effecting an intimate profundity while saying nothing, but doing it in the manner of high gravitas perfected by Connery's Bond. Above all, keeping a tight reign on all information, however trivial. Keeping secrets. Like all those fucking chefs, he thought, as he moved to circulate and chat casually to some vaguely known faces.

He'd quickly ascertained that this was the sort of do where looking over people's shoulders was not considered rude but obligatory. It was almost prestigious to show how bored you were in the company of your casual acquaintance. Your mouth spraffed away from a stock of responses based in one sparkling region of the mind, while your eyes wilfully scoured the other guests to see if you could upgrade your company.

It's an ugly, status-conscious survival of the shitest.

Now he was doing the same, as he was still engaged in tracing De Fretais's movements. He saw the fat chef talking to Roger and Clarissa and seized his chance, bounding across to them. — Excuse us a second . . . he nodded to the others. — Alan, can I have a quick word?

— It's our young Unionist friend, Clarissa purred, her eyes and lips scrunching into a couple of gashes in her face. — Did you enjoy your little . . . *union* at our last meeting?

— I'm incredibly busy right now, Mr Skinner, afraid it'll have to wait, De Fretais said, suddenly bounding over towards the bar area.

— It's important, it's about my moth– Skinner began.

De Fretais wasn't hearing him, though, and Skinner was about to set off in angry pursuit, when in an instant he was rooted to the spot and his heart nearly bounded out his mouth as he saw the familiar black sheen of a young woman's hair. She was dressed in a traditional white-and-black waitress's uniform, but with a short skirt, wrapped tightly around an arse he knew well, the look completed by black tights or stockings. Serving up some savouries from a tray, she turned in profile and Skinner caught a beaming toothsome smile.

Roger made some comment, which he couldn't hear through the pounding of the blood in his head, but he could tell it was a sarcastic one by Clarissa's mocking laugh.

Skinner turned distractedly to her. — Bet you were a looker in your day, he said, her imploding face telling him he'd got the requisite amount of sadness in his expression. — Long time ago now but, eh, he added. He moved away from them, behind the waitress, watching the curves of her buttocks in the tight skirt as he felt something stir inside him.

Kay . . . what the fuck is she . . . ?

And worse still, he saw that De Fretais was approaching her, with a big smile on his face. The chef put his hands around her waist. She gave a reluctant smile and tried to wriggle away, but she was unsuccessful, as she couldn't let go of the tray she was holding.

He's got his fuckin greasy mitts all over her!

No . . .

She's fucking well just standing there . . . just letting that fat cunt paw at her!

The bilious acid rose up in his guts as he felt the glass in his hand. He envisioned plunging it into the neck of the fat chef, like a dagger, watching him bleed on the floor; his vacant uncomprehending livestock eyes as he kicked out in his death throes. Skinner could feel his own blood bubbling warmly in his veins, but his thoughts were still composed and abstract. Fortunately, one of those notions was to wonder how many previously socially functioning men had killed in such circumstances, and this was enough to make him abruptly exit the bar.

Outside, the street was full of small groups of people between hostelries. As he filled his lungs with the cool, night air, he realised the champagne glass was still in his hand. He hurled it to the ground, his loud curse drowning out the sound of the glass shattering, and he flagged down a passing taxi, oblivious to the nervous stolen looks of passers-by.

That boy is a typical alkie, Mark Pryce, the sales assistant at Victoria Wine, thought, as Brian Kibby shuffled into the shop, now so desperate as to be devoid of his normal furtiveness. He asked for two bottles of whisky: one Johnnie Walker Red Label, one The Famous Grouse.

Mark was a second-year psychology student at the university. He thought deeply about some of the regular customers he served in the shop. In a sane society he would have referred many of them to the local health and social services rather than sold them alcohol.

That boy doesnae have much time left, Mark considered in a sombre evaluation, as he bagged the bottles and handed them over to a wilting, trembling Kibby. He felt so strangely moved by the subdued but intense disconsolateness of this particular customer, he almost felt like saying something. But when he made eye contact with Kibby, he could see nothing, just a dark void once inhabited by a human soul.

Pryce took the money and rang up the sale and made a mental note to get another part-time job. *Somewhere more socially rewarding, like McDonald's or Philip Morris.*

Arriving home, Brian Kibby entered in clandestine silence, anxious to avoid his mother and a potential scene about his drinking. Fortunately, nobody was in. He tried to pull his frame up the aluminium stepladder to his old hiding place, but after a few steps he felt giddy, the blood throbbing in his head, and he knew that he wouldn't make it. Descending slowly, he went to his room where he abjectly drank one bottle of the whisky, and made a respectable dent in the second before passing out.

Morning rolled in as the seagulls squawked in the mottled light that faded up slowly over Leith. Danny Skinner was feeling very rough already, suspecting Kibby, but his discomfort was massively augmented when the phone rang and Shannon McDowall greeted him with some devastating news. — Bob's in the Infirmary . . .

This galvanised Skinner, and fighting through a sickening hangover, he made his way up to the hospital. He almost vomited on the bus and drew disapproving stares from a woman with a small boy who wore the new green Whyte & Mackay whisky football strip that had replaced the Carlsberg lager one.

At least when it was only beer the poor wee bastard had a sporting chance . . .

When he got to the hospital and up on to the ward, he saw the prostrate figure of Foy, unconscious, lying back in a bed, hooked up to an electrocardiograph, a tube coming from his nose. Not good, Skinner thought.

Amelia, Foy's second wife, was sobbing by his side, along with Barry, his teenage son from his first marriage. — Danny . . . Amelia blubbered, rising and hugging him tightly, the smell and proximity of her causing an awkward Skinner to remember that time, in a drunken session some months ago, when he'd ended up round at the Foy household.

After a formidable drinking binge, Foy had passed out on the couch, and Amelia had grabbed Danny Skinner and had practically tried to force him to fuck her on the kitchen worktops. Skinner had pushed her away, leaving her with Foy's slumbering body. They hadn't spoken since.

Wonder if she still wants it. Probably now more than ever. At least there's somebody I can fuck . . .

Amelia seemed to sense something in him, some hint of the sewer, and quickly pulled away. Stealing a fretful glimpse at the depressed-looking Barry, she explained in a fluster, — I found him lying in the garden. He'd been sweeping up leaves. I was trying to get his diet sorted out, the doctor had said that his cholesterol levels were way too high . . . he wouldn't listen, Danny, she bubbled, — he just wouldn't listen!

Skinner squeezed on her hand, caught Barry's eye over her shoulder and gave him a lugubrious nod. Then he looked at Bob Foy, lying there, but where was he? In the bed? No, more like trapped on some strange mezzanine floor between life and death.

He wondered if Foy could hear him, if he should say anything, if the doctors had said that he could hear. Skinner thought of that old council epitaph: *He knew his way around a menu in French.*

It's certainly been a diet heavy on the arteries. But then Bob never had a Brian Kibby.

Then he felt the ache in his kidneys. It seemed like Brian Kibby was realising that *he* had a Danny Skinner.

The bastard fuckin kens awright.

39
Alaska

His head thumped and his stomach went into dry spasms as he bent down to pick up the mail. A letter from the sheriff officers informed him that the bailiffs would be applying for a warrant to gain entry to his home and seize goods to auction in order to pay off the large amount of debt he'd accumulated. He couldn't bear the thought of his expensive goods being sold so cheaply to the extent that they wouldn't even dent the debt.

It's just a fucking show of strength . . .

As fate would have it, he had been approached to come back to the council for the duration of Bob Foy's illness. The last thing Danny Skinner had wanted to do was to recommence his employment, but the pistol was at his head. He resolved that he'd return and get started paying off the arrears, to get the sheriff officers off his back. Then he'd sell everything he could and resume his career break in California.

Might be there for a long fuckin time as well.

It had been, he realised in his guilt, a while since he'd responded to Dorothy's last email. This was almost exclusively due to Caroline and his fascination with her and the Kibbys. As he couldn't tell Dorothy about them but had done little else, there was simply nothing to report to her. But now he felt an overwhelming need to see her.

Although Caroline's good looks were readily evident to him and the rest of the world, he found her oddly sexless. He couldn't even get hard thinking about her, but whenever he contemplated Dorothy's nose and hair, he thought that his cock was going to explode. His head rattled and pounded. He thought about Kay, about how he'd so resented De Fretais touching her. Was it because it was her, or because it was him?

On his way up to the office for his first day back, he stopped off at the Internet café.

To : dotcom@dotcom.com
From: skinnyboy@hotmail.com
Re: Things

Hi Dotty Yank

Sorry I haven't been in touch for a bit. I don't like Internet cafés – the ones in Edinburgh are so grungy and crusty compared to the ones in Frisco. There's nothing been happening at all in Leith. Zero to report, except I'm still on wagon (that's why there's nothing to report – sad but true). I've been forced into going back to work temporarily, in order to pay off some debts. Obviously missing you and California very much. It's so dark and cold and dreary over here. Glad to hear that you're still thinking of coming over. I'm sure I'll find ways to keep us warm!

On that subject, see what you were talking about with the screws, well, the old baws are quite delicate but I'm always game. Agree that we shouldn't be thinking of involving other participants at this stage. Dot, to be honest, I just want to make love to you slowly, sweep back that curly mop and whisper in your ear 'mein liebling Juden Fräulein' or something like that. Skinner: sick or sexy? – you decide.

Love
Danny XXX

PS: Will phone later on.

PPS: Poles: born to suffer or what? Russia one side, Germany the other. Like sharing a railway compartment with a Jambo and a Hun.

PPPS: The Poles played a largely unheralded role in the history of Scottish football *and* were known as dapper dressers: Felix Staroscik at the now defunct Third Lanark, Darius 'Jackie'

Dziekanowski at that Irish diaspora multinational heritage corporation formerly known as 'Glasgow' Celtic.

I recall when we last made love we almost sucked the fucking breath from each other.

Aye, I'm better with Dorothy and California, away from all these terrible obsessions that drive my life; alcohol, my father's identity and, most of all, the fucking Kibbys.

Too fuckin right.

It felt odd stepping back into the office. It had only been a few weeks but it seemed like epochs to him. It was welcoming and disheartening at the same time. Shannon was still temporarily in his old job, with him having the same status in Bob Foy's. Cooper had retired slightly earlier than expected, and Skinner and Shannon's new boss was a thoughtful, bespectacled man called Gloag, who seemed fair and decent, if a little dull. He threw himself back into work, undertaking several tasks on his first day, mainly catching up with paperwork. One thing that he realised was how little Foy actually did, as it dawned on him that he himself, in fact, had effectively run the section. This was a mantle that would be passed on to Shannon.

After a late finish and a few beers it was time for him to meet Caroline for some Italian food at that old favourite of Foy's, the Leaning Tower. They shared a bottle of wine, at his insistence, a full-bodied Chardonnay from California's Sonoma County. Skinner felt he needed a good drink.

Gillian McKeith can get tae fuck.

As he sat looking at Caroline, he saw a row of three red spots, forming a crescent on her chin. She was picking at the skin around her fingers. There was an air about her: increasingly desperate and needy. Basically, he thought, she just wanted fucked, and he wouldn't, couldn't, do the business. And she was blaming herself. It wouldn't last of course, she'd soon get to the 'well, fuck you then' stage. Her self-esteem wasn't low enough to carry on like this for ever, although he had no reason to deny the veracity of her emotions when she told him how she felt about him.

But do I love her? In a way. But there's Dorothy, and I love her in a proper, non-fucked-up way.

— You okay, Danny? You look a bit rough, Caroline said.

— I feel like I'm coming down with something. Some kind of flu or the likes, he muttered. Then Paolo, the proprietor, asked him how Bob Foy was and he was forced to tell them both the story. They listened with sympathy and put Skinner's distracted manner down to shock.

The drop of white wine nestling in the bottom of Caroline's glass looks to me like the remnants of pish in a latrine. Things are becoming corrupted . . . no, they've always been that way. I've just noticed because the corruption has taken on a new hue. Now my cock's failed me. Nearly twenty-four and I can't fuck a gorgeous girl who's nuts about me.

Is that it, it that the answer to this fuckin mess? Can I only gain power in hate? No. I didn't hate Kay, or Shannon. I certainly don't hate Dorothy.

And Skinner thought he just couldn't go back with Caroline again, his head so messed with Dorothy, and with Kay and De Fretais. He couldn't subject either of them to more of that fumbling, tense, perverse psychosis. He needed distance, space to order his thoughts, so he made his excuses and headed home alone. Or intended to head home.

The city streets were morgue-like by this time. He saw the odd bunch of revellers but felt as forlorn and abandoned by his home town as he had been by the father he had never known.

As lonely as a bastard on Father's Day.

Part of him wanted to be back in his flat, with his books of verse for inspiration, but he found a vague sense of purpose gnawing through his ennui, as he walked through the city. He found himself murmuring a recitation under his breath:

The Devil went out a walking one day
Being tired of staying in Hell
He dressed himself in his Sunday array
And the reason he was drest so gay
Was to cunningly pry, whether under the sky
The affairs of earth went well.

The nature of his impetus remained opaque until he came by Muso. A light was still on. Without thinking what he was doing, he went round the back and pushed at the kitchen door. It was open. He heard noises; slow, gasping sounds, punctuated by the odd terse, sharp, cry, and followed them, gingerly tiptoeing round to the restaurant area. The sounds were coming from the bar.

It's De Fretais. He's shagging somebody. On top of them, on the bar. Somebody is underneath his sweating mass, pinned to the bar.

I know who it is. Kay. He's shagging her. Her heid's away from him, turned to the side, but there's no mistaking that long, raven-black hair . . .

He's fucking well shagging my Kay . . .

The fuck . . .

Instinct seemed to propel his movements. He stepped back into the shadows and climbed a set of stairs that led into the attic of the building. He could feel his heart pounding and his lungs forcing the air into his body as he mounted the steps.

The attic was partially floored with rough plywood. It was barely used, even for storage, and was all but empty barring a film of dust and some spiderwebs. The half-moon shone murkily through a Velux skylight, shedding its light on a bag of tools. A rubber torch lay on the bag and he picked it up and clicked it on. The light revealed a few misdriven nails in the floor and some overhead beams to avoid. There was a full-length mirror, propped along the outside wall. He could see two large bolts coming through a beam across the floor.

Of course, the piano. It's directly above them. That dirty creepy cunt . . . and Kay, my Kay . . .

He moved around in the darkness, saw a light filtering up from the grill of a vent. Looking through it he could see them, or rather De Fretais, his bulk obscenely smothering her, his ex-fiancée. All that was visible was her head. He tried to make out the expression on her face. Full of dread, or orgasmic? He couldn't tell.

And De Fretais's fingers in her mouth . . . to stop her screams . . .

The fucking rapist bastard . . . just like he did to my fuckin ma all these years ago, that's why she hates the cunt . . .

. . . to stop her groans of pleasure . . .

The dirty fucking hoor . . . couldn't resist the fucking lure of the dance, the fame she so badly wanted but wasn't good enough to get, so she thinks she can get it by proxy by letting a fat monster rifle her . . .

Danny Skinner couldn't tell. Training the torch on the bag of tools, he searched for something with which he could loosen those bolts.

It's so strange with Danny and me. He looked really down at dinner; he'd heard bad news about his friend. We're both worried about this sex thing coming between us. It's only a shag, but it seems to weigh so heavily on us. I want him so much, I think about him all the time, but when we get in each other's company I feel so . . . squeamish, when I think about sex. Like I was a daft wee virgin.

Sometimes Danny seems to carry the whole weight of the world on his shoulders. When he was telling me and the guy at the Italian place about his friend, it was so reluctant, like getting blood out of a stone. He should try to share his problems instead of keeping everything to himself.

My evening's ended earlier that I anticipated, so I decide to go back home to look for some old books I need for college, ones I've stored in Brian's attic, or what we know as Brian's attic.

When I get in Mum's sitting watching the telly. She's been crying, telling me that she found Brian drunk upstairs with two bottles of whisky. I tell her that I think this may have been at least part of the problem all along, that he somehow managed to conceal it from the doctors and from us. She argues weakly to the contrary, but I can tell that she's also reassessing things.

I leave her and go upstairs to look in on him. He's lying on his bed, fully clothed, mouth open, his breathing ragged and hollow. The room stinks worse than ever. I can barely recognise that thing on the bed as my brother.

I go into the hallway and pull down the hatch and the aluminium stepladder and scramble up. It's all dusty and neglected, due to Brian's illness. It's been ages since anybody was up here. Switching on the lights I can see the big model village rolling out in front of me. The trains, the station, the blocks of flats, the town growing around the hills. It is impressive, if you like that sort of thing. Even if you don't, I suppose.

One life gone, the other draining away, and that's their legacy. Dad's hills. He always liked Edinburgh for its hills, he said it was the hills that kept the city compartmentalised, kept us minding our own business, keeping our little secrets. He'd take me up them all; Arthur's Seat, Calton Hill, the Braids, and the zoo at Corstorphine Hill, the Pentlands.

Danny said something similar about San Francisco. He told me that he loved walking there; up and down its steep hills, getting a different view of the city each time. He even spread a big map on the table and talked me through them; Twin Peaks, Nob Hill, Potrero Hill, Bernal Heights, Telegraph Hill, Pacific Heights. He made it sound great, even said that we might go there together one day.

But we can't make love. We want to but we just seem to tense up around each other. I love him. I seem to really need to be with him, to be around him, so much. I've become the kind of pathetic lassie with him I said I'd never be. I want to fuck him, or I think I do. But, I wonder, what does he want, because he's as uptight around me when we get intimate as I am with him. Is it that American woman he's mentioned, does he love her? Does he have her on his mind every time we go to get it on?

I find the books, stacked neatly in a corner, select a couple and head downstairs. Mum has dropped off in the chair, her mouth open like Brian's. There's no point in waking her. I head out into the cold and wait for ages on a bus because when I count out the change in my hand there's only four pound coins and I can't afford a poxy taxi.

His hand gripped the spanner tightly as he wrenched at the large nut, feeling it give straight away. Then, without loosening it fully, he twisted on the other one. He could feel a twinge on the joist, hear the sound of the piano rocking.

I'm looking back to the grill of the vent, but from this angle I can't see their reaction, her and that animal that's on top of her, fucking her.

But do they see it, do they see the piano rocking, hear the bolts slackening?

Resuming his efforts, Skinner couldn't see them, but he saw himself in the meagre torchlight, reflected in the full-length mirror. His expression was devilish, but composed, like a rock-carved gargoyle from a medieval building that had suddenly come to life and was feasting slowly, with insect coldness, on the flesh of a warm-blooded animal it had just slain.

He watched himself unscrew the bolts and there was only one

heart-thudding, sickening moment when he wanted to stop but that was the futile split second before he felt the weight of the piano slip as it sprang from its mountings with two twisting, wrenching snaps.

There seemed a long pause between the release of the instrument from its ceiling berth to the almighty crash and horrible animal groan, which, even through the attic ceiling, was harrowingly audible to Danny Skinner.

Skinner froze, looked at his guilty reflection in the mirror. Then he thought about Kay, and the love they had shared, as the blood ran cold in his veins.

WHAT HAVE I DONE?

Maybe I missed her, or missed them. Surely.

They would have heard it, seen it loosening, got out of the way. She would have seen it. But . . .

But his hand was in her mouth, stifling her cries, her moans, his big, fat sweaty carcass on her . . . my dad's, no not my dad . . . but aye, it makes as much fucking sense as anything, this is how it has to fucking well be, this is how it has to end . . .

Skinner ran down the stairs, and he didn't turn back, didn't look in to see them, or the piano. But then he noted something, a white, ivory key that had shot out from the impact and ricocheted round the corner. There was no noise; no groans were coming from the room. For some reason he picked up the piano key and stuck it in his pocket. He kicked the back door of the restaurant open and moved out into the dark night. Heading down the road in haste, he was almost tempted to break into a run. Avoiding North Bridge, he scurried down New Street, past the abandoned bus depot, on to the deserted Calton Road, running alongside the railway embankment. His spine was almost rigid with fear as he drove forward, waiting for the pursuing police car that never came. Slowing down to a busy stride, he went past the new parliament, open for business at last.

Our toytown parliament: like looking for a father and being presented with a guardian from the social work department.

When he got closer to Leith he avoided the Walk and Easter Road, ghosting and weaving down the backstreets between them. He had taken a circular route across the Links and was down by the Shore when he stopped for a while and looked at the still Water of

Leith draining into the Forth. He felt the piano key in his pocket. When he picked it out he was shocked to see that his mind had been playing tricks on him, this key was not ivory white but ebony black. He chucked it into the Water of Leith, went home and sat up psychotic with exhaustion and anxiety, fretfully wondering just what exactly he had done.

Ellie Marlowe was a little late for work, and she hoped that Abercrombie the Zombie, as they referred to one of the line managers who never seemed to sleep, had not risen early in order to check on her. Even worse, the fat boy from the telly, him that owned the place, was sometimes prone to coming in, as it was his new venture.

There was something wrong . . . the door. It wasn't locked. Somebody was in. Ellie started to formulate excuses about buses. She couldn't run a car on cleaner's wages, they surely knew that as *they* were paying them, after all. She doubted whether Abercrombie or De Fretais had seen a bus timetable in their lives.

Ellie turned the corner with trepidation, walking into the main bar. As a pungent odour of urine filled her nostrils, she couldn't believe the sight that met her. She then thought that she might scream, or run out into the street, which surely would be coming to morning life by now. Instead she calmly lit a cigarette, then picked up the phone and dialled 999. When the operator asked her what service she required, Ellie took a puff on her Embassy Regal, paused for a second to consider, then said, — I think you'd better get the lot ay them.

The trickle of perspiration snaked down his neck in slow, flesh-crawling violation, setting off a quiver in his body. Brian Kibby slowly rose and saw the cold glint of the bottles by his bed, instantly knowing that they would not have escaped his mother's notice. Pungent aromas of old alcohol and stale body matter swept into his head, which then fell into his hands in deflated anguish.

Everything's falling apart. He's won. He'll destroy us all.

His heavy body thumped downstairs, as he saw his mother sitting at the kitchen table with a pot of tea and a Maeve Binchy novel. Kibby immediately blurted out an apology: — Mum . . . I'm sorry about the drinking . . . I was depressed . . . I won't do . . .

Joyce looked up, but without meeting his eyes. Staring off into space she said, — Caroline was here last night. Did you see her?

Why couldn't they face things? Brian Kibby's soul screamed. Yet he'd been the same, lying in a stupor, too drunk to even notice that his sister was in the house. — Mum, my drinking, I'm sorry, it won't . . .

— Would you like a cup of tea? she said, suddenly looking right at him. — I've nearly finished the new Maeve Binchy. She displayed the novel's cover. — I think it's the best one yet. Pity you missed Caroline.

Kibby nodded slowly in defeated resignation and lumbered wearily to the cupboard where he got a 'Hyp Hykers Do It Wetter' mug. It was Ken Radden who had got those mugs made. At the time Kibby had considered them as simply referring to their tendency to get sodden wet in the Highland rains on their hiking trips. Now they seemed to carry a risqué and close-to-the-bone *double entendre*.

He poured a cup of lukewarm tea and sipped at it, letting it part his lips by dissolving the gluing film on them.

Why was I so stupid? Why couldn't I see it for what it was? So many of them were just in it for sex. Like Radden and Lucy . . . like . . .

Caroline had probably gone away to be with Skinner. Most likely she was in his bed right now.

Suddenly Kibby felt a terrible resentment towards his sister, so extensive in its nature that previous sibling rivalry had only hinted at it. She was like her friends, all those girls that he had seen glow impossibly, defencelessly, with youth and beauty. With her creamy skin and sharp jawline, her hard breasts swelling and her small waist, she seemed like a walking insult to him, her and her friends. His very presence made them awkward and embarrassed, he just seemed to give off this stink. Yet he could cruelly see how Skinner would be so much at ease with them, how he could easily satisfy this ecstatic, puzzling need to take such beauty to you, to open it, penetrate it, and attempt to elicit its nature.

And Brian Kibby, with a dreadful insight gained through his own terrible decline, saw that there were not the boundless eras he had thought between Caroline's pellucid, imperturbable beauty and the sagging, haggard appearance of his mother. It was a tunnel made dreadful by its shortness, and you emerged from its other end in a confused dance at a velocity you could barely perceive.

Time is running short, slipping away . . .

He went upstairs and switched on his computer.

The chat room . . . was that horny wee bitch in the fucking chat room . . . ?

Yes . . . there she is . . . how many marks out of ten will I give this dirty wee slut . . . ?

07-11-2004, 3.05am
Jenni Ninja
A Divine Goddess

I've taken the plunge and got started on the new game. Magnificent! Has changed my life. Decided to marry Ann.

07-11-2004, 3.17am
Smart Boy
The Man in the Know

Ann's pretty cute in the new edition, but I still prefer Muffy. She's the hottest!

07-11-2004, 3.18am
Über-Priest
King of the Cool

I think you're the hottest, Jenni babe. Where do you hang out?

07-11-2004, 3.26am
Jenni Ninja
A Divine Goddess

Why, Über-Priest, I didn't know you cared! I live in Huddersfield and like skating and swimming.

07-11-2004, 3.29am
Über-Priest
King of the Cool

We should meet up and hang out sometime. I'll bet you're really sexy. I don't mind that you dig other chicks cause I like to watch, before I join in, of course. What do you look like?

Holding his stiffening cock, he eagerly waited for a response. None was forthcoming. Then, as he received a message from the board monitor saying that he was banned from the chat room, his erection crumbled in his sweaty hand.

Ellie Marlowe's contention had proved not to be so fanciful: they had indeed required the services of the fire brigade as well as the ambulance and police at the Muso Bar and Restaurant. The piano had fallen almost square on top of the Master Chef and the waitress, pinning them to the bar during their act of copulation.

Alan De Fretais had died instantly under its impact. At first it was thought that Kay Ballantyne had suffered the same fate, but they felt a faint pulse in her. Kay was weak but still very much alive, the considerable bulk of the chef absorbing most of the shock impact of the falling piano.

The fire brigade used power tools to cut the legs off the instrument, and then it took several strong, fit firefighters to lift it from De Fretais. It took almost as many to prise the chef's corpse from the comatose body of Kay Ballantyne. Blood ran from his mouth into her face; he'd bitten off his own tongue and it hung almost completely severed across her cheek. As they attempted to pull the corpse with its obscenely bulging eyes from her, they noted that Kay seemed to be coming to, murmuring deliriously. It was one of the attending doctors who saw that the motion of De Fretais's corpse was arousing her, given that his member was still inside her and had probably stiffened due to rigor mortis.

As Kay Ballantyne gasped into consciousness, one irreverent firefighter turned to a colleague and remarked, — You've got tae hand it to that fat cunt De Fretais. A top shag, even in death.

40

Persevere

He sat, staring out of his bedroom window, across the back-court, to the bare, spindly trees, their sooty-grey barks greening with moss and lit up by a semi-opaque shaft of morning daylight. Behind them were the five-storey tenements, the emerging sunlight bouncing off them, shining up their brown stone to a rustic Mediterranean terracotta.

The clock on the church steeple told him the time, his one piece of reality orientation. Otherwise Danny Skinner felt as rootless as the dead autumn leaves that blew aimlessly around his backcourt. He had sat up most of the night, snorting cocaine from an old wrap he'd found in his bedside cabinet, listening to Radio Forth, particularly anxious every time a local news bulletin came on.

Then, at around 9 a.m., Skinner heard about the two persons believed to be badly injured in a freak accident at a restaurant. He had no intention of going in to the job he'd just restarted and sat consumed by misery and regret until he went down to the Bengali grocer's on the corner, for a late-morning edition of the *Evening News*. The paper headlines were full of the grisly death that television celebrity and Master Chef Alan De Fretais had suffered. Skinner was jolted, but not surprised, to hear that the chef's real name was Alan Frazer and that he came from Gilmerton.

I've killed him. Killed my own father. He was a chef, a shagger; we even had the bond of hating Kibby. My ma didn't like him, but then he wasn't a likeable guy. I can see it now, she didn't detest him because he hated her; she loathed him because he was so indifferent to her, indifferent to me. She was just another silly wee tart who didn't take precautions that he'd got up the duff, so it was her problem. He probably got into her the same way he did tae poor Kay . . .

He didnae react tae me like I was his long-lost son. There was no vibe, outside a bit of morbid fascination on his part, which he satisfied after he'd met me a couple of times. He knew who I was from the start, but there was no vibe because he was just a selfish cunt . . .

. . . but . . .

. . . but when I got the promotion and went to his restaurant, and he brought over the champagne, maybe he did that because he was proud of me . . .

He got an old notepad and pen and practised writing the name:

Danny Frazer

The paper reported that Kay, whose identity was not disclosed until later issues, was in a stable condition. As soon as she was named on Radio Forth, Skinner made telephone enquiries to the hospital, stating he was her fiancé. A sympathetic nurse told him she was okay.

There were tears in his eyes as he read the glowing testimonies to the achievements and character of his victim. Shaking free of his maudlin inertia, Skinner took a taxi to the Infirmary, convinced that enough time had passed to put him out of the frame of suspicion. There had been no reference to potential foul play in the paper but the police would know that bolts didn't unscrew themselves. Or maybe they did, he didn't know.

When he got on to the ward he almost walked past Kay's bed. She was so battered-looking, like she'd been in a bad car accident. Her face and eyes were swollen and there was a bandage across the bridge of her nose.

De Fretais must have nutted her when the piano hit them.

Yet she seemed so pleased to see him, and he was just massively relieved to discover that she would be okay. He realised with an almost sickening force that he still loved her, and possibly always would. It was a doomed love of course, but one that would never be the less for that. He wanted to tell her everything, but fortune had it that she spoke first.

— Danny . . . I'm so glad you're here . . .

— I heard about it on Radio Forth. When they mentioned your name, I was so shocked, I had to come and make sure you were okay, Skinner gasped, now relieved that the moment for total candour had passed. — What happened?

— A piano fell on us . . . myself and Alan. He's . . . I was so lucky . . . Tears welled up in her eyes. — I was so stupid, Danny . . . we were . . . we were having sex . . . She spluttered it out. — What was I thinking about?

— It's okay, it's okay . . . Skinner cooed breathlessly, almost rendered speechless with guilt. Her nose was broken and so were two of her ribs and he had done this. Done this to someone he loved.

It was the hate.

It was the alcohol . . . the chefs.

It's not Kibby's curse, it's a curse to everybody, and it's consuming me and every single person I come into contact with. I've got to sack it all, got to get back to Dorothy in San Francisco . . .

Skinner sat for a bit until Kay's mother came in. She was an elegant woman, well groomed, who had obviously looked after herself. The type that aged well, he'd always thought. She seemed surprised to see him. It's probably because I'm relatively sober, he considered with a poignant ache.

He excused himself but was in no shape to return to work. He found an Internet café and emailed Dorothy, and then checked online for cheap flight tickets to San Francisco.

Ah'm fucking oot ay here. The Kibbys, Brian Kibby and *Caroline Kibby, it isnae right, it's well fucked. Ah'm gaunnae kill them all if ah dinnae get the fuck away. It's being here; it seems to lend itself to having strange, destructive obsessions with your neighbours, and you forget to get a life of your own.*

Naw, I'm hurting nae cunt else.

He contemplated the curse, how it was infecting everything. He thought of the old cliché, 'Be careful what you wish for', and considered whether he could, *compos voti*, achieve satisfaction.

While looking through the *Evening News* earlier, Skinner had noticed a feature on a white witch, Mary McClintock. Although now retired, it was claimed that she was an authority on spells. It took him a long time to track her down to her Tranent home in the sheltered housing complex. He called her and, after finding out his age, she agreed to see him.

It was uncomfortably hot in Mary's flat, but Skinner took a seat opposite the fat old woman. — Can you help me? he said earnestly.

— What's your problem?

He told her that he believed that he had put a spell on somebody. He wanted to know if this was possible, how he could have done this, and how it could be reversed.

— Oh aye, it's possible. Mary regarded him cannily. — I can help you, but I need payin first, son. Money's nae use tae me at ma age. Her eyes wrinkled. — You're a fine-lookin laddie, she said harshly. — A good cock, son, that's the payment I need!

Skinner looked at her, and shook his head. Then he broke into a broad grin. — This *is* a joke, right?

— There's the door. Mary raised her hand slowly and pointed behind him.

Skinner kept his gaze on her, his expression pained. He blew out some air through tight lips. Then he thought about Caroline, his terrible impotence around her. — Awright, he said.

Mary seemed slightly taken aback, then rose eagerly, letting her weight slump heavily on to her walking frame. Hobbling slowly through to the bedroom, she beckoned Skinner to follow. He hesitated for a second, and smiled crushingly to himself, before pursuing her.

The sparsely furnished bedroom, with an old brass bed prominent, was dank and musty. — Take oaf yir clathes then, let me see the goods, Mary rasped in lecherous cheer.

As Skinner undressed, the old woman removed her coat and began to struggle out of a series of cardigans, pinafores and vests. Lying on the bed, she looked smaller but still monstrous, wrinkled rolls of flab spilling over the mattress. Foul aromas rose from the putrefying pools of sweat and dead skin trapped within the folds of her flesh. — Thoat ye'd be bigger, Mary pouted as Skinner removed his Calvin Klein briefs.

Fuckin cheeky auld clart . . .

— Next time ah'll bring a strap-on, he said bitterly.

Ignoring him, Mary lay back on the bed and pulled away at the sagging corrugations of her body until she was able to locate her sex. — Ah've nae cream tae lubricate this. Ye'll huv tae use spit. Howk it up, she commanded.

Skinner moved across to the bed. Mary's bony fingers held her folds up, and he saw it between those surprisingly spindly thighs, which were so thin and sharp it was as if the thigh bone would rip through the papery yellow and blue-blotched skin. Amazingly, the hair was still as raven black as the hair on the woman's head probably hadn't been for many, many decades. With the skin around her pubic region angry-red and swollen, probably from some kind of infection, her genitalia appeared to him like the deformed newly born offspring of a life form not yet conceived.

In a gripping fascination, Skinner wondered how many frustrating sexless years she'd endured, relentlessly nagged by a body clock that refused to run down. In confirmation, he glanced at her head sprawled on the pillow, and she caught his eye with a coy look, enabling him to briefly glimpse the young woman in her, which rendered her all the more grotesque in his eyes. His knees sank into the mattress, as the waft of the yellow urine and slimy golden-brown faecal matter that lay saturating the incontinence pads underneath her rose in the cold air.

The smell was bad, but he thanked the cocaine blockage of his nostrils. He pulled phlegm up from his chest and sucked mucus down from his head, mixing them into a pungent cocktail before splattering it with violence on to her pubic area. — Work it in, Mary urged, as Skinner took his thick green slime and spread it like a chef might glaze some pastry, at the same time slowly breaching and exploring. A ludicrously distended clitoris popped out from nowhere like a jack-in-the-box, the size of a small boy's penis, and disconcertingly strangulated groans coming from the bed told Skinner that he was hitting the spot. After a while she gasped, — Pit it in now . . . pit it in . . .

In his total preoccupation with the macabre pantomime he'd become involved in, Skinner hadn't even begun to consider his penis, but it was rock hard, even after him having done half a gram of cocaine earlier. Without being conscious of it, he was framing yet another hypothesis to explain his alcoholism: he speculated that he possessed a libertine sexuality and attempting to swamp it with the bottle was a way of preventing situations like these continually arising. He rubbed some of the waste on to the tip, then the shaft of his cock and entered her with slow trepidation.

— Been that long it's probably sealed up, she said heavily, reading his mind as he forced his way in.

She took a lot of fucking; her desire might have been intact but if there was a climax in her it seemed to be well buried.

Fuck sake, I should get the morn's lottery numbers plus next week's racing results for this!

There were times when she was close to the brink but it seemed to slip away, and Skinner felt like giving up as the foulness of the situation hit him. He watched the old alarm clock by the bedside going from seven twenty to seven forty. As he felt the slurping of her wet skin on his stomach, thighs and testicles become the rub of coarse sandpaper then the jag of brittle old bones, he was forced to recall the old Leith motto: Persevere.

When she came it was accompanied by a long, nocturnal, wolf-like howl, and her bony fingers sank like meat hooks into the tight flesh of his buttocks.

Without coming himself, Skinner withdrew, climbing off Mary and the bed. Gingerly picking up his clothes and holding them out from himself at arm's length, he went to the toilet, knowing that if he looked at what he felt was splattered on his genitals, abdomen and thighs, he'd never be able to hold on to the contents of his stomach. There was a small shower at one end of the bath, with an alarm cord to call the warden in emergencies. There was no soap in the shower tray: it lay by the bath taps. Skinner suspected that Mary came from the generation where getting clean meant steeping in a tub of your own waste every Sunday. The water was tepid but he watched tendrils of mucus, faeces and other excretions weave a dance around the grill of the plughole before vanishing.

He dried off, dressed and returned to the front room. There was no sign of Mary, though he reasoned that she was just putting on all her layers; but then he feared that the old woman might be lying dead, so preoccupied was he with his destructive powers. Eventually, he heard her moving down the hallway and was relieved to see her appear. As she collapsed down into the chair, a huge smile changing her expression so radically it was like she'd had a facelift, she said, — Doon tae business. What's the problem?

It took Skinner a while to get into his story, aware of its ridiculousness. However, he found to his surprise that what they'd just been through seemed to make it easier for him.

And Mary listened attentively, never once interrupting until he finished. After his tale, Skinner felt cleansed somewhat, unburdened by the act of disclosure.

Mary had no doubt as to what the problem was. — Intentions, son . . . call them wishes if ye want, they can be so powerful in some people that they do become curses, become spells. Yes, you've definitely put a spell on this young man.

Having lived with this strange arrangement for many months, Skinner accepted this as given rather than just a fanciful notion. — But why do *I* have that power, and why just with *Kibby*? I mean, I've wished for other things tae happen tae other people but nothing's come of it, he explained, thinking about Busby, as he picked remorselessly at the skin around his nails.

Then Skinner felt a chill, the air seeming to cool, as Mary nodded slowly. For the first time he became aware of a certain power emanating from this old woman. — It's either something tae dae with the nature of what ye wished for or tae dae with the person you wished it upon. What does the spell mean tae ye? What does this laddie mean tae ye?

He shook his head slowly, stood up and prepared to take his leave. — Thanks very much, but I *have* been thinking about those questions, he said, his tongue dripping sarcasm.

Mary twisted her head round and said, — The more things in your life that are unresolved, the more powerful yir anger is, the stronger the potential fir ye to do this sort of harm.

Skinner stopped. — Kibby was a . . . he began, then halted as he had an abominable but opaque awareness. It was stark but somehow not envisionable. He had a sense that somewhere inside of him he knew the answer, but would never be able to dredge it into the realm of conscious thought.

But . . . one time I mind of this guy who always used to watch us play football. Inverleith Park, the Links. He always kept his distance though. One day he said to me, 'Good game there, son.' He was . . .

— I'm worried for you, she warned, — worried that you'll come to harm. Then her hand reached out and grabbed Skinner's wrist.

Skinner's heart flew to his mouth, shocked as he was at the sudden movement and the speed of the old woman's reflexes and the strength of her grip. Nonetheless, he composed himself and twisted his arm away, breaking her grasp. — Worry about the other boy, that's the one you should be concerned for, he scoffed.

— I fear for ye, she told him.

Skinner again scorned her, but as he departed he could not conceal his apprehension. Maybe he would go for that drink he needed.

41
Train Wreck

The whisky helped. It had given him the power and determination to embark on the arduous task of hauling his heavy, battered frame up the stepladder. The wasted muscles in his arms and legs burned like hot coals as the aluminium steps creaked, popped and groaned under his weight. A fuzzy rasp trawled through his lungs, which toiled to push in enough oxygen to feed his exertions as his pulse accelerated. At one stage he was so giddy he thought that he was going to slip off the ladder and crash to the floor. Then, with one last exhaustive heave, he stepped, trembling, into his old attic. It felt like breaking through a suffocating membrane into another world as his head spun with the drink and the effort of the climb. He gasped, struggling to regain his wind and senses as he tugged on the cord light switch. The neon strip lights flickered into action confronting him with the model railway and town.

Its delicacy and precision instantly mocked him. He stood there, housed in the wrecked and wretched soft machine of his body and raged at his pristine, useless creation.

What is all this? It's all I've done with my fucking life. It's all I've got to show that I ever existed on this planet. This fucking toy!

I won't get another job.

I'll never get a girlfriend, never find somebody to love.

This is all I've got. This!

It's not enough!

— IT'S NO ENOUGH! he screamed, his voice emanating from a buried, tortured part of his soul and ricocheting around the cavernous attic.

The hills his father had made, the houses he had built, the tracks he'd laid, the trains he'd bought, all looked back at him in an obstinate, contemptuous silence. — IT'S NOTHING! IT'S

NOWT! And he lumbered towards the town and found himself tearing it apart; kicking and pulling and punching at it with an energy and power he thought that he'd never, ever possess again. Brian Kibby smashed the buildings to pieces, tore open the papier mâché hills, ripped up the tracks and hurled the train engines across the room, ransacking the model town like a demented beast in an old horror movie.

But the adrenalin vanished as mysteriously as it had appeared and exhaustion suddenly took him, stranding him prone on the floorboards, leaving him crying softly in the rubble he'd created. After a bit his glassy gaze drifted across the floor to the glossy maroon-and-black engine, which lay smashed and strewn in the debris. He could see the gold-and-black plaque on its side branded with the words: CITY OF NOTTINGHAM.

The R2383 BR Princess Class *City of Nottingham*. Its axle was broken. He picked it up, cradling it like a first-born child that had been fatally hit by a passing car. As he wept slowly he raised his head and looked at his father's once magnificent hills, now levelled and reduced to trash.

The hills that Dad built . . .

NO . . .

What have I done?

And he climbed back down the aluminium stairs, now not worrying about the jarring thumps as his legs crashed down each step, and he thought that now was the time he was ready to die.

It would be better for everyone.

But perhaps there's somebody else who has tae die first.

It was as if both Caroline Kibby and Danny Skinner had realised that there was a kind of love so empyreal in its nature that the window of opportunity for real physical congress cracked open for only a short period of time. If, for whatever reason, you couldn't jump through it, it was slammed shut for ever.

The smell of her hair. Her lovely deep hazelnut eyes. That beautiful skin, how it all seemed to change under my touch, as if corrupted by my proximity. I can't be with her: not in that way.

Yet what other kind could there possibly be? he wondered as

they stiffly headed arm in arm down Constitution Street in the confused, beaten silence of doomed lovers.

Caroline dug into her make-up bag, produced the gold lipstick tube and twisted it. As that scarlet piece popped out Skinner imagined his cherry poking out of his foreskin in the same way.

If only . . .

It was the curse on her brother; that was what was messing them up. It had to be. He wanted to tell her so much, just scream it out: *I'm killing your brother, I've put a hex on him. I did this because I objected to his mediocrity, his blandness and how he would advance beyond me purely because he didn't have my demons holding him back. I won't be able to touch you until this curse is lifted . . .*

What could she say to that?

But who are they, this strange but so mundane family: the student daughter, bright and full of life; the stricken, nerdy hillwalker brother; and the crazy God-fearing anxiety-ridden matriarch? Who in the name of suffering fuck are those people? What the fuck was the faither like?

Skinner thought about the missing Kibby, the one who seemed to have cast such a large shadow over the others. — Caroline, what happened to your dad?

Caroline pulled to an abrupt halt under the orange sodium street lamp and looked quizzically at him with the same bewildering sense of intrusion she demonstrated when he tried to touch her. This moved Skinner to qualify his motivation. — Naw; it's just that Brian's illness seemed to happen shortly after your dad died. Did he have something the same?

— Aye, it was horrible . . . his organs had just seemed to rot away from the inside. It was weird, because, like Brian, he was never a drinker.

Danny Skinner nodded. After all he had been through with Brian Kibby, he began to entertain the notion that maybe there was no hex, perhaps it was all just the uncanniest of coincidences. Maybe Kibby had the same, rare degenerative disease that his old man had before him. Who had he been to assume that he had the power to put a hex on anybody? Perhaps it was all his own mad, twisted vanity, distorting everything he saw around him.

No, he had to get away from them, he'd kill them all, like he'd probably killed his own father. Only now Alan De Fretais seemed more alive than ever: it was reported that sales of *The Bedroom Secrets* had picked up dramatically in the last week, putting his aphrodisiac cookbook back at number one on the best-seller lists. *Scotland on Sunday*, the *Herald*, the *Mail on Sunday*, the *Observer* and *The Times* all ran big features on him. Stephen Jardine presented a television documentary on the life of 'Scotland's greatest culinary talent'. On this programme, one wag claimed that De Fretais taught us to look at food differently – holistically – relating to it in a completely cultural and social way. They referred to him as the 'Godfather of the Culinary Generation'.

He was simply a cunt, Skinner thought, thinking of the old joke:

Who called the cook a cunt?
Who called the cunt a cook!

The lights of the Shore flashed into view, dancing across the Water of Leith. Skinner had insisted that he return the compliment by taking the Kibbys out to dinner at his favourite seafood restaurant. Joyce was delighted but she worried about how Brian would react. Strangely, he had raised no objection, although he was far from enthusiastic. — I hope you have a good time, he said, albeit in a distant, hollow tone.

— But Brian . . . you're invited as well, Joyce had incredulously shrieked.

— I'll come if I'm up to it, Kibby said, the fight further knocked out of him following his deeply regretted trashing of the model railway and town. But even as he protested he realised that in his heart of hearts there was no way he was going to be absent, to be the subject of Skinner's one-sided propaganda. One thought burned in his brain: *I need to protect them from that bastard.*

As they crossed over the cobblestones, Skinner glanced down an alleyway, saw something move. It was a gull, and it appeared to be covered in blood, on its head and chest. It was hiding among the sacks of rubbish from the restaurants. — Look at that . . . poor bastard, Skinner said.

— It's only a seagull, Caroline scoffed.

— Naw, he's covered in blood . . . a cat must've got him while he was rummaging . . . It's okay, pal. Skinner crouched, moving closer to the wild-eyed bird.

The gull squawked, suddenly rising and flying past him, into the sky.

— It was tomato sauce, Danny, Caroline explained. — It had been scavenging, ripping open the bin liners.

— Right, he said, keeping his face away from her, so that she wouldn't see his tears, those strange tears for the lonely seagull.

When they got to Skipper's Bistro, they noted Joyce immediately, standing in the doorway outside the restaurant, too nervous to enter unaccompanied.

— Hi, Mum . . . Caroline pecked Joyce's cheek and Skinner followed suit. — No Brian?

— I haven't seen him today, he went into town . . . He said he might come.

— Here we go, Skinner nodded tightly, glancing over Joyce's shoulder. She and Caroline turned to acknowledge the source of his gaze. Through the fog and night an almost shapeless figure emerged, moving slowly towards them. He seemed less a real human being than a piece of the vapid darkness come alive.

— The man himself! So you made it then, Danny Skinner smiled warily as Brian Kibby approached.

— Looks like it, Kibby snapped curtly back.

Skinner opened the door of the restaurant and ushered Caroline and Joyce inside. He held it open for Kibby, mouthing a crisp and stagy, — After you.

— You first, Kibby bit again.

— I insist, Skinner said, his elongating smile disconcerting Kibby. It was cold and he was desperate to get inside and into the heat, so he stumbled through the door with Skinner following behind.

A girl took their coats and they had a drink at the bar, Kibby sipping a tomato juice under Joyce's approving scan. — Awright, Charlie. Skinner enthusiastically greeted the chef who had come through from the kitchen and they exchanged pleasantries for a bit.

— You must know a lot of chefs through your work, Danny, Joyce remarked, obviously impressed.

— One or two . . . though not as many as I'd like, he said, a sadness coating his words.

In her excitement Joyce didn't pick up on his lugubrious tone. She turned to her son, whose eyes were fixated on the spirits gantry. — I'll bet you know a few chefs from your council days too, Brian?

— Not at my level, Kibby said evenly.

They were shown to a table, where, at Joyce's instigation, they ordered some wine. Skinner was reluctant at first, then looked over at Kibby and said, — I'm not so much of a drinker these days, but maybe just one glass. What's it they say: a meal without wine is like a day without sunshine?

Brian Kibby looked hopefully at Joyce who screwed her face up. He filled his glass with mineral water instead.

Still a fucking sad mummy's boy, Skinner thought savagely. He saw the television in the corner burn with footage from the Iraq occupation, and proposed a toast. — *A buon vino non bisogna fasca.*

Not one of the Kibbys had an idea what he was talking about, but it sounded impressive enough, especially to Joyce's ears. She was highly thrilled by the food; she'd never seen or tasted sea bass like the one presented to her. Caroline, at Skinner's recommendation, Brian Kibby noted, joined him in the John Dory. Kibby himself opted for the lemon sole. The fish was excellent and the evening was a treat for Joyce, who seldom ventured out after dark. — The fish is very fresh, she said appreciatively. — Is yours nice and fresh, Danny?

— Fresh? I was squeezing my lemon on it, when the last rites were still ringing in its ears, Skinner jested.

Everybody laughed, except Brian Kibby, though Joyce was gratified that, although quite surly, he wasn't being overtly hostile to Danny. — Are you much of a cook yourself, Danny? she asked.

— I'm an unashamed glory hunter, Joyce. I'll pick up any TV chef's recipe book – Rhodes, Ramsay, Harriott, Smith, Nairn, Oliver, Floyd, Lawson, Worrall-Thompson – and faithfully strive to recreate their offerings, the exigencies of the local marketplace permitting . . .

— What about our old pal De Fretais? Kibby said in a sudden challenge. Skinner felt his pulse rise. His body was suddenly immobilised in shock. — The one who's kitchen was a midden! Mind that, Danny?

What the fuck . . .

— That was a terrible thing, Joyce said, — a man at the top of his career and a great chef.

De Fretais . . .

— I thought he seemed like a real creep, Caroline said.

My old boy . . . I killed him . . .

Joyce pursed her lips at her daughter. — Speaking ill of the dead like that!

. . . he was a sex beast, an exploiter . . .

— What did you think, Danny? Kibby urged.

Kay. She's such a lovely girl. All she wanted to do was to dance. To be good at it. What the fuck was so wrong with that in my eyes? I should have supported her. I should have . . .

Skinner thought of his former fiancée lying in the hospital bed. — It was very sad, he said sorrowfully, then he felt the rage coming back as he recalled the image of De Fretais on top of her. — I was critical of his kitchen, we all know that, and so were you, Bri. Unfortunately, we never got the back-up we needed from senior management. As you're aware, I was a long-time advocate of changing the reporting procedure to make it harder for officers to have inappropriate relationships with the De Fretaises of this world . . . He watched Kibby redden and squirm. — . . . but I didn't get the support. Personally, though, I have to admit that De Fretais was one hell of a chef. So yes, I unreservedly add him to the list of people whose dishes I've shamelessly striven to replicate in the kitchen.

Kibby's head was now bowed.

Skinner turned back to Joyce. — Alas, with little aplomb. So I try, Joyce, but I'm not quite in your league.

Joyce put her hand on her chest and batted her eyes like a schoolgirl. — Oh, you're very kind, Danny, but I'm really not up too much –

— Your soups are good, her son petulantly snapped.

— You're a wee bit too red meat inclined for me, Caroline interjected.

Noting the fish on Caroline's plate, Joyce retorted, — Some vegetarian, you, madam!

Caroline shuffled in her chair.

— I'm getting her off all that nonsense, Skinner teased, as Caroline nudged him playfully in protest. Both again wondered fretfully how it was that they were so able to display the intimacy of lovers while still trying to consummate that love.

Her pubic hair will be as blonde as her head, so sweet and delicate, and I'd love to graze on it like a spring lamb on the virgin grass of the season, but I'll never know it, not like I knew old Mary's sweaty mass . . .

— Aye, sure. That'll be the day, Caroline chided back.

Brian Kibby tried to meet his sister's eyes with a burning look but she couldn't even see him.

He's fucking controlling you!

Joyce was having a good time, and was drinking quickly, unaccustomed to the wine that Skinner kept pouring into her glass.

— Do you ever go to church, Danny? she asked him earnestly.

— Religiously, said Skinner, drawing a laugh from Caroline and a guilty grin from Joyce. Kibby remained stone-faced. — No, I have to admit that I don't, Joyce, he continued, dispensing with the levity, — but I hear that you're a regular attender.

— Oh yes. It was a great comfort to me when my Keith . . . She stifled an emotional tear and looked over at her son. — . . . and of course, when His Nibs there was really sick.

Kibby, in response to his mother's condescension, felt his inner thirteen-year-old kick in. He downed the mineral water and poured a glass of the white burgundy. — Just one won't hurt, he said to Joyce as she pouted, then he turned sardonically to Skinner and added, — A little of what you fancy, right, Danny?

Skinner looked from him to the disapproving Joyce and raised his hands in the air in the gesture of mock surrender. — I'm staying out of this one!

But there was a lot more than just one, as another bottle found its way to the table.

Kibby was becoming emboldened by the drink. He looked across at Skinner. — People criticise the police, until it's them that get burgled or beaten up, eh, Danny?

Skinner shrugged, wondering where Kibby was heading with this.

— No, I was just thinking of the time that you got beaten up at the football. You would have been glad of their intervention then.

— It would have been a relief . . . for somebody anyhow, Skinner smirked.

— Police? Joyce asked in concerned anxiety. — What about the police?

— 'Walking on the Moon'? Skinner winked, and Joyce grinned without knowing what he was talking about.

After a few more bottles of wine had been downed, it became apparent that Joyce Kibby was having a *very* good time. — I have tae confess . . . I feel a wee bit dizzy, she giggled, relaxed as she noted that Brian and Danny seemed to be getting on a bit better. Then the room started spinning and Joyce began to gag and redden. — Oh dear . . .

— Mum, are you okay? Caroline enquired, this bizarre but welcome circumstance of her mother's intoxication and her boyfriend and brother's civility, albeit forced, not being lost on her. Although her spirits were raised, a sense of duty called. — I'm going to take Mum home, she said, rising.

— Aye, let's call it a day, Skinner agreed, signalling for the bill.

Kibby threw back his double brandy digestif, and ordered another. — The night is but young, he smiled, vaguely sinister, his hooded eyes in shadow from Skinner's vantage, but gleaming under the candlelight nonetheless. — What's wrong, Danny pal, kin ye no stand the pace?

Only Danny Skinner saw something dark and ethereal in that aside, something which went beyond the semi-drunk banter of two old workmates.

The day it is passing in laughter and song . . .

— You two stay for a drink if youse want, Caroline said, trying to get her shaking and bemused mother to her feet.

As Skinner gently chided Joyce for being drunk, Brian Kibby turned to Caroline and yanked on her arm. She braced herself for another of his attacks on her beau, but he just looked sadly at her and whined lowly, — I broke it, sis. The railway. Smashed it all up. Dad's railway. I was depressed, I just went crazy, and I feel so bad . . .

Caroline saw the terrible pain in his eyes. — Oh Brian, you might be able to repair it . . .

— Some things cannae be fixed. They just stay broken, Kibby groaned miserably, turning to take in the other diners in the room and focusing on Skinner, who had caught the comment and returned his stare.

As the waitress came with their coats Caroline felt the tension rise like a rocket, and said a reluctant goodbye. But Skinner only saw her lips move, because that gesture and supposedly inoffensive remark confirmed his realisation that Kibby somehow knew about the curse.

He knows. And now he's going to kill us both with his drinking.

Panic seized him for a second or two, but Danny Skinner accepted the offer to drink on, feeling that he now had little option. He was tossed around in a maelstrom of sensations, but one thought dominated: they were destroying each other, and Brian Kibby had to be made to see that.

So the two strangest drinking partners bade the women farewell and retired to the adjoining pub. Skinner looked at Kibby. It seemed he was preparing for more than just a drinking bout; he sat up on a bar stool with the intensity of a gladiator.

Skinner's mind flipped and tossed as he looked across at his opponent. — Bri . . . this is daft. This kind ay drinking isnae good for either ay us. Trust me, I know.

— You do what the fuck you like, Skinner, I'm on the piss and I don't give a toss, Kibby said, gesturing to the barmaid.

— Look, Bri . . . Skinner began, but Kibby already had a pint and a double whisky by his side, so self-preservation compelled him to follow suit.

Kibby can't have that much left; another mega-session will make him so ill he'll be bedridden and unable to get near any pubs or offies, and therefore unable to damage me. Then I'll be able to convince him it's a mug's game.

— You won't be able to keep up with me, Brian, Skinner said, raising his glass, then added chillingly, — There's no way you can win.

— I'll have a fuckin good try though, Skinner, Brian Kibby spat in retaliation. — And you don't need to be all smarmy now that my mum and sister are away!

And he raised a glass of absinthe, which Skinner hadn't even noticed him ordering, to his cracked lips.

C'mon then, Skinner. Let's do this. Let's just fucking well do it. Absinthe, whisky, beer, voddy, gin, fucking meths, anything you want. Bring it on. Bring it on, you evil, smarmy, mutant bastard spawn of Satan!

Help me God.

Help me.

Skinner looked Kibby up and down. It didn't even sound like him any more. But fuck him anyway, he thought, seeing a phantom sweep of the old Kibby, the professional victim he'd extended the hand of friendship to, but who, frightened of life, had scuttled back into his wimpy shell. — Suits me fine, he said. — Oh, and incidentally, whatever you think I've done to you, it's no been anywhere near enough, he sneered as he slugged at the drink.

The thing was, even as he hissed out this abuse, he realised in paradox that he no longer actually disliked Kibby.

Now Kibby isnae the keen, sooky, irritating little arselick of old. He's caustic and bitter and vindictive and obsessed and just li– . . . no . . . no . . .

No . . .

Fuck you, Kibby, I've got a plane tae catch.

42
The Diary

When we get out the taxi and back to the house, I leave Mum sitting drunk and giddy in front of the television. I've never seen her like that before. She's rabbiting on about my father, telling me what a good man he was, and going on about Danny, saying that he's a good boy and that it's great that he and Brian are now friends.

I'm very doubtful about that, and I was reluctant to leave them together because there was something going on there, but they insisted and I really needed to get her home.

She's on about my dad again: going on about how much she loved him. Then she turns to me and looks almost angry as her voice drops and she says, — Of course, you were always his favourite. They always say fathers and daughters, mothers and sons. She coughs, and her eyes go wide in a fanatical zeal. — But I love you, Caroline, I love you so much. You know that, don't you!

— Mum, of course I do . . .

She rises and stumbles over and hugs me. Her grip is surprisingly strong, and she's clinging to me desperately, not letting go. — My wee lassie, my bonnie wee lassie, she says through her choking tears. Her convulsions are rocking me. I'm stroking the dyed curls of her hair, watching the grey coming out at the temples of her scalp in a morose fascination.

But I'm getting uncomfortable and I whisper in her ear, — Mum, I'm just going upstairs for a bit. There's something I said I would check. She looks at me agog for a second, so I add, — For Brian, which seems to placate her and she loosens her grip.

— Brian . . . she repeats softly, then starts murmuring something, a prayer or the recital of a passage of Scripture, as I leave the room.

I get upstairs and yank down on the hooked stick, opening the trapdoor and freeing the aluminium steps. I pull them down and start to climb. The bolt that attaches them has become worn and they rattle dangerously under my weight. I'm relieved when I scale to the top and step on to the attic floor.

I click on the lights and I can see that Brian has really wrecked the place. It's like the model town has been bombed. I don't know if it can be restored; I would think that anything that can be built can be restored, but it's going to be a big job. I doubt Brian's up to it now. Part of me thinks I should offer to help him, then I consider just how ridiculous that is. I wouldn't know where to start.

I sift through the mess, looking at the broken hills that Dad made with all that papier mâché. I remember helping him make it up in this big orange basin we used to keep under the sink. So I did contribute to all this, more than I realised. When I think about it now, we all did it together. I was just a wee girl but I remember that I was excited to help. Where did I edit out all that good stuff in our lives? When did all those lovely memories of togetherness and fun start to become uncool and embarrassing for me?

I try to pull two parts of one split hill back together. Something inside falls out and hits the ground with a thud. I think it's a wooden support from part of the frame or something, but I see what looks like a thick desk diary on the ground. It's not a diary though, it's a lined John Menzies notebook and the handwriting inside it is all Dad's. Inside the front cover there's a note attached.

> One day this notebook will be found. My wife and children will know the truth that I've lived with for so many years. Joyce, Caroline, Brian, please believe two things. Firstly, that the person I was then before you all came into my life was very different to the person that I am now. Secondly, wherever I am now, I love you all more than ever.
>
> God bless you all.

I start to read from the book. It's trembling in my hand so much that I have to put it on the floor. My blood runs cold at one passage.

> I can't believe that he said nothing. An accident at work, they

called it. We both knew better, and I suppose that she did as well.

I couldn't help it; I was demented with anger and the drink. It's important for me to write this down.

My name is Keith Kibby and I'm an alcoholic. I don't know when this started. I always drank. My friends always drank. My family always drank. My dad was a merchant seaman and he was away from home a lot. Now I can see what a great life being at sea was for an alcoholic. You can dry out at sea, the only place you don't have encouragement to buy drink. No pubs, no adverts, no booze. But nobody drinks like a sailor and when he came home he drank and drank. I find memories of him sober very few and fleeting.

I was mainly brought up by my mother. I had a younger brother but he died as a baby. One day I came home from school to find my mother crying with my Aunt Gillian, and the crib empty. Cot death, they said. People also said that my mother and father were never the same after that. They said that Dad drank more than ever.

Growing up, I started to hang around with some local boys. We got rowdy as we got into our teens, as boys do when they're in a gang. Some of us were tough, others just pretended to be. We called ourselves the Tolcross Rebels. We were proud of who we were. We fought other gangs and we drank a lot. I drank more than most.

I left Darroch School at sixteen. When I went to my careers officer he sat me down and gave me a card, which I took along to the railways. I trained as a chef on the railways, with British Rail. They sent me to Telford College on day release where I did the City and Guilds of London Institute's chef course.

I never, ever liked being a chef. I had no flair for it and resented being cooped up, sweating in a hot kitchen. I worked on the Edinburgh to London trains, in the restaurant cars. I wanted to be up front driving the train, not penned into a narrow kitchen, heating up pre-cooked food for businessmen. Like so many kids at my school, I got poor career advice.

The Tories had come to power under Thatcher and they

were shutting everything down. I got involved in the union, and became politically aware, or 'politically conscious' as we liked to refer to it back then. I went to meetings, took part in marches and demonstrations, stood on picket lines. I read a lot of history; a lot about socialism and how it offered working people the chance of a better life.

But I could see that so much of it was pie in the sky. The system would always win, would always be able to throw enough scraps from the rich man's table to keep ordinary people stampeding over each other to get to them. I grew disenchanted that the world would never be like I wanted it to, a fair and just place for all. So I drank more. At least that was the way I saw it at the time. It was probably just an excuse.

I needed excuses, as I didn't want to be like my father. He was abusive in drink. I stood up to him as a young man when he hit my mother. We fought, physically fought, in drink. My father was a brutal man, and I suppose that I learned to be too, in order to stand up to him. Once we both ended up in casualty after a battle. My mum would sometimes leave him but she would always go back.

There wasn't much love in my life back then, but I had music. Outside of politics, that was my big passion, specifically punk rock; when it came along I was in my element, as it sort of combined the both. It was stuff that was being made by ordinary young guys from the same sort of places as us, rather than remote, rich pampered superstars in Surrey mansions. There were some great local bands in Edinburgh at the time: the Valves, Rezillos, Scars, Skids, the Old Boys and Matt Vinyl and the Decorators.

It was strange that punk was portrayed in the media as violent, but it was going to punk gigs that got me away from the street violence of the Edinburgh gang scene at the time. Through punk I fell in love with this girl, I met her a Clash gig. Her name was Beverly; she was a true punk rocker. She had green hair and she often wore a safety pin through her nose. A really wild lassie, though she had her softer side as well. She stood out just by being a girl as, to be honest, there weren't many who were lookers that were into punk. Compared to her I suppose I was just pretending: I was a punk on Friday and then got togged up in disco gear to go to Busters or Annabel's on Saturday, in order to meet girls.

But I never met a girl like her at those places.

Beverly hated that; she was always calling me a plastic. She worked as a waitress in the Archangel Tavern, where she became famous for her green hair. They said it was a bohemian crowd that hung around there. I didn't like them though; they were too posh for the likes of me.

Not that I cared about them. For the first time in my life, I was in love.

Beverly was friendly with some of the chefs there. They were restaurant chefs and they looked down on a railway skivvy like me. That De Fretais boy was one of them, only he wasn't called De Fretais back then. He was in my class at Telford.

There was always a problem with my drinking. Put that together with Beverly's temper and we were a volatile mix. She did her own thing and was seeing this other guy at the same time as me. He was a chef as well, in the Northern Hotel. I didn't know him but I knew of him. Hotel and restaurant workers tended to socialise together because of the working hours.

Beverly fell pregnant right after we got together, wouldn't say whether it was mine or the other guy's. He was a drummer as well; he played with the Old Boys. I didn't know this guy but I hated him. Why not? He was a chef in a better place than me, a real punk who played in a band, and Bev, whom I was crazy about, she loved him more than she did me. I couldn't accept that.

One night, things just came to a head. I was drunk and I was really angry about the situation, and I did the most stupid thing I've ever done in my life. I went to see the other boy to try and sort things out. It was horrible. I went to where he was working and argued with the guy in his kitchen. Nobody else was around at the time. He didn't take me seriously, gave me the brush-off. As I went away, shouting at him, he flicked the V-sign at me and said, 'Fuck off, arsehole.' He said it so dismissively. Now when I think about it, fair play to the boy; a drunkard comes into his work shouting the odds, how else would he react? But in drink and crippled with jealousy, I was totally enraged and lost my head.

The boy had turned away from me and I ran back towards him, grabbed the back of his head and pushed it into what I thought through my alcohol haze was this pot of soup. It wasn't. It turned out that it was deep-fried fat. He screamed: I've never heard anything like that scream, but I suppose I screamed too, as it burned my hands. The pot cowped over and I ran out the kitchen without looking back. A porter saw me and I pushed past him and mumbled something about there having been an accident. I never even knew the boy's proper name at the time. Since then I found out it was Donnie Alexander. I went home and when I woke up it seemed like a dream. But my scorched hands told me that it wasn't. The boy had such terrible burns to his face, and was badly disfigured. For some reason he never shopped me, said it was an accident. I couldn't go to the doctor's with my hands. I was in pain for weeks; God knows what it was like for poor Donnie.

He didn't say anything, but Bev knew that I had done it. It didn't take a genius to figure it out. She wouldn't see me, even when the baby was due. Threatened to tell the police what I'd done if I went anywhere near her. She wasn't joking either. Beverly was a very headstrong lassie. I loved her but she really did love Donnie. Who could blame her? I was a drunk and the thing about drunks is that you always tire of them at some point. She was with him before me; it was just that they'd had a bad fallout. Sometimes I think she was just using me to get at him. I would have done anything for her.

Then the kid came along. A boy. I know that he was my son, I just do.

The worst thing, though, was when I heard about Donnie Alexander's death. I had disfigured him. He went away to work down in Newcastle, in a small hotel. Then I heard that he was dead. He'd committed suicide in his bedsit. It was all my fault; I as good as murdered the man.

It's important for me to write this down as honestly as I can.

I went to AA and straightened myself out and from there I got into going to church. I had never been religious, in fact I was anything but and to be honest I'm still sceptical, but it gave me the strength to continue life sober. I let go of politics, although I remained a union man. I stopped seeing all my old pals. I retrained with British Rail, first as a signalman, then as a driver. I loved the job, the solitude, and particularly the beauty of the West Highland line.

Through the church I met my Joyce and built a new life with her. We had two great kids. I only ever touched alcohol on a few occasions after that. In those relapses I could see the old me: bitter, sarcastic, aggressive and violent. I was a psychopath in drink.

I felt terrible about Bev's boy but I reasoned that he was better off without me. She had started a hairdressing business, which seemed to be successful. I went to see her at her shop once, a few years later. I wanted to see if I could do right by the kid. But Bev told me that she wanted nothing to do with me and that I was never to go anywhere near the boy; Daniel, she called him.

I had to respect her wishes. I did watch him play football sometimes, making sure that she didn't see me. It used to break my heart, watching the other fathers making a fuss of their laddies. Maybe I was just projecting my own hurt, but he often seemed such a lost, lonely wee guy. I mind of him scoring a goal in a game once, when she wasn't there, and I went up to him afterwards and said, 'Good game there, son.' A big lump stuck in my throat when his eyes met mine, I was choking back my tears. I had to turn and leave. It was the only words I ever spoke to him, although I've said thousands of them in my own head. But in the end I had to let go as I had my Brian and Caroline to consider, and, of course, Joyce. I had to try and look after them as best I could.

I told Joyce everything. I think that it was a mistake. They say that the truth sets you free, but now I know that it's just self-indulgent nonsense. It may set *you* free, but it can decimate those around you. It hurt Joyce so much that she had a nervous breakdown and I don't think she's ever been quite the same since.

Now, I suppose, I'm doing the same thing. Spouting self-indulgent truths to make myself feel better, when I know that it might hurt those I love the most. I feel that you should be strong enough to suck it up, keep it in. But when I do, I feel the burn in me, the need to go out and drink. I can't do that, and only writing it down helps. I only hope that when you all see this, it'll be at a time in your lives when you can understand it. The only thing I can say is that there are some kinds of mistakes you make that you never stop paying for, nor do those closest to you.

Now, Brian, Caroline, the chances are that you're reading this. Danny, you might even be too. If so, I missed having you around, believe me. There hasn't been a day that's passed in my life when I haven't thought about you. I sincerely hope that not having me around made absolutely no difference to you.

Joyce, I love you and could never apologise in a million years for all the hurt I've caused. I love you all and hope that you can find it within yourselves to forgive my stupidity and weakness.

God bless you all.

43

Leith Calling

The rain was now falling in cold sheets against the dark sky, rapping threateningly on the windows outside. Caroline ghosted into the room, which was lit only by the glow of the television set. She could barely make out the form of her mother, crushed into the big easy chair.

On the mantelpiece, through the flickering light, she could intermittently see the image of her father as a young man. She walked up to the framed black-and-white portrait picture and studied it as never before. There *was* something different about him; the eyes had a hitherto unnoted manic restlessness, the mouth was cast in an intemperate pout. Now it seemed to reveal him not as the quiet man who sat in the armchair, the upright, sober, churchy man, but as someone driven by great and sometimes terrible urges he struggled daily to repress.

She moved into the chair next to her mother's; the innocuous-looking John Menzies notebook, which contained those amazing confessions, pressed hard against her thigh. — Mum, what was Dad like when you met him?

Joyce looked up, interrupted from the steady anaesthetic drip-feed of the cathode-ray tube. The charge of the alcohol was running down, leaving her bleary and disorientated. In maudlin guilt she was now thinking that she had desecrated Keith's memory by drinking. And now there was something in her daughter's tone, something threatening . . . — I don't know what you mean, he was just your dad, he was –

— No! He was an alcoholic! He had a child by another woman! She stood up and dropped the journal into her mother's lap.

With wide, pained eyes Joyce looked from notebook to daughter, and then broke down, weeping uncontrollably as the journal fell to the floor. To Caroline she now seemed more of a dark, shapeless mass than ever. — He never loved her . . . he loved me! He loved us! Joyce said, her desperate timbre somewhere between a plea and a declaration. — He was a Christian man . . . a good man . . .

Caroline's stomach churned nervously, heavy with the food and drink. She exited to the hallway where a phone was mounted on the wall and a phone book and Yellow Pages sat on a shelf below it. She found Beverly's business phone number quickly enough, and just hoped that Bev Skinner kept her name in the residential phone directory.

There were quite a few B. Skinners, but only one listed for the Leith postal area of EH6: Skinner, B.F. She dialled the number with trembling care, and a woman's voice came on the other end. — Hello?

— Is that Beverly Skinner?

— Aye it is, came the aggressive reply. — Whae wants tae ken?

— Are you Danny Skinner's mother? Caroline asked, the woman's anger fuelling her own sense of indignation and giving her strength.

There was a sharp exhalation of breath down the phone. — What's he been up tae now then?

— Mrs Skinner, I think that I might be Danny's half-sister. My name's Caroline, Caroline Kibby. I'm Keith Kibby's daughter. I need to see you, to talk to you.

There followed a silence so long and deafening that Caroline wanted to scream in rage against it. Just when she suspected that Beverly Skinner might have put the phone down in shock, she heard the voice again, as pugnacious as ever. — How did ye get this number?

— The phone book. I need to see you, Caroline repeated.

There followed another silence, before a more resigned voice said, — Well, if it's in the phone book, you ken where I live.

Caroline Kibby did not even go back in to say goodbye to her mother. Joyce sat in a daze with the John Menzies notebook at her feet. As the front door slammed shut, she flinched only slightly.

Beverly Skinner put the phone on its cradle and sat back in her armchair. Cous-Cous the cat jumped up on her lap and Beverly found herself stroking the animal, which began to purr, a loud snoring noise, and then salivate over her.

For so long she'd been waiting for this day with a strange, gnawing dread. She had expected that when it came along it would be extreme: traumatic or even cathartic in some way. But in the event it was a total anticlimax. Beverly felt disappointed. She'd wanted to keep Keith Kibby's malign influence from her Danny for as long as possible. But Danny had managed to mess things up for himself, without that prick's help. The drinking, the fighting . . . well, she'd done her best with him.

That girl on the phone was the Prick's daughter. Him, that violent, drunken psycho! Him who'd dunked her beautiful Donnie's head into the chip fat. Disfigured him. That had finished him; he'd left the band, left his home, left her . . . and they found him dead. And now the Prick's daughter was coming down here to see her, no less! And it struck Beverly that the lassie sounded well spoken, not like the Prick, although he could be quite plausible sober. Mind you, such occasions were few and far between.

He'd probably given some other woman a life of hell as well. Perhaps we'll be able to compare notes. But it would be so bad for Danny if he knew about his father, if he knew he was . . .

Beverly heard a car pull up outside her house. By the heavy, tumbling sound the engine made, she knew immediately that it was a hackney cab. Knew who would be inside it.

She got up and opened the door to see a young blonde girl heading up the stair, looking up at her from the landing.

From Caroline's vantage she could see Danny in Beverly straight away, across the eyes and around the nose. — Mrs Skinner?

— Aye . . . come in, Beverly said. Her first impression of Caroline was that she was a very good-looking girl. But then the Prick was handsome too, it had to be said, when they first met. Even then, though, it was evident that the drink was beginning to destroy his appearance.

— So you're Keith Kibby's lassie? Beverly said, unable to prevent herself from making it sound like a challenge.

— Yes I am, Caroline said evenly.

— How is he? Beverly attempted to force a genuine equanimity into her tone. Once again she suspected that she had failed.

— Dead, Caroline said steadily. — He died just after Christmas.

For reasons she couldn't immediately ascertain, this information made Beverly feel oddly raw inside. After all, for years she had thought, albeit in the abstract, about dancing on Keith Kibby's grave. Yet in reality, she'd never actually thought of him as being dead.

But his daughter seemed genuinely sad at this state of affairs. And Beverly Skinner suddenly saw what was really upsetting to her; it was the idea that this terrible man might have somehow been able to redeem himself. That she had spent all those years hating someone who, in a real sense, had long since ceased to exist.

And as she talked with this young stranger, Beverly Skinner saw the evidence of that redemption with her own eyes, in the beautiful, poised and graceful young woman who sat opposite her.

It was the guest who eventually summed things up. — It seems like he was two men, Mrs Skinner, the one you knew and the one I knew. He never drank at all, he was a very gentle and loving man. But I read stuff in his journal . . . stuff I couldn't believe . . . he was never like that with . . . me . . .

Caroline was about to say 'us' but something stopped her. Brian. Did he ever have it different, ever see another side of their father?

Beverly let the words sink in. Tried to comb her memory to find another Keith Kibby, and just about succeeded. — Aye, we did have some good times at first. The Clash concert at the Odeon; that was where we met. A bunch of us were jumping around together, all out of it. I bumped intae him and spilled his cider. He laughed and chucked some at me. Then we were snogging each other's faces off . . .

Beverly stopped, noting that Caroline gulped at the thought. Then the older woman reddened at having inadvertently paraded a younger, unrestrained self.

— Aye . . . but Keith was that jealous, so possessive . . .

Caroline flinched again, aware that her father had never demonstrated this sort of passion towards her mother. It was a quiet love, between a strong, stern and sober man and a nervous homemaker, and it was based on shared values like duty and a commitment to family life. But passion, no . . .

Then Beverly was talking about how they used to go swimming together and it was bringing so much back for Caroline. How sometimes at the pool her father would lift her up and look at her and say with a ferocious intensity that almost scared her, like it wasn't him: *You're gaunny dae great things, lassie.*

There was almost a phantom 'or else' tacked on at the end, the idea that failure was not an option. Did Brian feel this more than her? Was he made to feel this by their father?

— Who was Danny's father, Mrs Skinner?

Beverly sat back in her chair and looked at this young woman. A stranger, asking that question of such impertinence, in her own home. Like many people who were overtly outlandish in their outward behaviour and appearance, Beverly Skinner was in constant flight from the part of her soul that was mind-numbingly conventional. Now there was no escape from it. She felt offended. Not angry, but simply offended.

— Was it the man with the burned face, or was it my dad?

Now the anger was present. In a rush it almost overwhelmed Beverly, forcing her to turn away. Not to do so would have meant her flying at Caroline Kibby with her fists. Instead she gripped the armchair.

The man with the burned face. That's my Donnie they're talking about. We had just got back together, patched things up properly, when that fuckin vermin Keith Kibby . . .

— Please, Mrs Skinner. Danny's with my brother Brian. They don't like each other and they've both been drinking heavily. I think that they might be planning to hurt each other in some way.

Beverly took in a sharp breath and panic rose in her chest as she thought about Keith Kibby's anger.

What that Kibby had done to ma Donnie in drink . . .

. . . and ma Danny. My wee boy. He's always had a temper.

As for that other one, the Kibby laddie, God knows what he's capable of!

Beverly grabbed the phone on the table beside her, called her son on his mobile number. It was switched off. She left a message on his answering service. — Danny, it's Mum. I'm with Caroline, Caroline Kibby; and we need to talk to you. It's very important.

Call me when you get this message, she said, then added in breathless urgency, — I love you, darlin. In some anxiety she turned to Caroline. — Go and find them, hen. Tell Danny to call me.

Caroline was already rising but as she got to her feet she stopped and looked Beverly in her eye. — Is he my brother?

— What do you think, Beverly snapped. — Go on, go and find them!

Caroline had no time for any more diversions. She quickly left the house, running down the stair and into the night, heading towards the Shore.

Beverly looked at the *London Calling* album on the wall, the signature and the date, and remembered with fondness and guilt that over the course of that bizarre evening she'd taken not one, or even two, but three lovers.

44

Stranger on the Shore

The scorch of the hard liquor enlivened his spirit, and in the toilets he'd also sneaked down a big line of cocaine. Perversely, Danny Skinner had the notion that he'd share it with Brian Kibby, then realised just how daft that would be.

His heart was thudding steadily in his chest, like the jungle drums of tribesmen preparing for war. But even through those rushes the stupidity of the situation was starting to eat at him. What was he doing here with Kibby? What could they possibly say to each other? Then, as he returned to his stool, Kibby noticed powder on the hairs of his nostrils. — Have you been taking drugs?

— Just a line of coke, Skinner said nonchalantly. — Want one?

— Yes, Kibby replied, trembling at the abruptness of his response. He was anxious to try the powder; it seemed important to experience it, important to keep up with Skinner.

Skinner moved back towards the toilet, bidding Kibby to follow him. They got into a cubicle and he closed the door behind them, chopped out a big line, then rolled up a twenty-pound note. The two men were crushed together in uncomfortable proximity. This was crazy, Skinner thought ruefully, as he watched Kibby snort it back; they were only going to suffer for this later on.

— Whoa . . . that feels fuckin good . . . Kibby gasped, his eyes watering as the cocaine rush fused through him, stiffening his spine. He felt so strong, like he was made of metal.

His reaction didn't escape Skinner. — People criticise the criminals . . . until it's them who want to get a hold of class-A drugs, he said in affected pomposity.

Brian Kibby had to struggle to repress a chuckle as they left the toilet and headed back to the bar.

Skinner caught the young barmaid's eye with a smile, and got one back. Kibby saw this, feeling something seethe inside of him. — It comes easy tae you, eh, he said bitterly, nodding towards the girl.

It made Skinner stop and think. In the past, when he was out with his mates, he – more often than not – was the one that pulled. Since he was sixteen, he had been more or less continuously sexually active, either with a girlfriend or through a series of casual flings. From the point of view of someone like Kibby, he considered, he *would* be regarded as highly successful with women.

But the real problem is relationships, which fucking social retards like Kibby can't grasp, because they're just so obsessed with getting their hole.

Skinner realised that he'd seldom thought about a woman in purely sexual terms. Even if somebody was an object of his desire, he invariably found himself thinking about her level of intelligence, music, clothing, film and book preferences, the sort of friends she had, her social and political views, what her parents did for a living. Yes, he had got involved in one-night stands, but casual relationships were always unsatisfying to him. He looked searchingly at Kibby. — I'm just interested in women, Brian.

— So am I, Kibby whined in urgent complaint.

— You *think* you are, but you're not. You read sci-fi magazines, for fuck sakes.

— I am! What I read's got nowt tae dae wi it! Kibby blurted.

Skinner shook his head. — You're not curious about girls, other than sexually. I know you fancied Shannon, but you never talked to her about anything that *she* might have been interested in, you just inflicted your own shite about video games and hillwalking clubs on to her. You're hiding, Bri, Skinner said, now feeling the coke rush and slurping a bit of beer back, — hiding in model railways and *Star Trek* conventions . . .

— I don't even like *Star Trek*. Kibby thought bitterly of Ian as his head swayed furiously. — I'm just shy, I've always been shy. It's like a fucking disease, shyness! You don't understand, he shouted, — the likes of you are never gonnae understand the daily humiliation the likes of me get in life, his voice rose, — THROUGH BEING FUCKIN SHY!

A few drinkers looked round at him. Kibby nodded semi-apologetically, grinding his teeth. — You don't *fear* humiliation, Brian, Skinner said, — you *invite* it.

— I'm just unlucky with girls . . .

Skinner nodded, and was powerless to stop a mischievous thought settling in his mind.

— What? Kibby said, catching his contemplative grin.

— I was just thinking that if you fell into a barrel of naked Corrs, you'd end up with the guitarist sucking your cock, Skinner guffawed.

Kibby glared at him, felt that anger sop in his veins again. Then it seemed to settle into something colder, crueller. — So how many marks oot ay ten would you gie Shannon . . . as opposed tae that lassie Kay you were engaged tae . . .

He watched Skinner's face freeze over.

— . . . or ma fuckin sister! he spat.

Skinner felt his own rage rising up in him, and forced it back down. He coolly regarded Kibby for a beat. — They're women, Brian, not fucking video games. If I were you, I'd get a wad of cash out and I'd go to a prostitute and get my fucking hole. Once you've got rid of the stigma of virginity and unwound a bit, you might achieve a more realistic perspective about people.

As Skinner turned towards the bar, Kibby felt those liberating thoughts of violence again, surging through him like an electric current, working with the drug. When you let go, he wondered, what actually happened? How bad could it be? He was in uncharted waters, and he loved it. He was longing to let go.

That bastard Skinner: he's fuckin well getting it. Maybe now isnae the time. But he's getting it!

Just like McGrillen and that nonce Radden and that dirty poof Ian even, all those wankers that've crossed or patronised or rejected me. And that Lucy slag, I should have knobbed her when I had the chance. Couldnae see that the filthy wee hing-oot was ganting on it! And that Shannon, if she let the likes of Skinner up her then she must . . .

He looked at Skinner, now in conversation with the barmaid. She was pretty and was laughing at something he said to her. And he's supposed to be with Caroline, he thought in a murderous rancour.

Ma fuckin sister . . . Skinner, you fuckin animal . . .

— See, if you hurt ma sister, Skinner . . . Kibby hissed in his ear.

Skinner turned to him, as the barmaid departed to get their order. — I would never, ever do anything to hurt Caroline, he said in such emphatic sincerity and conviction, Kibby almost felt foolish.

— Chattin up other lassies as soon she's oot the door . . .

— I'm just talking to the girl, I was getting us a round in. Skinner shook his head. — For fuck sakes, lighten up, Kibby, he snapped, his smile returning as he saw the barmaid advancing with the drinks.

Just as he was considering that he would tear into Skinner with all the power he could muster, Brian Kibby caught a glimpse of his adversary in profile and was stunned with a strange semi-recognition. He heard an old voice in his head:

I'll cut your fucking cock off. I'll dae that, cause it will fucking rot away and fall off anyway, if you put it anywhere near those filthy slags . . .

That dehumanised voice, the evil simplicity of the statement, spilling from a poisoned, spiteful mouth, it was so easy to see it coming from Skinner's. But it wasn't from Skinner's.

It seared so sharply into his brain. That time his dad had seen him with Angela Henderson and Dionne McInnes. They were just talking and laughing, that was all they were doing. His dad came down the road, hunched, shuffling and shot his son that terrible look; a satanic stare that chilled his soul. When he got into the house his father was angry, rambling and semi-coherent. Then Keith Kibby grabbed a hold of his son's arms with those claws of this, would not let him go. Brian could smell the alcohol on his breath, see the burning red wrath in his father's eyes, feel the spittle on his face, as Keith Kibby warned him about hanging out with those dirty wee hoors, how they carried Aids or got up the duff deliberately, how they could only mess up a laddie's life and how if he ever saw him messing around with that rubbish again he'd . . .

No. He wasnae well. He said so.

The next day his dad had approached him in a terrible sober guilt, restored to his normal self, exorcised from the horrible demon that possessed him. — I was silly last night, Brian . . . when I got on to you. I wasnae feeling right, I've no been too well, son. You're a good lad and I don't want you tae the make the mistakes that I've

. . . some other people make. I'm really sorry though, son. Still buddies, eh, mate?

He remembered how craven and apologetic his dad was, how he sadly tried to make things up. As they watched *Star Trek*, Keith Kibby conceded to the son that *The Next Generation* was better in every way to the original: deeper, more interesting and philosophical storylines, better characters and superior special effects. As he sat there on the couch, Brian Kibby was cringing again, this time for his father rather than himself, once again wanting this tortured man to just stop.

His father had been weak, and so had he, but there was no time left to stay weak. — Here's to mosquitoes in Birmingham, he smiled in sudden inspiration, raising his glass at Skinner.

Skinner briefly shuddered, looking at Kibby's sly grin with real fear for the first time, but then quickly raised his drink in defiance. — Broom-may mos-kay-toes, he said in a put-on West Midlands accent, then curtly added, — and not forgetting the sci-fi nerds of Ibiza!

It had the desired effect of stopping Kibby in his tracks and making him contemplate Skinner in bewildered awe.

She had been running in long bursts, down Henderson Street, as the Water of Leith came into view, the moonlight dancing across it as she succumbed to breathlessness and the weight of the food and drink in her guts. She held on to a railing and filled her lungs with air. Two boys passing her stopped and said something but Caroline was hearing only white noise as the contents of her father's journal and Beverly's disclosures, or the lack of them, flooded her mind.

Her father: an alcoholic thug. It seemed impossible, way beyond her conception that a drug could change a person so much. But some things were starting to come back, fragments of long-repressed memories from childhood. That one time when she heard shouts coming from downstairs, and her mother crying. She got upset and wanted to see what was wrong. Brian stopped her; he came into her room and cuddled her and wouldn't let her go downstairs. In the morning her mother was tense and her father silent, probably in his hung-over guilt.

Brian. How much had he known, how much had he protected her from? Her hands were shaking and her belly fluttered continuously, at one stage threatening to relinquish the rich food inside it.

In an almost splintering burst of empathy, Caroline realised that her brother as a young boy had probably witnessed at least some part of this mess, something that had almost completely eluded her.

The thick fog coming in from the sea had now been blown away by the storm, but the rains whipped at her in stinging bursts. She pulled her mobile phone from a pocket in her already soaked jeans, only to find that the credits had run out.

Top up . . . fuck!

Caroline got on her toes again, her feet cold, wet and sodden, but as she increased her speed, she regretted not changing into a pair of trainers as her squelching foot slipped on the wet stones and her ankle twisted in an audible wrench. She hobbled on, tears coming from frustration as much as the pain.

A crowd of girls staggered out of a restaurant right in front of her, their drunk laughter bellowing through the storm. — Don't come back, said a suited restaurateur in the doorway, holding open the door, as the last of them stumbled out into the street.

— How's yir cock fir lovebites? one girl with a sweaty face and long brown hair rasped at him and her mates let out accompanying volleys of shrieking laughter.

The man shook his head and went back inside.

Caroline approached the girls in appeal. — Have youse got a mobile I can borrow? It's an emergency . . . I really need to call somebody!

One chunky, nervy-looking girl with a short fringe handed over her phone. Caroline eagerly took it and dialled Danny's number. It was still switched off.

As the drinks slipped by the fight in them seemed to ebb and flow. When they met each other's eyes it was in a quizzical disgust, which appeared to come from a mutual disappointment. Indeed, to onlookers they seemed more like intense lovers who had just had a stupid, drunken row and were now embarrassed but unsure of how to make up without losing face. In both men the urge to drink had also taken a sudden flight. It was as though they realised that there was little to be gained by trying to poison themselves.

In a shuddering awareness, it dawned on Skinner in his fraught, jaundiced state, that his relationship with Kibby was now almost exactly the same as it had been with all his binge-drinking buddies.

We tried to poison each other. We were like lemmings, but instead of jumping over a cliff together, our suicide pact was long and turgid. We just wove the bastard imperceptibly into our social life.

They looked up at the television above the bar, at the sly, grinning face of the American President, re-elected as Skinner had been positive he would be, in spite of wishing Dorothy good luck as she had cast her vote for the other candidate, whose name he'd already forgotten. Danny Skinner and Brian Kibby, in private unison, both wondered where the next war would be. Skinner didn't want any more wars though. He was tired: very, very tired.

Somehow, through a combination of my intense hatred for Kibby and my burning need to carry on living the life, I was able to concoct a psychic spell so powerful it allowed me to transfer the burden of my consumption on to him.

I got someone else to fight my battles for me.

I look up at Bush as the US forces assault Falluja, the no-hopers; cannon fodder from de-industrialised places like Ohio with rising unemployment, who voted him back in. Down the line they'll be penniless jakeys like their betrayed forefathers who went to Vietnam and now panhandle in the Tenderloin. Their role is to be shafted for somebody else's dreams and schemes. The Iraqi children's corpses off-camera during the election, the rows of coffins with Old Glory draped over them, verboten for screening in the world's supposedly greatest democracy.

You can get away with it if you have the power and you're fucked if you don't. But it's all shite: who needs it?

— I'm gaun hame, Skinner suddenly said, climbing down from his bar stool. Kibby thought of a response, but he didn't feel like arguing, didn't feel victorious. He needed his remaining strength because he was going to do something to Skinner. He didn't know what, but he was going to do something to make him pay, to stop him getting to his family. He was beyond anger; now all he felt was cold certainty.

They staggered outside, both very drunk, but still keeping a distance from each other. The weather had changed again for the worse and a storm of lashing wind and cold, driving rain greeted them. The shock of the frozen reception to his system seemed to reignite Kibby, and a frustrated rage pulsed through him. He needed to know. Not even how, but why. — WHO ARE YOU, SKINNER? he shouted through the wind. — WHAT DAE YE FUCKIN WELL WANT WI ME? WHO THE FUCK ARE YOU?!

Skinner stopped immediately, relaxing the shoulders he had braced against the storm. — I'm . . . I'm . . . He couldn't answer the question. It burned in his head through the haze of drink and the whipping wind that swirled around it.

Brian Kibby seethed.

This . . . thing, this bastard who's all but destroyed me and will surely destroy my family . . .

Kibby suddenly charged towards Skinner and swung at him. Skinner quickly dropped his shoulder, stepping off, remembering the moves he'd learned as a boy at Leith Victoria Boxing Club. Frustrated, Kibby launched himself forward again, only to be met with a swift, solid jab, which snapped into his face.

— Fuckin well calm doon, Brian, Skinner said, somewhere between a threat and an appeal.

Feeling his split lip swelling up, Kibby backed away in shock. Then another surge of anger took hold of him, propelling him back towards Skinner. — AH'LL TEAR YIR FUCKIN FACE OFF, SKINNER!!

But Skinner clipped him with a jab again, stopping him in his tracks, then smacked him with a heavy right-hander which rattled his jaw and made his head spin. Before Kibby could react, a solid body punch squeezed the wind out off him, jackknifing him. He bent double and spewed up his rich food and drink into the street in solid, wrenching heaves.

— That's enough. I don't want to hurt you, Skinner said, realising that he really didn't. He was worried about Brian Kibby's new liver, his wound.

What the fuck was I doing hitting the poor cunt in the body!

Skinner felt almost as nauseous as Kibby, as if he had been the victim of his own blows. He moved closer and rested an arm's-length hand on his rival's shoulder. — Take deep breaths, you'll be awright.

Kibby breathed heavily, like a snorting, wounded bovine beast in a bullring. As the rain plastered his hair to his cranium, it dawned on Skinner that his bladder was going to burst. So he broke into a rubbery trot and lurched up to a large wall by the old dock gates and pissed up it, in a long, liberating expulsion of the steamy, hot yellow fluid that filled his bladder.

Skinner scarcely noticed that there was another man just a few yards down from him, doing exactly the same thing. He was a lorry driver named Tommy Pugh and he'd had a long day coming up from Rouen in France with his load, bound for Aberdeen. Good time had been made but now Pugh was exhausted. He'd parked up by the old dock gates and was anticipating a good rest in the cab of his rig, and a substantial saving on his B&B allowance.

Kibby gasped and raised his head, letting things come into slow focus through the rain. He saw the rig, and the huge silver petroleum tank it carried. He saw Skinner, urinating. Yes, the cab was empty, he noted as he shuffled over to inspect it. Looking inside, he saw that the door was open and the keys were in the ignition. And there was the lorry driver pissing against the wall, just a few yards downwind from Skinner.

It was a sign, it had to be, it was all it could be. And if Brian Kibby did not grasp this opportunity now, he just knew in his heart that the Fates would not give him another.

— Dae ah no ken you fae somewhaire? one of the drunk girls asked her, the one with the sweaty face, as Caroline stared at the phone. In mounting desperation she punched out a text message:

DAN, FOUND MY DADS DIARY.
HE IS YOUR FATHER TOO. U R
MY BIG BROTHER, SAME WITH
BRI. PLEASE DON'T HURT EACH
OTHER. C XXXXX

She sent it off as the other girl, the nervy one with the fringe who had lent her the phone said, — D'ye ken Fiona Caldwell?

— No . . . I need to send another text.

— Nup, gie's ma phone, the girl demanded.

— Let her send the text, another girl, a bit more sober than the rest, said. — It's Caroline, isn't it? As Caroline nodded in recognition, she added, — Caroline Kibby, she was at Craigmount with me.

Caroline realised that she had known the girl, Moira Ormond, from school. She was a shy goth back then, but not now. Nodding with more gratitude than she remembered expressing to anyone, Caroline punched out another message on the phone, this time for her brother.

The hardest part was hoisting his cumbersome, perspiring body into the driver's cab. Once again, the alcohol helped, dulling the terrible mortal pain of his flesh.

He quickly started up the lorry and drove it towards his blissfully unaware target, who was still relieving himself up against the wall.

Tommy Pugh heard the familiar sound of his engine starting up. *What the fuck . . . ?*

Tommy glanced round in terror as the lorry accelerated towards the wall, a few yards from him. He moved quickly in the other direction, as his stocky build found an athleticism that came from sheer desperation.

45

An email from America

To: skinnyboy@hotmail.com
From: dotcom@dotcom.com
Re: Love and Things

Okay, Skinner

I'm so glad you're coming back over. Why? Well, it's cards on the table time. I'm nuts about you too. I miss you so much. I know this could all just be cyberromance stuff but I keep seeing your face, that ski-slope chin that juts out and looks a bit like a half-moon in profile, those big black brows like you should be in Oasis.

I don't know where this is going to lead us, Danny my sweet love, but like you I know we'll be mad if we don't try it. And it just feels so right. I'm so happy and I can't wait to see my darling boy again.

Love you so much,
Dorothy xxxxxxx

46
Flame-Grilled

Caroline forced herself through the driving rain along the cobblestones of old Leith. Her footing almost went again, and she was now in real pain. There were very few people around, most had made their way home, some were still ensconced in the noisy bars and restaurants that lined the Shore at the Water of Leith.

Where will Brian and Danny be? Which one? The restaurant . . .

As she went to go into the bar attached to the place they'd been dining at, Caroline gasped as the explosion roared in her ears and the light from the fire bounced off the blue-black cobblestones around her. She hobbled towards the source of it, at the old dock gates.

Beverly Skinner turned up the thermostat in her front room. It seemed to have suddenly got so cold. She picked up Cous-Cous, feeling the animal's warmth on her lap. She looked up at *London Calling* once more and recalled that cold winter Sunday night back in 1980.

First Keith Kibby and her going back to that party at the Canongate and them having befuddled, unprotected sex in the hall. Then he'd got really inebriated – blindly, obscenely drunk – and passed out. She didn't want to go home to face Donnie so she wandered the dirty streets up the Royal Mile. The tourist area wasn't as complete as it is now, and she passed a couple of rough-looking pubs, heard two young men threaten each other as a mob spilled from a tenement door out on to the street. Even when she heard the sound of glass breaking and screams, she didn't look back. She passed the World's End pub, which, a few years previously, had been the last place where two girls were seen before their bodies were found strangled on a nearby beach, in a double murder that was never solved.

The strip changed, as the tourist and tartan kitsch shops started to dominate. As she passed the new Scandinavian-style hotel, she could scarcely believe her eyes as she saw three of them getting out of a car. That was when she approached him, told him how much she'd enjoyed the gig and loved the band. He was a gentleman, and invited her back for a drink. They went back to his room and he treated her well, and became her third lover that evening. In the morning, when they parted and he got ready to go back on the road and she prepared to start her lunchtime shift in the restaurant, neither one of them regretted a thing.

Her son was born nine months later, on 20 October 1980. Of her three lovers, her heart said that the first was his father, her head the second. And sometimes, only sometimes, when she put on a particular record, her soul would hint that it just might be the third.

As he shook out his penis with one hand, Danny Skinner fished out the mobile with his other and clicked it on. It showed three missed calls. He was about to stick it back into his pocket when it made a sound heralding a text coming in. He didn't recognise the number but called it up anyway, and read the message.

Then he heard a noise and turned round to see the manic face of Brian Kibby, up in the cab of a lorry, bearing down on him. Their eyes met and Brian Kibby saw something in Skinner, who just stood there and raised his mobile phone in the air, shrugged and laughed. Something in his glance and bearing instantly disarmed Kibby's murderous emotion. He slammed on the brakes but it only caused the lorry to go into a skid.

The HGV crashed into Skinner at speed, crushing him against the old dockyard wall. The back end of the vehicle then swung on the oily surface, the huge petroleum tank thrashing against the wall and springing several leaks. Just before it exploded, rendering Skinner's corpse almost unidentifiable, an ungainly man exited the cabin and moved off, before the flames could also engulf him.

Tommy Pugh, the only eyewitness present, said that he was a grossly fat man with dark circles under his eyes. He moved slowly, wheezing away from the blazing wreckage, where people who had come out from the bars to investigate the noise from the explosion saw him heading back in the direction of the Shore. It was thought that he went into one of the many waterfront bars.

When the police arrived and trawled the area, the only person drinking alone in the vicinity was a tall, thin man. He looked super-fit; a good ten years younger than the person described leaving the scene, or, police forensic scientists would later estimate, the bloated body burned beyond recognition in the fire.

The lone man was very drunk, but with a glazed expression, continually staring at his mobile phone. His back was to a desperate, fretful girl who had heard the explosion and come into this bar like the others before it, searching for a man who was him but who looked nothing like him. But he was drinking heavily: oh yes, Brian Kibby was drinking like there was no tomorrow.

Afterword

It shouldn't be required to state the obvious, but I've found that in this game it's sometimes necessary. This book is fiction. For instance, the 'Edinburgh Council' in the manuscript doesn't exist; like everything else here it's a figment of my imagination. I have no reason to believe that the real Edinburgh Council has employment practices or personalities like the ones in this book.

Thanks to my friends in the marvellous cities of Edinburgh, London, Chicago, San Francisco and Dublin for giving me the space and sustenance needed to write this book.

Special thanks to Robin Robertson, Katherine Fry and Sue Amaradivakara at Random House.

In Michael Kerr, I lost a good pal when I started writing this book. Following its completion, another two great buddies, William Orman and James Crawford have died untimely deaths. Edinburgh is a sadder and less colourful place for many people. Rest in peace and play in fun, Mikey, Billy and Big Crawf.

Acknowledgements

'We Used To Be Friends'. Words & Music by Grant Nicholas, Jon Lee, Taka Hirose & Courtney Taylor © Copyright 2003 Chrysalis Music Limited (80%)/Universal Music Publishing Limited (20%). Used by permission of Music Sales Limited. All Rights Reserved. International Copyright Secured.

'Something Beautiful'. Written and composed by Robbie Williams/ Guy Chambers. Published by BMG Music Publishing Ltd. Used by permission. All Rights Reserved.

'Ignition'. Written and composed by Robert Kelly. Published by R Kelly Publishing Inc/Zomba Music Publishers Ltd. Used by permission. All Rights Reserved.